He glared at that monstrous composite face and poured his hatred on it. The face of Ihya Khumnas with his hooked nose and gleaming white teeth, which even now bared themselves in a snarl; the face, too, of Yakob Mhireni, with its livid blaze of scar tissue; and what of the coarse, hairy trunk from the waist down, for the moment hidden by the wall between?

By the same author

BRIAN LUMLEY

Demogorgon

Grafton

An Imprint of HarperCollins*Publishers*

Grafton
An Imprint of HarperCollins*Publishers*
77–85 Fulham Palace Road,
Hammersmith, London W6 8JB

A Grafton Paperback Original 1987
9 8 7 6 5 4 3 2

ISBN 0 586 07031 1

Set in Times

Printed in Great Britain by
HarperCollinsManufacturing Glasgow

For the two Nicks –
'Young Nick and Old Nick!'
– and also for Guy, researcher
par excellence!

Demogorgon: a mysterious infernal deity, circa A.D. 4–500 to date. (Apparently Gk. – *daimon*, deity; *Gorgo*, Gorgon; *gorgos*, terrible.)

* * *

An error in ancient translation or transcription. Properly the Gnostic creator . . .

* * *

       . . . when straight behold the throne
Of Chaos, and his dark pavilion spread
Wide on the wasteful deep; with him enthroned
Sat sable-vested Night, eldest of things,
The consort of his reign; and by them stood
Orcus and Ades, and the dreaded name
Of Demogorgon; Rumour next and Chance,
And Tumult and Confusion all embroiled,
And Discord with a thousand various mouths.

                Milton's *Paradise Lost*

Part I

Chapter One

Late August, 1936. *The year in which the Oriental Institute of Chicago extended its activities to include a dig at Meggido in (then) Palestine . . .*

The four came out of the desert as evening turned to night. They might have been wandering Arabs, coming to the ruins with their donkeys, finding a place to camp through the hours of darkness. They *might* have been Arabs. But they came silently, the hooves of their beasts muffled with rags, and their silhouettes furtive against the early stars as they crossed a ridge and plodded down toward the shining inland sea. And though unwittingly they followed more or less a path Jesus of Nazareth had followed some nineteen centuries before them, that was the single way in which it could be said that they 'walked in the Ways of the Lord.' For in all other respects they were ungodly indeed, and one of them especially so.

Now they picked their way carefully through rubble on the outskirts of what had been, long, long ago, a village. Low, ruined walls stood up from stony ground; the rim of a dried-out well had caved in where once streets joined in an open plaza, and where now the bleached bones of a great olive, dead six hundred years, lay sandpapered and near-petrified under the darkening sky. The moon shone down on a desolation of tumbled stones and rude dwellings crumbled almost to their foundations; in the near-distance, Galilee was a sheen of rippled silver under the stars.

'This is the place,' said the leader of the group, slowly

nodding. His voice was the dry whisper of reeds, rustling up as from a throat full of dust. 'Help me down.'

The old man's followers silently dismounted, then assisted him from his donkey. He was light as a feather, desiccated, old as this old place itself. So he seemed. To any chance observer it would also seem that his retainers handled him with reverence; in fact, they handled him with fear – like a fragile bottle of some deadly virus which they dared not spill.

Hooded, all four, for long moments then they stood under the moon, the old man clinging to his donkey until he found his legs. Finally he stood unaided, put up a hand and threw back his hood. The others at once drew back from him. Age had made him . . . very ugly. Age and something else: black evil!

George Guigos was all old cracked leather and stained ivory. His lips seemed to have withered, drawing back from teeth which jutted from shrivelled gums and gave him an awful, permanent grin. Oddly, he seemed to have retained all his teeth. Above his mouth, a collapsed nose was a raw hole, the bridge between its great pits of nostrils almost completely eaten away by disease. Pits, too, his eyes: but these were yellow in the dark like those of a cat, with nothing at all of senility about them but a bright and terrible awareness, a luminous intelligence. Bald, his head was a brown walnut on a pipestem neck. He was frail as a twig, and yet his power was awesome; it was the power of evil in him.

'Are you sure, Mr Guigos?' one of the three, a little bolder, perhaps, than the others, stepped forward again. He put back his own hood, glanced all about with quick, dark eyes, as if to find some sort of landmark or point of definition. 'One mound of rubble seems much the same as any other to me.'

'But not to me, Ihya Khumnas,' Guigos snapped, his voice coming viciously to life. 'This *is* the place.'

'The place of the treasure?' another asked, his voice an eager hiss. This one was called Yakob Mhireni.

Guigos looked at all three in turn. 'The place of great treasure, yes!' he answered.

'You mentioned a map,' said Ihya Khumnas, licking his lips. 'But . . . you never seem to refer to one.' He shuffled uncomfortably.

'The map is in my head,' said Guigos. 'If you had such a map, wouldn't you keep it in your head?' He laughed a laugh that grated like a shovel in cold ashes, which finally subsided as he glared again at the three. 'But it seems I must remind you: you have no interest in the treasure itself. Only in its recovery. The treasure is mine. Or perhaps you think you weren't paid well enough?'

They had been paid half in advance, the rest due on completion. And it had been enough. Not a man of them would ever need to work again, neither them nor their children. They could all live in luxury on the interest alone. They were almost rich men, and would certainly *be* rich men when the account was settled in full. But last night Khumnas and Mhireni had conspired between them, and now they gave each other small, furtive glances before Khumnas answered: 'We've been paid well enough. It's just that we're eager to be done with this, that's all. We're tomb-looters, here under false papers, labouring through the day for the Americans at Meggido, who at any time are liable to see through our cover. That's enough to make anyone nervous. The sooner we can get out of here the better.'

'We are in complete agreement,' said Guigos. 'I do not any more enjoy your company than you enjoy mine. Anyway, that choked well back there – where the old streets cross – that was once the centre of this village.

13

There was a grapevine growing all along the under-branches of the olives, of which there were several. Figs grew up the wall of one of the houses. All in all, it was a very pretty square; the village was not unpleasant.'

'*Huh!*' Mhireni grunted. 'That lone tree's been dead a hundred years and more! When was this time you speak of, Mr Guigos?'

'Long, long ago!' Guigos rasped. 'As for the olive tree by the well: you are wrong, it has been dead six hundred years. In any case, the well is my marker. That and Polaris.'

He turned his yellow eyes up to the sky, sought out the Great Bear and its pointers, guided his donkey between low mounds of rubble. The others glanced at each other, shrugged, began to follow him.

Khumnas was a forger and confidence trickster; he had been recruited six months ago as he fled his native Iraq where the authorities were intensely interested in his head. Mhireni was likewise Iraqi: a thug and brutally strong, he was nevertheless devious and quick-witted and had thus eluded justice for most of his twenty-eight years. Guigos's third hired hand was no less a criminal, but he was somewhat different from the others.

Handsome, with typically Greek features and a phys-ique to match, Dimitrios Kastrouni was the youngest of the three. His twenty-two years had been spent mainly in Larnaca, a fishing village in Cyprus. The only son of a Greek-Cypriot vintner, two years ago he had been spurned by a girl who then married his rival. Sneaking into the wedding ceremony, as the two were joined, he had leaped forward to slit the bridegroom's throat before all the horrified guests. Then, barely ahead of the hue and cry, he had fled to the mainland in his father's boat, scuttling the craft off Haifa and swimming ashore by night. Under an assumed Jewish name he had got himself

14

a job driving for the British authorities, which was where Guigos had found and recruited him only a month ago.

Kastrouni was on edge, his nerves jumping. But his was a controlled nervousness; outwardly he appeared cool, almost emotionless. His internal agitation sprang from two years of flight and deception in a world where the storm-clouds of political unrest and the ominous stirrings of nations as they prepared for war had covered his tracks and given him freedom; but he remained unconvinced that he had escaped the consequences of his crime; while he did not relish the thought, still he anticipated his past catching up with him. Sooner or later it would, he was sure, and that kept him on his toes. But, basically honest, he was satisfied with what Guigos had paid and promised to pay; the alleged 'treasure' held no interest for him. Thus he was not part of Khumnas's and Mhireni's conspiracy.

Now, as the four picked their way carefully through the ruins, Kastrouni's flight-sharpened ears detected some slight sound, hopefully distant. '*Shh!*' he cautioned the others, coming to a halt.

'What is it, Dimitrios Kastrouni?' Guigos hissed.

They all held their breath.

'I heard – something,' finally Kastrouni answered.

'*Huh!*' Mhireni snorted. 'And who would be out here, under the stars, in a God-forsaken hole like this?' Although he was not a true believer, Mhireni came of a Shia Islamic family. His remark had no real significance; it was something he'd picked up from the Americans, who blasphemed as a matter of course. But while it meant nothing to him, Guigos was different entirely.

'Be *quiet!*' the old man hissed, then gave a deep, chuckling, rustling laugh. 'God-forsaken, indeed! Aye, Chorazin is that, all right . . .' And to Kastrouni: 'Well, what was this "something" you heard, Dimitrios?'

15

Kastrouni looked at him, scowled, rounded on Mhireni. 'Fool!' he said, keeping his voice low. 'Who would be out under the stars, you ask? This is British territory. They patrol constantly. To the north the French have border posts. The Arabs still inhabit a number of towns around Galilee. Fishermen sail on the night waters and nomads wander in the desert. Archaeologists scour the land, seeking out just such "God-forsaken" places as this. Who would be out here? Man, didn't you hear what Khumnas said? We're tomb-looters! This treasure Guigos seeks is not his to keep, but he will keep it. Therefore he is a thief and we are helping him. There are men enough in this land who would kill you for your gold earrings, let alone a treasure. And when I say I hear something, you had better believe I hear something!' He spoke Greek but Mhireni understood every word.

Mhireni's flush went unnoticed in the gloom, but Khumnas saw his hand steal inside his robe. The Iraqis had plotted to kill Kastrouni along with Guigos – but after they had the treasure. Khumnas caught Mhireni's elbow in a tight grip. Lightly he said: 'The Greek is right. Perhaps it would be better if one of us kept watch and scouted the land about.'

Guigos looked reluctant but finally agreed. 'You do it, Dimitrios,' he said. 'Your eyes and ears are sharp, and you seem to value your life and freedom more than these two. Keep a watch; go in a wide circle; but be back here by midnight. I'll need you then.'

'Back here?' Kastrouni looked all about. 'Back where?'

'Here,' Guigos grunted. 'Right here!' He stamped an oddly twisted left foot and pointed out three large boulders in a triangle where they supported a fourth. 'That is the marker.'

Khumnas and Mhireni tethered their donkeys, went to the boulders. Limping a little and moving more slowly,

Guigos followed them; he took a dry stick and traced a square in the sand of ages. Its sides were about six feet long and enclosed the triangle of boulders with their boulder apex. The sides of the square itself were parallel to those of a greater square formed of ruined walls. 'This was a temple,' the old man said, almost to himself. He nodded. 'A cursed temple in a cursed and doomed town.'

'And the treasure?' Khumnas couldn't help but lick his lips as he waited for an answer.

'Come,' said Guigos with a nightmare grin, 'topple that boulder and roll the others aside, out of the square. Then get your shovels. Twelve, fifteen inches deep there's a slab; beneath it are steep steps following a natural fissure. The treasure is down there – but I alone know where.'

Khumnas and Mhireni glanced at each other, ran to their beasts. Guigos chuckled, limped to one of the tumbled walls and sat down. He gazed at Kastrouni with sulphurous eyes. 'And you had better get on with your patrol. But carefully. And remember – be back by midnight. Join us below . . .'

Kastrouni nodded. He tethered his own animal and took some bread and meat from a pack. 'Midnight,' he nodded again. 'I have a wrist-watch. I'll be back.' He opened his robe, took off his belt, closed the robe and belted it to him. The broad leather belt supported a scabbard and sharp knife. Munching slowly on a piece of dried meat, Kastrouni melted into the shadows.

And George Guigos sat there under the brilliant jewel stars and chuckled obscenely, and watched his pair of Iraqi hirelings through hooded eyes where they struggled and strained to move the boulders . . .

Kastrouni moved south through the ruins, following the old town's crumbled mounds of debris to the head of a steep watercourse. A little water still trickled, falling in tinkling rills to the silver inland sea spread some eight hundred feet below. In its heyday, Chorazin had offered a superb view of the entire Sea of Galilee. Tiberias's lights were plainly visible to the south-west, some eight miles away, along with a sprinkling of others farther down the rocky eastern shore.

Kastrouni struck out west along the rim of the crags. He would walk maybe a third of a mile, clear of the ruins, then head north and make a half-circle back to the cliffs, and finally west again to bring himself back to this point, and so back to Guigos and the others.

As he walked, keeping back a little way from the edge of the cliff and taking care not to silhouette himself too much against the night sky, he felt somehow relieved to be out here alone. Old Guigos was a living gargoyle, a withered mummy of a man who but for his frailty would be terrifying. Even ancient and dried up as he was, still there was something nightmarish about him: the aura of evil, of a life spent in the pursuit of dark secrets and darker deeds, seemed to emanate almost physically from him. You could very nearly feel it like a fog on your skin. But . . . he had offered good money, and Kastrouni would use it to maintain, to perpetuate, his freedom. And maybe one day, under another name and disguised by the years, he would return to Cyprus. Not to Larnaca, no, but another place where he was unknown.

Under another name . . .

That was the funny thing about it. Or maybe not so funny. Kastrouni frowned in the night. He had chosen to call himself David Kammad when he arrived in Haifa. And while his features were not typically Jewish, still the assumed name and faith had seemed to turn the trick. The British administration had given him a job and issued an identity card, and that had been that. But then had come the night when Guigos found him, and immediately the man had seen right through him. Kastrouni remembered what the old devil had said to him:

'David Kammad? Ah, but that is not your real name, my boy. These eyes of mine are very old and very wise – in ways other than you'd suspect – so that I'm not so easily fooled. You are Greek, not Jewish. Oh, it's likely you've kept your initials, but only those. Now then, what is your *real* name, the name you're keeping secret?'

And Kastrouni had told him. As simple as that. It had probably been Guigos eyes, which were very nearly hypnotic; whichever, Kastrouni had put his life in the man's hands, and in return had got himself fixed up with this job. And a lot of money. When all of this was over he would head for one of the Greek islands, set himself up in a small business, and –

Kastrouni froze, his thoughts returning to the task in hand. Voices had carried to him on a thermal sweeping up from below. Arab voices, he thought, guttural and – excited? This was what he had heard before, back in the ruins, but it was clearer now and unmistakably a babble of conversation. There were people down there. But doing what?

He dropped to all fours, crept to the rounded shoulder of the cliff. Careful not to disturb any pebbles, he leaned forward and directed his gaze downward. Lights bobbed on the water, occasionally blinking as dark, laughing figures splashed about them. Kastrouni knew at once what was going on: he had seen this often enough in Cyprus. These were fishermen, luring fish into their nets by use of floating lanterns. They were wading in the shallow water at the rim of the lake where the night feeders would gather in small shoals. Nothing to fear from them: they had probably come here by boat from Tiberias or elsewhere, and would return by the same route. Anyway, he couldn't see that they'd have any reason to climb the steep, ancient watercourse to Chorazin. No, and certainly not by night. His fears allayed, Kastrouni drew back, stood up, turned north and commenced his semi-circular sweep.

Back where the cliffs went down to the Sea of Galilee, Kastrouni's wrist-watch ticked away the seconds. A soft link had snapped where his wrist had scraped over a rock as he crawled on all fours. With all of his senses keyed to what had been happening below, he hadn't noticed. The luminous dial said that the hour was fifteen minutes after eleven . . .

It had taken only ten minutes for Khumnas and Mhireni to clear away the loose sand and soil from the square scratched out by Guigos. A little more than fifteen inches down they had reached a stone slab and quickly cleared its surface until clean edges could be seen to form a rectangle some two feet wide by three long. A heavy iron ring at one end of the slab was large enough in diameter to allow both men to get several fingers through, but strain as they might the slab would not come up. By now, as they cursed and struggled with the ring, it was almost as if they had forgotten Guigos was there at all; their minds were full of what might lie below. The old man's chuckle seemed deliberately contrived to remind them of his presence.

'Ihya Khumnas, you were chosen to assist me because you are a cheat, a liar and an expert forger. Not the very best I might have obtained for the money, but you were also young and strong.' He omitted to add that Khumnas would not be missed in this world, not by anyone, but the thought crossed his mind and caused him to smile hideously.

'As for you, Yakob Mhireni,' he continued, ' – you are here because of your great strength, also because you are brutal and devious and utterly untrustworthy. Oh, don't worry: these are qualities I greatly admire, else you would not have been chosen.'

He stared at both of them, his yellow eyes glowing in the shadow of his terrible face . . .

'So?' Khumnas finally growled, sweat drying on his back and causing him to shiver. 'And what use to sit there like an ancient mummy and insult us? Do you want the slab tilted or not?'

'Of course!' Guigos snapped. 'And with your cunning and his strength it should have been the very simplest of tasks – and now I think perhaps I chose unwisely after all! If you are not clever enough between you, what now? Should I ask these poor dumb beasts of ours for help?' He turned his head and stared pointedly at the tethered donkeys.

Khumnas followed his gaze, frowned, finally believed he saw what the other was getting at. Mhireni merely scowled and stood watching while his companion took one of the shovels and weighed it in his hands. Khumnas propped the head of the shovel against a flat stone, jumped on it with both feet together and broke off the metal blade. This done he took rope from a pack on his donkey, passed it through the handle of the shovel and made a knot. He had left about five and a half feet dangling, which he now tied to the iron ring. At the other end of the slab, he jabbed the broken wooden stock of the shovel into the loose earth until it found purchase, then tested his device by hauling on the rope. The slab grated and moved a fraction of an inch, but Khumnas was not an especially strong man. The handle of the shovel formed a satisfactory fulcrum but Mhireni would prove to be the better lever; and if Mhireni's strength alone should not suffice, then they could always employ a donkey. Doubtless Guigos had meant as much with his cryptic comment.

Mhireni had got the idea at last; he took the coil of rope from Khumnas and wound it round his arm and shoulder, then leaned into it until the slab gratingly shifted and raised up an inch or two. Khumnas gave a small cry of triumph, jammed several stones under the rim, said: 'More yet. Pull, Yakob, pull!'

The big Iraqi strained, but though the slab shuddered and grated some more it would not lift. 'Donkey!' gasped Mhireni finally. 'Fetch a damned donkey before I break my back!' He stood panting until Khumnas brought one of the animals and tied the rope to its saddle, then together men and beast hauled on the rope until the shovel's handle came over and upright and the slab was suddenly yanked two-thirds of the way toward the vertical.

'Hold it there!' cried Khumnas. The shovel's handle was visibly flexing; before it could break he ran to the slab and threw all of his weight against it, standing over the hole beneath to do so. And at last the slab passed through the perpendicular and leaned back at a slight angle, jamming itself in that position.

'Done!' grunted Khumnas. 'We've done it!'

He stared down into the darkness of the pit, wrinkling his nose at the stenches which came welling up. 'All done,' he repeated then, a little less certainly. 'And the treasure's down there, is it?'

Mhireni went to stand beside him, and both men stared hard at Guigos in the darkness. One thought was uppermost in their minds now, and it was as if the gargoyle read it there:

'The treasure is *hidden* down there,' he said. 'Well hidden – and I alone know where.' He glanced at his watch. 11:25, and time growing shorter with every passing second. 'Come, let's get below.'

'Where's that idiot Greek?' growled Mhireni. 'Is there more hard work below? Are we to do everything?'

'I told Kastrouni to be back by midnight,' Guigos snapped. 'That's when I want him and not before. As long as he's back by then I'll be well satisfied. Meanwhile he's ensuring that no one can come up behind us – and that is important! Now get down there. Time's wasting and there's more to do yet.' He stood up, shuffled awkwardly to the hole where steps went steeply down into darkness.

The two Iraqis stood there undecided; the thought of a hidden hoard lured them magnetically, but the darkness and the odours wafting up from below deterred them. Khumnas took out a candle from his pocket, shielded it with a cupped hand, lighted it. He stooped low over the hole. The steps went down, down, well beyond the limit of the candle's illumination.

Khumnas gave an involuntary shudder. 'It stinks like hell!' he said, turning his face away. 'Like a charnel house. Like a corpse overdue for the worm.'

Mhireni didn't like that; irreligious he was, but he was also superstitious. 'Tomb-looters, you called us,' he prodded Khumnas accusingly. 'But I didn't think you meant it! Is that what this is, a tomb?'

'Dolts!' Guigos chuckled throatily, elbowing them aside. 'Out of my way, both of you . . .' He descended into the reeking opening until only his head and shoulders protruded. 'Well, are you coming? Or don't you want the rest of your pay?'

Without waiting for an answer, the grinning, half-crippled gargoyle stepped down out of sight. As he disappeared, so Mhireni's hand snaked inside his robe and snatched out a curved dagger. 'So help me,' he

23

harshly whispered, 'the moment my eyes light on that treasure, I'll slit that bag of filth open from his belly to his balls!' A deep scar on the left of his long nose and down his cheek almost to the jawbone glared white in the moonlight.

Khumnas's teeth were even whiter, twin bars of savage anticipation as he answered: 'Only if you reach him before me!' Then he controlled himself and grasped the other's arms. 'Look, we both hate the loathsome old dog, that's agreed; but just remember this: we can't touch him until after we have the treasure. Then he's fair game.'

Mhireni nodded. 'Right,' he growled. 'And the same goes for the Greek.' Then, Khumnas leading the way with his candle, they followed Guigos down into what was otherwise a Stygian darkness.

The steps were steep and narrow but dry; worn in the middle, as from the passage of countless thousands of feet over the centuries, they wound down in a semi-circle until the way suddenly widened out and grew straight. To the left the steps were hewn from a wall which overhung just above shoulder height, so that the two must go in a half-crouch; on the right stood empty space, inky black and echoing to their half-hearted footsteps. Mhireni deliberately kicked a pebble over the rim, listening for the rattle as it hit bottom. After several seconds his patience was rewarded, but with a distant splash. Water down there – a long way down there.

On the far side of the cleft the opposing wall beetled black and jagged, with stony projections throwing wavering shadows in the dim, flickering light of Khumnas's candle. A thought – how panicked they would be if the candle should go out – struck both men simultaneously; so that even as Mhireni grabbed Khumnas's shoulder, so the other half-turned and produced from a pocket a second stub of wax and wick.

24

'Have you counted the steps?' Mhireni whispered hoarsely, his great hands trembling slightly as he accepted fire from the other.

'Two dozen,' said Khumnas at once. 'Twenty-five with this next one.'

'Only twenty-five?' Mhireni was surprised. 'God! And already it seems we're half-way to hell! Anyway, how does he do it?'

'Eh?' Khumnas queried, his face pale in the candlelight. 'Old gargoyle? How does he do what?'

'See in the dark,' Mhireni answered. 'How does he *do* that? I mean, did you see him light a candle?' Damned if I did!'

'No, he didn't have one,' Khumnas frowned. 'I know he was carrying prepared torches under his robe; I prepared them, didn't I? But he didn't have a candle.' He shrugged. 'Anyway, I've heard of people like that, people who see in the dark. So what? Cats do it, don't they? Probably those bloody poisonous eyes of his! Come on, let's get on . . .'

In the space of another five or six paces the walls of the cleft came together again, even narrower than before, so that the two must turn almost side-on to proceed. But still the steps went down. And then, as they rounded a sharp bend, light blazing ahead! – and Guigos waiting for them, sitting on a boulder, where suddenly the cleft opened into a large cave . . .

Chapter Two

The light came from a pair of torches sputtering in brackets on the rough walls. The yellow, uneven flames eddied this way and that, as if from some intermittent draft. Khumnas started forward into the cave, and . . . yes, there was a draught; he could feel fresh air striking his face. Good, clean, fresh air – wholesome air – unlike the vapours of the cleft.

The cave was perhaps fifty feet long by thirty wide, roughly oval, low-ceilinged and obviously natural. There had been some work here: a single ledge circled the cave like a bench, cut where the walls met the floor; chippings from the work were still evident and had been packed down into the floor to give it something of an even surface. Equally obvious, the work was thousands of years old.

Khumnas, still looking the place over, put up a hand to touch the ceiling just above his head. His fingers came away cold and slightly slimy. In places the seepage had formed into stalactites, most of them long since broken off to allow headroom. A few large stones were bedded into the floor's centre; George Guigos sat upon one such.

The Iraqis moved toward him but, as they approached, Khumnas's eyes stared beyond the bent, withered form of the old man to the far extreme of the cave. It was darker back there, and yet strangely luminous in one small area. Khumnas had thought he spied, in that luminous area, tiny bright points of light glittering like diamonds in the upper darkness.

Diamonds? Guigos's treasure?

Passing the old man by without a second glance, Khumnas went into the farthest part of the cave. Mhireni followed close on his heels. Now, in the greater darkness, both men could see the points of light. Also, the influx of fresh air was stronger, colder. With his hands groping before him, Khumnas came up against the wall. On a level with his chin, a jagged hole two feet across looked out to a far, night-black horizon tinged with indigo where the earth met the sky. The bright points of light were stars. Standing on his toes and turning his eyes down, the Iraqi saw the same stars mirrored in the Sea of Galilee some seven hundred and fifty feet below.

'An observation hole,' Guigos's harsh whisper echoed gratingly in the cave's confines. 'Also, ventilation. Crawl out of there and the fall would turn you to jelly – literally!'

'What is this place?' growled Mhireni. He went back to Guigos.

'It's a place to hide,' the old man answered. 'Or at least it used to be. More than two thousand years ago, when first the town was built, tribal wars were frequent and bloody. The old men, the women and children, would come down here and sit it out in times of extreme danger. The all clear would be signalled from down there on the Sea of Galilee: the bright flash of the sun reflected in a mirror of polished bronze.'

None of this was guesswork; the old man knew irrefutably that what he had said was one hundred per cent correct, fact. The brutish Mhireni sensed the truth in Guigos's explanation, but by his nature he couldn't accept anything unless there was concrete evidence.

'Huh!' he grunted. 'Oh, you're an old 'un, sure enough – but not *that* old, George Guigos!'

At that the gargoyle laughed, a choking, croaking, gasping laugh that echoed and reverberated – and ended in a strangled coughing. The way he coughed, it was almost a death rattle. He rocked where he sat and fought for air, one bony claw clutching at his stone seat for balance and support, the other clawing at his robe where it seemed to obstruct his throat.

Ihya Khumnas came quickly from the darker part of the cave, stood over the old man and stared at him in the light of the flickering torches. Guigos's face was parchment now, with all the leathery texture seemingly leeched away. He looked bleached, dry as fretted bone; he looked as if a puff of wind would tumble him to dust. Something had happened to him in the last few minutes. Something terrible. It was as if his years had suddenly decided to catch up with him, all of them at once.

He is *a mummy, yes,* thought Khumnas, *except his metabolism works in reverse. They only crumble when you fetch them* up *from their tombs . . .*

But out loud he asked: 'Are you all right?' It wouldn't do to have Guigos die here, now. Not just yet, anyway.

Guigos's coughing bout was over. He stopped rocking, lifted a spindly wrist and blinked eyes which were now turned rheumy at his wrist-watch. It was 11.40. 'I'm . . . all right, yes,' he coughed. 'But now we must hurry.' With an effort he turned his face up and stared at Khumnas. There was a film over his eyes and his gaping, diseased nostrils were red raw in his papier-mâché face.

'The treasure,' said Khumnas. 'Where is it?'

'Help me up,' Guigos held up his spider arms. The Iraqis lifted him like a child, stood him upright, held him there so that he wouldn't fall. He lifted a skinny, gnarled finger, waggled it. 'There . . . there . . .'

They looked. At one side of the cave a fat stalactite came down to meet an upthrusting mushroom of dripstone, forming a column. Between the column and the wall proper was a darkness deeper than mere shadow.

Khumnas gasp was clearly audible. Was this a secret chamber, a second cave? 'I'll take Guigos,' he told Mhireni. 'You bring one of those torches.'

Guigos was in a bad way. All of his former strength, whatever it was that held him together, seemed to be ebbing out of him. Now he was more nearly what he should be: an ancient, near-senile bag of bones. His syphilis alone should have done for him years ago. But Khumnas knew no fear as he picked the diseased ancient up and followed Mhireni where he led the way with his torch held aloft; he merely averted his face from Guigos's reeking breath.

Behind the stalactite a low arch led into a second, smaller cave. It was empty, almost bare, much similar to its larger companion. But close to the base of one wall stood twin levers of bronze: massive perpendicular rods, tall as a man, whose lower ends slotted deep into regular grooves cut in the floor. Between the levers, in deep recesses, the tops of a pair of polished stone tablets stood up out of the solid rock. Perhaps five inches wide by eighteen long, the thickness or depth of the tablets was anybody's guess.

Khumnas approached the one on the right. Carved into its top edge was a single glyph, a 'U'-shape or descending node. The one on the left was carved with the same character but inverted. Guigos seemed reluctant to look at the first but turned his eyes back to the lever on the left. 'There,' he croaked. 'That tablet, that lever. They guard the treasure . . .'

That last word was like a spur on Khumnas's flank; he put the old man down, seating him none-too-gently on the stone floor. He went to the lever and tested it braced his back and pulled at it. The thing wouldn't move an inch. Whatever mechanism was involved here, it seemed that the years had welded it solid.

Mhireni jammed his blazing torch into the floor where there was a little loose rubble, went to assist his companion. Together they hauled on the lever. And as that great bar of bronze gratingly, squealingly gave an inch or two, so the stone tablet with the ascending node rose up a little, revealing a dusty line of carved characters along the top of its face.

Guigos tried to stand but could not. He crawled to the tablet and laid trembling fingers on its surface, his dried-up lips moving as if in silent prayer – or blasphemy too revolting to utter out loud. He seemed to draw strength from the polished stone, brushed dust from its graven figures with suddenly urgent fingers, turned his walnut head and gazed fire-eyed at the two where they strained at the lever.

'Rest,' he said, something of strength returned to his voice. 'The lever is on a rachet – it will not spring back. One line at a time – that's how it was designed.' He pointed at the first line of characters. 'Can you read it, Khumnas? You, Mhireni? No, but I can. Listen.'

His eyes went back to the tablet, and the words his writhing lips then formed were terrible to hear. They made no sense to the Iraqis, though certainly they contained sounds which seemed familiar. But that's all those words were, sounds. Primal sounds from the runebook of some ancient wizard, perhaps, or a cryptogram from a text of demoniac lore. In any event, they were terrible words, and as each one was formed so Guigos's voice grew stronger until he came to the end of the line.

Even as the alien-sounding, eery cadence echoed into silence, so there came a rush of wind from the other cave to set the torch madly guttering; and a moment later thunder rumbled like a peal of distant doom, finding its way into the caves through the vent which opened over

30

the Sea of Galilee and passing through them like the inner and outer chambers of a giant's car.

Guigos's eyes were feral in the flickering torchlight. 'A storm's come up,' he said, grinning fiendishly. He glanced at his watch – an eager glance, Khumnas thought – licked quivering, shrivelled lips, urged: 'Quickly, haul away! The next line, let's have it up.'

'What is this?' cried Mhireni, plainly bewildered and even a little frightened. 'What's going on? Words on a stone? What sort of treasure is that? And a storm? Why, the skies were clear and bright not ten minutes gone!'

Khumnas felt the other's unease reaching out to him. He fought the feeling down. It wouldn't do to lose his nerve now – and it certainly wouldn't do for Mhireni to lose his. The man was strong as an ox; without him the tablet could not be raised. 'Yakob!' he snapped, covering his own nervousness, 'Yakob, what's wrong with you? So there's a storm brewing – so what? As for this tablet: its message is in code – and the code tells where the treasure is hidden!'

Khumnas had worked out that last part for himself. It was the only answer . . . wasn't it? There must be a treasure of sorts, else Guigos had not gone to all this trouble. As for putting an end to the rotting old leper: it had seemed until a few moments ago that would no longer be necessary. Now, since Nature had not seen fit to take her course after all . . . they *would* kill him, at the right moment, and leave him down here for the ages to turn into dust.

Guigos glanced once again at his watch. 11:51 – almost time to read the second line. 'Haul away,' he commanded once again, his voice coarse with a sort of eager, barely controlled lust. The Iraqis strained; the great lever tilted a fraction; the tablet grated upward from its recess, revealing the second line. 'Rest,' Guigos rasped. And: 'Listen – soon you will begin to see . . . strange things.'

Khumnas and Mhireni glanced at each other, frowned; the latter opened his flabby mouth to form a question but Guigos saw it coming and cut it off:

'No questions, not now. Just listen. It is the air down here, which acts like a drug. It is that and it is the ancient protection of the place. Like the so-called "curses" on the tombs of the Egyptian kings: superstitious rubbish! But you may see things to frighten you – except you will not be afraid because you will know that these things are mere visions, hallucinations, ephemeral as mirages.' He lied, but he had to lie else they would flee. The 'freak storm' had been one thing, but what lay ahead was far, far worse.

11:52, and now Guigos read the second line. Thunder rumbled again in the hoary caves as he pronounced those weird words, his fingers tracing them even as he read. And now it seemed that strength definitely flowed from the tablet into Guigos's withered mummy's body. He got to his knees, lifted his head and laughed bayingly – then choked as something was ejected like phlegm from his mouth. But it was not phlegm.

Guigos clawed at his throat, fell on his side, coughed up an apparently endless stream –

– Of frogs!

The Iraqis couldn't know it but they were Egyptian frogs – the spotted frogs of the Nile, *rana punctata* – and they were not the product of hallucination but of black sorcery! Ash coloured, dotted with green spots, the things hopped and slithered everywhere, apparently fleeing Guigos's yawning, rictus-contorted mouth in terrific haste. They formed a squamous column, a batrachian army that streamed past the staggered Iraqis and out of the lesser cave into the greater; and at last it was over. The sound of their massed flopping faded away.

Guigos lay sprawled upon the stone floor, coughing blood now which he wiped from his mouth with the sleeve of his robe. Weak as a kitten, he somehow raised himself up on one elbow. 'Up!' he croaked. 'The next line. Fetch it up . . .'

Wide-eyed in flickering torch-light, gaping, the Iraqis were frozen in position at the lever, goose-flesh crawling on both of them. Finally Khumnas found his voice. 'What by all that's – ?'

'Hallucination!' cried Guigos at once. 'A fever-dream. I warned you what would happen, didn't I? It was worse for me than it was for you. Now come on, man – the treasure. We're nearly there!'

'Pull,' Khumnas hoarsely ordered, prodding Mhireni in the ribs with a sharp elbow to startle him from his trance of horror. 'Pull, Yakob.'

'But – ' Mhireni began to protest, his lower lip trembling.

'It was a vision,' Khumnas cut him short. 'Think of it, of what you saw. It could *only* be a vision – you know it!'

Mhireni shook his head, said: 'I have a feeling about this. I have a very bad feeling.' But he joined Khumnas in straining at the lever. And again the bronze rod pivoted an inch or two, and a third line of runes rose up into sight.

Guigos grasped the upper six inches of protruding tablet and blew dust from the graven characters. He silently read, his yellow eyes blazing, then laughed like a madman.

'What does it say?' Khumnas was eager as Guigos himself. 'Does it mention the treasure?'

'The greatest treasure in all the world, aye!' Guigos nodded his skull of a head. 'But a good many visions, too, before the secret is revealed in full – and none of them pleasant. Now listen – and watch!'

He read the line again, out loud, and there was a power in his voice that gave the lie to the feeble body which housed it. Something had entered Guigos, was entering him even now. Something from the tablet and its hieroglyphs. He drew an awesome strength from them. They gave him renewed life, and they drove out the death in him. They drove it out in many forms.

As he came to the end of that third line of morbid runes, so Guigos collapsed again, drawing himself into his robe so that he almost disappeared under it. At the same time the inner cave was lit, however briefly, sporadically, with livid flashes of white light: lightning so bright and close that its light blazed in through the observation hole in the outer cave and penetrated even here. Then came the thunder, seeming to shake the very rock with its booming and sending down rivulets of centuried dust.

But while the thunder and lightning were stunning in themselves, there was that about Guigos which fixed the Iraqis' eyes upon him alone. For beneath his robe the mummy writhed and wriggled, causing the entire hummock of cloth to twitch and jerk. It fluttered and billowed as if disturbed by myriad small movements. Then the folds of that garment parted and a cloud of leaping motes sprang away from the almost naked, frantic figure beneath. A cloud of lice!

Unlike the frogs, the lice did not pass Khumnas and Mhireni by. They settled on them, a biting, scratching, lousy itching cloud of them that set the two yelling and leaping all about the small cave, tearing at themselves in their panic and their passion. It lasted only a few moments before the lice departed, streaming out of the cave as one individual, but that was sufficient time to leave the terrified Iraqis bleeding from countless small bites. And this time it was Mhireni who recovered first.

'Visions?' he panted, choking the word out as he advanced menacingly upon Guigos. 'Mirages? You lying old bastard! I don't know what sort of trickery you're up to, but *that* was no vision, no mirage.' He held out his arms, dribbling scarlet on the dust. 'This blood is mine – and it's real!'

'Treasure, Yakob Mhireni, treasure!' crooned Guigos. 'Think only of your wages, man. *If* you are a man . . . ?'

'What?' Mhireni scowled, baring his teeth and raising one great fist like a club.

'No!' cried Khumnas. 'Don't hit him. Let him get on with it. Can't you see he's crazy? But he'll lead us to the treasure, sure enough.'

'Huh!' grunted Mhireni. 'Crazy, him? Crazy like a fox. And treasure? I see no treasure in any of this.'

'But what if there is?' Khumnas pressed.

'Aye,' Guigos crooned. 'What if there is?' Then his voice hardened. 'Enough of your threats, Yakob Mhireni. You've been well paid, and there's more yet to come. Now get on with it.'

Mhireni gritted his teeth, stalked back to the lever bleeding and scratching himself, at flesh which already tormented with its small stings and fires. Guigos watched him go, checked the time, and his face grew livid with rage. He snarled something under his breath, and Khumnas thought he heard him say: 'Three, I need three! Where's that wily Greek got to?'

Out loud he rasped: 'Come on, you two, come on! Up with it. It must be up by midnight.'

They hauled on the lever and it moved easier now, and line by line the tablet came up – that monstrous carved stone with its ten damnations. Ten of them in all, before this thing would be finished; and their number was significant. For when the Lord had given the world the great boon of His ten commandments, Satan had answered with this . . .

Dimitrios Kastrouni had gone back for his watch. He did not want to lose it; it had been a gift from his father on his nineteenth birthday and formed his single connecting link with his past. When he had discovered its absence he'd remembered his wrist snagging on something as he crawled to the edge of the cliff. That was where the watch must be. And of course he'd found it there – and in the same moment found that time had narrowed down. Now he would get back only minutes before midnight, and then only if he hurried. Still, a minute or two could make no difference.

So Kastrouni had believed, but that was before the storm came up. Storm? It was the weirdest freak of a storm that the young Greek-Cypriot had ever seen – and in Larnaca on the east coast of Cyprus he'd seen some bad ones! But even they had kept themselves to their season; this one wasn't seasonal at all.

The lightning seemed centred over Chorazin. Indeed, the entire storm had its centre there; where black clouds boiled like a slowly revolving wheel low overhead, in a sky grown dark in less than fifteen minutes. And yet there was no rain: just the brilliant white lightning and its accompanying peals of thunder. Not that the thunder bothered Kastrouni, for he'd experienced as bad before – or very nearly – but the lightning was different.

Up here over the Sea of Galilee Kastrouni was exposed: exposed to the lightning and by it. Every flash limned him against his surroundings indelibly and marked him as an intruder. He had come out alone to ensure (ostensibly) Guigos's and the Iraqis' security, but now in this storm he could have the opposite effect: if he was seen he could

36

well attract attention. Which was why he was obliged to go circuitously, moving from hummock to crumbling wall to whatever broken ground he could find, always trying to give himself cover and at the same time attempting to gauge his movements so that they coincided with the utterly dark lapses between lightning flashes. And it was slowing him down.

With minutes left before the midnight hour, suddenly Kastrouni recognized his surroundings, saw the donkeys huddled together and trembling where lightning turned them into momentary spectres. And still no rain.

It was strange . . . *very* strange. It seemed to the Greek-Cypriot that the air was charged with a force akin to electrical energy: he could feel his skin creeping to its touch, except that this wasn't dry like an electrical charge but slimy as the skin of a long-dead fish.

He found the slab where it stood open over the gaping dark entrance to the secret place, went quickly forward and began to descend the steps, then paused to light a candle. As he did so and while the flame on the wick sputtered up to cast its light ahead, so he heard something from far below. Kastrouni's sharp ears fastened on those sounds; they froze his blood, froze his feet rigid to the steps. Eyes bugging, his hair prickling on the nape of his neck, he craned forward, listening.

There it was again: mad laughter welling up, almost but not quite drowning out . . . screams? What in the name of . . . ? Laughter, and screams, and . . . buzzing? The buzzing of –

Of countless flies!

They came up out of the darkness like a cloud, swarmed toward Kastrouni – flew round him so close he felt the wind of their wings, so massed together that they became a blue-black metallic sheen of motion – before passing him by and streaming up and out of the entrance into the night and the storm. Flies, yes: blowflies big as bees! Carrion flies, born in rotten meat or the running sores of living beasts!

Horror crawled on Kastrouni's spine. Whatever was down there was not for him. He would not go down. He backed up the stone steps, ran to a crumbling wall and crouched there trembling, his eyes glued to the dark opening of the vault. And no sooner was Kastrouni out of the place than the screaming welled up once more, screams such as he'd never heard before and hoped never to hear again. They told of agony, those screams, of pain unendurable, of Death's sure approach. But what *sort* of death?

Money could not keep Kastrouni here now. Neither money nor treasure nor any kind of promise. He was not especially superstitious, no, but neither was he a fool. Men were dying down there, in a way or ways unimaginably cruel. Guigos had to do with it, he knew, for it was the old man's laughter he heard – or would have been his in his youth! Strength was in it, a hideous strength not born of earth but hell, and it welled up even louder than the now frenzied screams of the dying Iraqis.

And as the laughter and screams faded away – even as Kastrouni gathered up the reins of a donkey and numbly untied the beast to lead it away – so there came the whirring of many wings. Smoke boiled from the opening under the slab; no, not smoke but an almost solid black column that jetted up like oil from a well, except that oil has no volition. For this jet scattered, spread, whirled like a new cloud under the greater clouds in the sky, then fled into the night on a million wings.

Members of that aerial horde struck Kastrouni and the donkey where they crept away, and one flew full in the Greek-Cypriot's face. He thought the thing was a flying cockroach and struck it down, but it felt big as a sparrow in his hand. Then, as lightning flashed again, he saw what the whirring cloud was made of: locusts!

First flies and now locusts? Kastrouni thought he must be nightmaring. What sort of Pandora's box had the three opened down there? Treasure? More like the font of everything unclean! He made to mount his donkey . . . then dragged the beast quickly into the shadows cast by a mound of rubble, as a new sound pricked up his ears. It was a mewling, a moaning, a sobbing; it was all three sounds in one, and it grew louder as something came gibbering out of the depths and into the night. Mhireni!

Mhireni, the strong one, the scarface. But not Mhireni as Kastrouni had last seen him. No, for this was a madman, a man driven mad by fear! He clawed his way up from the darkness, jaws gaping, dribbling froth. His eyes were brown bulging marbles in a purple, bloodied face where his scar stood out like a jagged stripe of white paint. What he had seen, what had happened to him, was beyond imagining; but without the slightest doubt he was totally insane.

Out in the open air what little strength remained in his massive frame now fled him; he crumpled to the ground, lay sprawled there beside the raised slab, babbled and sobbed like a child as he hugged the earth – but only for a moment.

For in the next instant there came a voice – a monstrous voice like the belch of some titan frog – and the name it croaked was that of the fear-crazed Iraqi:

'MHIRENI! YAKOB MHIRENI!'

The – voice – came from below, and it seemed to pick Mhireni up and stand him on his feet with its sheer force. Also, it was the voice of George Guigos, but amplified and intensified ten times over.

'*No!*' Mhireni babbled. 'No, not me. Take him, take Khumnas, but not me!'

39

'IHYA KHUMNAS IS NO MORE, YAKOB. YOU KNOW THAT. BUT HE WAS NOT ENOUGH. I NEED THREE. I NEED YOU, YAKOB!'

'*No!*' Mhireni cried again, frantically shaking his head. He tried to run, his feet pumping in a slow-motion parody of running. But he was exhausted, by terror, by loss of blood, whatever. His feet pumped and his arms flapped and his chest heaved, but he merely staggered. Watching, Kastrouni felt sick for the Iraqi – felt sicker yet a moment later as something else bulged into view up that demon shaft.

What it was *exactly*, Kastrouni could not say. Not then or ever. But it was nothing out of any sane or ordered universe. It was the blackly glistening stuff of nightmares!

It frothed, it lapped, it came up like inky jelly through the gap under the slab. And it was alive – and it laughed with George Guigos's voice! Ropes of black jelly whipped out from it, knocking Mhireni's lurching feet from under him. He went down screaming, and the stuff flopped over him like sentient black slime. He came upright with a blanket of the stuff clinging to him, his head and hands poking through. It tried to drag him down again. He tore at it, bounded against its elastic constriction again and again. But uselessly.

The stuff laughed. Even as it ate Mhireni alive, it laughed hideously.

Kastrouni could not, dare not move. He must stand and watch. He was ill; the earth and the boiling sky reeled about him; he saw but knew that what he saw could not be. And whatever else happened he knew that he must not scream or make a sound, and he knew that he must *not* faint. Not here, not now . . .

Still Mhireni bounded, but weakly now. And still the doughy ink-thing threw its ropes and flaps over him. And it burned, that stuff. Like acid, it sluiced away his flesh,

40

flensing him where he strained with his every last ounce of strength. He was a thing of bone and raw flesh now, a black and red blob of a man that heaved this way and that and tossed and shuddered and gurgled as it went down. Mercifully went down, for Mhireni was no longer anything human. And at last there was only the amoeba-thing pulsating half-in, half-out of the vault under the slab.

'MIDNIGHT!' the voice came again, and Kastrouni knew that it talked to itself, in the habit of Guigos. 'MUST HAVE A THIRD,' the thing said.

It strained upright, took on a vaguely manlike shape – but huge, massive, lumpy and loathsome. The other three donkeys were rearing, kicking, braying their terror to wake the dead. The man-shaped black amoeba heard them, turned lumberingly in their direction.

'MIDNIGHT – NOW!' rumbled that awful voice.

It might well have been an invocation – a call to the dark gods of the storm – and it was at once answered. Lightning walked the land on jagged, brilliant, searing legs. Lightning with a mind of its own. It *literally* walked, coming out of the east, each steaming stab at the earth a pace in the direction of Chorazin, toward the nightmare thing which even now reached out impossibly elongating pseudopods toward the donkeys.

Kastrouni saw it all: bright as day in the white light of the stalking lightning bolts, it seared itself upon the balls of his eyes – and upon his mind forever.

Still more or less upright by the open vault, the man-amoeba stood or slumped, with great ropy arms twenty feet long reaching out to the screaming animals. Two of the donkeys broke flee and fled before those black, vibrating arms could reach them, but the third was tethered much too securely. It could only rear and kick and bray. And yet, easy victim that the poor creature was, the doughy pseudopods held off.

'A . . . A DONKEY?' the awful voice questioned. 'FATHER, IS IT FITTING? THIS IS THE BEAST THAT CARRIED THE GOOD ONE!'

The lightning had paused; but now, as if by way of a command or a threat, it stabbed again – a massive bolt that struck the upright slab and hurled it flat over the yawning vault, sealing the secret place shut once more. The amoeba-thing staggered back from that blast and cried:

'I . . . I HEAR, FATHER – AND I OBEY!'

The elongated, vibrating pseudopods fell at once upon the donkey. It screamed like a man in its agony, as its flesh was absorbed and the shuddering thing at the closed vault grew larger still. Now the lightning flickered in eery traceries along the undersides of the clouds, for all the world as if the elements tittered! And by the light of that weird coruscation Kastrouni saw that which finally broke the spell to send him running into the night, then bounding onto his beast's back, then riding as if all the devils of hell rode at his heels – which indeed they might have. A sight to scar a man forever, which in fact it did, for his hair turned white in the space of that single night. It was this:

The ink-black thing where it stood with its outstretched tendrils began to shudder more violently yet – *and at the same time it began to change!*

Where a monstrous leech had imitated the shape of a man, now the head and shoulders of a *real* man became clearly visible. His face, lit by the flickering energies of the sky, was lifted in peals of awful laughter – laughter in which George Guigos's voice was still all too obviously present. But the face itself was not Guigos's face! It had the gleaming white teeth of Ihya Khumnas and his hooked nose, but it also had the white blaze of Mhireni's scar! And worse, as the metamorphosis continued down the length of that re-born thing's body, and as the donkey finally succumbed and was reduced to a sack of steaming bones . . .

. . . It was *that* which sent Kastrouni flying wildly into the night. The sight of those hairy limbs which ended not in feet but the horny black hooves of a beast. The Guigos-thing was only half man – and the rest of it was donkey!

It was only with the dawn that Kastrouni and his mount, both of them exhausted, quit their panic flight. And it was then, too, that the young Greek-Cypriot discovered it was Guigos's animal that he had taken.

Later, when he had rested, he opened and wonderingly inspected the contents of the beast's packs. And slowly but surely things began to make sense. If 'sense' was the right word for it . . .

Chapter Three

Cyprus, *July 1957*

It had been twenty-three years since Costas Kastrouni last saw his only son. In that time his two daughters had married and now had grown-up children of their own; his wife had sickened and died at only thirty-one years of age; his wine business had been reduced to a single corner store in Larnaca, where because of 'the troubles' even his trade with the British service families had fallen off. A shame, that last, because Costas had always liked the British almost as much as he now hated EOKA.

EOKA – hah! Cyprus would be in ruins before that crowd of untutored thugs and juvenile delinquents were through – and not the ruins at Kouklia and Koravastasi, either! The 'Island of Love,' indeed! Kastrouni locked up his shop early, uttered another bitter '*hah!*' and set off for his home just this side of the Turkish sector not five minutes walk from the bars and tavernas of the seafront.

The 'Turkish sector': that was worth a third '*hah!*' in itself. Many of Kastrouni's oldest friends were Turks. Turks in the business, the wine trade; Turks in shipping and transport; Turks who were his *customers* – and that last was all-important. A business needs its customers whoever they may be. But all of them ordinary Turks, unthreatening, wanting only a little peace and quiet in which to live their lives. And now – why, the Turkish-Cypriot communities were almost in states of siege! They would not cross the line for their lives, let alone a bottle of ruby-red Commanderia!

Bloody EOKA! Dumb, ignorant, swaggering, fat-arsed

terrorists! Kastrouni dug his hands deep in his pockets, cursed into his moustache, strode home under the blazing sun with his floppy hat pulled down low over his brown eyes and the neck of a bottle of good Keo brandy projecting from a string bag on his shoulder. Damn them all: them and Makarios and Grivas, and damn all the shit and snot and scummy pus they were made of! Rotten stuff, all of it.

Boys on bicycles rode along the dusty, narrow, bazaar-like Larnaca main street. They had cheap Italian spear-guns across their backs and their catch in baskets under the high sit-up-and-beg handlebars of their bikes: strings of red and grey mullets, and an octopus or two still sluggishly mobile. They held up handfuls of pink-suckered tentacles for Kastrouni to admire, and he nodded his approval as they pedalled off, triumphant and laughing.

Those had been the days, when young Dimi had used to come home just like those two, all salty from the sea and proud as a young lion with his catch of small fishes.

Dimi, ah, Dimi!

To hell with EOKA and all that; the troubles were only Kastrouni's excuse. He knew what had really been upsetting him these last few days. It was the Armenian, Khumeni. (At least, Kastrouni suspected the man was Armenian.) It was what Khumeni had said that upset him. It was the hope he'd held out, and the frustration. But . . . now he must put it from his mind, for he was home.

Home. The old house, where Dimi and his sisters had grown up; where their mother Cleanthis had lived with him, and died in his arms; where he now lived with memories, faded photographs and too much brandy. He let himself into the tiny courtyard under the vine, crossed to the door of the house, reached up and felt for the key over the door lintel – and the key wasn't there. Kastrouni frowned, shrugged, allowed himself a nod and a small smile. One of his daughters had come visiting. That must be it.

He pushed open the door and entered into cool gloom, calling: 'Hello? Who's come to see me, eh? And are there grandchildren here, too?' He stared into the room, letting his eyes grow accustomed to the contrast of shadow after brilliant sunlight – then drew air in a sharp, audible gasp.

This was the main room, sparsely furnished, low-ceilinged, fairly large by Cypriot standards. Kitchen led off to the right, bathroom and shower to the left, wooden stairs climbed a side wall to three small bedrooms above. But against the shuttered rear windows the shadow of a man was striped with thin bars of light, and there was something familiar about his posture, the way he held his head, that –

'No,' came his voice, deep and low. 'No grandchildren, father. Only a son.'

A son? *Dimi!* But it couldn't be. Dimi was little more than a boy and this was a man full-grown, and –

Suddenly Kastrouni realized how old Dimitrios would be now, and how much older he himself was. He *felt* old, weak at the knees, and staggered a little as he moved uncertainly forward across the familiar room. His son came to meet him, clasped him in that dim room of bright memories, hugged him tightly.

Because he had grown tall and his father had shrunk down a little with age and worries, Dimitrios Kastrouni's hot tears fell on the old man's leathery neck, while Costas's were lost in his son's jacket.

'It was . . . an omen,' the elder Kastrouni finally gulped. He pushed his son away, held him at arm's length, stared at him. 'An omen,' he repeated, nodding. 'I heard your name spoken not three days ago. A man

46

called Khumeni told me he knew you in Israel many years ago. He asked after you. I told him I knew nothing, not even your address – not even if you were alive any more. Your last letter is – oh, two years old now?' There was reproach in the old man's voice, but not too much. Before his son could begin to make excuses, he quickly went on:

'Listen, Dimi, it's all right. Just to know you're alive, here, home, makes everything all right! You're my son . . . my son . . .'

The old man was over-excited, the younger Kastrouni could feel it. He drew him close again, held him tight. 'Father, I won't be able to stay – you have to understand that. I'm as much wanted now as I was – then. I'm a murderer, remember?'

'Murder? More than twenty years ago? You should have stayed. You'd have been out in no time at all. Why, in France they'd have called it a crime of passion! It was your hot blood. The Kastrounis have always been hot-blooded. We should have expected it.'

'Not good enough,' Dimitrios smiled wanly, shook his head. 'None of it. A pack of excuses, and there's no excuse for murder. Her family will never forget – or forgive. And as for his . . .'

'His? The boy you killed? *Hah!* And maybe you weren't so wrong to kill him at that! His two younger brothers have turned into worse murderers than you could ever be. At least you had reason – by this island's standards, anyway – and you did it cleanly, out in the open. But they are members of EOKA – the Ethnike Organosis Kyprion Agoniston – which means that they're glorified butchers!'

Dimitrios nodded. 'I know about EOKA, father. Everyone knows. We get all the news on the mainland. It's one of the reasons I'm back, because I was worried

47

for you and the girls. But on the other hand . . . Listen, I live in Athens now, where in fact I'm doing very well – but I have to tell you this: if it wasn't for EOKA I couldn't have come back at all.'

'What?' his father was shocked. 'You came back with them?' His voice had grown angry in a moment, shaking with outrage.

'*Shh!*' Dimitrios cautioned. 'With them? What do you mean? What are you thinking? That I work for Grivas? How could you think that of me? I'm a businessman like my father, not a thug! No, I only came back to see you and my sisters. But if EOKA hadn't sort of prepared the way for me . . .' He let it tail off.

'I . . . I don't understand,' Costas Kastrouni shook his head.

'It's easy,' said Dimitrios. 'Listen: for fifteen years I've looked for a way to come back, but could never find one. Even though my face changed, even though *I* changed, someone might just recognize me. Because, of course, the people here are curious, and they had nothing better to do – nothing better to occupy them. A stranger was always a source of terrific interest. You know that. But now . . . now people have a lot more on their minds. That's what I meant when I said EOKA have paved the way for me. Do you see what I mean? It's unwise to look at anyone too closely in Cyprus these days.'

Costas agreed, gave a curt nod. 'Except the wrong ones,' he added. '*They* look, all right!'

'Let them look,' said Dimitrios. 'The British have outlawed them anyway. They have their own problems. But this is my plan: I'm going to spend a few weeks in Troodos.'

'Troodos? The mountains? But I'll want to see you! And what about your sisters? You're an uncle four times

48

over, Dimi. Don't you want to know your nephews and nieces?'

'Of course I do,' Dimitrios smiled, clasped his shoulders. 'They can come and see me in Troodos – and so can you! I have money, father. More than enough for all of us. We'll stay in a Troodos hotel, in Platres, perhaps. Separate rooms. I'll be a visitor from the mainland, a stranger, and you'll be up there for your health, the fresh mountain air . . .'

The elder Kastrouni slowly nodded, began to grin as the notion caught on. 'It's a good plan, Dimi, yes. And it's the truth: I could use a holiday. Your sisters, too.'

'Good!' the other was pleased. 'So I'll go up to Troodos in a few days and you can follow at your leisure. And you'll let the girls know about me, too – but discreetly! Make them understand that they mustn't breathe my name to anyone.' He released his father, stepped to the shuttered windows and laid his hands on the catches.

'Is that wise?' It was Costas's turn to caution. 'I mean, the window?'

'I can't live in the dark, father,' his son smiled. 'Not even here in Larnaca. And it *is* your courtyard; I don't suppose anyone's out there. Anyway, I want to see my father – and clearly, with the light of day on his face!' He opened the shutters.

Costas Kastrouni was sixty-five but looked ten years older. His son studied his lined face, forced a broad smile, tried not to show his concern. But he blamed himself, at least in part. His running away had taken the old man hard; on top of which there had been the death of his mother, harder still, and now these damned troubled times. But –

'You look good, father,' he lied. 'Hardly a day older than when I last saw you.'

'Huh!' the other was pleased – but he was also more

truthful: 'I wish I could say the same for you, Dimi. But your hair! It's quite white. You must have worried terribly over the years, son.'

'Worry? Oh, I've worried, I suppose. But that's not what bleached my hair. That was something that happened in Israel, in a ruined town on the Lake of Galilee.' And now he frowned long and hard.

'Son?'

'Father, I wasn't listening to you properly when you first came in here out of the sunlight. But I remember you said something about an omen, and you mentioned someone who had known me in Israel. Who was he, this man? I believe you spoke his name . . . ?'

'Khumeni. George Khumeni. He's Armenian, I think. It's a strange name, though. I know most of the Armenian families in Larnaca, but none of them called Khumeni. This one says he's here on holiday – for the sun and the sea. He's rich, certainly; he has three men along just to look after him. And he's old, too. Or maybe he's not too old, I'm not sure . . .'

Dimitrios frowned again, his interest gaining ground. 'But what has he to do with you, this Khumeni?'

His father shrugged. 'He has the villa on the coast. Hired it for a fortnight. Moved in just two days ago. There was a nice British family in there, a Warrant Officer from the garrison in Dhekelia, but they went to Germany a month ago. There'll be another British family taking the place over in just a few weeks; till then – ' he shrugged again, ' – this Khumeni offered good money.'

The 'villa' he mentioned was in fact a second house he'd built on the coast, very privately situated between Larnaca and Dhekelia, a roomy place to which he'd intended moving, leaving the house in Larnaca to his son if and when he took a wife. After Dimitrios had fled the island, however, he had started letting the place and had

50

continued to do so for over twenty years. His daughters hadn't needed it; they had both married men with property of their own.

'Khumeni,' Dimitrios rubbed his nose, still frowning. 'And he said he knew me in Israel? By my Greek name? That's hardly likely. I don't recall anyone called Khumeni. In fact, I don't remember any Armenians at all!'

The old man sniffed. 'Perhaps he was just making conversation. After all, he didn't seem to know anything of you or your personal circumstances – and I certainly wasn't going to tell him. Anyway, he didn't ask. Why should he?'

Why indeed? But . . . 'Khumeni,' Dimitrios said again, sourly, his nostrils flaring, which they always did when he was confronted with anything suspicious. 'George Khumeni, *hmm*! What's he like?'

'Like? I don't know. We did our business by telephone. He was in Nicosia when we spoke. He arrived the next day in a hired car. I was at the villa to greet him, but his entourage swept him in and I hardly got a glimpse of him. Then one of his men came out, gave me my money and that was that.'

'So how did my name come up?' Dimitrios pressed.

'It was just that when I spoke to him on the phone he mentioned having known a Kastrouni in Israel.' The old man was growing impatient with all this. 'Look, what is this, Dimi?'

His son slowly shook his head. 'I'm not sure. It just seems funny, that's all. I'm probably being over-cautious.' He deliberately put aside his worried thoughts and smiled. 'Anyway, how is the villa? Do you look after it?'

'Every year, before the really hot weather comes in, I go up and give it the once over. A touch of paint here, a new stick of furniture, you know? It was a good investment, so I look after it.'

'I remember it was finished the summer before . . . before I got myself in trouble. I used to go up and watch them working on it. There was a space under the flat roof I could crawl into. Sometimes, after spear-fishing, I'd go up under there and gaze out to sea – and often fall asleep! I liked the villa. I was proud my father had two houses and I was jealous of you that you'd be living there when I was married, and I'd only have this place.' He laughed, however wryly. 'And now? What I'd give to have spent the last twenty years here – right here, in this little house!'

There were tears in his father's eyes. Dimi had awakened old memories. The elder Kastrouni tried to answer but could only gulp loudly. Finally he nodded. 'What you'd give? What *I* would give! But too late, it's done.'

Dimitrios changed the subject, tried to console him: 'Father, we can talk now and have a drink together, and make our plans for Troodos. Tonight I'm going out, but after dark. Don't worry, I'm not staying in Larnaca but going somewhere I'm not known. But I have to go for I've people to see and one or two things I must do.'

'People? Things?'

'Just things, father. Nothing to get concerned about. I've learned how to be very careful. Anyway, I'll be back long before morning.'

'But – '

'Just trust me.'

To which request the old man could only acquiesce . . .

When night falls on Cyprus it comes down like a shutter. From the sky's sharp, bright blue with its solitary line of black on the sea's horizon, to darkness sweeping shut like a curtain hung with stars, and all in the space of a few minutes. The ever-present chirping din of the cicadas takes on a strange clarity whose rhythm seems full of secret meaning, like a cryptic insect Morse-code rising up in the heat of the night.

It was the sudden intensity of the cicadas' songs – that and night's muffling of other sounds – which brought Dimitrios Kastrouni bolt upright in his old room upstairs in his father's Larnaca house; but it was mainly the cicadas. And it was their drilling, sizzling song of hot fat frying which brought the sweat starting in salty solicitude from his body's pores. Insects had that sort of effect on him . . . now. He'd felt that way about them ever since Israel. He could take them one at a time, on their own; but *en masse*, when they seemed joined in this weird single-mindedness of purpose or pursuit, that was too much for him.

To get it off his mind he got up, quickly dressed, stole downstairs. The old man slept in his chair, empty glasses standing on a wooden table close at hand, just where father and son had left them. They had talked until Costas had had his fill of brandy and nodded off, and then Dimitrios had gone upstairs to sleep, until nightfall and the cicadas had woken him up. But now there was something he must do, and until he had done it there'd be no more rest for him. He had to know about this man Khumeni. There could be no connection, no, of course not, but still he had to be sure. And he had good reasons for wanting to be sure . . .

Over the years, ever since that monstrous night in Chorazin, Kastrouni had thought long and often on what he had seen there in that dead, doomed city. Much of it was still very clear in his mind, seared there, but his mind *itself* had long since stopped believing in it. It had been hallucination, nightmare, a bout of madness – any or all of these things – but it had not been real. How could it have been? And Guigos, George Guigos: whoever he

53

had been, he could not possible be alive now. Could he? No, of course not, for he had been ancient even then. By now he would be bones picked clean by the worms. Surely . . .

And yet there had been the contents of the packs on Guigos' donkey: those esoteric books, old parchments, fragments of half-forgotten, long discredited or 'forbidden' incunabula. Oh, yes – and at various times Kastrouni had studied all such in great depth over the years.

Guigos had been a diabolist, beyond doubt, and he'd wrought diabolic things. But his magic, however 'black,' was still only magic: stage-trickery dressed up to look real. For all Kastrouni knew, the things he *thought* he had seen that night had been rigged to frighten him off, so that he would have no claim to the balance of the money Guigos had promised him. And perhaps the other two had been dealt with in a like fashion. Perhaps Ihya Khumnas and Yakob Mhireni had been similarly frightened off, thus forfeiting their wages also. That must be the truth of the matter . . . mustn't it?

Sometimes, rather than face an unthinkable truth or an untenable situation, the human mind will fashion all kinds of excuses for those things it does not want to believe. Kastrouni's mind was no exception to this rule, but it did retain its great curiosity. And because he was still a fugitive, it was a curiosity which the years had taught him to temper with wariness. The curiosity of a fox, and stealth to match. He was a fox now as he drove a battered hire-car along the coastal road from Larnaca in the direction of Dhekelia . . .

About half-way between town and garrison he drove past Yanni's Casino, a sprawling concrete bar and taverna standing midway between the road and the sea, and remembering the place from his boyhood he smiled. 'Casino,' indeed! The only gaming he'd ever seen in the place was in the shape of a trio of one-armed bandits! Actually Yanni's wasn't intended to be a casino at all; it catered for weddings and other receptions, political meetings, social and ethnic festivities of many sorts, and so forth. Its main attraction was its large, open hall, which doubled as a restaurant, and its views of the ocean.

The smile quickly slipped from his face. This was where the man – the youth, really – he'd killed would have brought his new bride. And since then twenty years had flown by, and now here he was, Dimitrios Kastrouni, back on the island from which he'd once fled for his life. Back to see his father, his sisters, the place where he'd grown up in what now seemed a different age. And back to come face to face with this ominous coincidence: this man who said he had known him back in Israel.

The bright lights of Yanni's Casino faded in his rearview. One or two cars passed him, heading for Larnaca. The road was fairly quiet, and that suited him perfectly. Another mile and he'd be there.

Khumeni . . .

George Khumeni.

And this stranger – this man who rented his father's villa – he had three along to guard him, did he? That other George had also had three men to do his work for him. And over the years . . . hadn't Kastrouni had his suspicions? Hadn't he time and again suspected that someone, some*thing*, tracked him – sniffed at his heels, followed his spoor as he constantly changed his identity, covered his tracks and moved on?

Of course, it could simply be that he'd developed a morbid phobia, a sickness of the mind. He supposed that there would be a name for it, this fear of being tracked down and brought to justice. It wasn't just a persecution complex, for there was guilt there, too. After all, he *had* killed a man; but did he fear retribution for that, or for

55

something else? Whatever it was, he supposed that the great Nazi war criminals must all have suffered from it – until the day they *were* tracked down. And now the thing was in him, too. Either that . . . or there really had been someone on his trail ever since that night in old Chorazin.

And what if that someone and this George Khumeni were one and the same? And what if Khumeni was also one and the same with . . . with someone else?

'That can't be!' Kastrouni snarled out loud. 'It *can't* be!' But again that niggling doubt in the back of his mind, asking: 'Oh, can't it?'

Where the road swung a little away from the sea, in a fenced grove of pomegranates and olives at the foot of a long, wide garden, there stood the villa. It had a dirt path leading to it for maybe a hundred yards, then a gravel drive through the garden to the front of the house. Of fairly modern design – or at least of a design still greatly in fashion – it was a low and spacious bungalow, very clean and attractive, airy, uncluttered.

Kastrouni saw it from the road, slowed down, stared hard into the night. He wound down his window, slowed his car's pace to a crawl. The sea made a low, barely audible *hush, hush,* where it breathed against the land like a great sleeping head on a pillow. The sea and the cicadas, nothing more. But a light shone in the villa.

Kastrouni spotted a vehicle's headlights moving toward him from Dhekelia. He picked up a little speed, turned his face away as the other car sped by, watched it in his rearview. Its braking lights came on and it turned down the track to the villa. He hadn't seen the occupant or occupants and presumed they hadn't seen him; probably one or more of this Khumeni's henchmen.

Less than a hundred yards farther on there had used to be a sparse copse of Mediterranean pines standing just off the road. If the land hadn't been cleared . . .

It hadn't.

Kastrouni parked the car under the trees, made his way back toward the villa along the beach. He knew every inch of the way, seemed to be familiar with every washed pebble on the shore. Nothing had changed. But as he approached the house a second car came down the path from the road, causing him to duck low as its lights cut a swath in the night over his head. Perhaps this Khumeni was throwing a party or some such. If so, the house seemed oddly quiet. Whichever, he would soon know for sure. And he would know for sure about Khumeni, too.

The villa was probably unique on the island for its roof, certainly in the Greek sectors. Dimitrios's father was originally Rhodian and had wanted incorporated into his new home the ceiling beams peculiar or special to that island; but at the same time he had known that the winter rains along the Larnaca coast – often violent as monsoons – would demand a roof sturdier than those of village houses on Rhodes. Hence the double roof: a slightly sloping concrete slab roof on reinforced supports over a flat Rhodian roof of thick pine tongue-and-groove planking, sealed on top with bitumen and white gravel. Inside, the pine ceiling was varnished and supported by the carved and beaded Lindian beams the old man so fondly remembered from his childhood. The villa was weatherproof and well insulated, cool in the summer and warm in the winter. And between the two roofs – a space where a man could hide. Or a youth, anyway. The way Kastrouni remembered it, it hadn't been too tight a squeeze; but he guessed he was a lot bigger now, bulkier. Certainly he was heavier . . .

At the ocean-facing fence – a wire trellis held up on red-leaded iron staves, itself supporting a vine extending all the way to the house – Kastrouni took off his jacket, bundled it up and put it down in shadow. His shirt was black and merged with the dark mass of the vine where he reached up, caught hold of a thick, gnarly branch, lifted his feet like a circus acrobat and swung them through the gap between the trellis and a ceiling of blue-shining, almost ripe grapes. Then, when he soundlessly lowered his feet, he was inside the garden.

And that was when he once more became aware of the cicadas. Or rather, it was when he noticed their silence; a silence like that of the tomb. Kastrouni shuddered. Most tombs, anyway.

He brought his mordibly wandering mind back to the present: the cicadas were still as the night, their voices switched off like a single light, as if someone had thrown a universal switch. Even the sea was silent, its *hush, hush* against the shingle beach suddenly stilled.

Kastrouni held his breath, listened. And it was as if all around him the night, too, held its breath.

The thing lasted for only a moment; it was over when a third car approached the front of the house, the purr of its engine opening a door in the silence and allowing the sea and the cicadas once more to breach the threshold of reality. Kastrouni heard the car's engine switched off, heard two of its doors open and slam shut one after the other, and was glad sound had returned. But for all that he jiggled his little fingers in his ears and shook his head to clear it, still the sea didn't sound quite the same, and there seemed a new, timid note in the song of the cicadas.

He moved quickly through the dark garden to the house. The lights on this, the ocean-facing side, were out, but still he was careful to keep low and not put his silhouette on the silver sea, the floating moon or the stars. Above him the straight edge of the concrete room loomed blackly, a shutter on the Milky Way, where beside him a stepped wall of fancy breeze blocks formed

58

his ladder to the gap between inner and outer roofs. He climbed carefully, noiselessly. Up there, between the roofs on the external perimeter of the building, he knew there was a facade of varnished marine plywood; but he also knew where a section of the ply was hinged to allow for inspection of the inner roof. In a corner where the breeze-block wall met the actual wall of the house, he wedged himself firmly in position and put both hands to work in the darkness searching for the flap. He found it, lifted the vertical trapdoor on hinges which nerve-grating squealed a little, for they hadn't been oiled in years, and squeezed himself in through the gap. Lowering the trapdoor behind him, he found himself at once plunged in utter darkness.

The gap between the roofs was such that Kastrouni could barely crawl, and even then his shirt dragged on the rough concrete above. Cobwebs were thick and the dust his movements stirred up choking; also, the gravel finish over the bitumen was sharp on his hands and knees and in places loose, so that he must be careful not to disturb it for fear of the harsh, sandpapering sound it would make. For the moment, however, he'd stay perfectly still and make sure that the squealing of the trapdoor had not attracted anyone's attention, and while he waited give some thought to his next move.

The darkness was not total after all. Some little starlight filtered in through ill-fitting joints in the ply panels, and ahead of Kastrouni at the front of the house, lamplight came up in dusty beams through several small knotholes in the pine boards. He knew those knotholes well enough: he was the one who had poked his fingers through them, knocking out the hard cores, when this pine ceiling had been brand new! Yes, and he'd counted on it that they'd never been stopped up. For now they were to be his peepholes on this Khumeni.

Now from below, also from the front of the house, came the low murmuring of voices. Kastrouni could make nothing of what was said. On elbows and knees he began to make his way toward the dust-filtered beams of light – and at once collided with something in the gloom, his right elbow sending it sliding and clattering on the gravel. He stopped moving, stopped breathing, even tried to stop the sudden wild hammering of his heart. And he listened . . .

The low murmurings had ceased. He could detect nothing, and yet it was as if a large dog had suddenly, silently pricked up its ears. And in the next moment: 'Was that outside? The back of the house? Take a look. I want no snoopers!'

That voice: was there something in it that Kastrouni recognized? It was mud and oil, that voice, thick and glutinous, but yet viscously fluid as treacle. It had not spoken Greek or Armenian but more nearly Iraqi. Kastrouni's nostrils flared and his flesh grew cold. He felt he knew the owner of that voice.

He lay perfectly still, listened to soft but hurrying footsteps below and the clicking of switches as lights were put on almost directly beneath him. Thin light at once filtered up through poor joints in the pine boards, and thinner beams through nail holes and other tiny apertures. Then the sound of a door thrown open, and a moment later muted voices from the garden where minutes earlier Kastrouni had crouched.

He listened attentively:

'Should we go onto the beach?' (American, that voice.)

'Hell, no! It's almost clear as day under these stars. If there was a kitten on that beach you could see it from right here. And if there was someone here he's long gone. No good to look for footprints: it's all pebbles.' (This one, too, American; but where the first had been cautious, this second voice contained something of a sneer. The voice of a man too sure of himself.)

'What about those trees along the beach, between the road and the sea?' inquired the cautious voice. Kastrouni gritted his teeth: that was where he'd left his car.

'You want to take a look, take a look,' snorted the other, disgustedly. 'I say you're too jumpy. *I* say: you check around that way to the front of the house, and I go this way. We meet at the front. If there's nothing in the garden, that's it. Me, I'm not going anywhere. I want to know what our Georgie is up to with those women!'

The first voice growled a warning: 'Yeah? Well, OK – but watch your lip. He hears you taking the piss like that and he'll have your balls!'

'It's been tried,' the other grunted.

'The guy you replaced used to say the same thing. We still don't know what happened to him . . .'

Footsteps were soft in the night, dividing, circling the house to the front. Kastrouni remained perfectly still, prayed that cramp wouldn't set in, wondered what it was he'd bumped into in the darkness. As voices drifted up to him again – the oily voice with its Iraqi accent and one other, polished, English – he reached out his hand in search of whatever it was he'd sent skittering. And the moment his fingers made groping contact he knew. The plastic-coated steel body; the pistol-grip, safety-catch; the long, heavy projectile itself still seated in position atop the barrel: it was his speargun!

He fingered the rubber hurlers and found them in tatters, rotted away. But beside the gun a hinged tin box, and Kastrouni's memory flooding now with pictures twenty years forgotten. He'd used to keep spares in this box and maintenance gear: spare rubbers, trident heads for the spear, some talc and a small bottle of oil.

Spare hurlers . . . Kastrouni wondered if they'd kept.

He waited until he heard the two at the front of the house, heard them enter and their voices join others in a low conversation, then opened the box and took out the spare rubbers. They were still good! Trying to catch all of the conversation – or if not its substance, at least its mood – he removed the old rubbers from the speargun, replaced them, began to lightly oil the mechanism. The spear itself felt rusty – its trident welded to the shaft – but the gun still seemed in working order. Praying the rubbers wouldn't snap, he slowly stretched them and loaded the weapon, then carefully placed it to one side. Just knowing it was there made him feel a lot easier in his mind.

The voices were louder now, and it seemed to Kastrouni that two of them were a little heated. He crawled soundlessly, laboriously forward until he found a knothole over the main entrance hall. Putting his eye to the hole he saw that four men stood below him in the porch. He looked down almost directly on top of their heads. On a wooden bench against one wall there half-reclined a woman whose features and clothing defined her as one of the island's upper class Turkish-Cypriots. Her head lolled back a little and Kastrouni could see that she was quite young and very beautiful – and either very drunk or drugged almost unconscious! To the right of the group an open door led to a corridor with two bedrooms leading off.

Now one of the four men – a figure with a lop-sided, peculiar half-crouch, who had his back to Kastrouni – spoke up in that volcanic mud voice of his: 'In there, I said – put her in the second room, on the bed beside the English girl.' His voice contained a note of authority – and a barely veiled threat. This could only be Khumeni.

One of the Americans, a tall, thin man with slicked-back blond hair, stepped closer to the one who commanded. 'And I asked why! Look, Georgie, I don't mind the work and the money's good. Also, I get to travel. But see, I like to know what I'm doing. I hate working in the dark, you know?'

'Oh?' said Khumeni. 'And did your last boss spare you so much time? Did the Mafia treat you *that* well? Did they tell you all the whys and wherefores? Listen, Garcia, the only reason you're alive now is because I needed a man with your talents as they were described to me. A talent for kidnapping, and possibly a talent for killing. How long have you been with me now? Three weeks, a month? The only talent you've shown until tonight is an unhealthy curiosity! Be careful – I might yet send you back to the tender mercies of Mike Spinneti.'

The man Garcia was suitably cowed. He backed off, looked down at the floor, said: 'I only thought to – '

'You think too much!' Khumeni snarled at him. 'And mostly you think of women. That's your trouble, isn't it? Women! You like to think you're getting your share – even when you've no share coming. It's what got you on the wrong side of The Family. Shame on you, Garcia! And she was one of theirs, too. Well, *these* women are mine – mine, you hear? If only for tonight. And I'm far more jealous of them than ever the Mafia could be. Now, when we fly out of here back to America, will you want paying in gold, Garcia – or would you prefer some other heavy metal?'

That visibly shook the other man. He sputtered, made vague motions with his hands. He might have started to protest, but again Khumeni cut him off: 'Now do as I say! Take her to the second room and put her on the bed next to the English girl. And try to keep your grubby fingers off her. 'You – ' Clumsy as a cripple, he half turned to look at the closest of the other two men. 'You help him.'

The two Americans picked up the doped, unprotesting

63

woman between them as if she was a sack of potatoes. Grunting, they carried her through the open door and out of sight. Khumeni reached out and closed the door behind them, then stumblingly turned to the Englishman. 'Willis,' he gurglingly whispered, 'I think this Tony Garcia is going to be a problem – if we let him. When this is over, remind me to think of a suitable solution.'

The other nodded. Immaculately dressed and straight-backed, he flicked imaginary specks of dust from his sleeve. And in his pure English he said: 'Like sulphuric acid? That is a solution, isn't it? I was always very bad at chemistry.' His voice was cold as ice, so perfectly metrical as to be almost mechanical.

Khumeni chuckled. 'That's what I like about you, Bernard Willis,' he said. 'Even your jokes are quite emotionless! Perhaps I'll let you deal with Garcia, eh? Maybe that will give you a real laugh . . .'

Chapter Four

Kastrouni's flesh was crawling again.

There was something about this Khumeni, an impossible something which he, Kastrouni, had to find out about, had to discover one way or the other beyond any reasonable doubt. But the way the man talked, the way he stood – like a cripple – his arrogant attitudes of command, authority, threat: they were all identical to that *other* figure, that figure whose presence at the back of Kastrouni's mind was like a corpse rotting, whose stink kept wafting up from a mental grave which by now should lie forgotten. Impossible, yes – but there were the books, the paraphernalia from the packs, and there was . . . there was this Khumeni.

Kastrouni controlled himself, resisted for the moment the temptation to find a new position; but he desperately wanted to get a good look at Khumeni's face. The others – the American thugs and this Englishman – they were only ciphers; well, perhaps Willis was a little more than that; but Khumeni was the key, the focal point about which all else revolved.

The Americans came back. 'Done,' said the one with the cautious voice. 'All done, Mr Khumeni. What now?'

'Now, Gillfellon?' Khumeni answered. 'Now you two can get out of it. Take your cars back to Nicosia. We're all four booked on the 2:00 A.M. flight. Wait at the airport and keep a low profile. Willis and I will be there in plenty of time.'

'And meanwhile – what will you do?' (This from Garcia.) 'You and Willis?'

'Willis will wait for me and bring me to Nicosia, of course.'

Garcia licked his lips, brushed fingers through his grease-shiny, slicked-back hair. 'And . . . the women?' he inclined his head toward the open door to the bedrooms.

'You never learn, do you?' said Khumeni quietly, gratingly. And to Willis: 'Bernard, if this lout isn't out of here and in his car by a count of ten, I want you to put your gun in his right ear and pull the trigger!'

Garcia stepped back, reached toward his inside jacket pocket, froze. Willis held a weapon on him, its blocky silencer unwavering. The gun had seemed to appear from nowhere. Cool as ice, Willis inquired: 'Can I put one in his belly first?' He casually aimed the automatic in the general direction of Garcia's navel.

Khumeni appeared to ignore him. 'One,' he said. And: 'Two . . . three . . .'

Garcia didn't wait for four. He left the door swinging open on the night. The man Gillfellon backed out after him, looking sickly and shrugging apologetically.

'Actually,' said Khumeni when he heard the engines of their cars start up, 'I don't like either one of them. Make a note of that, Willis.'

Willis pocketed his weapon. 'Where shall I wait for you?'

Khumeni gave a lop-sided shrug. 'Here, if you like.'

Willis shook his head. 'No, I think I'd rather be a little more remote than that. You're in a devilish mood, George, and I've been with you long enough to know how unhealthy that is. For anyone too close to you, I mean.'

Khumeni laughed like the gurgling of an underground sump. He nodded. 'As you will. Then go somewhere and park your car and smoke a cigarette or two, but be back in an hour. By that time it will be over. By then, too, we'll do well to get ourselves off this island. Tomorrow it will be a bad placc to be. The situation, as they say, will be deteriorating. Or if you like, all hell will be breaking loose here.' And again he laughed.

Willis visibly shuddered, then controlled himself. 'I have a feeling it will be breaking long before then,' he said. 'Indeed, shortly . . .' He headed for the door. 'Very well, I'll go for a little drive – but tell me,' he half turned, paused at the door. 'Why here? Oh, I know that you want to turn Greek and Turk and British soldier each against the others – but why here, this house? You were very specific about that: that it should start in the house of this Costas Kastrouni. And you've named him in those messages you've arranged. But why him? What's he done to you?'

'The old man? Nothing,' said Khumeni. 'It was his son, a long time ago. As for what he did . . . you've seen me, Bernard. You know!'

Khumeni's words froze Dimitrios Kastrouni rigid. Even with his monstrous suspicions, still he believed he could no longer trust his own ears. But he could see Willis's face: it grew pale as the Englishman said, 'The old man's son had something to do with . . . with that?'

Khumeni nodded. 'Yes, he had everything to do with it. I suppose you could say he made an ass of me, eh?' But now there was no laughter, not even a chuckle. 'I'm just settling an old score, that's all. I haven't yet tracked down the man who did this to me, so I'm exacting payment from his father. Payment in full!'

Up above the two, Kastrouni's thoughts whirled. Feverishly, he tried to make some sense of what he'd heard. It had formed, in effect, a confirmation of everything he'd feared most in this world. And now, as further confirmation, what he wanted most of all was just one good look at Khumeni's face. Oh, he knew well enough how that face would look, but he must see it anyway. And then there would be only one thing left to do, one last act to perform if Dimitrios Kastrouni was to know any peace at all on this earth. And that would be the killing of the man who now called himself George Khumeni.

As Willis left the house and Khumeni went through into the corridor leading to the bedrooms, Kastrouni squirmed backwards like a lizard until he could reach behind him and locate his speargun. He fondled the pistol-grip and gritted his teeth in the confines and the dusty gloom of the space between the roofs. And awkwardly carrying his weapon before him, he crawled forward again until he was over the first bedroom. There he brushed away a shroud of thick cobwebs and carefully put his eye to a tiny knothole. Any small sound he might have made was drowned out by the crunch of gravel under the tyres of Willis's car as he drove away from the villa; by that and by Khumeni's own activity in the room below; or so Kastrouni must hope.

But if he'd thought that at last he might see the supposed Armenian's face, here he was cheated. The small bedroom below was lighted with a single oil lamp; not only was the light dim but fumes rising from the lamp stung his straining eye where he gazed down into the dusky gloom of the room.

Khumeni was there, a shadow standing at the foot of the bed, head bowed almost as if in supplication. Then, as he began to mumble harshly, Kastrouni saw that it *was* supplication of a sort. Entreaty, yes. Prayer – but to whom? Or to what . . . ?

'Master,' Khumeni's voice gurgled up and mixed with the oily smoke of the lamp. 'Most Devoted Servant of Shaitan – Avatar of the Great Fallen One, Whose Beauty is Unbearable – His Messenger on Earth and among men – Father, aid now Thy son, this wholly worthless one whose only desire is to prosper Thy will abroad, in the Name of Our Lord, Shaitan! Demogorgon, let Thy great lust come into me, that tonight I may father men in my likeness as Thou fathered me in Thine! I call upon Thee in the name of Ab – which was my first name – and by the Unholy Tablet of Power, writ by Shaitan Himself!'

As the last words were spoken – invocation to forces Kastrouni knew now existed, and not merely in some mazed corner of his mind – so there came . . . a change. It was as quick as that: there was an immediate alteration in the atmosphere (in the ether?) and a terrific and very tangible depression of Kastrouni's spirit; his soul at once felt weighted with lead. The knothole, which only a single tick of a clock ago had issued thin oil fumes and a weak beam of light, now vented a continuous icy blast, so that the hidden watcher almost cried out loud as he jerked his face to one side and dabbed furiously at his watering eyes with the back of his wrist. But as the blast of frozen air died down a little, determined to discover exactly what the man – the creature? – below was about, he once more lowered his face into position.

And at once some of the words Khumeni had spoken made sense. 'Let Thy great lust come into me,' he had begged, and certainly something appeared to have come into him. His outline was dimmer now in the guttering light of the lamp, but it was an outline filled with motion. As Kastrouni watched, so the shape below seemed to swell larger as Khumeni literally tore off his clothes and hobbled to the single bed. Upon it, for the first time, Kastrouni saw the sprawled form of a female: one of the women Garcia had mentioned, but not the Turkish-Cypriot woman. This one seemed dressed more in the mode of a Greek peasant girl, though in this poor light Kastrouni couldn't be sure. In any case, he was more interested in Khumeni.

Glaring through his knothole in red-eyed, morbid fascination, he strained to make out the figure of the man more clearly. His figure and his face. But uselessly; the room below might as well be in total darkness.

Now Khumeni had stripped the woman, turning her face downward, mounting her like a beast where he stood upright beside the bed and gripped her to him. And his grunting and laughter and bestial slobbering almost completely drowned out the moaned and sharply gasped protests of his only half-conscious victim. Hearing those protests, Kastrouni saw that indeed she was Greek-Cypriot; he felt the hot blood surge in his veins, gripped his speargun tighter yet. It could be of course that these women were here of their own free will, but he doubted it. Then, with a final cry from the girl and a howl from Khumeni – of pleasure and seeming agony combined – the throbbing shape below split in two parts as the girl was thrust aside, to lie sprawling half-on, half-off the bed. And as Khumeni staggered to the bedroom door, opened it and went out into the corridor –

It was the merest glimpse, only that – the sight of Khumeni silhouetted like a blot against the comparatively bright light of the corridor, a glimpse almost as brief as a camera's shutter opening and closing on its subject – and yet it drew that loud gasp which had been threatening to break from Kastrouni's lips with each passing moment, so that only the slamming of the bedroom's door and the moaning of the raped girl drowned the sound out.

Then Kastrouni was rolling, holding his speargun before him in both hands and rolling as silently as possible, trying in this fashion to cover the greatest distance in the shortest time. Calculating that distance, and as he heard from below the opening and closing of the second bedroom door, Kastrouni stopped rolling, began searching for a peephole. Nothing!

He peered all about, saw close to the plywood perimeter a thin crack of light streaming upward, crawled swiftly, silently to that vantage point. Then a desperate pause as he fought to hold back a sneeze brought on by a sudden puff of dust, and precious seconds wasted as he pinched his nose to clear it and wiped spontaneous tears from his eyes.

This second bedroom came up against the end wall of the house; to its front was the corridor, to one side a shuttered window looking out on the garden. Kastrouni remembered well the layout of the villa and wished now that he was down in the garden, where he might be able to look in on what was happening. Instead . . . all he had was this narrow crack where a board had warped and split. He put his eye to the fault and viewed an empty corner of the room. That was all, and no way to change the angle of view. Except –

No, the corner wasn't empty: there on the wall hung an old mirror! And the scene in that tarnished glass was one of such sheer unnatural horror as to cause Kastrouni to doubt his very sanity – or would have had that effect if he had not twenty years ago seen something equally monstrous – or might have if he had not at least half expected it. However distorted that picture, however warped by the bad glass and flattened by the angle through which it was viewed, still its content could not be disguised. The light in the second bedroom was electric and good; Kastrouni's worst suspicions were suspicions no more; his eyes told no lie.

Khumeni, as he – as *it* – called himself now, was finished with the Turkish woman. As he withdrew himself from her, Kastrouni should not have been surprised by the size of his erection – but he was anyway. And now it was the turn of the English girl. She was dressed in uniform (that of the QARANC as it would later turn out,

71

Queen Alexandra's Royal Army Nursing Corps, but that meant nothing to Kastrouni, except that she must be from the garrison at Dhekelia) which the lusting thing in the room must first at least partially remove. This he did while still the watcher gawped, paralysed by shock and horror. And when the girl lay naked, her clothes from the waist down literally ripped from her, once more Khumeni turned her to the preferred position of the beast.

And as he entered her without pause . . . that was when Kastrouni knew that this thing had to die. Ab, Guigos, Khumeni, spawn of Satan: whatever he was, he *had* to die. And Kastrouni would never have a better opportunity than the one he had right here and now.

Heedless now of any noise he might make, he turned on his back, swivelled his legs round until his feet came up against the perimeter of ply panels, bent his legs at the knees and drove his feet forward. The panel gave at once, shattering from its fixtures as it was driven out into the soft starlight of the garden; and Dimitrios Kastrouni following it, tossing his speargun into the lower branches of a pomegranate tree and lowering himself by his fingertips, then dropping lightly to the ground. Up on his feet in a second, he tore his weapon from where it was tangled in the trees, turned to the shuttered window of the bedroom.

But as the speargun had come free, so its hurlers had slipped from their notch in the spear's shaft, whipping forward and cracking against Kastrouni's knuckles. He cursed, dropped the weapon, and at that precise moment heard Khumeni's muffled cry of surprise and outraged inquiry from the room beyond the shutters:

'Who . . . ? WHO . . . ?'

The English girl, perhaps part-shaken from her drugged state by Khumeni's hoarse shouting, gave a cry of pain and protest – cut off by a curse from Khumeni, a ringing slap and a dull thud.

Frantic motion then inside the room, and the sound of someone snatching at the catches on the windows. Khumeni must be going to take a look outside! Kastrouni quickly wrapped a handkerchief round the numb, bleeding knuckles of his right hand, grabbed up his speargun and somehow managed to reload it, started to come upright holding the weapon awkwardly in his left hand. But he was much too close to the window, and that was a mistake.

He had expected the startled creature in the room to move with a degree of caution: he knew it was half-crippled – indeed, only half man – and fairly slow-moving. Also, the memory would not leave him of the *other* Khumeni, which had been called Guigos: that ancient, diseased and infirm bag of bones he had known in Israel. He could not yet wholly tie that memory, that mental picture of the cripple together with this new, much more vigorous incarnation.

But the Khumeni avatar *was* vigorous, so that when the louvred shutters smashed open outwards – smashed into Kastrouni and knocked him from his feet – he was taken completely by surprise. On all fours, dazedly he looked up. And there at the window, silhouetted against the bright light of the bedroom, stood Khumeni glaring down on him. His eyes found Kastrouni, *knew* him, and in the next moment the look on his awful face changed from outrage through astonishment to vengeful triumph.

Looking at that face, Kastrouni knew that hatred was mutual, knew now why Khumeni was here in the first place. Just as he wished Khumeni dead and would now try to kill him, so the monster wanted *him* dead, and that was the real reason for his being here. He had not succeeded in finding Kastrouni and so would do that which must surely bring Kastrouni to him: he would strike at Kastrouni's very heart, strike at his family, his home.

Khumeni filled the window, arms wide where they held back the shutters, eyes glaring down on Kastrouni from a face filled with poison.

And now those eyes filled with something else: a terrible malice, an awful intent.

'You?' Khumeni growled, bending to reach down his arms and hands. 'But of course. Who else would it be?'

His eyes, his voice, his very presence – all were hypnotic, like a snake's hypnosis when it holds a bird in thrall. As the hands reached down for him, so Kastrouni felt this hypnotic paralysis – felt and fought it. He glared at that monstrous composite face and poured his hatred on it. The face of Ihya Khumnas with his hooked nose and gleaming white teeth, which even now bared themselves in a snarl; the face, too, of Yakob Mhireni, with its livid blaze of scar tissue; and what of the coarse, hairy trunk from the waist down, for the moment hidden by the wall between?

Khumeni! Something suddenly clicked in Dimitrios Kastrouni's mazed mind. Khumnas and Mhireni, of course! Not only had Guigos taken them, but he'd taken something of their names, too. 'Khum' from Khumnas and 'eni' from Mhireni. And that was the realization which broke the spell. What would this beast's name have been if he had also succeeded in taking Kastrouni? Kashumeni? The thought enraged Kastrouni: his hatred and strength were doubled.

This was no man but a hell-spawned beast formed of the parts of others, and this paralysis wasn't hypnosis but fear! Kastrouni had been unmanned by his own knowledge, his own terror – almost. But now, as Khumeni's hands clamped onto his shoulders, in that same instant his own fingers closed on the pistol-grip of his speargun. But before he could even begin to bring that weapon to bear . . .

Effortlessly Khumeni lifted him up and dragged him in through the open window, his hands like clamps crushing Kastrouni's shoulders. The creature was – *powerful!* Of course he was, for had he not invoked the lust and strength and power of Demogorgon? Who or what Demogorgon was Kastrouni did not know or could not be sure, despite what he'd read in the works found in Guigos's saddle-packs; but he considered it likely that at least part of Demogorgon was Death, for certainly he now stared directly into Death's face.

Khumeni held him helpless in the bedroom – held him upright, arms fast to his sides – held him a foot off the floor and glared at him from only inches away. Kastrouni was literally immobilized from the waist up. But he could move his head.

He glanced down, saw the bowed, upright hind-quarters of a donkey and its huge genitals. This in an instant, and in the next the beast had hurled him away, against the wall, to crumple winded to the floor. But still he held the speargun; and as the power- and sex-crazed Pan of a figure loped unevenly toward him, terrible hands again reaching, so he shakily lifted the weapon, aimed it and without paused pulled the trigger.

The spear was armed with a trident, its tines about three inches long and brown with rust. If the head had been of the single-point variety, then certainly it would have gone right through Khumeni's shoulder. As it was, the horizontal bar at the base of the trident stopped it. Nevertheless three rusty barbs went home, deep into the hobbling beast's right shoulder just below the collar-bone, and the force and pain of the impact spun him off course, flailing wildly, he tripped and fell to the floor, and lay there threshing his legs – both hairy, one at least part-crippled – while he screamed and yanked at the spear in his shoulder.

Even injured, Khumeni would be more than a match for any normal man; knowing this, Kastrouni grabbed at his one opportunity for escape. He struggled to his feet, leapt for the door. He would have done better to dive straight out of the window. Khumeni ignored the pain in his shoulder, shot out a leg which ended in a hoof, tripped him only half-way out of the door.

Out in the corridor Kastrouni scrambled to his feet, fell, jumped up again and bounded for the porch. Khumeni – still roaring with the strange raw quality of a large, wounded animal, still wrenching at the shaft of the spear – was right behind him. A hand fell on Kastrouni's shoulder, hurled him sideways. He crashed in through the door of the first bedroom, shattering its thin louvres as he went. Then the beast was in the room with him.

In the gloom of the single bedroom, where the lamp had guttered so low that its light was very nearly extinct, Kastrouni saw his pursuer outlined in the broken door, saw that the spear was no longer in his shoulder and that blood flowed freely from his wounds. Then the creature had advanced and cornered him. Kastrouni saw again those terrifically powerful hands reaching – and heard the low moan of the naked Greek girl on the bed.

Khumeni was momentarily distracted; his feral eyes turned toward the bed; Kastrouni smashed into him shoulder-first and caught him off balance. The beast-thing crashed into a small table bearing the lamp and toppled it. Flames at once gouted upward, sending the shadows flying. A lace coverlet was burning fiercely, setting fire to other bedclothes.

But then a strange thing: instead of returning to the attack, Khumeni merely glared at his adversary, gave a single snarl (of frustration, Kastrouni thought), then rushed to get the Greek girl off the blazing bed. Since she, like the others, had simply been used by the beast, and since presumably she was no longer of any earthly importance to him, Kastrouni would have thought he'd give first consideration to his own skin. But in any case it was all to the good, allowing Kastrouni a second opportunity to flee – out through the shattered bedroom door in a flash, from corridor to entrance hall, and so into the clean night air.

And behind him the bright glow of a fire rapidly spreading, showing as an orange glare through the corridor's louvred windows, and Khumeni's hoarse cries from within. Scrambling over a low garden wall to one side of the villa's frontage, Kastrouni crouched down and looked back.

Out through the swinging front door staggered Khumeni, carrying the Greek girl and tossing her down on gravel well away from the building. And straight back in he went, through a thickening screen of smoke that gushed from the door and flowed in streamers from the louvres. Kastrouni had seen and done as much as it had been possible for him to do; he turned to make away, was brought to a halt by Khumeni's hoarse shouting. The beast was calling his name! Again he looked back.

Khumeni stood at the open window to the second bedroom. He tossed the English girl out into the night, the top half of her uniform still clinging to her shapely form. Obviously he intended to save all three, only pausing to shout this threat from the burning house:

'You, Kastrouni. You, Dimitrios, son of Costas. I was beginning to think you must be dead, but now I know differently. Well, you've interfered with my plans for the last time. I'll find you now, Kastrouni, wherever you go, and then you'll wish you really *were* dead!'

Kastrouni knew that this creature's threat was not an idle one. He backed off, turned and ran into the darkness, headed for the beach. And from behind, fading: 'Do you doubt it, Kastrouni? Dare you doubt it? Then see if you can doubt this – ' And he uttered a guttural, barking command in some ancient or alien tongue, a command – or summons? – which ended with one sharp and clearly audible word: Demogorgon!

The summons was answered at once.

As if that earlier preternatural silence had been prelude or practice for this, the cicadas went silent on the instant and the sea, lapping in small wavelets one moment, grew utterly still in the next. An electric tension was immediately present, heavy and tangible as a rank odour on the night air.

Kastrouni slowed, skidding on pebbles, took cover beneath a lone olive tree. But took cover from what? He felt his fear hammering in his chest without knowing what he feared. Oh, he feared the beast Khumeni, certainly – what man in his right mind would not? – but now it seemed he also feared the very night and its sinister silence.

Out over the silver sea there was movement. Kastrouni saw it from the corner of his eye, jerked his head round to stare. Clouds were swirling together, forming from nothing in an otherwise clear sky, where no clouds should be. At first mere wisps, they rapidly assumed a bank of cloud in the shape of some strange spiral galaxy – and it was drifting shoreward!

Drifting? No, it was *impelled* shoreward – but as yet there was no wind!

Kastrouni stared harder. There were small lightnings in that weird, spiralling cloud, flickering veins of white light that grew brighter by the second. And as the thing approached the shore, so its core took on a definite density – an outline. What that outline was Kastrouni could not, would not think – but it seemed to have eyes that glared down like sentient points of hellfire from on high! And in another moment the traceries of energy were no longer mere traceries but purposeful flashes of lightning that seemed for all the world to walk over the sea, to walk like –

– Like something he had seen before, one monstrous night in a strange land more than twenty years ago!

Kastrouni ran.

He ran for the copse of pines, for his car, for his life.

The lightning was white, its accompanying thunder deafening, and it brought a wind that lashed at Kastrouni as if to snatch him up and dash him down. The still sea had been whipped to a frenzy in seconds, and sand from the beach formed dust-devil clouds that chased each other in all directions. In January or February, Kastrouni might have expected such – but mid-summer?

The cloud was almost overhead now but the fleeing man dared not look at it. Lightning flashed and struck the sea almost at the shoreline, sending steam boiling skyward. Another bolt, landing this time on dry land. And yet another, right at Kastrouni's heels. The thing was going to walk right over him, stamp him flat!

The copse of pines seemed to grow out of the swirling sand and pounding thunder. Kastrouni flew forward into the trees. His car was waiting. *Two* cars were waiting!

He flattened himself to the bole of a pine, sensed rather than saw someone close to him in the night. Then something crashed against the base of his skull and everything dissolved in pain and icy, inky darkness . . .

Windblown, the Englishman Willis stood over Kastrouni and pointed his pistol with its ugly silencer at him. The man on the ground remained motionless where he had fallen, was out like a light. 'Good!' whispered

Willis, his pronunciation perfect as ever, however shaky his voice. 'Very good. You could never have outrun *that*, my unknown friend. It followed your fear as remorselessly and unerringly as a hound tracks the blood of a wounded man. But unconscious you're also unafraid, and so the scent is lost.'

Baffled, the lightning was retreating down the beach, the whirling cloud already beginning to lose something of its cohesion. Willis used the toe of an immaculately styled shoe to turn Kastrouni over onto his back. 'So you see, you really ought to thank me for that tap on the head. No?' He shrugged. 'Have it your own way. But who are you and what were you doing, eh, that he should call something like that down on you? Were you spying on him? Ah, you sneaky, grubby, dirty-minded little Greeks!'

The cloud was drifting out over the sea, retracting its fiery legs, beginning to disperse. The wind had died away as quickly as it came up and the cicadas were tentatively starting up once more. Willis wiped a brow shiny with cold sweat. He considered putting a bullet into the unconscious man's brain, then thought better of it. He had no instructions, didn't even know who the man was. Nobody, probably. Khumeni had been enraged at finding someone spying on him, that was all. And as to why Willis had saved this stranger's life: really, he'd had little choice in the matter. In fact he'd been obliged to save himself! A direct hit by the lightning – on the unknown Greek, or worse still one of the cars – and it could easily have killed both of them.

Willis bit his lip. Perhaps he should kill him after all. He went down on one knee, aimed his pistol at a spot central between Kastrouni's closed eyes, and –

Down the beach a previously unnoticed orange glow turned red and demanding. And suddenly the acrid smell of smoke was in the air. Distantly, harsh as the bark of an angry dog, Willis heard Khumeni cursing and calling his name. He stood up, put away his gun. The villa? On fire? What the hell – ?

Willis moved to his car and jerked open the door. He glanced one more time at the figure stretched out under the trees, then got in. Whatever had happened back there at the villa, so close to the road – a fire in the house, whatever – it was bound to attract attention. And soon. That had been Khumeni's plan, of course: to attract attention and stir old fears, old hatreds, but not while he was still on the island.

Willis switched on his engine, lights, put the car in gear and picked his way through the pines to the road. By the time he got back to the villa flames were leaping from almost all of the windows – and Khumeni, clad only in baggy trousers and a dressing-gown, was raging where he loped to and fro on the gravel drive . . .

Part II

Chapter One

Late May 1983; a little before midnight; a private country estate near Radlett, just north of London.

Set in wooded acres behind high stone walls, the house was restored Elizabethan, three-storey, timber-framed with high-peaked dormers, very attractive and impossibly expensive. Its single incongruity was a large modern porch, mainly glass, extending like a foyer to meet the tarmac of the drive where it wound to the house from tall iron gates.

The owner of the place was a long-retired big-time crook, August 'Gus' (or more often, in his youth, 'Cat') Carter, one of London's gang-bosses from the city's criminal heyday, and one of the few to come through it all hale and hearty and rich with spoils. He was one of the exceptions proving the rule that 'crime doesn't pay.' It had paid him, handsomely. Another exception to the same rule was Charles Trace, 'Charlie' to his small circle of friends, who even now emptied the display cases in Carter's locked top-floor study. The doors of the study were locked, anyway, if not the dormer window through which Trace had gained entry.

Cat Carter and his much younger wife were in the Bahamas, enjoying the first week of a three-week holiday; and while Cat was away the mice – his three grown up children from a previous marriage, two half-breed hoorays and an educated-to-order deb – were playing. Downstairs the spacious olde-worlde rooms were a riot of upper-class rovers, rangers and ravers, and all-or-nothing groupies, 'dancing' to the much amplified heavy metal pounding of Glue in Persons, in person. The outrageous group's van was parked in the grounds with the cars of the guests. A stubby Volkswagen with gaudy Glue in Persons legends daubed on both sides and on the roof, it stood out like a sore thumb amidst Jags and Mercs and Porsches. There was even a Roller complete with chauffeur, hat pulled down over his eyes where he slept in the back.

Trace had been quiet in his climbing and breaking in. The climb had been easy: all ivy and ledges and corners, and the dormer window – warped in its frame until the catch no longer fitted – had opened at a single push, opened inwards at that. And no alarms. Three storeys up, Cat Carter had thought the place secure enough; of all people, he should have known better. Trace had climbed inside as easily as that.

Now he grinned as he loaded up the zip pockets of his cat-suit with some of the choicest items of Carter's collection. His gold collection. For forty-odd years the old thug had been getting this little lot together: fine lockets and miniatures in gold; filigreed chains and fancy snuffboxes; golden guineas, medallions and pendants; fob-watches and rings, and even tiny German ingots. A large fortune in this their original state, and even melted down a small fortune. Trace would settle for the small fortune; there wasn't a fence in London who would try to pass Carter's stuff as it stood, but there were many who'd take it in small, rough, anonymous ingots.

Gold: a lifelong foible of old Carter, and a way of life for Charlie Trace. The first had lived to gather it and admire its great beauty, while the second cared nothing for its beauty but stole it to live, which was the thing he did best. Stole it to live, yes, and very likely to die, if Cat Carter should ever discover the author of this little job . . .

His pockets loaded with about eight pounds in weight of trinkets (if loot such as this could ever be described in such a way) finally Trace was satisfied. Briefly he toyed with the idea of making two trips, then dismissed it. That would be to push his luck too far. He'd known about old Carter's being in the Bahamas, but the party had been a bonus. Best to leave it at that.

Since the noise from the party downstairs was now deafening, blasting up through the house with its own dully shuddering vibrations, Trace could allow himself to relax a little and get out as quickly as possible. He could descend at speed and not worry too much if he jangled a bit. That was all to the good, for he knew from experience how eight or nine pounds of gold could weigh a man down.

Fortunately Carter's study was situated at the back of the house and the back bedrooms on the first floor weren't in use yet, or at least they weren't illuminated. Bypassing one such window, Trace peered in and saw that he had been wrong in the first instance: three naked, marble bodies twined on a bed in the darkness. Some bloke with a pair of birds. Lucky sod! But Trace didn't wait for his eyes to grow accustomed to the darkness in the room. In any case, he'd rather partake than peruse. And moments later he was on the ground.

Then, sticking close to trees and shrubbery as much as possible, he was through the grounds in minutes and climbing the perimeter wall. There, hidden in bushes, his Black Bess awaited: an ancient but excellently maintained 500cc Triumph Speed Twin fitted with a Slickshift gearbox. Quickly he loaded up the bases of twin panniers and eased the false bottoms into position, then donned his crash-hat and wheeled the bike through the bushes to the road. Very little traffic about at this time of night, but there would be more as he rode into London.

Before kick-starting the motorcycle into life, he patted his top right-hand pocket, checked the presence there of the small documents-wallet which contained his driver's licence, insurance and registration documents, and allowed himself a satisfied nod. His road tax, of course, was right up to date. It wouldn't do to get pulled in for some minor traffic offence, not with all that yellow stuff hidden in his panniers. Nor, for that matter, would it do to have an accident.

So, despite the fact that his machine could do a ton without even breathing heavily, he took it easy all the way home, riding carefully through the summer night and arriving at his moderately attractive Highgate address a little after 1:00 A.M. He garaged the bike in a shed in the tiny plot of a garden, took the panniers and let himself into the house, passing through the communal hall and quietly upstairs to his own place.

Without emptying the panniers of their loot, he changed into a dressing-gown poured himself a drink, sat down by a panoramic window looking out over London. From here he had a prominent view of the city: it was all twinkling lights and night-haze, and the warmth of millions of people going up into the night, and even at this hour a rumbling one sensed rather than heard: the throb of a gigantic heart on the verge of sleep. It always had a calming effect on Trace. It cleared his mind and let him think slowly, methodically, clearly.

Now he thought about tonight: the job he'd just pulled in Radlett. The entire thing had gone without a hitch. Hadn't it? But something niggled. Trace found and held down the niggling thing, examined it closely.

It was a car, shiny-black, quiet, squat on the roads and strangely menacing, like a creature rather than a machine, whose eyes were hooded yellow lights. In the eye of his memory Trace saw the car again. He saw it in his bike's mirrors, like a big mechanical woodlouse tracking him one hundred and fifty yards to his rear. Foreign, French maybe. It had picked him up almost immediately after he left Carter's place, following him (or seeming to) almost half-way home. He'd worried a little about it. An unmarked squad car? An off-duty copper, suspicious about night-riders? Or worse still, some watchdog of Carter's . . . ?

But then the car had accelerated to pass him like a shadow and just as silently, and the shadowy driver hadn't even looked at him, just sat there staring straight ahead. And in a little while Trace's nerves had stopped jumping.

Then, on the North Circular just this side of the Golders Green turn-off, at a junction where the lights were just turning against him . . . that car again, or one very like it. Crouching there at right-angles to his path. Its eyes half-lidded. Its driver a soft black blot behind the sheen of glass, the brain of the beast. It was funny how the car had seemed more important than its driver. And yet not funny; it had struck Trace that quite obviously the machine was merely an extension of its driver; he would be a most mechanical man, a cold man, whoever he was. Trace remembered thinking that just before the light turned green for the car and it surged forward, inches away from his front wheel, crossed and disappeared into darkness. And again the driver hadn't so much as glanced at him, and once more his nerves had been left leaping . . .

Trace poured himself another drink and sipped at it, ran the sequence of events through again in his mind. Coincidence, that was all. And an overactive imagination. The car had been a Citroën or some such, a recent model or at least one with which Trace wasn't familiar. And in all likelihood there had been two cars and not just one.

The thing had seemed sinister because of the circumstances: an uncomplicated case of conscience. Trace dismissed it from his mind.

He finished his drink, put a well cared for, old but unscratched Ray Charles blues long-player on the turntable with the sound turned down low, hid the loot from his motor-cycle's panniers in a compartment behind a loose polystyrene ceiling tile and then had a hot shower. Towelling himself dry just as the record was finishing, he put it carefully away, switched off the lights and went to bed . . .

. . . And came awake in an instant. After being asleep for only a moment or two. Or so it seemed.

For a moment chaos.

He had been dreaming.

About last night.

About gold.

About the black car.

And then . . . the telephone.

It rang again, its jangling voice demanding that he pay attention. Trace sat up in his bed. 9 A.M., and someone ringing him? At this hour? What the hell . . . ?

His friends knew he was never out of bed before 10:00. So, if not a friend . . . who?

He swung himself out of bed and went unsteadily to the telephone, resisting the impulse to snatch it from its cradle. 'Yes?' he growled.

'Charles Trace?' enquired a male voice Trace didn't know, whose accent was possibly Greek. Or maybe he did know him; there was a Greek smelter he sometimes used in Dockland.

'Who wants him?' he asked, stifling a yawn.

The voice seemed to sigh – in relief? – then said: 'You

90

don't know me – but I know you. Something of you, anyway. Can we meet?'

There was an ill-concealed urgency in the voice; however cryptically, silently, nevertheless it begged that there be no questions, no arguments. Trace felt his heart pick up a little speed, knew that this was important. 'Do you know where I live?'

'Yes, you're in the directory. It's where I got your number – but no, not there. Somewhere else?'

Trace considered it. 'Close to where I live there's a pub – a big one – on the corner. It's quiet and I know the landlord. We can meet there if you like. When?'

'I . . . I'm not sure. I'm at Gatwick Airport. How long will it take by taxi?'

'Eh?' Still not fully awake, Trace was now intrigued. 'Jesus, I don't know!' He shrugged. 'An hour, hour and a half. Look, when you get there just sit tight. I'll let the boss of the place know you're coming and he'll give me a ring. Just tell him you're waiting for Charlie, right? Hey, and are you sure you've got the right Charles Trace?'

'Oh, yes, I'm sure. See you soon . . .' And the phone went dead in Trace's hand. Just like that. Weird . . .

He phoned The Ship and spoke briefly to the landlord, then half-heartedly breakfasted on a poached egg, toast and coffee. After that he splashed cold water in his face, shaved, got dressed. And he wondered.

A Greek, at Gatwick – probably just off a plane – who didn't know London but knew him, and wanted to talk to him urgently. About what? Trace hadn't wanted to ask on the phone. There might be something he didn't want to hear – not without knowing who was saying it. He had no connections in Greece, did he? No, he didn't. What then?

What about last night and the black car? Someone putting the squeeze on him? But if so, why call from

91

Gatwick? And wouldn't there have been just a hint of dirty-dealing in the other's voice? The suggestion of a knowing sneer?

Trace wasn't given much longer to think it out, however, for as he finished dressing the telephone rang again, causing him to start. He wasn't used to a lot of traffic on the phone.

'Charlie?' This time the voice was female, soft and mildly seductive.

'Jilly? Hi!' Jilly was his current lady. Great fun but a little short on grey matter. She had picked him up in a bar a month ago. They would see each other two or three times a week and later spend the night either here or at her place, whichever seemed right at the time. He wasn't serious about her and hoped it was mutual. Too heavy would be too much and he would have to get out. He hadn't the time for permanent relationships; or rather, that sort of relationship didn't appeal to him. Certainly not with Jilly. A beautiful body is great, yes, but there should be something of a mind in there, too. Trace didn't consider this a cynical attitude. If he used her, it was no more than she did to him.

'I gave you a ring last night,' she said, and he could picture her pretty mouth forming a meaningless pout, 'but you were out. And I couldn't sleep so I phoned you again at half past twelve – and you were *still* out!'

Trace sighed. This sounded a lot like he had feared might happen. Heavy. 'Oh?' he said. 'I mean, I *do* go out, you know?'

'OK,' she said airily. 'I'm not prying. Shall I come over?'

'What, now?'

'Well it is Saturday! I thought we'd go out.'

Trace tossed his head in annoyance, said: 'Look, Jilly,

I'm busy this morning. Why don't I give you a call tonight, eh?'

'Oh!' she sounded disappointed.

Trace nodded to himself, felt himself starting to turn sour. It would soon be time to get out. But sweetly, if that was at all possible. 'I'll book us a meal,' he said. 'Then we'll go on to a casino for an hour or two. And finally back to your place. OK? We'll use your car.'

She brightened up. 'OK. About 8:30?'

'Fine. See you.'

As he put the phone down he heard her blow him a kiss. Normally he'd respond to that in like fashion, but now he didn't. A slow breakaway was the answer. Anyway, right now Jilly was the least of his problems.

He phoned a fence in the Holloway Road, a 'used bookshop', and when he heard the familiar voice said: 'Joe, this is Charlie. I told you I'd have some books later. I have them. There's no real urgency but I'd like to get them to you soonest anyway.'

''Ow many books, Charlie?' Joe Pelham's voice was all Cockney, gruff as gravel, just a trifle cautious.

'Almost four kilos.'

'*Phew!*' said Pelham. And: ''Oo's been a naughty boy, then? You must've raided a bleedin' library!'

'When?' said Trace, unable to keep back a grin.

There came a scraping sound as Joe scratched thoughtfully at his permanent stubble. 'Tuesday's about the earliest I can take 'em, mate. Depends on the books, really. I mean, will I 'ave any bovver shiftin' 'em? Are they first editions, mint, or what? Are they the sort of fings people will be on the lookout for?'

'No,' Trace answered, 'not immediately. But I shouldn't think you'd hang onto them too long. They may have a bit of worm and you'd want to avoid contagion. I got them job-lot from the widow of a collector. Maybe you'd like to speak to someone in the trade, split them up, like . . . ?'

'You let me 'andle that end of it, my son,' said Pelham. 'Incidentally, 'oo was the deceased? A collector, you said? Anyone I'd know?'

'You really wouldn't want to know that, Joe,' said Trace. 'It's morbid. Anyway, what will you give me?'

'The usual: 60% face value. Best I can do in the circumstances – probably too good, in fact. What wiv worm and wotnot. But in any case that's a fair bit, which is mainly why I can't do it till Tuesday.'

'OK. Tuesday, then. Give me a buzz when you're ready.'

'Too right, son,' growled the other. 'S'long . . .'

The Ship's upstairs rooms and bar were done out like the interior of a galleon, allegedly. It had always looked wrong to Trace, however, and he preferred to drink downstairs where there were four-seater booths which allowed something of privacy. When he walked in off the street in answer to the proprietor's telephone call, he saw half a dozen regulars at the bar where the boss pulled pints, and an elderly, but sprightly, tall and rugged type sitting in one of the booths nursing a virgin pint. From behind the bar the boss caught Trace's eye, nodded toward the man in the booth. Trace ordered a beer, took it with him and slid in opposite the stranger.

They stared at each other for long moments, and Trace got the impression that the other sought for some mark or sign in his face, some pointer to his identity.

Trace saw a Greek, but darker than the average London variety, whose handsome, leathery features were no strangers to strong sunlight. His aura was all Mediterranean; there was only one exception to a general impression of yellow walls, olive groves and donkeys hauling water, and that was his hair. His hair was white. There was no trace of black about it at all. It couldn't be more white if he'd been an albino. Even for a man in his late sixties, which the Greek must be, still that snowy whiteness was somehow unnatural . . .

Other than that . . . the Greek could easily pass for fifty. For his eyes were brown, very alert, almost anxious. In fact they were very nearly feverish, with a sort of trapped animal awareness about them. Young, worried eyes in an old face. A young spirit in an old body. That was how Trace saw him.

In the coolness of the booth and under Trace's close scrutiny, the Greek shivered a little. His suit, despite being very lightweight, was expensively cut; the ring he wore was heavy, solid gold; when he lit a cigarette from a fresh pack of Karelias, Trace saw that his lighter was also of gold. Obviously he wasn't short of money. Obvious, too, that he'd come here straight from Greece. To see Trace. But why?

What the Greek saw was this:

A man he knew to be about twenty-five years old, but one like himself who looked younger than his years; a long, slim man, narrow-hipped and sinewy; a man quick to frown and very slow to smile, with some great, invisible weight on his narrow shoulders, seeming huge out of all proportion to his strength, but which he yet carried uncomplainingly. A pale man with a brush of fine, light-brown hair and thin brown eyebrows over intelligent green eyes, and a nose very slightly hooked, but not so as to spoil the generally clean lines of his features. A young man, yes, but entirely self-sufficient and far, far wiser than his years might allow. Or perhaps far more foolish. And a man who didn't much like being studied like this.

'I'm Charles Trace,' Trace abruptly introduced himself without offering his hand. 'And you – ?'

The other shook his head. 'For the moment my name is unimportant. Indeed, just knowing my name could place you in great danger. And you already have problems enough.'

Trace's thoughts and emotions whirled but he allowed no external sign of his agitation. This could only be the squeeze, blackmail. The Greek had something on him and was about to threaten him with exposure. That must be it. What else could it be?

He forced a smile, said: 'I have no problems, Mr, er, Unimportant? *You* have the problems, or else you wouldn't have come to see me. And since I'm not much of a one for other people's problems, it sort of looks like you're on a duff mission. Or at best acting on duff information. But just for laughs, who sent you and what is it you want from me?'

'I want nothing *from* you. I bring you something. A warning. And you think I'm on a mission, like a messenger? No one sent me, Charles Trace. Indeed I must be crazy just to have come here – because by doing so I may well have put my own life in jeopardy.'

He was in earnest, Trace could see that. But a warning? And all this talk of danger and lives in jeopardy . . . ?'

'Look,' Trace said, 'this is getting us nowhere. Are you going to tell me what this is all about, or am I going to walk out of here?'

The stranger leaned forward across the table, drew back his lips from clenched teeth and glared at Trace. 'Perhaps you didn't hear me,' he hissed. 'My life is on the line just being here! Be grateful I've come, you English bastard, or *I* might be the one who walks out!'

Trace made to stand up but the Greek grabbed the sleeve of his jacket, drew him back down with surprising strength, hit him with a sudden burst of information – about himself:

'Your name is Charles Gordon Trace and your mother was evacuated out of Cyprus in early 1958 to give you birth. Her name was Diana Trace. She was unmarried, a nurse in the QARANCs, a very lovely girl. I know because I saw her, just once, on the night you were conceived. I also saw your father – and vowed to kill him! Since when it's been as much as I can do to avoid being killed myself! Soon your father will come for you, and I know why. That's why my life is on the line, and it's why you're in such danger. I mean it, Charles Trace – terrible danger!' He released Trace's arm, sat back, visibly calmed himself. 'And now if you want to walk away – ' and he nodded curtly toward the door. 'Go on, walk.'

Trace remained motionless but glanced toward the bar. They were too far from it – too insulated by the booth – for their conversation, however heated, to attract much attention. That was good, for now he could feel his own blood rising a little.

'See,' he said to the Greek, 'I don't like being kept in the dark. A little knowledge is not enough, not for me. I don't want to know just part of it but all of it. And I'm only interested in the truth, for lies only lead to confusion. Up to now you've been both secretive and a liar. It doesn't inspire much confidence.'

'Mr Trace,' began the other at once, 'I assure you, I – '

'You lied about getting my number and address out of the directory. Oh, they're in there, all right – along with God-only-knows how many other C. Traces! So how could you be so sure you had the right one, eh? Is it likely that you'd have come all the way from Cyprus or wherever without first doing a little homework? No, I think you've been interested in me for some time. You've had me watched, checked out' (the black car?) 'until you think you may have something on me. I think that right now you're building up to some sort of blackmail demand,

and that the rest of it – the "danger" and "lives in jeopardy" bit – is just so much shit!'

'Mr Trace,' the other started again, 'I – '

' – But so far you're not doing too well. For one thing your homework has let you down. You say my father will come for me? But my father died out there in Cyprus, in a car crash in the Troodos Mountains in September 1957. At the time he was my mother's fiance, a young lieutenant in the RAMC. That's why she was unmarried when I was born. His name, incidentally, was – '

' – Lt Gregory Solomon, RAMC, wasn't your father,' said the Greek, which stopped Trace dead in his tracks. 'Your real father's name – ' he paused, shook his head, brushed back suddenly damp white hair from a leathery brow. 'Your real father has had many names. Look, the story's a long one. It will take me all of an hour, maybe two, to tell it all. But be sure I'm not here to blackmail you, and I'm not a liar. Oh, I admit I knew about you before I came here. Certainly I've done my homework – I've *been* doing it for quarter of a century! – but I couldn't let you know too much too soon, for that might scare you off. So please believe me now, Charles Trace, that you have nothing to fear from me. But that soon, very soon, you will have much to fear. And I am the single person on the face of this entire world who can help you.'

Trace was feeling more and more uncertain with each passing moment and it was beginning to show. Seeing this, the Greek urged: 'Let me try to find some small but significant item which might convince you, something which no other man might reasonably be expected to know about you.'

Trace narrowed his eyes. 'Such as what?'

'Such as this: the fact that you are not physically . . . perfect?'

Trace felt a sympathetic tingle in his left foot, fought

himself not to glance down at it. 'Is anyone physically perfect?' he asked.

The Greek seemed to have expected a stronger reaction. He was sweating profusely now. 'Look, we can't stay here. This is almost as bad as being out in the open. He may be having you watched even now.'

'Who?'

'God *damn* you – if you're not already damned!' the other leaned forward and clutched his sleeve again. 'Haven't you heard anything I've said? I'm talking about your father – your *real* father!'

And suddenly Trace wanted desperately to know what it was all about. There was something about the Greek: an intensity that demanded belief. Certainly it demanded an audience. But before Trace could say anything more to him:

'One last thing,' said the Greek, 'and believe me I use this only as a last resort. I do not enjoy it . . .' His tone of voice had changed; now it was full of compassion, full of . . . pity?

'Go on,' said Trace, staring deep into the other's eyes.

'Your mother,' said the Greek. 'She's in a Swiss madhouse.'

Trace jerked back in his seat, wrenched his arm from the Greek's grip, went white in a moment. 'She's . . . resting!' he hissed. 'She had a breakdown when I was a child, and – '

' – She's a lunatic,' the other insisted. 'She will never recover.'

Trace shrank down in his seat, glared at the Greek. 'You bastard!' he spat. 'What the hell are you up to?'

'Listen, I didn't want to hurt you,' the other held up his hands placatingly. 'And it's really not important that she's mad, for there's nothing we can do about that.' He saw Trace's eyes blaze up like fires and quickly went on,

'What matters is this: I know what drove her mad and it's the same black evil which threatens you!'

Trace shook himself, struggled up straighter in his seat, reached out a trembling hand for his beer and drained the glass in one long pull. 'Well, you've got me,' he finally admitted and gave a weary shrug. 'Where can we talk? Where can I listen to you while you get this – this thing, whatever it is – off your chest? My place is no good, you said?'

The other shook his head. 'No, it may be watched. Call a taxi and we'll go to my hotel. On the way here I stopped at a place and booked a room. Also, I left my cases there. There are things in those cases I want you to see.'

Trace nodded. 'OK,' he agreed, 'and the sooner the better. I want all of this sorted out – right now!'

Chapter Two

In the taxi Trace asked: 'Did you come here direct from Cyprus?'

'No,' the other shook his head. 'I did not come from Cyprus at all, except in the beginning. I arrived here from Athens – but I might just as easily have come from Karpathos, Rome, even Paris. I have business in all four places. That is, I'm a silent partner in businesses in these places. That's how I manage both to finance myself and stay out of sight. You see, Mr Trace, I'm a fugitive. I've been one for almost fifty years, and in half a century you get to be good at it. My money works through a numbered Swiss account – just like yours.'

Taken aback, Trace couldn't subdue a single nervous twitch. The Greek saw it and for the first time smiled. 'Homework,' he said.

Trace chewed his lip and made an effort to cover his confusion. 'Karpathos? Isn't that in Rumania?'

'You're not much travelled, Charles,' the Greek snorted. 'You're thinking of the Carpathians – that's a mountain range. No, Karpathos is an island of the Dodecanese group in the Aegean. It has one main town, one or two villages. Until recently it was very much a nowhere place, forgotten on the edge of civilization. It's a little more lively now, through tourism. I have a profitable wine shop in Pighadia, the town.'

'Hardly cosmopolitan,' said Trace.

'My interest in Karpathos isn't purely business,' the Greek answered, his tone souring. 'No, for there's more to the island than first meets the eye. A monastery in the mountains, for one thing. At least it was, many years ago. There's just an old man and a handful of servants there now – a man old before his time, and the thing he watches over . . .'

That was far too cryptic for Trace. Doubtless the Greek would get around to unravelling all of this thing in time, but in his own time. It was going to be very frustrating, Trace decided. And he was becoming far too dependent upon thinking of the Greek as 'the Greek.' So: 'Before we get any deeper into all of this,' he said, 'I still don't know your name. And incidentally, I don't like being called Charles.'

The other shrugged. 'Then I shall call you Mr Trace.'

'I meant that my friends call me Charlie.'

'Are we to be friends, then?' he raised an eyebrow.

Beware Greeks bearing gifts! Trace said to himself, and out loud: 'At least until you prove to be otherwise.' For to be honest, he couldn't help liking the man. 'So what do I call you?'

The other nodded. 'Very well, hear my name and use it when you speak to me; but in all other instances forget that you ever heard it. I am Dimitrios Kastrouni.'

It meant nothing to Trace. 'OK, Dimitrios,' he said, 'and you're also a fugitive, right?'

'That's correct. I am two sorts of fugitive. A long time ago I killed a man. But that was fifty years ago. I don't think there's anybody who cares much about that now, but it served to teach me a great deal about survival. I needed that, for since then I've also become a fugitive from your father. And he is utterly relentless!'

'See,' said Trace, exasperation showing again, 'while on the one hand I'm inclined to hear you out, statements like that last seem deliberately designed to put me off! You killed a man; you've been running for fifty years; you're now on the run from my father – who I know died before I was born, died thousands of miles from here in a car crash! How in hell am I supposed to take you seriously?'

'In hell, yes,' said Kastrouni, nodding. He glanced out of his window and saw that the sky was darkening at what looked like the start of a summer storm. Anxiously, his eyes flickered from one quarter of the sky to the next; a nervous tic tugged the flesh at the corner of his mouth; and again he said: 'Yes, in hell . . .'

Trace sighed, tried a new approach. 'You said Greg Solomon wasn't my father. But I've had it from my mother – many times, times without number – that he was. Why should I believe you? What's your evidence that you should make such a claim? Who *was* my father if not Solomon?'

'Who?' Kastrouni gave him a sharp glance. 'Rather you should ask what. "What" is he, not "who".'

Trace took it to mean that his father was something – someone – big, at least in Kastrouni's world. 'OK, "what" is he?'

'Demogorgon!'

'Eh? Never heard of it.'

'Untravelled,' said Kastrouni, almost to himself. 'Not especially well read. Cynical. No real vices – except perhaps he likes too many girls. But these days . . . ?' (A shrug.) 'And no blemish, no *stigmata*, apparently, upon his body. On the surface I might seem mistaken. But his mother was Diana Trace, and while he does not appear to have any sure means of support, still he is not poor and keeps a numbered Swiss account. So what does he do for a living – and why does he fear blackmail? So maybe there's something of his father in him after all.'

From beneath knitted brows he glanced at Trace, then out of the window at the darkening skyline. He drew himself down in his seat at the sight of thunderheads

103

gathering over the heart of London. In the far distance, lightning flashed. Kastrouni shrank down farther yet.

'Does lightning bother you?' Trace asked.

Apparently startled by the question, Kastrouni sat up straighter. 'Doesn't it bother you?' he countered. And: 'Did you know that in the Holy Land in biblical times – and in parts of the Mediterranean even today – people believed that the devil walked the earth in lightning storms?'

They had arrived at their destination – a motel sort of place near Brent Cross, nothing special – and while Kastrouni hurriedly paid off the driver Trace sprinted for the lobby. It had started to rain: warm, heavy droplets that marked light clothing like splashes of ink, and thunder had become audible even over the heavy rumble of traffic. Kastrouni was spotted like a Dalmation when finally he joined Trace under an awning outside the lobby.

'What's your drink?' he asked, leading the way inside.

'Whisky,' said Trace, 'with a little ice and water.'

Kastrouni crossed to the desk, spoke to an untidy, uniformed young man with pimples, beckoned Trace to follow him upstairs to his room. Surprisingly, the room was clean and well set up: it had good wide windows that let in plenty of light, was equipped not only with a large bed and its own bathroom but also a couple of comfortable chairs. The obligatory Gideon Bible stood on a small table beside the bed; there was no TV; the carpet was wall to wall and looked new. It was probably as good a place as any for a private conversation.

Trace excused himself and used the toilet, and when he came out saw that Kastrouni had drawn the curtains and put the light on. Before he could comment the Greek said: 'Yes, you are right, I don't like storms.'

There came a soft knock at the door and Kastrouni

answered it, returning with a tray containing glasses, a jug of iced water and two half bottles. One of the bottles was Courvoisier, the other Johnnie Walker.

'Courvoisier?' said Trace, raising his eyebrows in question.

'Mine,' said Kastrouni. 'I'm for anything in brandy or cognac. All other spirits are second-class citizens. And I should know because I'm in the business. My family has been in the business since . . . a very long time.' He poured drinks, passed a glass to Trace. 'Cheers!'

'Cheers!' Trace returned, lifting his glass and sipping.

And without further pause, except to light the occasional cigarette or freshen their glasses, Kastrouni told his story: how he had come to leave Cyprus in the first place, about Guigos and Chorazin, then on to Khumeni and that night of discovery and horror confirmed at the villa on the coast road north of Larnaca. He offered little by way of explanation, told it just as it had been, or as he believed it had been, left the rest and a great deal of unnecessary detail to Trace's own enquiring mind and imagination. If Trace wanted to know more, surely he would ask.

He did:

'What are you on, Dimitrios?' he said quietly when it seemed Kastrouni had finished.

'On?' the other looked puzzled.

'What's the monkey on your back? What is it you take? What poison is it you're addicted to?' Trace watched his reaction closely – and was disappointed.

'Addiction?' And at last Kastrouni's eyes widened in understanding. 'Ah! – Drugs, you mean?' He shook his head. 'I have no strong vices, never have had. Unless you class tobacco as a vice.'

Trace fingered his chin, took a sip at his drink. He had sat here patiently for a long time. Perhaps for too long. 'I

105

can't believe in satyrs,' he said. 'I don't think you saw what you think you saw.'

'Not a satyr,' said Kastrouni, 'except perhaps in the sexual sense of the word. No, for a satyr is part goat. Like Pan, you know? Pure myth, as far as I know. Khumeni is no myth . . .'

'Then he's simply deformed. You saw a cripple with badly deformed legs, or maybe legs burned in a fire, an accident.'

Kastrouni was shaking his head in denial, but before he could give that denial voice Trace went on: 'And you say he raped my mother?'

'He raped three women that night: a Greek girl, a Turkish woman, and your poor mother.'

'But they didn't know it was happening? They were drugged?'

Kastrouni half looked away. After a moment he said, 'I know what you're getting at. Just in case I am telling the truth, you want it confirmed that your mother didn't suffer. Well, from what I saw, she would not have suffered physically – not right there and then – not a great deal. They knew very little of what was happening to them, those women. Later they would be hurt, would need medical attention. But your mother was in the best possible place in the world for that. She worked at the BMH: the British Medical Hospital in Dhekelia.'

Trace nodded, tightening his mouth, said, 'One of the things you said that hooked me – the main reason I came here with you – was that you knew what drove my mother mad. I take it you meant this rape? And yet now you say she wouldn't remember it, that she was doped to the gills. That doesn't connect, Dimitrios.'

The other made vague, frustrated gestures with his hands, finally said: 'If Khumeni had been any ordinary sort of a man it wouldn't connect. How can I explain? I

106

don't wish to hurt you more than I have already. We're talking about your mother, after all! I – '

'Don't hide anything from me,' said Trace abruptly. 'If you know or think you know something – anything – then tell me. I can always make up my own mind about believing or disbelieving.'

'Very well,' Kastrouni answered. 'But first you tell me something: are you a religious man, Charlie? I think not.'

'I think I believe in God, yes. I mean, not the God who sits on a marble throne in the clouds attended by a flock of winged harpists. Maybe the God I believe in is part of me, part of us, the group goodness in all of us. Our intelligence, perhaps? Our compassion? I don't know. It's too deep for me. Anyway, I don't go to church. That would be sheery hypocrisy. I'm no angel.'

Kastrouni nodded, slitted his eyes a little, quietly commented, 'Indeed you are not.' Then, with more animation: 'Very good. So, you believe there is good in the world. The root goodness in mankind. The intelligence of men. Their compassion. But for everything there must be an opposite, Charlie, every plus has its minus. Day and night, black and white, good and evil. Good, with a capital "G" – and Evil with a capital "E". Do you also believe in evil?'

'Of course. Look around you. Isn't it far easier to believe in evil than in good?'

Again Kastrouni's nod. He was eager now, warming to his subject. 'But I mean an ultimate evil. I mean the devil himself! The horned one, yes! You believe in the good in men, their compassion, their intelligence. You are not sure about God, but you agree there is something that lifts us up. And what of that which bubbles and seethes and blasphemes and strives to maintain the balance? What of that which drags us down? Evil, you say, is far more evident than good, and I agree.'

Trace was looking weary now, his mind full of strangeness, his head packed with pictures and impressions and ideas which hadn't been there before. It made him feel tired, but still he would hear Kastrouni out. 'Go on,' he said.

'Just let us suppose that Jesus was a focal point for Man's goodness – let us say that in this way he *was* the Son of God. Incidentally, I personally have no doubt of that last: this conjecturing is merely my way of putting it to you. So let us say that Jesus came to bring God's light to men – to "save" them, if you like. My question is this: who would maintain the balance, Charlie? And *how* would it be maintained?'

Trace shrugged, said the first thing that came into his mind: 'An antichrist?'

Kastrouni sat bolt upright in his chair, almost spilled his drink. Eagerly he grabbed Trace's arms, stared at him wide-eyed. 'But you understand the concept! A man was here who could live forever – if he desired. With all the powers of – of God, on his side. He had only to will it and we couldn't hurt him, nothing could. And yet he let us kill him, cruelly. Why? To teach us a lesson, Charlie. To lift us up. So that today we would remember and believe. Do you see?'

Trace could have argued but merely nodded. Best to let Kastrouni get on with it. 'So?'

Kastrouni released him. 'Satan is quick to learn, quick to take advantage. Jesus – Jesus the ultimate martyr – was the biggest blow he'd ever suffered. People knew there was evil in the world – it was self-evident, as you've pointed out – but until Jesus they had had no proof of the existence of good. Now they *knew*! Satan had to retaliate, and quickly. And so he, too, gave the world a son.'

'Khumeni?'

'Khumeni *now*!' said Kastrouni at once. 'But first there

was a creature called Ab. And later there was Guigos. And in between – how many more?'

'I don't understand.'

'Reincarnation! Resurrection! He is a black phoenix rising from his own putrid ashes. I saw just such a foul rebirth in Chorazin . . .'

Trace sat back. 'This doesn't explain my mother's madness.' He gave a snort. 'In fact that could be strictly hereditary, for all I know. Certainly *I* must be more than half-crazy – I *must* be, just to sit here listening to all of this!'

'Certainly it explains her madness,' Kastrouni insisted. 'Charlie, she wasn't merely raped by Khumeni. She was utterly defiled by him – she was desecrated – penetrated to the core by the son of Satan himself. It wasn't only her body he raped: it was her mind, her soul. She had been *joined with him*! The very fact itself was a cancer, something which grew in her just as you grew in her – but more slowly. She knew she'd been used, defiled. But by whom, by what? She must have wondered; and over the years perhaps there were vague recurrent memories of that night, of the *thing* that took her like a beast. The *thing* that – '

'Shut up!' Trace shouted.

Kastrouni started as if he'd been slapped. He pushed his chair back, stood up, went shakily, almost staggering, to the window and parted the curtains a little. Outside, the storm had long since retreated. It was mid-afternoon and the sun was steaming dry the roads and pavements. They had been here for a little over two hours. Their half-bottles were almost empty. Kastrouni turned, leaned backward against the window-sill, tiredly said:

'I don't blame you for reacting like that.'

Trace stood up. 'You're a crazy man,' he said.

Kastrouni hung his head, ran his fingers through his

white hair. 'You were right,' he said without looking up. 'I did come to you for help – but also to offer help. But you mustn't go yet. We're not finished.'

'Yes we are, and I'm going now,' Trace answered.

'I want the beast dead,' Kastrouni continued, as if he hadn't even heard Trace. 'I want him dead! – but I can't do it alone.'

'Goodbye,' said Trace, heading for the door.

Kastrouni looked up, looked washed out, weary to death. 'At least I've warned you,' he said.

'Never come anywhere near me again,' Trace told him. 'You're an old man and crazy, but if I do see you again – and if I ever hear you mention my mother's name again – I swear I'll shove you under a fucking bus!' He went out and slammed the door behind him.

But there was a door in his mind, opened by Kastrouni, which for all his anger he knew he could never close. Not completely. For the moment he had turned his back on that portal, refused its invitation. Beyond its threshold lay fantasy, and Trace's feet were set firmly in reality.

Waiting for his taxi under the awning outside the lobby, he became aware that he was tapping his left foot nervously on the pavement. Kastrouni had wanted to tell him more, show him things. What things? Stuff from Guigos's saddle-packs? Had there ever been such a man as George Guigos? What difference did it make anyway? Kastrouni was crazy, possessor of a few facts around which he'd constructed an entire realm of nightmare and . . . and fantasy. Sheer fantasy.

Balls to him and his bloody story!

But Trace's foot – his left foot – kept on tapping for all that . . .

Trace rarely slept during the day, but that Saturday he slept right through what was left of the afternoon. Slept like a dead man, dreamless and motionless as a log, so that when he came gropingly awake he found his bed untumbled, with only the long, single hollow his body had made to show he'd been there at all. A roll of carpet may just as easily have lain there, would have moved as much or more than he had.

It had been the whisky, of course. Half a bottle of the stuff: like an anaesthetic to a mind suddenly assaulted by an unknown past, or more properly by someone else's warped fancies. Kastrouni and his bloody mumbo-jumbo.

Kastrouni . . .

All the way from Athens.

Words leaped to the forefront of Trace's mind. Words from a fantasy, but unforgotten. Ab . . . Demogorgon . . . Chorazin . . .

'Stigmata . . . ?'

He got out of bed, checked Yellow Pages for the number of Kastrouni's motel and started to dial it – then stopped. Hell, *no*! His life was complicated enough without getting mixed up in someone else's nightmares.

And anyway, he was supposed to be at Jilly's place in – (he glanced at his watch,) in fifty minutes!

Frustration and momentary panic came together in an explosion of confused mental activity and frantic physical motion. Trace knocked over the telephone table, tripped on the TV cable, banged his shins on the washbasin's pedestal before he could bring himself under control.

Then . . . he deliberately printed up Kastrouni's name on the computer of his mind, and even more deliberately erased each letter of it one by one. That was that. And as for Jilly – she could damn well wait!

He put his mind and body into a lower gear, took an hour to clean up and get dressed, arrived at Jilly's place exactly one hour and twenty-five minutes late . . .

* * *

Jilly was blonde and beautiful, long-legged, big-eyed and just three inches shorter than Trace. Her breasts were classically pear-shaped, with nothing of sag to them, and when she and Trace made love she had this habit of putting her arms up over her head so that he could see them displayed to their best. She liked sex as much as he did and no position was taboo. She did have a brain but had largely lost the use of it after discovering her normally devastating effect on men. Nor was she unacceptable to women: her model looks and natural flair for style had made her top salesperson at a well-frequented shoe shop in Oxford Street. She worked every other Saturday and this had been one of her 'off' days; which meant, to her way of thinking, that Trace's refusal to spend the day with her had been a complete waste.

His turning up late didn't go down very well either, and he hadn't booked a table as promised; but he *had* taken her to a top restaurant for an expensive meal, and at the casino in the Cromwell Road he had diligently directed her in the placing of her chips at the roulette tables. In an hour she'd won more than three hundred pounds which he insisted she keep ('Buy yourself some knickers or something . . .'), following which he'd driven her red Capri back to her place.

That was where his preoccupation – which he had thought well hidden – finally got through to her: the fact that his mind wasn't on the job.

Normally they'd have a drink, bathe each other and stretch out naked on huge cushions in front of her video watching soft-porn films until they got caught up in it. But tonight was different. They got through the preliminaries but then . . . after tempting him for the best part of an hour she'd suddenly asked:

'Where are you, Charlie?'

'Eh?'

'I mean, your things are here – almost – but you're somewhere else!'

He'd turned from the screen to look at her, and slowly his eyes had focused. 'My things?'

She'd stroked his genitals, barely touching him with only the tips of her fingers, and kissed his chest. 'These things. But where are you? Have you met someone?'

He had started to make love to her then but half-way through had paused, as if on afterthought, to answer: 'Yes, I've met someone.'

'Oh!' And she had pouted in typically mindless fashion.

'A man,' he'd explained. 'Business.'

Then she had put her hands up over her head and Trace had concentrated long enough to bring them both to climax. Afterwards she'd said: 'It's funny, that's all. I mean, you've never let business interfere with "business" before.' Which for Jilly was uncommonly clever.

But then she'd said something to spoil it, something to annoy him out of all proportion. 'Have you hurt yourself, Charlie? I mean, ordinarily you walk so straight, but tonight I've seen you limp now and then. Is your foot giving you trouble? Your funny foot?'

His 'funny' foot. He'd told her before about saying things like that to him. But her dejection had been obvious when Trace dressed and phoned for a taxi. On his part it wasn't so much pique as the fact that after what she'd said their nakedness seemed suddenly obscene.

While he waited for his cab she put on a dressing-gown and sat smoking, saying nothing. Normally he would stay the night and they'd make love over and over. So maybe he really had met someone else. But she kept her thoughts to herself and when he left she hadn't asked when she'd be seeing him. And Trace had been glad for that.

Now, in the taxi where it headed east on the North Circular, he lay back and considered the day's events.

They hadn't been especially strenuous – grotesque, but not strenuous – and yet he felt thoroughly exhausted. And this after an afternoon spent sleeping! He was normally this way on the night *before* a job, not the night after. All the planning, the tension and suspense as the time drew closer.

But this Kastrouni – him and his half-told tale – and his alleged too-intimate knowledge of Trace's beginnings . . .

And his very genuine fear of summer storms.

Of course if there was a single grain of truth in his story (there couldn't be, but if there was) then it was only to be expected that he'd be afraid of lightning. The rumble of thunder must sound like the very knell of doom to him, and –

– And what the hell! Trace gave a loud snort, sat up straight in the back of the taxi. Why, he'd actually let the crazy Greek bastard get through to him! Ridiculous!

He looked out of his window at the night-grey buildings drifting by. And talk of the devil, there over the rooftops the sudden bright flash of lightning.

Talk of the devil.

Satan.

Ab.

Demogorgon.

Stigmata . . .

'We're driving right into it, Guv!' the cabby commented, glancing at Trace over his shoulder. 'The storm, I mean. Bleedin' weather!'

Trace nodded, said nothing. His left foot ached, felt trapped in its specially modified shoe.

The taxi arrived at his place dead on 2:15 A.M. and just as it started to rain. Five minutes later Trace was in bed and almost as quickly asleep . . .

* * *

114

. . . And almost as quickly awake.

What was that? A knock on his door – at this time of night?

He got out of bed, went to the door and used the fish-eye lens to stare out onto the dark landing. He stared harder, blinked, brushed a stray hair from his brow. A shadow, descending the stairs and so out of view? Some-one had softly knocked, certainly, for listening intently Trace now heard the accustomed creaking of tight treads from half-way down the stair-well. Then the banging of the main door on the ground floor confirmed it, a banging almost immediately drowned out in a long, rumbling peal of thunder. The storm was now at its peak.

But who would have come here in this weather and at this hour? Trace opened his door, moved to step out onto the landing and put the light on – and went sprawling!

He had tripped over something lying immediately beyond the threshold, something both bulky and heavy. On the gloomy landing on all fours, the shuddery thought flashed across Trace's mind that perhaps it was a body. Where that idea came from he couldn't think, but it had him up on his feet in a moment and groping desperately for the light switch.

And then he was gulping air thankfully, and tremblingly reaching to touch the battered old brown leather suitcase where it stood against his door. A sheet of notepaper had been rolled up and pushed through the time-blackened handle. Trace saw it, snatched it free and read:

Trace,
   He is here and knows that I too am here. Once more I am pursued. I know you think me a madman, but the contents of the suitcase may yet serve to convince you. This is as much as I can do for you. Good luck!

D. Kastrouni

Kastrouni! It had been him. But why had he run? Why hadn't he waited for Trace to open the door, let him in? Trace started downstairs, a cry rising to his lips – which died as he realized he was naked. Cursing under his breath he hurried back into the flat, ran to the bathroom. The window there opened over the street and the main entrance to the house; Trace threw it open, stuck his head out.

Down the street a running figure in a light suit drew up to a waiting taxi. Getting into the taxi, the figure looked back once, turning its face toward Trace. It could be Kastrouni, but Trace wasn't sure. Again Trace went to cry out, and once again found himself stalled. A wind had come up, was blowing in his face, would whip his words uselessly away and waste them. Anyway, the man was already inside the taxi, which was drawing away down the street.

But it wasn't only the wind that had stopped Trace calling after the man in the street, neither the wind nor the huge pellets of rain which seemed to deliberately slap him in the face. They were only products of the storm, after all. But the storm itself, that was something else.

It was alive. It had purpose. Crazy, yes, but Trace could feel it. It pricked at his skin, brought up gooseflesh on his naked arms and legs. It swirled in past him and filled the flat. The wind was full of strange energy, alive with a monstrous sentience. Trace felt himself scrutinized.

The taxi had reached the corner, was indicating a turn and slowing down. Its brake lights glowed red. Around that corner was an open space, a park, where the tops of tall trees showed over the rooftops. The topmost branches of those trees were in a frenzy now, whipping to and fro. And that was when lightning came striding from the north, marching on legs of white fire from a low ceiling of boiling clouds.

Trace had never seen anything like it. Only a second or two separated the flashes, which seemed to head in a straight line directly toward him – no, *toward the taxi* where it turned the corner and passed behind the brick bulk of a building. The sudden violence of the storm was terrifying as a hissing, crackling bolt struck down into the street and ran in rivers of molten light down the gutters – followed immediately by another that sizzled down to strike at something just around the same corner!

The thunder and the detonation came together: the first from the sky, a drawn-out roll of drums that rattled the tiles on all the rooves, and the second from the exploding taxi. The red rim of a fireball blazed briefly from behind the corner house, lighting up walls in an orange glare, and in the next moment flaming fragments of the car itself were blown back into view.

A twisted door bounded in the street, spraying glass. An axle with a blazing wheel intact performed ill-balanced pyrotechnic somersaults among the higher branches of the trees. Black smoke shot with fire boiled upward and outward.

'Christ!' Trace heard himself croak. 'Jesus H. *Christ* . . .!'

But down inside he knew that this had had little or nothing to do with Him . . .

Chapter Three

Trace's hands were shaking so badly he had difficulty getting dressed; by the time he was down on the street at the scene of the shredded, burned-out car, a redundant ambulance was already in attendance, police cars, even a fire-engine damping down shrubbery which blazing debris had set on fire. Windows in the corner house and its neighbour had been blown in; the damp pavements were full of people in dressing-gowns and slippers; the road was cratered where smouldering remains hissed and crackled as hot metal and small pools of glass cooled and contracted. Nothing in the mess much resembled human remains, for which Trace was glad. But in any case it had been instantaneous; no one had suffered and nothing could possibly have lived through it.

As for the lightning storm: it had passed on, burned itself out. The sky was bright and clear above a perfectly normal summer night. Perfectly normal . . .

Knowing there was nothing he could do and having no wish to get himself involved – not wanting his name in any way in the limelight – Trace stayed only a few moments before returning to the flat. There he opened the suitcase and tipped its contents out on the floor of his bedroom, sat staring for a long time at a mass of books and documents and fat envelopes. The fruits of Kastrouni's lifelong obsession, the bulk of his 'evidence', the accumulated substance of a phobia which, ironically, in the end had killed him. That was what all this stuff must be, Trace thought. And that was the strangest part of it: he'd been frightened of lightning, and sure enough lightning had done for him.

Phobia? said a voice at the back of Trace's mind. *Obsession? The crazed fancies of a madman? Do you really believe that, Charlie? What is it, Charlie? What are you afraid of?*

His left foot was aching abominably, felt confined in the soft warmth of his slipper. Trace kicked off the slipper, drew his feet up under him cross-legged on the bed, sat glaring at that left foot. In general outline it was very much a human foot, but its sole was thicker by half an inch, and the small toes were all joined. Not webbed, joined. Only the bones themselves were normal, the bones and nails and the cleft between the big toe and the rest of the foot. It fitted into a shoe, yes – albeit a special shoe – but in fact it was more a hoof than a foot. A cloven hoof . . .

'Not physically perfect . . .'

'Stigmata . . .'

And that monstrous sentience he had felt in the storm. There had been no denying that. No avoiding it, either. Black magic? Hallucination? There had been more than enough of both in Kastrouni's story.

Trace got up off the bed, sat down again on the floor amidst the jumble from the suitcase. And slowly he began to examine each item, piece by piece. 'This is as much as I can do for you,' Kastrouni had said in his note. Well, and now Trace supposed it was the least he could do for him.

There was a slim notebook, its flyleaf bearing the neatly inscribed initials D.K., Kastrouni's initials. Trace glanced into the pages, let his eyes skip over the entries without really seeing anything, laid the book aside for now.

And there were maps. A good many. Some of them

were little more than sketches on ancient scraps of parchment; others were modern and presumably accurate, of the Ordnance Survey sort and possibly to that standard; there were even battle-maps (plainly Israeli) showing areas of good natural advantage, elevated observation points, harbour areas for troops, tanks and so forth. And with very few exceptions all were of the same region: the Sea of Galilee. Chorazin had been clearly marked on all of them, lying at the central points of inked crosses.

There was also a map of Karpathos in the Aegean, not recent – not in the last ten years, anyway, for on the legend the island's name was spelled with a 'C' as opposed to the more romantic 'K' of the travel agencies – but fairly detailed for all that. It, too, was marked with a cross, the location of some ruin or other in the coastal mountains of the south-east, and there was also a name inked in but it was in Greek and Trace couldn't read it.

Then there was an A-4 sized manila envelope of cuttings, even entire pages, from several Cypriot newspapers, all dated either 27th or 28th July '57; and stapled together with these was a poor photocopy of a six-page report in English, addressed to the GOC Cyprus District and signed by the Deputy Assistant Provost Marshal, Middle-East Land Forces. Remembering Kastrouni's story of what he believed had occurred that night at his father's villa north of Larnaca, Trace decided to read this report first, but not before he'd at least glanced through the rest of the suitcase's contents.

There were Holy Bibles, some huge and antique and full of explanatory notes, others Trace could hold in one hand, whose print was minuscule. He remembered seeing a list of biblical references in Kastrouni's notebook and made a mental note to check it out later. But what on earth could anyone want with more than one Bible? It could be, of course, that Kastrouni had fooled around with bibliomancy or some such (certainly he had been a 'true believer', as he himself had readily admitted) but to Trace a Bible was simply another book.

He began to go a little more quickly, barely glancing at the stuff now. There were several crumbly parchments marked with esoteric designs that looked decidedly occult; these were preserved against further disintegration in plastic sleeves or between stiff laminates; and a very worm-eaten book in Arabic, held together by rubber bands, whose leaves almost without exception had come loose from the spine and flaky bindings; a fat bundle of papers in a large clear-plastic envelope labelled 'Demogorgon & Associated . . .'; several volumes of world history since biblical times, with special reference to wars, invasions, disasters and the like . . .

There were, too, a number of books on ritual magic – gibberish to Trace – and one bulky leather-bound tome in what looked like ancient Hebraic, stamped or impressed on its age-blackened cover with the six-pointed Star of David. Finally, there was something called *My Journeys & Discoveries in the Holy Land*, a slim privately printed book by one Morgan Selby, bearing the subtitle: *Myths of the Bible, and the Great Biblical Myth*. Well, at least Trace should be able to read that one! As for the rest of it . . .

Trace shook his head, snorted his frustration. Much of this stuff was completely beyond him. He went back to the Military Police Report, began to read it:

Sir,
By now you have doubtless read several accounts or versions of the occurrences of the evening of 26th July of this year, including the Interim Report of my investigating NCOs, dated the morning of the 27th. This current report is not meant to be all-embracing, neither does it draw much in the way of conclusion; detailed conclusions must wait upon thorough and

121

possibly lengthy investigations. It is in the main a Situation Report, giving an overview, as it were, of the occurrences from a purely Provost viewpoint, and partial assessment of the damage on a diplomatic level and in terms of internal security.

First the facts of the occurrences themselves:

1. On the evening/night of the 26th–27th July a Greek-Cypriot bungalow residence standing not far from the coast road between Larnaca and Dhekelia was burned down. The fire may have been set deliberately, in which case the arson was probably in connection with the whole crime, one of a series of serious offences by person or persons as yet unknown.

2. A Military Police Mobile Patrol returning to the garrison from Larnaca spotted the fire and went to investigate and/or lend assistance. The patrol discovered three women in the close vicinity of the burning house, one of whom was Turkish-Cypriot, one Greek-Cypriot, and one regrettably British, a young and respected member of QARANC, the fiancée of an Officer serving with the RAMC at the BMH. All three were in a sorry state, heavily drugged and scantily clad – 'dishevelled' at best – and medical examinations at the BMH showed all to have been raped very brutally and probably repeatedly. On alerting the respective authorities, the Greek and Turkish women were later taken from BMH by their relatives and civilian doctors from Larnaca. The usual warning was applied: that we would no longer be responsible for their welfare once they were released, but of course there was no way we could legally detain them.

3. Statements recorded at the earliest opportunity (copies of which you have subsequently seen, including those obtained from the local Greek and Turkish authorities) show a striking similarity: all three females were apparently abducted – Diana Trace, the QARANC, from the grounds of the BMH in the Sovereign Base Area itself – and chloroformed, following which they remember little else of what occurred save general impressions upon partial and eventually full recovery of consciousness at BMH. You will appreciate that the nature of the crimes against them (I refer specifically to the island women) preclude any detailed statements such as the one obtained from QARANC Diana Trace. We have, therefore, been more or less obliged to rely solely upon her account. Unfortunately that account seems to have been coloured (perhaps not unnaturally) by recurrent nightmares which have plagued her ever since. At present she is undergoing a course of psychiatric treatment.

4. Motive:

While the motive for the offences will not be known until the offenders are detained, still we may make some educated guesses. The intention of the author of these crimes could have been to bring about shame and general demoralization – but *to* whom *by* whom? We could (as the leaders of most local Turkish communities have done) point the finger at EOKA; except that the abduction and rape of one of their own – i.e. a Greek-Cypriot girl, and the daughter of an influential man and suspected EOKA sympathizer at that – must of course damage EOKA's cause enormously. Is it likely that EOKA would make such a blunder? I for one doubt it, and they themselves (in several hastily circulated pamphlets) have made much of this inconsistency in the Turkish accusation. It is all a Turkish plot, they say, to dishonour them and detract from their credibility. And they ask: what clean-limbed Greek would force himself on a filthy Turk anyway? But the suggestion that a Turkish group is responsible seems even more unacceptable; the involved Turkish woman is the wife of an ex-mainland diplomat; any Turkish involvement in her abduction, rape, etc., is simply out of the question. The penalties would be unthinkable, deterrent enough for even the most degenerate of criminals. Any felon or felons apprehended in this respect by the island's Turkish authorities could expect only the very harshest treatment, and if caught by one of the Turkish vigilante groups . . . why, they would simply disappear forever! Their nationality would not matter greatly, but if they *were* Turks . . . then may God help them!

And finally, to further complicate the incident, we have the English girl's involvement. Certainly the rape of a serving member of QARANC could be the work of EOKA; but in all truth, are the Turks any less capable of such a crime? And of course we know – we are absolutely *certain* – that this could never be the work of serving members of HMF. We are as certain of our own innocence as the Greeks and Turks would seem to be of theirs . . .

Personally, as the head of your Provost Staff, I have tried to take a step back and view the entire incident from a position external to all mutual enmities and prejudices. We do not yet know who is to blame and may never know their real motives, but it seems to me that if some entirely anonymous outside agency or agitator were bent upon fermenting even more bloodshed on this already troubled island, he could hardly have chosen a better way to do it. Nor is this attempt at some sort of conclusion entirely unfounded:

You will recall that on the night of the 26th a telephone message was received by Provost in the garrison threatening that from that time forward EOKA would shame all British women on the island when and wherever possible. It might therefore be construed that the unspeakable acts of that same night were committed by them as proof that they had issued no idle threat – if they issued the threat in the first place. For as you are aware EOKA has stated that on the night of the 26th *they* received just such a threat from the British Forces against *their* women. Purely terrorist propaganda, of course – but at the same time the Turks likewise stated that they had been warned of punitive action against their women by an hitherto non-political Greek Faction! Did everyone take it into their heads that night to go threatening everyone else? In this light my proposition (that perhaps some outside agency is at work here) does not seem so far-fetched.

And as we have seen, in the week gone by since the incidents occurred, there has been more than enough violence on both sides – even, unfortunately, on our side.

Initially, on the morning of the 27th, the wineshop of one Costas Kastrouni was looted and vandalized and Kastrouni himself murdered at his home. He was the owner of the burned house where presumably the women were raped on the previous evening. He was a pacifist and was known to be friendly with many Turkish customers. There is some evidence to suggest that Kastrouni had let the house in question to persons at present unknown, but nothing positive. He kept no records. In any case we are reasonably sure that he was murdered by EOKA as a Turkish sympathizer.

Then, on the 28th, a Turkish observation post on the Greek-Turk boundary was fired upon and burned out with the loss of three lives. Also, our patrols have come increasingly under fire (apparently from both sides) and there has been at least one case of an apparently random shooting by a member of our own forces. In general, there has been a definite and accelerating deterioration of relations and communications between all parties; I am at a loss to know what action may be taken to defuse the situation. If this *was* the work of some outside agency,

124

agitating for its own purposes, then someone, somewhere, must be very pleased with himself indeed.

5. The security of the Dhekelia Garrison –

– And so on – but Trace wasn't interested in the rest. He went back and read again the facts concerning his mother, trying to find something he'd missed the first time. The report seemed to bear out much of Kastrouni's story.

And Kastrouni's father – murdered! The Greek hadn't made mention of that. But no wonder he'd wanted this man, Khumeni, dead. If such a man existed.

Trace stood up and eased his legs, put the report aside, went to make coffee. And sipping hot coffee he made himself a promise. Tomorrow was Sunday. No good trying to do anything on a Sunday. But first thing Monday morning . . . the Army kept records, didn't they? And QARANC? It had been twenty-five years ago but must still be worth a try. He nodded determinedly. He'd check back, find out for himself about his mother's 'disturbance' back there in 1957, discover exactly what had been wrong with her that she'd required psychiatric treatment.

Whatever it was, they'd failed. Psychiatrists, doctors, shrinks! *'Hah!'* Trace snorted. He'd been only eight years old when finally it all came to a head. He remembered that much at least, but even as a small child he had known his mother was strange. She used to have those terrible nightmares, would wake up screaming night after night.

Trace concentrated, tried to pin down elusive memories, things his child's mind might have demanded he forget. Her nightmares; how he used to go to her in the night, hold her in his small boy's arms; how he'd tried to comfort, console her as she sobbed of his twin, the brother who had died even as he and Charlie were born.

125

'And I was glad, Charlie, glad! I only saw him once, just once. But he looked like . . . he looked awful, Charlie . . .'

Her nightmares, yes: of his brother and of something else. Something coming at her. Of being pinned down. Of a bestial *Thing*. A thing that looked like . . . like the devil!

And as suddenly as that Trace remembered, and small, icy feet hopped and slithered on his rigid spine. Memories came faster:

He had been eight, just eight, when they'd gone on holiday, out of the city to the countryside. Devon, if he had it right. It was autumn but the sea and the sky were still summer-blue, and one evening as they'd walked back from exploring a tiny town on the coast to the old, rambling boarding-house where they'd stayed . . . that had been when it happened. He remembered how they'd passed a field where ponies rolled in the long grass and chased each other in sport. Or perhaps not in sport.

It had been then that her collapse had come, that final breakdown from which she'd never more recovered to this very day. Trace remembered how she'd suddenly screamed and run headlong, crashing through hedges, across ditches, blindly, hysterically, screaming all the way. And when finally, tearfully, he'd found her, how she had seemed huddled down into herself, all scratched and bleeding and sobbing.

'It was nothing, Mummy,' he'd told her earnestly. 'Nothing at all. It was only the ponies. They were playing, that's all, just playing!'

In fact they hadn't been 'just playing' and he knew that now, but then he'd been a child and had understood nothing of that. He had laughed to see the thrusting rump of the pony where he had mounted his quivering mate. He'd laughed, and thought his mother laughed, too, but remembered now that it had been more a

126

choking gurgle. Then the mare had gone to her knees and the stud had looked almost manlike standing there upright with his hooves in her back as he continued to thrust at her. And he'd tossed his mane of coarse hair and neighed his lust for all to hear.

Yes . . . and it was not until then that Diana Trace had really gone crazy.

Reliving the final events of that holiday seventeen years in the past had wearied Trace beyond the point where he could any longer keep his eyes open. He awakened the next day around noon, had a shower and a bite to eat, and only then returned to the various books and documents from the suitcase.

First he went to Kastrouni's notebook. It hadn't seemed extensively used when he'd glanced through it last night, containing mainly single-word entries under each of its alphabetical headings. Under 'A', for example, Trace found a few names, (including 'Ab',) several addresses and/or locations, and other entries apparently chosen at random from a mass of esoteric or occult sources. But nothing that appeared immediately as being of any great importance to anyone seeking clues. 'B' covered Biblical References and a further list of names, such as Bethsaida, Baal, Beelzebub, Belial, and so on. Trace was not totally ignorant of such things; he knew that the last three of these first four names were those of supposed demons, false gods or fallen angels – evil spirits, at any rate. Under 'C' he found Christ, Capernaum, Chorazin, 'Curses,' Crucifix, (and other Crosses,) Cabbala, and so forth.

It seemed the notebook was simply a directory: its contents were pointers to a far greater store of knowledge or information.

Well, he had to start somewhere. Better men than Charlie Trace had drawn alleged strength and inspiration

– and intelligence – from the Bible. Against 'Bethsaida,' 'Chorazin' and 'Capernaum' he had seen biblical references and a cryptic 'See MS, 62.' That last might mean 'Manuscript No. 62' or 'Morgan Selby's book, page 62.' He would look into that later. But for now let's see what the Bible had to say about this riddle:

Trace's first choice was a poor one: a fist-sized Bible he picked up purely for ease of handling, which proved to contain print so small that he'd have difficulty reading it. Instead he went to the opposite extreme, settling for a massive Family Bible in two volumes, published by Sangsters of London somewhere at the turn of the century, a superbly scholarly work by one John Kitto, DD, FSA.

Trace had several references, the most comprehensive of which seemed to be Chap. X, verses 12, 13, 15, and 18 of St Luke. Opening the massive Vol. II he turned to that Chapter and page and read the verses indicated:

12: But I say unto you, that it shall be more tolerable in that day for Sodom, than for that city.
13: Woe unto thee, Chorazin! woe unto thee, Bethsaida! for if the mighty works had been done in Tyre and Sidon, which have been done in you, they had a great while ago repented, sitting in sackcloth and ashes.
15: And thou, Capernaum, which art exalted to heaven, shalt be thrust down to hell.
18: And he said unto them, I beheld Satan as lightning fall from heaven.

Trace read that last one over again . . .

Finally he closed the great book, laid it carefully aside, returned thoughtfully to Kastrouni's notebook. But that phrase played itself over and over again in his mind: 'I beheld Satan as lightning fall from heaven.'

And, *is there a pattern to all of this?* he asked himself. *Is there?* But if there was, what sort of a crazy pattern was it?

The notebook opened – almost with a sort of familiarity this time, as if it had been opened here many, many times before – at 'A', and Trace's eyes seemed drawn directly to 'Antichrist'; it was as if the word had been waiting for him. Odd, because he'd already looked at 'A', when apparently he hadn't noticed it. It was the very last entry on the second page of the 'A' section, except for a terse note: 'See "Reincarnation."'

Trace turned the pages to 'R', ran his finger down the entries there until he found 'Reincarnation,' frowned at what he discovered: merely a list of numbers and another reference, 'See MS, 47.'

He studied the numbers:

347 A.D.	– less	20
327	– ..	25
302	– ..	30
272	– ..	35
237	– ..	40
197	– ..	45
152	– ..	50
102	– ..	55
1936		

The table meant nothing to him. He shook his head in frustration, looked closer. Trace had a good memory. Kastrouni's story had started in 1936 – at Chorazin. He pursed his lips and just for the hell of it totalled up all the numbers above that date – and discovered that indeed they added up to 1936. So what?

Twenty minutes later he was still trying to make something of the list of numbers when his telephone rang. By then he was so deeply engrossed (he believed he was just starting to see the light) that he gave a massive start as the silence of his flat was abruptly shattered.

He snatched up the phone, snapped, 'Trace?'

'Charlie? Are you OK?' It was Jilly.

'Am I OK? Of course I'm OK! Why shouldn't I be OK? What the hell do you want, Jilly?'

'Well, if *that's* your attitude . . .'

He relented. Before she could slam the phone down on him, he said: 'Jilly, I'm busy, that's all.'

'No you're not. You're mad at me for running off at the mouth last night. For going on about your foot and calling it "funny". Well, I'm sorry, Charlie. And I missed you, last night. I woke up and wanted you in me, Charlie, but you weren't there.'

'Jilly, I – '

'Charlie, is it finished? Is that it? If it is I'd like to know . . .'

He could finish it right here and now if he wanted to. He was tempted to say yes, this is it. But . . . hell, Jilly was some sort of sanity in a world rapidly going mad. He couldn't just *say* it, not just like that.

'Charlie?' She sounded far, far away.

'Fancy a drink?' he said – and at once hated himself for his weakness.

That was better. 'Your place?'

He looked around the flat, curled his lip at the chaos of books and documents, said: 'No, the Ship – about an hour?'

'OK. And then your place?'

'We'll see,' said Charlie. And he noticed how she hung on to her end until he put the phone down.

Then he stamped around the flat for a moment or two, picked up Kastrouni's notebook . . . and at once hurled it down so hard that it bounced on the carpet. What the hell had gone wrong with his life? Where was the peace and quiet? He'd always known where the action was, but now and then he liked a little peace, too!

Quickly he got ready to go and meet Jilly, then did something completely alien to his nature. Something just a little bit reckless. He got down his cache of stolen gold from its holding place and chose a single piece – a tiny antique matchbox strung on a fine, intricate golden chain for a necklace – to give her as a parting gift.

Reckless, yes, but . . . what the hell! The odds against Jilly ever meeting up with old Cat Carter must be a million to one at least.

By the time Trace was ready to leave the flat there were still some twenty minutes of the agreed hour left to run. He opened Kastrouni's notebook again, frowned at the list of numbers.

$$347 \text{ AD} - \text{less } 20$$
$$327 \quad - \; \therefore \; 25$$

Well, 347 less 20 was certainly 327; and 327 less 25 was likewise 302. And so on. But what was the AD? Anno Domini? (Or 'After Death', as he'd learned to remember it in school.) After the death of Christ?

'See MS, 47.'

Trace took up Morgan Selby's book, *My Journeys & Discoveries in the Holy Land*, turned to page 47. But here Kastrouni had left nothing to chance: the information he had desired to pass on – or at least, that information which had most interested Kastrouni himself – had been clearly indicated down the margins by thick strokes of a pen. Most of pages 47 and 48 were marked up in this way, and certain words and phrases were likewise ringed about in the same ink.

It was a long passage and referred to a 'lost' scripture, a scripture so blasphemous (which seemed to Trace almost a contradiction in terms) that it had never been set to print. Where the author had acquired this information wasn't explained, but he gave his version of the alleged contents of the missing scripture in the following manner:

ACCORDING to the scriptures Jesus damned Capernaum, Bethsaida and Chorazin. More recently, scholars of the occult and the infernal have generally agreed that Chorazin will be the birthplace of the antichrist. How this can possibly come to pass considering that Chorazin has stood in ruins for some fourteen centuries is hard to understand. But in fact the occultists are geographically correct: they are only at fault in their temporal calculations. For according to the natives and local superstition, Chorazin, on the shore of Galilee, *was* the birthplace of the antichrist.

The lost scripture (according to my sources) alleges that:

The Gadarene swine were not all 'choked' in the lake; one at least, a sow, survived. The legion of devils which were in possession of the drowned beasts all fled into this survivor, which was later impregnated with the devil's seed by Demogorgon, Satan's emissary. At the very hour Jesus died on the cross, an ugly child in human form was littered by the sow.

Growing up, the child was adopted by a witch dwelling in the wilderness close to Chorazin. The boy 'spoke in tongues' and had 'many demons in him.' His fostermother, a learned woman and necromancer,' encoded from his mouthings two texts of demoniac power, one to propitiate the strength of Demogorgon and the devil, the other to rob them of their strength and so put them down or exorcise them. Under the ascending node of the first, all hell might be unleashed; and by the descending node of the second, Demogorgon is made impotent. These texts, graven in stone, are like the scripture supposed 'lost', but in fact a rare Gnostic rite of exorcism employs a 'spell' or 'curse' of alleged Palestinian origin, which in every respect seems derived from the second Chorazin tablet.

As for Ab, son of Demogorgon (or more properly Satan's son, the antichrist): as a youth he spent half of his time mad, half sane; his witch fostermother used him as an oracle and made great profit from his utterances. For all that he was malformed, having a withered left leg, he fathered many children upon the witch, all of them monsters and every one dying in the light of its first day. Grown to a man and gross in all respects, still Ab and his witch fostermother cohabited; but as

132

she aged, so his lust grew ever more bestial. When she was seventy-seven, in a fit of sexual frenzy that lasted for whole days and nights, the changeling killed her and villagers from Chorazin found her torn up the middle as by an animal; following which Ab ran off into the wilderness and lived as a hermit, practising black magic.

Thereafter, a great many crimes were ascribed to him, including the abduction of girls and women, and their subsequent murders; the slaying of beasts, often in a manner best left undescribed; the defilements of temples and the haunting of all the countryside around. He is supposed to have lived, as did many other biblical characters before him, an inordinately long life: namely 347 years! His actual death, not on record, is also a matter of legend: again according to immemorial lore, in the year 347 A.D., on the night of a fearful lightning storm, Ab entered Chorazin and put a spell on three of the younger men of the village. The result of his spell – and perhaps more importantly its purpose – are not known, except that Chorazin's inhabitants fled the place *en masse* that same night, only returning after several weeks.

Thereafter, for one hundred and fifty years, gradually the village fell into decay until it was finally deserted for good. Wandering tribes made their homes there down the centuries, but none settled. When I saw the place it was in utter ruin and abandonment. The tribesman I had much of this from would not enter Chorazin with me but kept his distance. The place was cursed, he said.

In this respect it can be seen that Jesus's prophecy was borne out fully: 'Woe unto thee, Chorazin!' indeed!

Trace glanced over the text again; the words ringed about were these: 'Chorazin tablet', 'withered left leg', '347 A.D.', 'lightning storm', and the word 'three' in 'three of the younger men of the village.'

According to Kastrouni, George Guigos had also taken three young men with him into Chorazin on that night back in 1936. And here again was that date, A.D. 347 – the date of Ab's death? And yet Selby had clearly stated that Ab's actual death was not on record . . .

Trace glanced at his watch. It was time he went to

meet Jilly. The rest of the puzzle would have to wait. But one thing was certain: now that he'd started it he would finish it. If there was one thing Trace couldn't abide it was an unsolved riddle . . .

Chapter Four

Jilly was waiting for Trace at The Ship; a couple of yobby strangers were trying to chat her up at the bar, which was nothing unusual; the place was packed with arty types, queers, and Irishmen from Crouch End and Hornsey. Trace rescued Jilly, grabbed drinks – whisky for himself, a gin and tonic for her – and was lucky enough to take possession of a booth as its 4-person gaggle of spike-headed punks careened squawking out of the place on shoes like columnar clogs.

He wasted no time but gave her the necklace; her mouth fell open as she took it from him, opened up the tiny matchbox and looked inside. Trace hadn't thought to do that, but anyway there was nothing in there. The interior of the matchbox had been done out as a locket. 'I can put a tiny picture of you in there,' she said. 'And the chain is just long enough to dangle in between my breasts. That way you'll always be touching them.'

Trace knew it was now or never. 'Jilly, I'm moving on.'

She looked up from putting the necklace carefully into her handbag, her eyes slowly coming up to meet his. 'You're what?'

'That's to say goodbye,' he told her. 'Put someone else's picture in it. I'm not for settling down, Jilly.'

She let it sink in, said: 'You give with one hand, take with the other.'

'We said there'd be no strings,' he felt impelled to remind her. 'But if we go on the strings will come – and then when it's over they'll choke us off. I've loved you, but I don't love you.'

As if she hadn't heard, quite conversationally, she said, 'You know, I've often wondered what it was that attracted me to you. I do like you a great deal. But I'm damned if I know why. You're not especially handsome – in fact you're quite skinny – and you're not terrific in bed. I think it's because you're . . . I don't know, mysterious?'

'Deep, you mean?'

'I suppose that's what I mean, yes,' she said. 'Yes, deep.' Trace sensed she was about to get up and go. She looked deep into his eyes. 'Charlie, you're sure?'

'Yes,' he nodded. And with Kastrouni still on his mind, colouring his words, he lied: 'See, I've a girlfriend in Paris. We holiday together every year in Greece. I'm meeting her in Athens and we're going on from there – the Greek islands. A week, maybe two. I didn't want to have to cover up for my absence, so . . .'

'And when you come back?' She stood up, looked down on him. Her nostrils were pinched and her eyes were slitted as he'd never seen them before.

'It's no good, Jilly,' he said, shaking his head.

'I'll keep the necklace and locket,' she said. 'Always. To remind me of you.'

'Thanks.' He didn't know what else to say.

'To remind me how easy it is to make mistakes.'

'Jilly, I – '

'Fuck you!' she said without malice, turned and melted away into the bustle of customers.

Trace finished his drink, let himself settle down *into* himself, gradually began to feel good. It must be like this when they take off the handcuffs, he thought. He went to the bar, ordered another drink. And as he swirled the whisky in his glass and let the babble of the pub wash over him, so he slowly became aware of someone watching him. A man at the bar, tight in a corner where the bar met the wall.

136

Trace looked at him out of the corner of his eye, then openly glanced at him. But just a glance. That was all it took. A mental photograph etched itself into Trace's brain, was locked away for future reference in some cranial filing cabinet.

The stranger was straight as a ramrod, his suit expensive, his general image impressive. He could be anything between forty-five and fifty-five years old, with iron-grey hair, blue eyes, pale, unblemished skin. Not quite as slim as Trace but a little taller, he managed to look somehow remote, cool – no, cold – and his voice as he looked away from Trace across the bar to order a brandy was very correct and Old Etonian. Trace wasn't sure what ex-Guards officers looked like – except for vague TV stereotypes – but he suspected that this must be very much it. Or maybe a male model for the glossy ladies' magazines?

Anyway (he gave a mental shrug), he must be mistaken, the man hadn't been watching him after all. On Trace's other side a very attractive girl was getting giggly on vodka. That's who the stranger was watching. Maybe he contemplated a cradle-snatch.

Behind the bar The Ship's boss, Freddie, held up a bottle of whisky questioningly. Trace shook his head, signalled that he had all he wanted. Freddie went off to serve someone else but was back moments later, 'Blower,' he said. 'For you.' He tilted his head toward a door at the side of the bar. The door led to a corridor, the corridor in turn to the telephone, the toilets and the street.

Trace raised his eyebrows. The telephone? For him? He shrugged, headed for the corridor. Probably Jilly telling him to fuck off or something. In the corridor the telephone hung loose, bobbed up and down on its coiled plastic lead. With the dregs of his drink in his right hand,

Trace took the phone awkwardly in his left, stuck it in the crotch formed of his neck and shoulder. 'Hello?'

'Charlie Trace?' inquired a coarse voice faintly tinged with some unrecognized foreign accent.

'That's me,' said Trace.

'Just thought you'd like to know,' said the phlegmy voice. 'Mr Carter is cutting his holiday short by a week. He'll be on the first available flight home. Next Thursday, I believe.'

Trace came close to dropping his drink, grabbed the phone tightly to stop from dropping that, too. His mind whirled as he answered: 'Carter? I don't know any Carter. Who's speaking?'

There was a throaty chuckle. 'It seems Mr Carter has received a very annoying – one might say worrying – anonymous message concerning an interest of his back here in England. A warning, as it were, just like this warning.'

'Warning? What the hell are you talking about?' Trace snarled. 'I tell you I don't know any Carter! Who is this?'

'Goodbye, golden boy!' said the voice – and the phone went dead.

The door to the street opened, letting in traffic sounds, and Trace looked up in time to see the ex-Guards officer flicking imaginary dust from his sleeve as he stepped out into the street . . .

It was Sunday and it was hot. Trace considered packing a few things, getting out his Triumph and going for a spin out of London. Blow away some of the cobwebs, think things out. He could go up to Yorkshire, stay at old country inns, spend a few days sitting in orchards sipping ice-cold beer, or soaking up the sun on a blanket stretched out over springy moors heather. No, he couldn't; on

Tuesday he had to deliver the stuff to Joe Pelham in the Holloway Road.

It was just that he suddenly felt like getting away from it all. Getting away from everything. Running away from everything. It was all getting to be too much.

Memories had been shaken awake that should lie sleeping. He'd been handed a past he didn't want, an unsolvable riddle he couldn't rest until he'd solved. He'd heard a wholly fabulous story (or mostly fabulous) about a monstrous creature who was something more, or less, than human; he'd seen freak lightning strike a taxi and blow it to hell; he'd been threatened or 'warned' by an unknown someone about a job he'd done which no one else on earth could possibly know about . . .

Could they?

If he'd given Jilly that bloody trinket yesterday, then there might – just might – be an explanation. Someone could have seen it, recognized it, asked her where she got it, put two and two together, come up with four. But not in five minutes. Not by any stretch of the imagination. And as for getting in touch with Carter, *and* knowing he would be back home on Thursday . . . !

So Carter was breaking off his holiday, was he? So what? He couldn't connect his loss with Trace. He didn't even know Trace. And *nobody* – with the exception of a handful of fences, smelters and iffy jewellers – knew of Trace's penchant for raffling.

'Raffling': that was a word he'd coined himself. It meant doing a Raffles. And it rhymed with snaffling. Oh, Charlie Trace was a high-class tea-leaf, all right – an ace thief – but no one knew it. Or at least they shouldn't . . .

These were some of the thoughts Trace turned over in his head as he walked London's dusty summer streets, his jacket over his arm. He hadn't gone straight back to the flat but had taken a long detour instead, through a park and down avenues of trees, keeping to the shade wherever possible, just letting things buzz about and find their own level in his mind.

'Buzz about', yes. Like bumble-bees. But so much had happened in the last two-and-a-bit days that he felt his head must be starting to resemble a hive of the bloody things!

And there was Jilly, too. At another time he mightn't have broken it off. Not just like that, anyway. And that story he'd told her. He snorted: *'Huh!'* and almost wished he really did have a French girlfriend. As for holidays in the Greek islands: he'd never been anywhere near the Mediterranean. What was it Kastrouni had called him: 'Not much travelled'?

Kastrouni: on the run for almost half a century. According to him, anyway. Afraid of storms, and now cindered in a weird blast from summer skies. In London, of all places!

In a street of shops Trace stopped to stare in through the window of a travel agency. Almost of their own accord his eyes ran vacantly, then avidly, down the glossy, gorgeously adorned covers of the neatly displayed brochures. Girls, girls, girls. And beaches. And a sea so blue it was almost painful to the eyes. Even here, reproduced on paper, painfully bright and glittering.

CRETE: 'The Island That Dreams Are Made Of!'

And, CORFU! – with a full-page view of a place called Kaminaki Beach that made your mouth water.

SKIATHOS.

SKOPELOS.

ALONISSOS.

And all of them with scenes of empty beaches. Beaches deserted. Except, of course, for those nearly nude nymphets dipping their toes in the blue, blue sea, or gazing thoughtfully, with brown-tipped breasts a-tilt, into incredible sunsets.

I should have been a poet, Trace thought.

And, RHODES! – 'Historic, beautiful Rhodes, with 300 sunny days in every year . . .'

And, KARPATHOS: 'Darling of the Dodecanese!'

Karpathos . . .

Yesterday morning Trace hadn't even heard of Karpathos.

But as he turned away from the window and headed his feet in the direction of home . . . an idea, several, quickly blossomed in his quicksilver mind. After all, when had he last had a holiday? What? He'd *never* had one! Not a proper holiday. And it wasn't as if he couldn't afford it, now was it?

Growing excited with the idea, Trace unconsciously allowed his feet to pick up speed. And as he paced out the mile and a half to his home, so he made his plans and plotted a way to cover his tracks. That was something he'd never really had to do before: create alibis for himself. But now . . .

If someone – and it was still a big if, surely? – if someone suspected he'd done that job in Radlett, and *if* that someone should try to finger him for it . . . oh, yes, it would be as well to be prepared. For then, if Trace could show that he'd been out of London, even out of England, at the time of the theft . . . ? A lot of ifs.

How many people had he talked to in the last week? How many who knew him well or would remember him? A handful, that's all. And all of them trusted friends. Almost all of them, anyway.

Tomorrow he'd find out about a holiday abroad, the Mediterranean, the Aegean . . . yes, Karpathos. He'd be out there inside a week, even before Cat Carter had returned to England and discovered his loss. And before then:

Before then Trace would contact that handful of friends of his (who were, let's face it, all a bit iffy themselves) and use up a little of his native charm on them. And if anyone should later question them about his whereabouts just recently . . .

Karpathos.

Why not? He could use the trip to kill two birds with one stone. It would provide the foundations for his alibi, and at the same time he might visit a certain old monastery in the mountains there. Kastrouni's words came back to him:

'At least it was a monastery many years ago. There's just an old man there now – him and the thing he watches over.'

What thing? Trace could kick himself for having failed to ask. There was a great deal he might have asked, and probably a lot more he should have listened to. He quickened his pace again, scowled at the pavement beneath his feet, ignored the shaded places in his haste and sweated profusely.

Home before 4:00 P.M. he showered, put on his dressing-gown, returned to Kastrouni's suitcase of books and documents . . .

Demogorgon.

When Trace had asked Kastrouni who his real father was, if not the young RAMC officer Greg Solomon, the Greek had said, 'Demogorgon.' Trace hadn't understood this to be a genuine response to his question, just something on the tip of Kastrouni's tongue, which had come out instead of an answer. But now he wondered. And what would that make Charlie Trace?

A bastard, yes, but what else? Son of the son of the

antichrist? Satan's grandson? In which case, a right evil little bastard!

What do you call a man who scratches himself at his mother's wedding? Trace recalled an old, old joke. *A lousy bastard!* Ha, ha, ha! But it wasn't amusing.

He snorted, shrugged his shoulders irritatedly. Evil, him? Well he was no angel, that was for sure, but . . .

He'd said that to Kastrouni, too: 'I'm no angel.' And the Greek had answered, enigmatically, 'Indeed you are not.'

Demogorgon.

Morgan Selby had called Demogorgon Satan's emissary. He was separate from the devil but was gifted with his potency and carried his seed. Trace frowned, shook his head at that. That would never do. To have someone else sow your wild oats for you. But if the Lord could send down an angel to do the job for him, why shouldn't Satan send up a demon to –

– Beyond Trace's window, far away across the city, lightning flashed silently in a sky suddenly darkening.

Trace gave an involuntary shudder – then shook himself. God, but it wouldn't do to pry too deep into stuff like this! It was what nightmares were made of.

And again: Demogorgon.

He opened the clear-plastic envelope marked 'Demogorgon & Associated . . .' and separated the contents on the floor of his living-room. He threw down a cushion for his elbows, propped himself up and started to read.

The first item was simply a browning page torn out of some book or other; probably a work on demonology, Trace thought. At its top, the page carried a paragraph on 'Demodocus', crossed through with a slash of ink. Then, heavily underlined, 'Demogorgon' as a heading, and the following text:

ATTENDING the throne of Chaos and his consort, 'sable-vested Night', Satan found 'Orcus and Ades, and the dreaded name of 'Demogorgon.' Orcus was a strange and menacing giant of a monster. Ades? – Hades, of course! But what was Demogorgon?

Naturally, Milton offers no explanation; but Statius in his *Thebaid* speaks of a 'Most High One', a god or power so dreadful that we are forbidden to even know he exists. The sinister speculation this very likely aroused was probably satisfied by a revelation in Lactantius (*c.*250 A.D.) that Statius's 'Most High One' was Demogorgon. Later, it was believed by certain medieval thinkers that this was in actuality the name of Satan himself, 'dreaded' because to speak such a name aloud might cause a materialization of the actual elemental!

On the other hand, H. J. Rose, Albert Wanke, Thomas Curle and other scholars are of the opinion that in fact Lactantius's 'Demogorgon' should in fact have been 'Demiurgus', the Creator! 'Somewhere along the line,' Albert Wanke concluded, 'there was probably an error in translation or transcription . . .'

And then the heading, 'Demophon', ink-slashed through like 'Demodocus'.

Trace read the passage on Demogorgon through again. 'Milton offers no explanation . . .'

The poet, Milton?

He put the loose page aside, picked up another. This was simply a sheet of A-4, but it confirmed Trace's guess. For scrawled upon it in Kastrouni's own hand:

. . . when straight behold the throne Of Chaos, and his dark pavilion spread Wide on the wasteful deep; with him enthroned Sat sable-vested Night, eldest of things, The consort of his reign; and by them stood Orcus and Ades, and the dreaded name Of Demogorgon; Rumour next and Chance, And Tumult and Confusion all embroiled, And Discord with a thousand various mouths.

. . . Chaos and Night, (the unformed darkness?): Rumour, Chance, Tumult and Confusion. And 'Discord

144

with a thousand various mouths.' Bodeful things, all of them. And the demons or evil *foci:* Ades and Orcus – and the 'dreaded name' of Demogorgon.

There was more: on a second sheet of A-4, information first on Orcus and Ades, then a long list of the names of demons, a veritable pandemonium or pantheon of hellish characters. Trace merely glanced at this last:

Abbadon, Asmodeus, Astaroth; Balberith, Beelzebub, Belphegor; Carnivean, Carreau, Coskarna; Demogorgon (of course), Destus, Diabis . . . and so on, where Kastrouni had seemed to wish to group the demons in threes under each character of the alphabet. And at the end of this list a note:

'By no means complete; Johan Weyer says that there are more than *seven million* demons, serving seventy-two princes of hell!'

At that Trace was tempted to throw the lot out – everything: books, documents, manuscripts and all – with his rubbish; only Kastrouni's own exclamation mark at the end of his note stopped him. Obviously the Greek, too, had seen that this endless listing of so-called 'demons' was to go from the sublime to the ridiculous. But for all that Trace remained scornful, still he was aware that his scepticism was gradually weakening. Kastrouni had, after all, feared for his life. And he was (after all) now dead – of a freak blast of lightning from the sky!

Trace forced himself to go on. He would look at one more item before wrapping it all up for the day. And after that: suddenly he felt lucky. A visit to Cromwell's Mint? On his own, this time, with a couple of hundred pounds in his pocket. Why not?

He'd play big, chance his luck on two or three spins of the wheel, see how quickly he could double his money and then get out of the place.

That decided, and bolstered by thoughts of what might

prove to be an extremely enjoyable, profitable and even relaxing evening, he took up more photocopies from the 'Demogorgon' envelope. There were seven or eight much copied sheets in all, most of them concerning devil-worship of one sort or another in various parts of the world; but one of them in particular caught Trace's eye. It bore one of those passages which Kastrouni had thought important enough to ring about in ink, a page photocopied from something called Guazzo's *Compendium Maleficarum*, written in 1608.

Headed, 'Of the Six Sorts of Demon', the passage ringed about concerned itself with the second sort, of which Guazzo said:

'The second is the aerial, because these dwell in the air around us. They can descend to hell, and, by forming bodies out of the air, can at times be visible to men. Very frequently, with God's permission, they agitate the air and raise storms and tempests, and all this they conspire to do for the destruction of mankind.'

With God's permission? But of course, for in 1608 most God-fearing men seriously believed that *everything* was done 'with God's permission'. Else it were not allowed to be done in the first place . . .

But at last Trace had had enough of it. He bundled all but the map of Karpathos, Kastrouni's notebook, and one small Bible back into the battered suitcase, took it into his bedroom and shoved it under his bed. *Out of sight, out of mind,* he thought. For now, anyway.

And then he started to get himself ready for an evening's gambling. By the time he had given himself a leisurely shave and got dressed the evening had turned fine and a still hot sun dipped toward the west. The distant storm had quite dispersed itself, but by then Trace had forgotten that it had ever threatened . . .

* * *

Trace was in the casino by 8:00 P.M., out by 10:00, home before 11:00 – cleaned out! He had put his faith in an old 'system' with which he'd once 'cracked it', but which this time cracked him. And ruefully he told himself for the millionth (the hundredth, anyway) time, there are no systems where roulette is concerned.

He watched TV till closedown, went to bed and slept soundly. That surprised him, for he'd thought he was bound to dream; certainly there was enough on his mind. Or at least at the back of his mind. But (he'd told himself) what would be, would be, and no use worrying about it. And apparently he'd believed himself. So much for gullibility.

Monday morning was mainly eaten up in a trip to a local travel agency: yes, there were a few empty seats on a flight from Gatwick to Rhodes this Wednesday; and yes, Trace was fortunate, a late cancellation had left a gap in bookings for rooms at Amoupi Beach on Karpathos. The place wasn't so much a hotel as a taverna on the beach, with rooms. But all the more, well, Greek, for that. A very beautiful spot, yes. Self-catering was out, unfortunately, but the food at the taverna was quite exceptional. Homely but . . . exceptional. Was he interested in one week? It would be far cheaper (in the long run) if he went for two . . .

Trace took one look at the brochures and booked for two weeks. From the look of the place – quite literally a beach with a taverna and what looked like a block of flats behind, and nothing else! – this really was a holiday which would save him money. For one thing, there wouldn't be any casinos on Karpathos. In fact there wouldn't be much of anything on Karpathos. But plenty of sun, sand and sea, for sure.

147

And an old monastery . . . an old man . . . and the thing he guards.

Leaving the travel agency with his ticket and as he kick-started his Triumph into life, he thought he recognized someone across the quiet road. When he glanced that way again, however, the figure – that of a man, tall and straight and immaculately dressed – had turned away to walk down a side-street. The ex-Guards officer? Unlikely. But then again, why not? He might live around here, for all Trace knew. He put the sighting out of his mind and rode home.

At the flat he made a list of everywhere he'd been, everyone he'd spoken to or spent time with since last Wednesday. There were surprisingly few of the latter. Then he systematically called them on the phone and spoke to them, or left messages for them to contact him, and so began to put his alibi together. An alibi which was simply this: that he'd been out of the country, on holiday, since Wednesday last. No one gave him any problems over this: Charlie Trace was 'all right'; he would return the favour some day. Some things he'd done, however, couldn't be changed.

For instance: the necklace he'd given to Jilly. Best simply to forget that along with Jilly herself. To try and get it back would only arouse her suspicions; and besides it would mean talking to her again, which he wasn't up to; and anyway Jilly was just another girl, and there were millions of girls in London. Then there was Cromwell's Mint.

Trace had been to the casino twice since Wednesday and his name was in their book. But again, who was there to know he was a member? Why should anyone even want to know? In any case the place was miles away and unlikely to attract anyone of Cat Carter's standing. No, it would be the Ritz for Carter, if he gambled at all.

148

Last of all Trace went downstairs and had a cup of tea with the old girl who owned the house. Old enough to have been his mother, still he knew she fancied him enough to keep his rent low. But Trace had always managed to fend her off without causing offence. Now he cooked up a story about a girl he was trying to avoid, used it as a foundation for his alibi:

'So you see, Betty,' he finished, 'I'm off out of the country for a couple of weeks. She has a couple of big brothers, you know? *Big* lads! But the way I reckon it two weeks should be enough. She's a bit of a flighty piece, see? She'll have forgotten me by then. Anyway, if anyone gets after me, I'd appreciate it if you'd tell them I'm away. In fact, you can tell them I've been away since, oh, the middle of last week? Do you think you could do that for me?'

Betty Kettler was busty, brightly daubed, beginning to creak a bit but not nearly past it. And she was still trying. Arcing her eyebrows, she answered, 'I would do most anything for you, Charlie my lad. Think no more of it.' And she'd leaned forward over her cup of tea to let her housecoat fall open an inch or two.

And on his way out (but not too hastily) Trace said, 'Cheers, love,' and handed her a bottle of Bell's as a reminder.

Following which there was nothing much else he could do. Best not to go out any more before Wednesday – or at least not until tomorrow, when he must deliver the goods. And between times . . .

Suddenly he remembered his plan to get in touch with QARANC about his mother. He checked in Yellow Pages under 'Army', got in touch with London District Provost Company. The Chief Clerk there gave him the number of QARANC Records; he dialled and immediately got an answer; after a moment or two he was told:

Yes, a Diana Trace had been a serving nurse until her discharge back in 1958. This had been voluntary on her part, following her confinement at the maternity ward in St Mary's General Hospital, Portsmouth.

Trace knew that his grandparents had been Portsmouth people, so that must be right. His mother had stayed with them after he was born. If they were alive now . . . but they weren't. He contacted St Mary's, asked his question. What he wanted to know was fairly detailed; he made the girl on enquiries write it down; he impressed her with the importance of his call. And in a little while:

They would see what they could do; he must realize, of course, that it was a long time ago; could they ring him back? And could they please have his address?

He gave the hospital the necessary details and rang off.

After that he watched TV and waited for their call, but none came. It made for a very boring and frustrating evening and night. He slept poorly and was up at the crack of dawn. By 11:00 A.M. he had taken his loot down to the 'used bookshop' in the Holloway Road, where Joe Pelham hung a 'Closed' sign on the door, locked it, and escorted him through into a familiar back room. Out back, beyond grimy, almost opaque windows, an ancient van stood forlorn in cobwebs and shade under a lean-to in a high-walled yard, the locked gates of which closed out the street.

And, 'OK,' said Pelham without preliminary, 'let's see it, then.'

When Trace cleared a space and emptied his panniers onto the table, the squat, scruffy-looking fence gulped audibly and his eyes bugged. But then he grabbed Trace by the arm. ''Ere, son, I recognize some of this stuff! It's been through my 'ands before, some of it 'as.'

'Oh?' Trace tried to remain noncommittal.

'Yers. 'E's bound to be in touch, yer know. I mean, 'e

150

knows I do a lot in the trade. We've 'ad business before, as I said.'

Trace looked at him for a moment, began to shovel the stuff back into the panniers. 'No sweat, Joe,' he said. 'I'll take it somewhere else. I'd hate to involve an old friend in an iffy deal.'

''Ang on, son, *'ang* on!' said Pelham at once. ''Ell's bells, I only said we'd done business, Carter and me. I didn't say I liked the old bastard, now did I? Anyway, the lolly's already in. Most of it will go direct to your number' (Trace's Swiss account) 'as soon as we finish up 'ere. And I've got a couple of thou cash for you.'

Trace tipped the panniers out again, but slowly. 'You're sure?'

'Yers, course I am.'

Pelham weighed the stuff up, got out Trace's money. Trace knew the fence had already cleared a massive profit, but still he counted out and gave him back two hundred.

'No need, old son,' said Pelham, pocketing the cash anyway. 'I'm sweet enough.'

'It's for being a pal,' said Trace. 'And to be honest, it's for keeping mum and remembering that I've been out of the country since last Wednesday.'

'Oh, yers? On 'oliday, are you?' Pelham grinned. His grin quickly slipped from his face as he continued: 'As for keeping mum – 'ere's me about to turn this lot into roughage, an' you think I'm a good lad for keeping mum? If old man Carter were to find out I'd seen 'is stuff melted down 'e'd 'ave my balls for castors! Jus' you be sure *you* keep mum, my son!'

'Too right!' Trace agreed, and minutes later he was on his way back to his flat . . .

* * *

That night before retiring Trace packed a case, arranged an early morning call on the telephone to get him out of bed, booked a taxi to Victoria for 6:30 A.M. It was going to be a bloody hour to be up and about, but –

Tomorrow it would be the airport train from Victoria to Gatwick, and the 8:15 flight from Gatwick to Rhodes. On Thursday there would be a further flight – more a short hop, really – from Rhodes to Karpathos. And then . . . ?

Then we'll have to wait and see, thought Charlie Trace as he drifted into sleep.

Part III

Chapter One

Trace discovered that in fact Kastrouni had been right: he wasn't much travelled. A couple of hovercraft trips to Calais and Boulogne hadn't prepared him for this. The trouble lay, he knew inside (though he wasn't about to admit it up front, not even to himself), in the fact that this was only the second time he'd ever flown. The first had been seven years ago, before he'd become a thief full-blown: a disastrous week in Hanover, Germany, with a pimply teenage pen-pal. But things had moved pretty fast in the seven years which lay between.

For one thing, the sheer size of the aircraft surprised him; and the dawning realization that he was actually growing excited – like a kid with a new toy – only served to make him feel foolish and, for the first time in as long as he could remember, self-conscious. Yet big as the aircraft was where it stood in view of the departure lounge, still Trace had thought that the jet must be cramped; it seemed to him that an inordinately large number of people had been swallowed up in it ahead of him. But when he himself went aboard through the extending boarding tunnel (another new experience; what the hell had happened to those great, trundling steps?) the interior of the plane seemed more like a small cinema than something which very soon would be miles high in the sky, flying east at a speed in excess of five hundred miles per hour!

Then the seat-belt gave him trouble and an air-hostess had to show him how, and as for following life-jacket instructions as they were given just before take-off . . .

Trace could only hope that the plane would stay in the air all the way to Rhodes. If not – well, he would have to be one of the first casualties.

The beginning of the journey was not especially memorable: the take-off wasn't as smooth as he thought it should be; 'breakfast' was pure plastic; even the duty-free whisky seemed to taste just a bit off, and the mixers weren't right. But later, for consolation, there were wonderful views of the Alps as the plane soared effortlessly high above them, and fantastic glimpses of tiny turquoise, gold, azure and mother-of-pearl islands off the coast of Greece, in the Aegean, and down the Sporades to Rhodes itself.

And then the landing, (better than the take-off) and as quickly as that the flight was over, leaving Trace wondering just exactly where almost four hours of time had gone to. Finally came the deplaning, the stepping forth into blinding sunlight and blasting heat. Trace half-shuttered his eyes and shrugged: well, this was what he'd come for, wasn't it? Among other things . . .

No tunnel here but metal steps down to the cracked concrete flags of the strip, and airport buildings a little less than impressive, where sweaty, tattily uniformed customs officials peered at passports, probably failed to understand, but stamped them anyway. And beyond the barriers:

'Karpathos!' called a plump, jowly girl in knee-length shorts, holding aloft an imperative mill-board. Her voice rose strident over the general babble of disembarking passengers. 'All for Karpathos, to me!'

'*Heel, boy!*' thought Trace. '*Sit! Roll over!* GOOD *dog!*' Balls to that! He wasn't even *about* ready to be regimented. If he'd wanted that he could have joined the French Foreign Legion – or gone to a holiday camp in

Torbay! But he went to her anyway, his jacket draped over his suitcase, heat sticking his shirt to his back.

Three others were there before him, two men and a woman. He had seen them before ('seen', in the case of the two men, rather than noticed especially) at Gatwick and on the plane, but then he'd been far more interested in what was going on around him. In any case, they were simply three fellow passengers; though to tell the truth the woman, whose looks were really quite striking, had caught his eye more than once or twice. Now, however, he paid them more attention, and was pleased to note that all three seemed to be travelling separately. That is to say, the woman did not seem to be attached to either of the men.

Of the woman:

She was a green-eyed redhead, slim, tiny-waisted, maybe five feet six inches in height and beautifully proportioned. Her eyes were slightly tilted almonds, long-lashed, and she wore her hair forward, cut in a fringe over her eyes, and in two long plaits behind her elfin ears and forward to fall inside the fold of her shirt's collar. She wore flat white shoes, blue slacks and a gauzy blue puff-sleeved shirt open to the beginning of the valley between her slightly loose and obviously unfettered breasts. She was dusky, looked half-oriental, half-Arab; there was mystery in her; Trace believed he'd never before seen anyone quite like her. And she was going to Karpathos.

But so, too, were the two men. Of them:

One was thirtyish, sallow, thin as a pole and balding, whose expensive clothes seemed ready to slide from him the moment he exhaled. His accent was strongly American and nasal, reminding Trace of a jingle he'd heard somewhere or other, designed (he understood) to illustrate the language of New York's Bronx district:

'Toity poiple boids, sittin' on de coib,
Choipin an' a-boipin, an' eatin' doity woims!'

Normally he'd find an accent like that charming and amusing, but somehow not from this fellow.

The other man was short and fat, jowled like a bulldog, wheezy in his breathing and slow in his movements. He reminded Trace a lot of Sidney Greenstreet in those old black and white 'tough dick' gangster films. His hair was black, unruly, full of dandruff. He wore a silk handkerchief flopping three-quarters out of his breast pocket; his trousers were too tight and showed a lot of his socks; his shoes seemed tiny on feet far too small to adequately balance his lumbering body.

While Trace had checked them over, unconsciously committing them to memory, the chubby travel agency rep had ticked their names off the list clipped to her millboard. Trace had missed the names the men gave her, but he was all ears about the woman. Her name was Miss Amira (A-mee-rah) Halbstein. German? Trace would never have guessed it. Looking at her more closely, he saw that her nose was perhaps a fraction too large and very slightly humped, much like his own, in fact. Jewish? Hard to tell. *He* wasn't, for sure!

Then it was his turn. He mumbled his name, saw it struck through with a biro on the list. 'Just the four of you, then,' the rep smiled. 'Well, you've all got seats on the Lindos coach, out there,' and she pointed through the arrivals lounge windows to where coaches stood, waiting on the shimmering tarmac road. 'We'll drop you off at our transit hotel in Rhodes town for the night. A nice place but pretty basic – and it's just for one night, of course.'

'And tomorrow morning?' Amira Halbstein asked, her voice softly husky – *like the fuzz on a peach*, Trace thought.

'Tomorrow you'll be called at 7:00,' the rep answered. 'You'll breakfast at the hotel, if you require it. Transport: you can arrange transport individually, if you wish, but the cheapest – and friendliest way – would be to organize a taxi between you back to the airport. Whichever, just as long as you're back here for 8:15, OK? As for tonight: you'll find Rhodes town a wonderful place and very interesting. If you've been here before you'll already know that. And if you haven't . . . well, I won't spoil it for you. Will you excuse me now?' And off she strutted with her mill-board, calling, 'Lindos? All for Lindos – to me, please. To me!'

After a moment's hesitation, merely glancing at each other, the two men picked up their cases and made for the glass doors – together? But the woman had three small cases and seemed to be having some difficulty with them. Trace said, 'Can I help?' and was surprised how deep his own voice sounded. His offer, however, had been spontaneous, genuine. He wasn't simply trying it on.

'Oh!' she said, looking up at him. 'Why, thank you. But I couldn't help noticing your limp, Mr Trace, and – '

'That's nothing,' he said at once. 'Nothing at all. I must've got cramp standing around so long.' (Had he been limping? That damned left leg of his; his bloody 'funny' foot!) But how had she known his name? The list, of course. Stupid of him. But then again, that could mean she'd been as interested in his name as he'd been in hers. Things were really looking up.

He picked up her third case (and found it light as a feather), led the way out of the lounge and to a coach with a sign for Lindos hanging from its door handle. Already the coach was filling up with what looked like a pretty decent, obviously excited bunch of holidaymakers. They were mainly Brits off the same plane as Trace, but there was also a handful of Germans and several Scandinavian types, even a French couple. Trace waited for the driver to stash all four cases away in the compartment under the bus, then turned to look for the girl. No sign of her . . .

People were still boarding and it seemed to Trace he'd be wise to get aboard and grab a double seat. Harder than he'd thought, that last: all the doubles were taken, mainly by people on their own, with hand-luggage on the seats beside them. The two other men for Karpathos were seated in the back, each on opposite sides against the windows. They didn't look at Trace where he stood peering about. In the end he chose a seat behind the driver, next to a small, middle-aged lady who smiled at him as he sat down beside her.

And still no sign of Amira Halbstein.

'She went back inside the arrivals lounge,' informed the small woman beside Trace, touching his elbow.

'Eh? Oh! Did she?' (Was he *that* obvious?)

'Yes. The attractive girl, I mean. Are you together?'

'Er, no – I just helped her with her luggage, that's all.'

Trace half stood up, looked toward the arrivals lounge through the dusty window; and as the driver climbed aboard and started up the engine, so she came running, a carton of two hundred Greek cigarettes clutched in her hand. So that's where she'd been: to buy smokes.

As she came aboard Trace smiled at her but she hardly seemed to notice him, brushing past and taking a seat beside a florid German half-way down the coach.

'*Ah, well – and so much for that!* thought Trace. Except he suspected he wouldn't be giving in that easily.

The trip into Rhodes took maybe twenty minutes, was completely uneventful in itself. Gazing over the top of the little woman's head out of the window, Trace wasn't much impressed. There seemed to be a lot of building

160

going on: blocks of holiday flats going up, ghastly concrete things in the modern mode; and the locals looked a mainly dowdy lot, wandering about in their black shirts, black lace shawls, dark trousers and skirts. And as for the tourists – they were everywhere, in gaudy shorts and T-shirts, burned brown and often almost black by the sun.

But as the bus sped through the town he began to catch sight of massive walls, Moorish buildings and minarets, and suddenly things looked better. He knew that Rhodes had a fabulous history, began to actually feel something of the antiquity of the place seeping in to him through the windows of the coach. Why, the entire island was history itself – yes! The Crusaders had landed here, and stayed; signs of their handiwork, the *feel* and *atmosphere* of their time and culture, were everywhere; the modern concrete was soon forgotten, couldn't stand up before the stern reproval of ancient stone and towering fortifications.

So that Trace very quickly fell into a sort of drowsy reverie – broken by the abrupt arrival of the coach at the hotel in a narrow street near the docks.

The street was busy and the chubby agency rep got off first to usher her charges off the coach, up steps and into the hotel's reception area. 'Pretty basic,' she'd called it, and Trace could see why. Back in England he'd give it two stars – maybe. But his room had a shower and a huge bed, and the windows were shuttered to keep out the sun and let in a cooling breeze off the sea, and after all it was only for one night.

And what the hell! – from what he'd seen in the brochures, this was luxury compared with what he could expect on Karpathos.

He showered, changed into a white shirt, faded fawn jeans and sandals, headed for the hotel bar. It was closed, or at least there didn't seem to be anyone in attendance. 'Shit!' Trace muttered as he turned on his heel, intent on leaving the hotel and finding himself a quiet bar in the town.

Except – there behind him stood Amira Halbstein. The sight of her stopped Trace dead in his tracks. He looked at her, at the bar with no one behind it, back at her. He hoped she hadn't heard him swearing.

She came forward into the barroom, smiled at him, said: 'Did you want a drink? Me, too, before I eat. I'm told there are lots of good tavernas in town.'

'Drinks are out, I'm afraid,' Trace answered ruefully. 'Here, anyway. Place looks deserted. No one at the desk, and no barman.'

She laughed openly and Trace liked her laugh. 'Who needs a barman? The Greeks are a very understanding race, Mr Trace.'

'Oh?'

'Of course. Here, let me show you.' She lifted the bar flap, stepped inside, took glasses from beneath the bar. 'Yours is – ?'

'A whisky, please, with a little ice – if there is any. But don't you think this is a bit naughty?'

Again that laugh as she made drinks, perched herself on a tall stool on her side of the bar, leaned forward to stare at Trace from where she propped her face in her palms. 'Naughty? Not at all. I came down earlier and spoke to one of the staff. He said that if I wanted anything . . .'

Trace nodded his understanding, sipped his drink appreciatively. 'Ah, what it is to have a pretty face and figure, eh?'

'Not at all,' she answered coolly. 'It's like I said: they're understanding, that's all. And very accommodating.'

She was used to flattery; Trace's comment about her

looks had passed right over her head, without touching her at all. It was an approach he'd avoid from now on. 'Where were you thinking of eating?' he asked.

'Oh, anywhere. A Greek salad, a glass of retsina, that will be sufficient. But I also want to walk a little. Somewhere in the Old Town, I think. I'm told it's crowded with ghosts. Romance and magic and history rub shoulders here, you know.'

He nodded. 'I sensed that on the coach. So we're both first timers, eh?'

'In Rhodes? Yes. I've been to others of the Greek islands, but this is my first time here on Rhodes. Karpathos, too.'

'Miss Halbstein, I have to warn you that I don't speak Greek,' Trace began, 'in fact I don't know very much about Greece or the islands at all, but – '

' – We'll get by,' she cut him off, smiling again. 'I take it you'd like to be my escort?'

'Well, since we're both strangers here . . .' He let the sentence hang there.

'Very well, it's settled,' she shrugged. 'Shall we have another drink first?'

'No,' Trace shook his head, unable to believe that it was this easy. 'I mean, I don't think so. Not here, anyway. But you can introduce me to retsina, if you like, when we find a place to eat.'

'We'd better introduce ourselves first,' she answered. 'I'm – '

'Amira,' he cut in, his turn to smile. 'I know who you are – if not what.'

The smile never strayed from her small, pleasing mouth, but he thought he saw her tilted eyes narrow just a fraction. 'What I am? I don't think I quite . . . ?'

'Your nationality,' he held the bar flap open as she

163

came out from behind. 'You embarked in England, but I'd guess you're not English.'

'No, I'm Israeli originally – but I was educated in England. See how I get about? Anyway, I can tell you all about me later, but what about you, Mr Trace?'

'Call me Charlie,' he responded at once.

'Charles?'

'No, it's Charlie – to my friends, anyway.'

'Charlie Trace, from London, England,' she said as they left the bar, walked through the reception area and out into the bustling street. 'Fine, so now we know each other.'

In the street she unselfconsciously took Trace's hand, which made him start just a little, but she didn't seem to notice. 'Where to?' he asked.

'Well, if we follow the waterfront we'll be able to trace it back again later,' she said, logically. 'That way we won't get lost. I suggest we get as far away from the hurly-burly as we can, and then just walk. City centres are far too noisy for me. And sooner or later we're bound to stumble over a quiet little taverna.'

In less than ten minutes they found a market, wandered between stalls selling fruit and vegetables – which Trace noted didn't seem of especially high quality, except perhaps for the potatoes and melons, the latter being huge and glossy – and trinkets in bright, alleged 'coral', and fancy lace which old Greek ladies were fashioning right there and then, and ice cream, soft drinks, cigarettes and postcards. There was food, too: little shops round the outer ring of the stalls issued mouth-watering odours of spiced lamb and chicken sizzling over charcoal.

Trace could have eaten right there and then, but not his companion. Still holding his hand, almost dragging him along behind her, she struck out uphill, along narrow, high-walled, winding streets badly in need of restoration,

164

climbing away from the new and into the old. And she was quite right: here if anywhere romance and legend and the lore of the ages intermingled and lingered over; and as she finally slowed her pace and they walked side by side, there was little pressure to talk but simply a desire to soak up something of the timeless aura of the place.

Here and there the beds of the narrow alleys had been concreted over, where watercourses had been driven underground and now gurgled unseen. But in other places, where the streets were neatly cobbled and still in good repair, the original channels or gutters ran along the sides of the streets as of old, with tiny outlet holes, like mouseholes, jetting water from the gaunt stone houses along the sides. These were simply water channels, not sewers. Trace didn't know what happened to the sewage here, but obviously it was dealt with adequately. In a place where the streets were crowded and mazy, winding under tottering stone arches and high walls that fought a desperate fight against the invading beams of sunlight, he might reasonably have expected to smell the natural stenches of life, but they were quite absent. Obviously the Greeks had found the answer to this problem a long time ago. Trace said as much to Amira.

'Not only the Greeks,' she answered, 'though of course they've always been here, from classical times to the present. Can you imagine? But under all this rock and rubble and concrete the Italians found temples to Zeus, Athena Polias, Apollo? It's thought that the Cretans were first here, three and a half thousand years ago, then the Mycenaeans from the Peloponnese. Probably the two races intermingled. Anyway, the peoples we know as the Mycenaeans are the same race as the warlike Achaeans. Rhodes was very prosperous under them; so says Homer, anyway, and Pindar. According to them Zeus loved the

Rhodians. And the legends: did you know that Tlepolemos set off from here on his Trojan expedition? He took nine ships to Troy.'

Trace listened, fascinated – and a little lost. He wasn't much on world history, classical or otherwise. But that voice of hers: gold-dust blown in soft eddies from her pulsing throat. And he knew his fascination wasn't at all historic.

'And earthquakes,' she went on. 'Rhodes has always suffered from them. The Colossus fell in an earthquake. And all of this hundreds of years before the first Christian. The Goths invaded in A.D. 269, but by A.D. 620 the Persians were in occupation. Three hundred years later it was the Saracens, who sold off the fallen Colossus as scrap metal! Just think – his pieces had lain on land and in the water for over eight hundred years! And in another century and a half, along came Aroun-al-Rashid and his Seljuk Turks.' She paused abruptly at a crossroads of alleys and caught Trace off-guard, dragging him to a halt. 'The Turks, yes! Did you know that right here where we stand, the Turkish mainland is less than twenty miles away?'

She was so clever, so close. Trace couldn't resist the impulse but drew her to him and kissed her. She drew back, seemed to ignore the fact of his kiss, hurried on with him whirled along behind.

The alleys were almost empty of people here. Occasionally, at street corners, they would see distant tourists ogling old arches or peering at maps and guidebooks. 'Charlie,' Amira said over her shoulder, 'have you been listening at all?'

'Of course I have,' he answered indignantly.

'Are you sure?'

'Too right. Greeks and Turks and Achaeans and all that. Temples to Zeus and Apollo and wot-not . . .'

166

Amira sighed, ducked through a low doorway into a tiny, shadowy taverna. They had passed several but this one seemed to please her. The sign outside had said 'Theos' Restant', and the menu seemed similarly conjectural – to Trace, anyway:

> Very Salletts!
> Lamp Cattles!
> Staffed Tomates!

And:

> Red Snapers . . . ?

Amira laughed at Trace's reading of the thing, and translated: 'Various salads, lamb cutlets, stuffed tomatoes, and red snappers. The snappers are fish, and delicious!'

They each had a small Greek salad: mainly cool tomato pieces and sliced cucumber with a few black olives over a shredded cabbage base, topped with chunks of soft fetta cheese and liberally doused in olive oil and wine vinegar. Trace had tried similar dishes in Greek restaurants in London, but here –

'This really is delicious!' he said, dipping a crust of brown bread in the moist residue on his plate. 'This retsina, too. And yet back in London – I'd have to be bloody hungry to go in for this!'

'Greek food,' she informed, ' – more so than any other, I think – suits its natural surroundings. Do you know what I mean? It's more *right* than a bratwurst is in Germany, more *suitable* than even spaghetti would be in Italy. I mean, I have eaten octopus and squid in Famagusta, but I'd hate it in Genoa – and yet the Italians are supposed to be the experts!'

'Tell me more about Rhodes,' said Trace. He ordered

a second bottle of retsina; they were small bottles, and anyway the stuff didn't seem especially lethal.

'You *were* interested!' she said.

''Course I was!' (But it had been her voice, mainly.)

'Your own Richard the Lionheart came here,' she said. 'He recruited the Rhodian fleet into his crusade. Then, in the early 12th Century, the Byzantines. Fifty years later the island was still Byzantine, though in fact it was controlled by Genoese admirals. In 1306 they sold it to the Knights of St John of Jerusalem. After that . . . in 1480 the island was beseiged by the Turks, and forty years later Suleiman the Magnificent took it by force. Then the Turks ruled for almost four hundred years. Between 1912 and 1945 the Italians ran the show, but in 1947, finally the island went back to Greece.'

'Quite a history,' Trace commented.

'Oh, yes! Would you like a cigarette?' She offered him one from a Greek pack.

'I don't usually,' said Trace. 'But I rather feel like one right now. Thanks.'

They smoked and finished off the rather bitter, resinous wine in silence. Then it was time to go.

On their way back to the hotel she refused Trace's arm, was quiet, seemed more distant somehow. He decided she was happier talking, said: 'I still don't know anything about you.'

'My father was a German Jew,' she told him. 'He still is, if you know what I mean, but not in Germany. My mother was a Jewess living in Switzerland. During the war he got across the border and they met in Luzern. At the close of the war they married, and in 1950 went to live in Tel-Aviv. There was no hardship for they both had money. They hadn't wanted a family but I came along anyway. That was in 1955. My mother died two years ago but my father still lives in Israel. He's retired now but unofficially – you could say as a sort of hobby – he looks after the sites of old excavations and archaeological digs around Tiberias and El Hamma.

'But Israel has always had its problems. My father lived with some of them, saw others coming, sent me out of the country for my education. I grew fond of travelling, meeting people. It's a life that suits me, and it suits my father. He loves me very much, but likes me safely outside Israel, you see? Every now and then I go home, like when this present holiday is over, but mainly I live in Richmond, London. It's my father's house really; I keep it up for him, in case he ever needs a refuge.'

'And you're . . . on your own? I mean, you're still single?'

'There have been boyfriends, but nothing serious. Nothing lasting, anyway.'

'Story of my life,' said Trace.

'Oh?' she said. 'Well, we have plenty of time, both of us.' Following which she seemed even more withdrawn.

'What about tonight?' said Trace.

She raised her eyebrows. 'Tonight?'

'I mean, do you have plans? It will be a beautiful night. There are night-clubs, discos, shows I should think. I believe there's even a casino somewhere.'

She gave him a fleeting smile, a sad one, he thought. 'No, I don't gamble, Charlie. Life's a big enough gamble, isn't it? As for night-clubs and shows: I don't think so. I came out here for some peace and quiet. Anyway, we're off early tomorrow. I for one would prefer a clear head. We won't be flying to Karpathos in a modern jet, you know.'

'Oh?'

'No, indeed. A flying rabbit hutch, more likely! Wait and see.'

Their conversation during the remainder of their walk

was trivial, lacked zest. Trace delivered Amira to the hotel where she at once went up to her room, and then he restlessly headed back out into the streets. He was, in fact, feeling tired but guessed he wouldn't be able to sleep. Not yet. First he must burn off a little of his excess excitement. Sexual? Probably . . .

But on their way back something strange had happened and it was still on Trace's mind. It was one of those things which only register later, which come up clearer on reflection.

It had been as they'd passed an old lace lady's stall close to the dockside, when Amira had paused to pick up a piece of fine work to admire. The old girl had got to her feet, held up her work against the blue sky to emphasize its intricacy – and in doing so she'd stared deep into Amira's eyes . . .

. . . Then she'd backed off, stumbled and almost fallen. And Trace had heard her say: 'Ai! Kallikanzaros! *Kallikanzaros!*'

A youth, possibly the old lady's grandson, had caught her, seated her again in her chair. But Amira had quickly turned away and walked off. Trace had had to hurry to catch her.

Now he let his feet take him back that way. The old woman was no longer in attendance but the Greek youth was still there, putting away her lace and closing up the stall. Trace spoke to him:

'Er, do you speak English?'

'Eh?' the boy looked up. 'English? Oh yes, me speak.' Then he recognized Trace, went wide-eyed for a moment. 'Ah! Your lady, yes? Me sorry. The old woman . . .' He scratched his ear, then held out his hands palms up, put his head on one side and shrugged. 'Me sorry.'

Trace took out a fifty Drachma note – small change, in

170

fact – and handed it over. 'Tell me, what is, er, Kallikan – , er, Kallikan – '

'Kallikanzaros?'

'Right, Kallikanzaros! What is it?'

'Bad thing,' said the boy at once. 'Devil!' He made
horns with his forefingers.

Trace frowned, began to turn away, muttered: 'Crazy
old woman.' But the boy had heard him, came scrambling
round to confront him.

'Not crazy!' he shook his tousled head in emphatic
denial. 'Not she. She *i kali gynaikes!*'

Later, at the hotel, Trace got it right. He asked the
English-speaking boss of the place what *i kali gynaikes*
meant.

'I kali gynaikes is a "good woman,"' the man told him,
smiling. 'A clever woman, gifted. A woman who can cure
with her hands, who sees – everything. Things we cannot
see. There are still a few left on Rhodes.'

And: 'Oh,' Trace had said.

But when he would have turned away the man stopped
him. 'Excuse, but you were out walking, yes? With the
Miss Halbstein?'

'That's right,' said Trace. 'Yes, we were walking.'

'She came down and left this for you.' And he handed
Trace a guidebook to Rhodes. The frown lifted from
Trace's face at once. Amira had said she was new to
Rhodes and he'd thought she must be lying, but the
guidebook explained everything. It was all in there,
everything she'd told him.

Devil? No, not Amira Halbstein. Or if anything, a
rather clever little devil, a rather beautiful one.

But although Trace now felt easier about things, still
he limped all the way upstairs to his room . . .

Chapter Two

Flying rabbit hutch! thought Trace. A pretty good description. Square-bodied, square-winged, with the door at the rear like a hatchback, the plane didn't inspire confidence. A mini-van with wings, painted battle-ship grey and silver, and a pilot who looked like yesterday he'd been herding goats somewhere!

Trace had had his early morning call – and had then gone straight back to sleep! When finally it had got through to him that someone was banging on his door, and that the time was 7:40, then he'd come off the bed like a rocket. And into his clothes without washing or shaving, and downstairs with his case to cram himself with cold eggs and bacon washed down with tepid coffee, and into an ancient Mercedes taxi whose engine sounded like an asthmatic dinosaur.

8:25 when he got to the airport. They pushed him through a caricature of customs, hurried him across the tarmac and concrete carrying his own suitcase. But halfway across, with sand in his eyes and sweat dripping from every pore, then he'd stopped hurrying. He'd seen the plane by then – seen the pilot kneeling on top of its squat body, feeding it Avgas from a hose! And beside the stubby-looking winged thing a fuel truck, its driver sitting on the front bumper with an unlighted cigarette dangling from his bored mouth.

For God's sake don't light it! thought Trace, climbing aboard into a seating area just a little bigger than a large bathroom. There was only one seat left, his. It was at the back, just in front of the 'luggage compartment', which consisted of wooden shelves bolted to the walls. Someone had stood a large whicker basket on one of them; it was full of live chickens, all individually trussed to keep them from moving about too much. They didn't look especially happy about it.

As for the other passengers: they were made up of a Greek priest, a pair of peasants, Laurel and Hardy from the hotel, two middle-aged Greek women, a young German couple already beautifully bronzed, and Trace himself. And Amira. She was seated up front but didn't look back as he boarded.

He was only on board a moment or two and had just got comfortable when the pilot took his seat in the front, fiddled with switches until a flashing light came on over his head saying:

'NO SMOKE – BELT UP!'

Great! thought Trace. And: *am I really going to fly in this?*

Almost as if the thought had been read, the pilot turned in his seat, smiled and nodded at everyone, said, 'Hello – we go!' and that was that. They went.

But as the plane taxied, turned, revved-up and finally took off, Trace's bad mood fell away along with the concrete runway beneath. The take-off was smooth as silk; the throaty roar of the engines quickly fell to a soft growl; the plane gained altitude with ease and clipped south-west at a steady, reassuring, one hundred and fifty or so m.p.h. And Trace actually found it exhilarating.

The windows were square, gave good views; all the shades and colours of the land, the shoreline and ocean seemed painted by some magical, luminous brush; the aircraft's shadow was a dark blot flowing first over the earth, then the ocean, all the time growing smaller until

173

at last it merged with the sea as the plane climbed steadily into the sky.

But Trace had only sufficient time to begin to enjoy it; for in a short while the plane's nose came around and the island of Rhodes itself slid from view, after which there was only the ageless sea. That alone might be enough to lull him, ease his mind – that incredible, glinting, inviting Aegean ocean – but since the two airports were less than a hundred miles apart . . .

. . . It seemed only moments before distant, rocky ramparts rose up in the south-west – the long crag which was Karpathos – and then the nose of the plane dipped as the pilot commenced his approach run.

In his pocket, Trace had Amira's paperback guide-book. He'd skipped through it last night before sleeping, noting that as well as Rhodes it also contained a map and history of Karpathos. He'd marked the location of Kastrouni's 'monastery' on the map and now hoped to glimpse the site on the way in, but he soon saw that this was out of the question. Not knowing exactly how or where geographically the aerial approach was made, he found he couldn't orient the map with the actual island. Instead he read up on a few Karpathian points of interest.

The island was forty-seven kilometres long, ten wide at its widest. Lots of orchards, vineyards; plenty of water, with ample shade from the ever-present crags and outcrops. And mountains, of alveolate – honeycombed – rock. Volcanic, certainly, or at least the result of once-terrific volcanic activity. There were a handful of villages, some virtually cut off or largely inaccessible through difficult mountain trails. Main town: Karpathos, previously Pighadia, or Pigadhia, or Pigathi. Amoupi, or Amopi – not a village but simply 'a place', a bay – lay a few miles to the south of Pighadia. And south again, where great craggy cliffs rose straight out of the sea, there stood or should stand Kastrouni's monastery, its tenant, and 'the thing he watches over.'

Suddenly Trace realized that he didn't know where Amira Halbstein would be staying. Pighadia? Somewhere else? It would be too much of a coincidence if she, too, had booked a room at Amoupi beach. No, she'd probably be staying in Pighadia, which meant that Trace would be trapped between two desires and interests: the alleged pile of the monastery on the one hand, and the girl (woman, really, for in fact she was Trace's senior by three years) on the other.

Trace's thoughts had arrived at this juncture when the plane banked steeply, rapidly lost height, sped slantingly inland across a flat stretch of coast. And as the ground came up, so the speed of the aircraft seemed to increase, though that was purely illusory. The plane lost more height, and –

– *Where the hell is the airport?* Trace wondered. Which was just a moment before he saw it.

Touching down on cinders and dirt, and as the plane completed its perfect landing and taxied to a halt, he saw it – and almost didn't believe it! There, at the end of the single landing strip, a shack. Literally – or almost literally – a shack, with a fence projecting forlornly to one side and ending in a few broken, leaning boards. Customs? Baggage checks? All the other normal airport procedures? Forget it!

As Trace and the rest disembarked, so a fuel truck lumbered into view from behind the shack; with a grin and a wave to his departing charges as they entered the shack, the pilot climbed up out of his cabin and onto the plane's roof, ready to refuel for his return trip. His new passengers were already moving toward the plane – all six of them. Four Greek peasants (was it right to keep thinking of them as peasants?) and a pair of golden-brown Swedes in shorts and T-shirts. Trace couldn't help smiling as he noted that one of the Greeks carried a large polythene bag of red mullets!

In the shack the newcomers milled around and bumped into each other, shook hands with some sort of island dignitary, a little man with a huge moustache and a grin as wide as his face, and were offered coffee or cold drinks. Trace accepted a Coke and an additional map of the island, and in another minute or two he and the rest were let out through a back door to stand in the brilliant sunlight and watch a small caravan of taxis come trundling like so many bugs down out of dusty hills.

Laurel and Hardy (or Peter Lorre and Sidney Greenstreet?) and Amira Halbstein got the first one, asked to be taken to Pighadia. As their car drove off she spotted Trace looking at her, waved, mouthed carefully articulated words at him: 'Be – see – ing – you.'

'To – night?' he mouthed back; but already a cloud of dust had been thrown up by the taxi's spinning wheels, and the car had made a sharp turn. So that Trace was left with only a picture of her smile – and her nod of agreement?

The young German couple were speaking to the driver of the second taxi. Trace heard Amoupi mentioned, joined them. And suddenly he was tired. Determined not to favour his left leg, it had been a strain to sit, walk, act as if there was nothing wrong with his left side. But there was. What it was he couldn't say – some muscular disorder, a problem associated with his club foot, (*let's face it*, he thought, *that's what it is: a clubbed foot*,) – but sooner or later he was going to have to have it seen to.

Sitting in the front passenger seat, he shielded his eyes against the sun blazing through the window, lay back his head and closed his eyes. And stayed that way until, maybe half an hour later, the driver gave his shoulder a shake and said:

'Mister? Amoupi!'

The brochures hadn't lied. There was a long narrow curving beach with stubby, low-lying rocky bay arms at each end. To the south of the beach, on a rising, jutting bluff overlooking the sea, a tiny, dazzling white church with a domed tower stood as if in silent appreciation of its location. The taverna was a house, really, with a seaward-sloping roof and a large kitchen in front; and in front of that, a large vine-roofed patio where square tables were set out in the shade. Ten paces from the patio the sea lay like a big blue pond, with a tidemark less than twelve inches wide. Along the beach to the north some driftwood – bleached, skeletal trees – had been washed up right to the edge of where the scrub started. Obviously the sea wasn't always so calm.

Forty or so paces to the north and rear of the taverna, a modern-style building (no-style, in fact: a double-decker oblong of white concrete with up-and-over doors, like a double row of small garages, one above the other) was set at the foot of hills that drifted back into rising terrain, and farther back yet into low mountains. In fact the mountains seemed to ring the entire scene about.

But the sun . . .

The sun bounced off everything like the inside walls of an oven. It was hard to see how anything grew here, and yet this small valley and bay supported a large field (orchard?) of gnarled olives whose branches were laden, and the vines were green and thick with tiny grapes, and the scrub and coarse grasses weren't desiccated at all but yellowy-green and springy with sap. Like the guidebook had said, there was good water here.

The place was worked by an energetic Greek couple in

their early forties. An old lady, the mother of one of them, dressed in the inevitable black dress and shawl of the aged, sat in the patio's shade and peeled potatoes. Later Trace would learn that she'd sit there all day; working on a lace, darning some garment or other, cleaning vegetables; normally doing something. But at other times she'd just sit, staring out across the sea . . .

Gratefully he took shade under the vines, sat down at one of the tables and asked for a beer, waited to be shown his room. He was on the ground floor of the concrete block of garages, and in fact he had seen better appointed garages. He had a washbasin, a shower, a toilet. They were in the back, behind a sliding door. In front there was a bed and a wardrobe. And in front of that the up-and-over door. No windows; if you wanted light you kept the door open, which also provided shade.

Trace didn't even unpack his case but simply took out a pair of bathing trunks and put them on, then walked slowly back to the beach and into the sea. He'd never been much for swimming and hadn't used the trunks for two years or more. It surprised him that they still fitted him and weren't moth-eaten. When *had* he last worn them?

– All of two and a half years ago; a girlfriend used to drag him to the swimming pool in Crouch End. She'd been crazy on swimming, and very good at it, so that Trace had looked like a clown in the water by comparison. It hadn't lasted long. Swimming? – it was for fish and ducks!

But here . . . ?

Here it would be almost criminal to ignore the sea's languid invitation. He couldn't understand why there was no one else in the water. But it was true: he had an entire beachful of Aegean all to himself. There they sat, the other guests – maybe a dozen of them, total – under the vines in their bathing costumes or shorts, sipping their drinks and chatting, and Trace the only one of them in the water.

He swam, floated, paddled himself to and fro in the warm water of that great bath for almost an hour, then noticed some activity in the taverna. A meal was being served, and Trace had worked up something of an appetite. He came out of the sea, shook the water off his body, was very nearly dry. He'd left his sandals – the ones with the enclosed toes – on the beach at the edge of the water. Now he slipped them on, stepped into the patio's shade, found an empty table.

It was odd, but suddenly he noted that everyone seemed to be looking at him while speaking to each other in low voices or from behind the backs of their hands. He began to feel uncomfortable. But at last Fodula, the female part of the partnership, came for his order. She was pleasant, moon-faced, quiet and polite. Trace ordered a small salad, stuffed tomatoes and spiced Greek sausages. And a cold beer.

As he finished ordering, the young German male from the taxi came over from where he was sitting with his girl. 'Excuse,' he said, bending over Trace and touching his arm. 'Is first time in Greece?'

'That's right,' said Trace.

'Ah!' said the German. He nodded his blond head wisely and Trace began to frown.

'Why do you ask?' he said. 'Am I doing something wrong?'

'Wrong for you,' said the other. 'Please take.' He handed Trace a brown plastic bottle of suntan lotion. The bottle was two-thirds empty, was obviously no longer required – not by the German couple, anyway. Trace looked at the label on the bottle: a high protection factor.

Then, as the German went back to his own table, he looked at himself, his bare arms and legs.

So that was why they didn't venture out much at midday! He understood it now, why they sat in the shade like that, keeping cool and sipping their drinks. Already he was turning a blotchy red. And he remembered from somewhere a song that went:

'Mad dogs and Englishmen go out in the midday sun . . .'

After eating he returned to his room, shaved and showered, emptied the remainder of the suntan lotion onto his body and limbs wherever he could reach and smoothed it in. Then he dressed himself in shorts and a T-shirt, put up his door and sat there in its shade for a while. And as the soothing lotion did its work, so he began to make his plans.

He'd noticed that taxis came down out of the hills every now and then, often two or three of them at a time. Amoupi was a popular place with the locals, possibly as a direct result of the female visitors sitting there under the vine in their skimpy little bikini tops. Well, Trace couldn't blame the taxi drivers for that. But he decided that when the next one came he'd take a ride into town. There were two or three things he wanted to do there. Even as he made this decision, so a lone taxi arrived in a cloud of dust, its driver signalling his presence with a blast on a fancy horn that played the five-note communication sequence from Close Encounters of the Third Kind.

Trace stuffed paper money into his shorts pocket, locked his up-and-over, hurried across to where the driver was sitting on a low wall smoking a cigarette. His luck was in: this was the same taxi, same driver, who had taken Amira Halbstein to Pighadia. Not only that but he also spoke half-decent English. As they motored up into the hills Trace asked his questions about Amira.

180

'Oh, yes – she very pretty,' the driver answered, grinning. 'She at Villa Ulysses.'

'Good!' said Trace. 'I'll look her up. Also, can I buy booze in Pighadia?'

'Booze?'

'Drink – liquor – spirits, you know? I mean wine, whisky, er, ouzo?'

'Ah, *ouzo!* Cocktails! The bars . . .'

'No, not bars, shops.'

'Oh, yes – sure! Good shops. Three, four of them. All sell wine, whisky.'

'And can I find them easily, these shops?'

'Oh, sure. Small town. You walk, you find . . .'

The ride took ten minutes; they couldn't have covered more than four or five winding miles; Trace got out in the 'town centre' and paid his fare. So this was Pighadia.

A main road followed the coastline for something less than a mile, with the line of the harbour lying more or less parallel. In the central area the road sprouted several side-streets; there were shops, hotels, a handful of restaurants. In the harbour boats bobbed gently on an almost imperceptible swell. It was like a small, outlying district of Rhodes town, transplanted here. Except it didn't have so much of the ancient stone, the steeped-in-legend aura. Take away the sea, thought Trace, and you could shoot a good spaghetti western here. And if a man didn't want to be found, this would certainly make as good a place as any in which to disappear.

Then he thought about Amira Halbstein. But –

– First things first.

Trace wandered the streets, got the general layout of the place fixed in his head. Then he began checking the shops that sold drink. There was only one that he could find which stocked booze as its main business, and this was close to the harbour. Run by a thin, sour-looking

181

type, its metal shelves were crammed with all the best brands at incredibly low prices. Trace marvelled at a two litre bottle of Grand Marnier which was labelled at 1,700 Drachmas – a little over eleven pounds sterling!

There were two or three customers in the place but he went on checking and comparing prices until the last of them left, then turned to the surly proprietor. 'Excuse me,' he said, 'but do you understand English?'

'Little.'

'I'm looking for a wine-shop owned by a man called Kastrouni. Is this the shop?'

'Eh?' the man's thin face revealed nothing; his eyes were half-lidded, snakish.

'Kastrouni,' Trace repeated, louder. 'Is this his shop?'

'*My* shop!' the other thumbed himself in the chest. 'Who this Kastrouni?'

'Thanks anyway,' said Trace. 'Don't worry about it. I'm looking for someone, that's all.' He bought nothing, went out into the street, walked away from the harbour to a smaller shop. There were one or two tourists about, nothing like a crowd.

The owner of the second shop was youngish, over-weight, jolly-looking. He was handing out free sweets to village kids as Trace entered. Trace let the kids hurry off, laughing, then repeated his question.

And yet again he was met with a blank stare. Except –

Was that a nervous twitch he had seen at the corner of the man's mouth? And he noted that as the man repeated that name, Kastrouni, then that his hands started to tremble until he leaned his weight on them atop his counter.

Trace looked round the shop. It sold a lot more than just booze. There were cartons of cigarettes, cigars; sweets and candies in many varieties; tinned foods, packets of biscuits, even local eggs and cheese. Casually, as he examined the label on a bottle of Grants, he said:

'Kastrouni was my friend. He came to England to see me, to tell me something. But now he's dead.' And out of the corner of his eye he saw the other start, saw his jaw drop as if someone had just walked up to him and slapped him. Quickly he turned fully toward the man, but already the other had regained something of his composure.

'Dead? Someone is dead? That is very bad, but – ' and he shrugged.

Not very convincing, thought Trace as he paid for his whisky and left the shop. *Not at all convincing.* But that was all he had wanted from him, and now he gave a mental nod. Oh, yes. If Kastrouni had indeed been part-owner of a shop here in Pighadia, then this was that shop. It *was* this shop, there could be no doubting it. And certainly he had impressed his partner with the need for secrecy . . .

Out in the street, not looking where he was going, Trace bumped into someone staring in through the shop's window. This person, a fat man in a white suit, was just turning away as they collided. 'Sorry,' said Trace at once as the other stumbled. 'I wasn't looking where I was going.'

The other recovered, turned to stare at Trace from under a wide-brimmed hat. It was Mr Hardy – or Sidney Greenstreet. 'That's all right,' he wheezed, his accent mildly American – or poorly disguised as American. 'Hell, no – my fault. There's just too damned much of me. I get in everybody's way.' He waved his hands for a moment, apologetically, nodded and waddled off toward the harbour. Trace hurried after him.

'Er, excuse me?'

'Yeah?' the other waited for him.

'That girl who shared your taxi from the plane, Amira

Halbstein. I'm supposed to meet her. I know she's staying at the Villa Ulysses, but – '

'Hey, sure!' the fat man wheezed. 'Yeah, right. A real looker. She has one half of the place and we have the other half.' (Trace noted the 'we'.) 'You wanna know where it is, right?'

'That would be very helpful.'

The fat man gave simple directions and went on his way.

Quarter of a mile to the north of the town and set back against a hill, where it nestled in the lee of a rocky outcrop, Trace found the Villa Ulysses. It was a modern place but tasteful in an almost Spanish hacienda style which fitted in just right with its picturesque setting. With high-walled courtyards on both sides, the place looked exclusive and expensive. Bougainvillaea bunched up in green and purple clumps along the tops of the walls, falling outside here and there in cascades of blossom and leaf.

Less than a hundred yards away across the main road, the shoreline had been sun-blasted into a shade varying between pure white and faded yellow, where shallow shelves of rock slid like a tilted deck of cards into the sea. Trace looked at the villa, looked again toward the sea. He knew Amira had the northern courtyard and rooms, but he'd spotted a lone sun umbrella at the edge of the Aegean's blue expanse. One umbrella in maybe a half-mile of shoreline. And hadn't she told him she was here for peace and quiet?

He found her under the umbrella with a book. Her bikini was just decent and she was stretched out flat on a rush mat, propped on her elbows. Her skin glistened golden with oil and the smell of coconut wafted to Trace even before he was close enough to speak without raising his voice. Before his shadow could fall in her view and perhaps startle her, he said:

'Hello, there. I thought it would be you.'

She looked up over the top of her sunglasses, sat up cross legged in a fluid movement, put down her book. 'And I thought it would be you,' she smiled. 'Even if you are a couple of hours too early.' Then she looked at him more closely, took off her glasses and looked again, said: 'Better come under the shade. What on earth have you been doing to yourself?'

Trace snorted. 'No one told me the Greek islands were just big microwaves in disguise,' he said. 'I see you're wearing coconut this year. Me, I'm into German stuff. Hedgehog pee, I think. The Krauts aren't into how it smells, just if it works.'

She laughed. 'So what's your place like – at Amoupi, I mean?'

'I didn't say I was at Amoupi,' he answered.

She shrugged, half-looked away. 'Where else would you be? There are so few resorts on Karpathos.'

'But plenty of villas and apartments in Pighadia.'

'In which case I'd expect you to use the same taxi from the plane – so you'd know where I was staying. And how do you know I haven't already checked to see if you were in Pighadia? And incidentally, how *did* you find me?'

'A little bird told me,' said Trace, sitting down beside her. 'Well, a damn great fat bird, in fact!' And he wondered if she really had checked him out. He hoped so, for he found her increasingly attractive. 'Anyway, to answer your question, Amoupi is bloody awful. Not the place itself, the beach or the taverna. The *place* is idyllic. But the rooms . . . no windows, not especially comfortable, hardly room to swing a cat!'

'You poor man,' she said. 'And sunburnt to boot! And

here's me at Ulysses living in the lap of luxury. Would you like to see my apartment?'

Too right! thought Trace. 'That's very kind of you,' he said. 'And if you've ice I can offer you a drink,' he showed her the bottle of whisky.

She nodded, 'Plenty of ice, yes. OK,' she stood up, pulled on a cotton shirt, 'you can carry my umbrella.'

The lap of luxury, she'd said, and Trace considered it no exaggeration. The courtyard was almost a garden, with a vine, masses of bougainvillaea, flowers in Greek vases along the walls, paths and seating areas of small black and white cobbles laid on edge and set out in classical and geometrical representation of octopuses, dolphins, fishes, men and maidens. Amira's 'rooms' were in fact just one huge, high-ceilinged room, but laid out in such a way as to serve the functions of three. Wooden open-plan stairs led up the back wall to an open bedroom which took up half the upper area under varnished ceiling beams; the 'downstairs' area was divided by an archway almost as wide as the room, the smaller side of which hid a tiny, quite separate toilet, and a shower recess with ceramic tiled ceilings, walls and floor. Beneath the stairs and behind a bead curtain there was a tiny kitchen area, with a three-ring cooker run from a gas cylinder, a porcelain sink, some cupboards and drawers in varnished wood, and a small refrigerator. The wall away from the sea, where the ceiling was at its highest, was immensely thick; recessed into it was a stone platform with a mass of cushions, above which the stone arched in a style decidedly Rhodian. Light flooded in through high windows in three walls, as well as from smaller windows looking out on the courtyard. The place was delightful.

'I didn't know there were places like this,' Trace said in open admiration as he looked about. 'I won't ask how much it's costing you. And what does it matter anyway? It's a bargain!'

'There's ice in the fridge,' she said. 'Make yourself a drink while I shower, else I'll taste of salt when you kiss me. You will want to kiss me again, won't you?'

Trace was in the kitchen area; he stuck his head out through the bead curtains but she had already gone through the arch and presumably into the shower cubicle. Her bathing costume lay in two diminutive pieces on the polished pine floor. 'I didn't think you'd noticed the first time,' he called out, and heard her bright laughter ring out a moment before the *hiss* of jetting water.

'Oh, I noticed,' came her voice, panting a little, shivery from the effect of cold, stinging water. 'I thought it a little early to start a holiday romance, that's all.'

And Trace sensed, as some men can, the invitation. With most women merely bringing him back here would have been a signal, and certainly stripping and showering while he was here; but not with this one. No, the invitation had just been made – this minute, a single second ago. It had been in her voice, in that indefinable something which passes at light-speed between a man and a woman who *know*. But even so, even now, it was a tentative invitation – it would depend on his response. On the *way* he responded. And the last thing he must do was respond as a timid schoolboy.

'A little early?' he repeated her. 'And now?'

She made no answer and he knew he was right. But still Trace felt like it was someone else who removed his shorts, stripped him naked and walked him under the archway.

She stood there silently laughing at him from the water, which fell over her and rivered from her like a liquid glass curtain. And her laughter confirmed it. He looked at her, enjoyed her. Her breasts looked perfect to him;

they were large-nippled and hung ripe as splendid fruits. The V of the hair between her thighs was deep, the curls bushy, beaded now and glinting; she held up her arms to the source of the water and Trace was reminded of Jilly, but briefly. Jilly was Jilly, but Amira was real.

He stepped into the shower with her, gasped as the water hit him. She took his waist and turned him round, pressed herself to his back for the merest moment and then, as the water began to run warm, started to soap his back from the nape of his neck to his backside. And: 'Now?' she said, ' – now you're still a couple of hours too early.'

For a moment he felt her breasts again pressed to his back – felt waves of pleasure rushing through him, the full length of her leaning on him – and then she stepped out of the water, took up a towel from somewhere and wrapped it round herself.

'Wha – ?' said Trace from the shower, warm water streaming into his mouth. For he knew she had backed off, but at the same time knew he'd done nothing wrong. 'Amira, the last thing I need right now is a tease!' he said.

She towelled at her hair, bit her lip, turned her face away. 'I know,' she answered. And then, just a little desperately: 'But if we make love now we'll spend the rest of the afternoon, the evening and night in bed – and you know it. Oh, I think I want you, all right, Charlie Trace – but all in good time. I mean, I don't know you, do I? Not properly. And anyway, what do you call a girl who just falls into bed as easily as that?'

'Good fun?' Trace suggested, getting out of the shower as she handed him a second towel. If she had noticed his foot she failed to mention it. He was glad for that, anyway.

'No,' she shook her head, 'I was being serious. You

call such a girl a bag, a tart, a "hot piece". But on the other hand these are the islands of love, romance. So I suggest we split the difference.'

Trace's disappointment made him flippant, even a little sarcastic. 'My idea entirely,' he growled. Then he checked himself, conjured a half-genuine wince, bit his lip. 'A play on words,' he said. *'Double entendre* – and a poor one.'

'You're annoyed with me,' she said. 'I can't say I blame you. But if you don't want to hear my plan – the way I think it should go – ?'

'By all means,' said Trace. 'Let's hear it.' He began to towel himself dry.

'Well, my suggestion is this: you go back to Amoupi and dress yourself for the evening, just as you would in London. Then, about 8:00 tonight, call for me here and take me "on the town". Or take me on what there is of a town, anyway. You can wine and dine me, and try to convince me of your undying whatever. If there's a disco we might sit under the vines and the stars and watch the dancing for a while, and we'll drink exotic things and let the night close in on us. Then, if the spark is still there, if we're compatible – if we're "in love", for however brief a moment – we'll come back here and let things take their course. How does that sound?'

Trace nodded. 'Like a distant tinkle of water in a desert,' he said. 'It's promising – but there's always the chance that the spring will run dry before you get there.'

'Only if we discover that we really don't care for each other,' she said, sensibly. 'In which case it would be wrong, pure lust. Simple animal sex.'

Oh? thought Trace. *But sometimes there's a lot to be said for simple animal sex, my love. Certainly it's better than waking up all sticky from a wet dream!* And then he got dressed again . . .

Back in town looking for a taxi, Trace was attracted by a babble of excited Greek voices, and the 'Oohs!' and 'Aahs!' of holidaymakers, to the street with the two wineshops. Rounding a corner he saw a crowd gathered outside the smaller shop, the one where he'd bought his whisky – the one owned, or silent-partnered at least, by Dimitrios Kastrouni. A man was being led away, his arms locked firmly up behind his back, by three hard-faced, official-looking types. One of the three, the eldest, cleared the way ahead as the other two manhandled their prisoner through the crowd. They could only be part-time policemen.

Trace got a good look at the protesting prisoner's face: he was the surly, sour-looking proprietor of the larger wineshop. But what had he done; what had been going on here?

'What happened?' Trace asked a young British couple.

'Dunno,' said the man, slack-jawed and staring. 'Somebody said there'd been a murder, so we came to see.'

Murder! And the thin-faced type obviously involved. Standing on tiptoe to look over the heads of those between, Trace saw men come staggering out of the open door to the shop. They carried a stretcher, whose length was partly stuck in the entrance by a frantic woman who cried and babbled and beat her breast, all the while running her hands up and down the body on the stretcher. The woman was red: her white face was smeared with red, her fluttering hands, the front of her dress.

Then the whole picture snapped into focus and Trace felt his own blood drain to his feet. The man on the stretcher was quite obviously dead; his head lolled strangely and was tilted back at an odd angle, as if his neck was broken. It wasn't, but there was no longer any tension in it. The tension had gone when someone had drawn a razor across the throat, ear to ear. The body's front was sticky and scarlet and hellish where his life had gushed out and lay upon him, quickly clotting.

It was the happy, fat man: Kastrouni's partner . . .

Chapter Three

Trace was feeling greatly subdued when he picked Amira up at her villa. He had been doing a great deal of thinking and didn't much care for the conclusions he'd come to. Kastrouni's warning, about him being in great danger, kept coming back to him. And now the fat man from the wineshop, dead. On the other hand it seemed his murderer was another Karpathian, and that the murder itself was probably simply the result of rivalry. But it played on Trace's mind and Amira wasn't slow to notice it.

'You've been very quiet,' she said, as they sat in a taverna overlooking the harbour, where the lights of a handful of boats were reflected in the water like so many additional stars. 'Is something wrong? Have I disappointed you so badly?'

'You?' He realized he'd been miles away. And he must have seemed very withdrawn through their meal. 'No, you haven't disappointed me. Actually I feel completely at ease with you, so much so that I don't feel I have to keep trying to impress you. If that doesn't sound very flattering, you know that's not the way I meant it. But disappointed? – hell, if we hadn't bumped into each other in Rhodes, I'd probably be going round the twist right about now!'

'Oh?' she toyed with her drink, a milky ouzo climbing over large chunks of ice, and cocked her head on one side. 'Is that all I am, then? A playmate to amuse you and keep the boredom at bay?'

He smiled, reached across to pinch her chin between thumb and forefinger, said: 'You know that's not what I meant either. But see, just like you I came here for a little peace and quiet. For that and . . . for a couple of other reasons. And now there's you. So you see, you're a complication. A very sweet, very beautiful complication . . . but a complication anyway.'

'You'd prefer not to have met me?'

'You know,' said Trace, 'If you're not turning my words round the other way, you're doing it with my thoughts! Prefer not to have met you? Hell, no! No, that's the last thing I'd wish. But I know there'll be times – a day at least, maybe two – during this coming week, when I'll not be here. I won't be around. And then I'll think about you.'

'You mean you'll worry that I'm being chatted up by some other handsome young man,' she said, wrinkling her nose. 'I know.'

'That, too,' he nodded his agreement. 'And then I'd have to rough him up, and he'd probably rough *me* up!'

She propped her chin in her palms. 'I think I quite like that,' she said. 'The idea of men fighting over me. But what is this secret thing you have to do? Where is it you have to go?'

Trace looked at her, saw her very clearly for perhaps the first time. It wasn't simply the attraction between strangers now, and it wasn't the blurred sexual impressions cast by a lovely girl in a shower. It was that he looked at a warm, live, real person. Of flesh and blood. Fragile, as all human beings are. And vulnerable. For some strange reason Death had strayed into close proximity to Trace and seemed to be following him around. He spoke to someone, and that someone died. Then he spoke to someone else, and . . . same story. And now he was talking to Amira. She should at least be warned. She should know something of the sinister nature of what she was playing with.

'Do you want to know why I'm here?' he asked. 'Why I'm really here?'

'If you want to tell me,' she shrugged. 'I imagine you're running away from a love affair that's caving in on you; or maybe you're just getting out, for a little while, from under the weight of your everyday life. That's how you've looked: at the airport in Rhodes, in Rhodes town itself, even tonight. Almost a fugitive, a man who can't relax, who keeps looking over his shoulder. Not literally, figuratively.'

'Me, a fugitive?' Trace grinned, was on the point of denying it, impulsively decided to go straight-up. He shrugged, let the grin slide from his face.

'Am I right?' she pressed.

'Maybe, partly. Sometimes it seems like I'm a fugitive several times over. To quote you: not literally, figuratively.' And he quickly sketched in the bare bones of the story of his meeting with Kastrouni, of the Greek's freakish death, and now of the second man's murder just a few hours ago. He filled nothing in, painted a sketchy picture indeed, left out all the fine details.

Through it she sat listening (only half attentively, Trace thought, even fidgeting a little, as if silently urging him to get on with it; perhaps not believing him?) and when he'd finished she said:

'And is that it? A Greek gives you a mysterious warning in London and gets killed in an accident. You come out here to check up on something he said to you, and a person you've spoken to gets murdered.'

'You think it sounds weird,' said Trace. 'Maybe you don't believe it.'

'Of course I believe it!' she snorted. 'Actually, I've already heard about this murder. The whole town has been buzzing with it. But do you want to know what I think? It's all coincidence, that's all.' Then a thought

194

struck her and her eyes went wide. 'And is that what's been worrying you? That now you've met me, I too will fall under the influence? Do you think that maybe I'll be the next victim of this . . . this curse of Charlie Trace?'

He gave a shrug, began to feel silly. 'Something like that, perhaps.'

'Coincidence!' she insisted. 'Listen, Charlie, let me tell you something. A few years ago when my mother died, I spent a little time in Israel. There was a young man I was interested in – in a military kibbutz. We weren't lovers, just friends. But we were going to be lovers. We knew, you see? But one day I spent some time with him and a bunch of other young soldiers. That same night a terrorist raiding party came over and killed them all. Including the boy I hadn't slept with yet. A week later my uncle died of cancer. Death seemed to be everywhere that year, everywhere I went. And do you think it had anything to do with me?'

'This is different,' said Trace.

'How? Why is it? What exactly did this mysterious Greek tell you?'

Trace wasn't going to involve her. He felt he'd said too much already. And, hell – she could even be right! 'Nothing,' he said. 'You're right, I've let my imagination run away with me. Forget it. And as for my taking time off from you – forget that, too. Put it out of your mind. I won't be going off on my own, and you won't be getting chatted up – except by me. Anyway, I'm not much for crumbling old monasteries at the best of times.'

He was leaning back, looking out across the water as he said this, and Amira had just taken a sip of her drink; but her spluttering and sudden violent coughing had him on his feet in a moment, thumping her back, steadying her, full of concern. 'Are you OK?' he asked anxiously as the bout subsided. 'What happened?'

'Went down . . . the wrong . . . way!' she choked it out. Then: 'Thanks, I'm all right now . . .'

Following which conversation Trace felt easier in his mind, so that the mood lightened and the night quickly became enjoyable and exciting. They left the taverna and found an open square with coloured lights strung overhead, where Greeks in local costumes danced to bozoukis and swigged ouzo from a bottle which they passed around; and finally, more than a little tipsy, they strolled back together to the Villa Ulysses.

In the morning Trace wished he could remember more about their lovemaking, but he couldn't. It was then, over coffee, that she suggested he go and get his things from Amoupi and move in here. And Trace couldn't think of anything he'd like better.

Already he was looking forward to tonight, but this time he intended to remember everything . . .

He took a taxi back to Amoupi and arrived there about 10:30. The sun was sizzling its way across the sky again, of course, and all the smart-arses were under their vine, sipping their iced drinks as usual. All except one: a lone girl, topless, so brown that the sun ignored her, splashing in the sea and fooling with a beach-ball. Trace stood watching her for a moment, then turned toward his 'garage' – and at once turned back again.

Watching the girl as she'd moved in the water, Trace's eyes had settled briefly on a thin man sitting at a corner table on the taverna's patio. He wore tinted glasses, a 'Hawaiian' shirt and a straw hat, but he was still Mr Laurel.

Toity poiple boids, thought Trace at once, and: *What's he doing here?*

Mr Laurel didn't appear to be looking his way, but as Trace went to his tiny room so the thin man got up,

196

approached Trace's taxi where it stood waiting. Trace shrugged. It could be that he'd simply been checking the place out, seeing what he could see. Now he'd probably be wanting to return to Pighadia. Trace wasn't concerned for he'd asked the taxi driver to wait for him, and anyway he didn't mind sharing.

Trace's case was on the bed where he'd left it, and –

– No he hadn't. He'd left it on the floor beside the bed. Also, he'd locked the up-and-over door. But when he'd entered just now it had been open. He looked about the tiny room. What else was different?

On the foot of his bed he saw the guidebook given him by Amira. He hadn't left it there, open, face down like that. He could swear he hadn't. He flipped the open book onto its back, and in the instant before the pages readjusted themselves saw the map of Karpathos – on which he'd marked the approximate location of the monastery. Someone had been in here looking at this book, had seen his mark.

He went through his suitcase. It seemed in order, and yet –

No, it was *not* in order. Far from it. Kastrouni's notebook – gone!

Trace had brought just three of the 'Demogorgon items' here with him: the notebook, Kastrouni's map of Karpathos, a small bible. The bible was still here but the map and notebook – both gone, disappeared. But why?

Someone had come in here, searched through his suitcase, taken the map and notebook. Then he (or she?) had seen the guidebook. It, too, carried a map of Karpathos, which Trace had also marked. The unknown intruder had seen little point in stealing the guidebook: since Trace had marked it, he obviously knew where the monastery was . . .

Kastrouni was dead.

And the happy fat man from the wineshop was dead.

And up there in the mountains was a man someone thought was important to Trace. And damn it all, he *was* important to Trace – in the last five minutes he'd suddenly become more important to Trace than anyone else in his entire life!

Including Amira Halbstein? he asked himself. But that was a question he couldn't answer. Not yet. It was a question which now would have to wait. Until afterwards.

He quickly repacked the suitcase, took his key to Fodula where she worked in her kitchen. She looked surprised. 'You leave? But you have paid, and – '

'It's OK,' he said. 'I stay with friends in Pighadia.'

'OK, but – something wrong here?'

'No, no,' he said quickly, and forced himself to smile. 'No, everything is great. But – tell me, has anyone been in my room?'

'Eh? Been in – ' her eyes went wide. 'Something stolen?'

'Yes – *no*!' said Trace. 'No, nothing that I can see.' Too late he'd noticed the thin shadow just beyond the kitchen's threshold, thrown there by the sun. The shadow with the hat. Mr Laurel's shadow.

'Mr Trace, I sorry if – ' Fodula began, taking his hand.

'No, really, it's OK,' he cut her off. 'But from now on I'm staying in Pighadia. This place has been very nice – wonderful – but I have friends in Pighadia. Thanks . . .' And as the thin shadow melted away he made slowly for the kitchen door.

He made sure Laurel had plenty of time to get out of the way, then strode out into the sunlight. When he got to the taxi, the thin man was already seated in the back. Trace got in the back, too, said: 'Pighadia?'

'Eh? What? Oh, sure!' the thin man seemed surprised. 'Nowhere else to go on this rock, s'far as I can see.'

198

'It's just that this is my taxi,' said Trace, trying not to snarl. All of a sudden he hated this obnoxious bastard, wished he dared grab hold of him and turn out his pockets. But –

'Say, gee, I'm sorry!' the other seemed genuinely concerned. 'Hey, I'll wait for the next one.' He made to get out but Trace stopped him.

'It's OK, don't bother,' he said. 'And I agree with you. It is a rock of an island. So few birds.'

'Boids?' said the other, just as Trace had thought he would.

'Sure, girls. There's damn few about . . .'

'Goils?' the other shrugged his thin shoulders. 'Yeah, well goils is goils. Me, I'm here for the ozone – the smell off the sea. It helps my nose, you know? I get these blocked sinuses, see.'

'Yes, I see,' said Trace, and thought: *I'll block your bloody sinuses, you skinny little bastard!*

That was the end of their conversation, but as they pulled into Pighadia Trace asked: 'Tell me, do you know if it's possible to hire a motor-cycle around here? There's a place I want to visit in the mountains.' He was looking directly at Mr Laurel's face, but . . . not a twitch.

'Motor-cycles?' the other shook his head. 'Naw, I don't think so. Who needs one, the taxis are so cheap! So what's in the hills, eh? More goils, maybe?'

'No,' Trace shook his head. 'Just some old ruins. But I'm very interested in old ruins.'

'Yeah? Well, goils and ruins, that's your bag. Me, it's the schnoz, you know?'

Trace nodded, and to the taxi driver: 'Can you stop here? This is fine for me.' He got out in the main street, watched the taxi drive off.

It took only a matter of minutes to find a place where he could hire a small motor-cycle. The shop was in a tiny courtyard just off the main street; crammed with bits of bikes; where an old man and his son tinkered and pottered and put together machines from the junk. And yes, there were two motor-cycles free, a red one and a blue one. Trace chose the blue one. The other was just a bit too bright, too noticeable. He would have driven the machine off there and then but the old man wouldn't let him.

'Brakes need fixing,' he explained. 'Bad brakes, you fall, get hurt. Red one got good brakes. Or I fix this one.'

'How long?' Trace asked.

'Half hour?' the oldster shrugged.

'OK, I'll be back.'

Trace found himself a restaurant. He had coffee, a huge slice of swordfish and a side salad. The swordfish left a taste in his mouth which he washed away with a can of ice-cold beer. Then he went back to the bike shop. The blue machine was ready but . . . something was missing.

'Where's the red bike?' he asked.

'Red bike gone,' said the old man, wiping his hands on an oily rag. 'Hired out.'

Alarm bells started to ring in Trace's head. 'Oh, yes? Could that have been my friend who took it?'

'Friend?' the old man wasn't greatly interested.

'Yes, a thin man with a bright shirt and a hat?'

'Ah! That him. He want hurry, your friend,' the old man grinned gummily. 'I old. I not hurry.'

The alarm bells were louder. 'How long's he been gone?'

The old man shrugged. 'Half hour?'

Trace felt a lump rising in his throat. Had he taken that long over his meal? He supposed he had.

He took a pair of binoculars from his case – the ones he used at the races back home – and hung them round his neck; also Amira's guidebook, which he tucked under his belt. Then he gave the suitcase to the old man and paid him an extra hundred Drachmas to take care of it for him.

Heading his mongrel mount back out of town along the winding hill road to Amoupi, Trace tried to look ahead, see what was coming next. It was all too bizarre, too cloak-and-dagger, too incredible. And it was certainly too dangerous. As for where he was going: there was only one place he could go now. It was what he'd come here for. And he'd looked at various maps of the island often enough to know roughly where it was. No need to waste any more time on that. In fact he sensed that he daren't waste any time at all. Time was suddenly all-important.

But half an hour's start! How far ahead of him was Mr Laurel now? Or was it Mr Lorre after all?

> This skinny, doity boid,
> On his way to kill the thoid,
> Not Laurel, no, but Lorre –
> Or is that just absoid?

Trace was caught up in this now – guessed that he'd been caught up in it all along – and had come to the conclusion that merely half-hearted participation wouldn't be good enough. Not good enough? – it looked like it wouldn't even be allowed. Too much was at stake; indeed, if Kastrouni had been half-right in what he'd said, then he, Trace *himself*, was at stake. Those were pretty high stakes! They made tenners on the wheel at Cromwell's Mint seem a bit tame. And Trace's excitement, the adrenalin-inspired fever of his body and brain transmitted itself through him to his machine.

Actually it wasn't a bad little bike. Not a bit like his powerful old Triumph, no, but nippy enough for roads like these. With a full tank – all of twelve pints! – Trace could have done a complete circuit of Karpathos, if there'd been coastal roads. There weren't; the island was 'unspoiled'; much of the coastline consisted of cliffs rising sheer from the sea into mountains. But he would stay on the roads until they became paths, and on the paths until they became tracks, and so on. It might even end up with him doing a bit of uphill cross-country, but he'd done some of that, too, in his time; only for his own amusement, of course, but there weren't many who could handle a bike like Charlie Trace.

Full of confidence, he put his little machine through its clattering paces on the rough roads, and in no time at all Pighadia, then Amoupi were left behind in clouds of dust; by which time he was already climbing into the foothills. Then, too, he caught his first glimpse of the man he tracked: the brilliant flash of early afternoon sunlight glancing off a driving mirror high on a steep hillside. With practised ease Trace slammed on his freshly adjusted brakes, skidded to a halt at the side of the road, yanked up his binoculars to his eyes. The distance was probably one and a half, not more than two miles, but the glasses brought it down to mere hundreds of yards.

It was the red motor-cycle, yes, and the thin man riding like a demon, hunched over his little fuel tank. The old man at the bike shop had been wrong, it couldn't have been half an hour; more like ten minutes, if that. But the old boy's grasp of English wasn't much; he probably said 'half an hour' to any question regarding the matter of time. Trace got a decent focus going, looked closer at the rider up ahead.

He had something over his shoulder: a long cylindrical bag, like a thin golf-bag. Fishing tackle? But what sort of fish would he be after up here? Trace watched until, with a wobble and a jerk, the red machine was up the hill and dipping down the other side out of view.

Then he let the binoculars dangle, took out Amira's guide-book, opened it to the map of Karpathos. There was a pass through the mountains up ahead. The road went right through it. On the other side it dipped down into a valley, where there were several lesser tracks off to the left, toward the sea, one of which – just one – led up into more foothills right on the coast. And it was there, between the foothills and the second range or spur of the mountain, that the ruined monastery kept its lonely vigil. Against what?

That was something Trace had to find out. And if it was at all possible he must get there first, before the other rider. He stuffed the book back under his belt, revved up his machine, went spurting up the hillside like some strange mechanical squid . . .

Mr Lorre must be a better rider than Trace had credited, or his machine a better machine. For as Trace crested the range of foothills some three or four minutes later, already the red bike and its rider were across the flat and into the pass, disappearing from view in a puff of dust where the way led over a hump-backed saddle. Now, however, Trace's route lay slightly downhill for maybe half a mile, and the road was more or less straight, so that he could really 'open her up.' He did, and his machine responded with all of fifty-five or even sixty miles per hour; so that in less than a minute he was once more ascending, and in twice as long again was into the pass and riding in shadows.

Until now the cicadas had been cheering Trace on, strident as hordes of tiny fishwives in the coarse under-growth, the heathery thyme and spiked grasses alongside the road; but now in the brooding pass, where cliffs rose

203

up precipitously close at hand, the song of the cicadas was absent; and as the upward slope of the saddle grew steeper, so Trace's machine began to labour and its rider to regret his choice of mounts. He dropped a gear, gradually wound up the throttle, actually gained a little speed before coming over the saddle and down out of the pass. And at last it was all brilliant sunshine and dusty roads downhill again, but very windingly, so that Trace felt frustrated that he was unable to build up any real speed. And far down in the valley a flash of red, and bright glancing shafts of light as once more the sun taunted, striking fire from the machine of the rider he so desperately pursued.

Down into the furnace valley rode Trace, the wind of his ride keeping him cool, and once more the bike in front was lost to him as the land flattened out and Mediterranean pines grew up in clumps along the winding road to block his view ahead. Precious seconds were wasted on another glance at Amira's guidebook, following which Trace was on the lookout for tracks leading off to the left. It had seemed to him (if he could rely on the map at all) that the third or fourth such track was the one he wanted. But what was a track and what was not? There were paths galore to both sides – goat trails, probably, tracks used by local herdsmen – and all of them looked exactly alike.

Then, coming around a gentle bend and slowing down a little to avoid deep, criss-crossing ruts in a road which was now hard-packed earth, Trace passed the entrance to a somewhat wider track on his left – and at once throttled back and applied his brakes. He'd seen a snake lying there, maybe five feet long, all black and hissing and writhing in agony in the centre of the track. And its middle had been crushed and split open.

Manhandling his bike about-face on the rough surface,

Trace backtracked, looked again, nodded his approval. 'Thanks, snake!' he said.

The agonized creature had done him a favour and now he returning it, driving the wheels of his machine directly over its darting head as he followed the track east toward the sea . . .

The valley rapidly narrowed down as he stood up on his machine's footrests and jiggled the bike forward, manoeuvred the track's ruts and rocks; and while he hardly noticed it, soon he found that he'd got himself into a second, narrower, deeper defile than the main one; which is to say that he now rode parallel to the bed of some old, dried-out watercourse. Then the track petered out completely and he bounced the bike down a rough bank to the bed of the dead stream itself.

At least it was cooler here, where trees and bushes whose growth likewise followed the stream gave shade; so Trace decided to stick with it right down to the coast, if that was possible, then see what he'd see. Which turned out to be a good plan, as plans go.

In another half-mile the stream had levelled out and merged into dry scrubland; headlands of rock jutted out into the sea to north and south; Trace found himself in a natural bay where cliffs came straight out of the water to a more or less uniform height of about twenty-five or thirty feet. But from here at least, because of the curve of the bite and his somewhat elevated position above the sea, he was able to scan right along the rocky coastline to the south. Or rather, he was able to scan its heights.

For to the south the walls of the mountains rose mainly sheer and yellow and apparently inaccessible, for all the world like great bastions of dry, crumbling cheese, all cracked and caverned, where mould was represented by clumps of dusty growth or the occasional tree whose roots had found purchase in some half-secure crevice or other.

And this secret monastery of Kastrouni's was somewhere up there? In which case Trace might just as well give up the chase right here and –

Something glittered up there, something bright, reflecting the sun dazzlingly.

Trace snatched up his binoculars and trained them on a seemingly sheer wall of rock about half-way up the first stage of a two-tier system of tall cliffs. The distance was something a little over a mile; the picture lay crisp and clear on his eyes; it was Mr Lorre, *still* riding his red machine! Then for the first time Trace realized his error: he had thought that like himself Mr Lorre was *looking for* the monastery; but now he guessed that the other had known of its location all along, and that finally he had been forced into going for it. And he *was* going for it – straight for it – like a bullet to its target!

Trace stared harder through the binoculars, sought to achieve an even better focus. Ah! Yes! Now he could make out a ledge where it climbed like a shallow groove along the face of the cliff. It must be considerably wider than it looked, that ledge – at least Trace hoped so! But anyway, if the skinny American could ride a motor-cycle up there, so could Charlie Trace. He snatched Amira's guide-book from his waist-band, tore it open to the map, found a faint dotted line leading from roughly his present location to the foot of the cliffs. Now if only that line of dots represented a path . . .

. . . It did!

Five minutes later Trace paused briefly, throttling up his machine and threateningly feeding it revs, while he stared bleakly up the ragged incline ahead. On his right hand the rock rising sheer to the sky, and on his left, soon, a dizzy drop to more rocks. And between the two the track – literally a track, cut out of the cliff itself – and no more than six feet wide at best and much narrower than that in places. This was going to be one dangerous ride. Trace gritted his teeth. Bollocks to danger! And what the hell, you can't live forever, can you!

One slip when you're up there, Charlie Trace, he answered himself, *and you won't have to worry about living forever. You'll have just enough time for one good, long, loud yell!*

Then he was on his way, standing up and leaning forward, balancing the bike like a circus act as he stayed dead centre in the middle of the track. And as he rode so he thought daft thoughts, like: *I hope to God that old boy in Pighadia has these machines of his insured!* But mercifully it wasn't as bad as it looked; not at this stage, anyway. Not for all of two hundred yards distance and a hundred and fifty feet in height. But that was where the track doubled back on itself, and it was also where Mr Lorre had finally wised-up and ditched his machine.

There it lay, on its side under a clump of thyme, forsaken now that the race had entered its last and most deadly lap. And little wonder: Trace looked at the second section of track rising to a jagged horizon of cliff and sky. The way was steeper here, layered with dirt and scree from above, and something less than four scanty feet wide. Surely it would be madness to try and take a bike all the way up there, wouldn't it? The American had thought so. But there again, the American was still well in the lead.

Trace manhandled the bike round the bend, glanced down over the rim of the track as he did so . . . and told himself not to do that again. If ever there was a place designed to induce vertigo in a man, surely this must be it. And this, too, would also be the place where Trace found out just how well he really could ride.

He sat on the bike with one foot on the track, gritted his teeth and revved-up, gradually let out the clutch. The back wheel began to turn, kicked out dust and scree and smoke, and Trace said, 'Shit, shit, *shiiit!*' as he stood up again on the footrests, leaned sharply forward, went jetting his way up that final, fatal stretch. But not fatal for Charlie Trace, not this time. There were wild moments, certainly, but then at last it was over. And at the top . . .

. . . No time to sit down and rest and wait until he stopped trembling, for that would be to waste what little time and distance he'd gained. Instead he merely sat back in the saddle, sucked air deeply into lungs that seemed starved, looked all about.

He found himself on a wide flat ledge like a penultimate plateau. Two hundred yards in front the second stage of the cliffs rose up, higher still, to what looked like a flat summit. And half-way up those cliffs, toiling headlong up a narrow footpath, there was Mr Lorre with his long black bag still over his shoulder. Even as Trace spotted him, so the man looked back and down, looked directly at his pursuer. Trace couldn't see the man's eyes but he could feel them burning on him, their resentment, their hatred that he had put Mr Lorre to so much trouble. Oh, yes, for Trace had given Mr Lorre a real task, that much was obvious. But what *was* that task? And what was he carrying in that long black bag of his?

Trace jerked the bike into gear, went to move off and stalled. And in the immediate and startling silence which followed he heard from below and behind the clatter of falling rocks. He turned in his saddle, leaned toward the rim, craned his neck and looked down.

Below, just this side of the place where the track bent back on itself, another figure toiled upwards. Now who would this be?

Dressed in a black shirt and black, baggy breeches, the man looked young, unkempt, Greek. A goatherd? Some local character who'd spotted the crazy foreigners and wondered what was going on? Or a colleague of the thin American up ahead? Trace couldn't hazard a guess and he certainly wasn't waiting to find out! He kicked-started the bike into life, revved up, rode without further pause to where the second path or track rose narrow and crooked up the face of the cliff.

No hope of taking the bike any farther, for the route ahead was quite simply a goat-track with steps roughly hewn from the rock, some of them all of twelve inches and more deep. And already Trace's quarry was three-quarters of the way to the top. Trace unceremoniously ditched his machine, went on afoot. And where before he had driven the bike mercilessly, now he did likewise to himself, literally hurling himself into the final stage of the ascent.

No twinges now from his left leg and foot; indeed, they seemed full of a vitality all their own, as if to make up for Trace's previous concern. So that he scrambled up the narrow, dizzy way with all the strength and agility of a goat, recklessly ignoring the fact that death lay only the space of a misplaced foot away.

Mr Lorre was gone now, over the top, invisible; but down below the Greek youth was long-striding it across the half-way plateau, his hair flying behind him as he quite openly raced on Trace's heels. And the sight of him – the single downward glimpse that Trace allowed himself – was sufficient to propel him upward with even greater urgency.

Finally he reached the top, took in the scene at a glance:

The roof of the double-decked cliff was fairly flat. Seaward, one hundred and fifty yards away, a final tower of rock jutted up at the very rim, carved by time and the elements. And beyond that lone sentinel . . . Trace could just make out the edge of a now skeletal structure of what was, or had once been, a large man-made building of huge square blocks of stone. At the base of the natural spire of rock, out of sight of the ruins, there sat Mr Lorre on a flat boulder, frantically engaged in something or other.

Trace whipped up his binoculars, looked. The long black bag lay empty to one side; its previous contents were being assembled by Mr Lorre. Trace recognized the weapon at once: the rifle-like stock, slender, dull metal cross-piece and flighted bolt. He gasped and let the glasses fall. A crossbow!

Trace was winded, but still he forced himself to run, sucking at the air as he commenced lumbering forward. If he had had the wind he might have yelled, but he was sure anyway that the American would pay him no heed. He might be wrong: it could be, of course, that the crossbow was for him, but he doubted it. And in fact the thin man was now on the move again, ignoring Trace, hurrying round the base of the rocky tower and once more disappearing from view as he closed on the ancient monastery.

On flat, springy turf, Trace might have covered the distance between in something less than twenty seconds – that is if he were fresh and his legs weren't wobbly as columns of jelly – but here the way was strewn with rocks and boulders, and Trace, by his own terms, was very nearly knackered. Still it wasn't much more than half a minute before he, too, was cutting round the base of the tower. And it was then, as the ruins came into full view, that his headlong speed very nearly did for him. For between the massive rock pinnacle and the ruins proper –

– A chasm that went sheer down to the sea!

Trace reeled back from the rim, his back slamming against the worn-smooth rock, and stared wide-eyed around the tower's curve. Fifty feet away, a stout wooden

210

bridge with a handrail crossed the gap; and between Trace and the bridge . . . there kneeled Mr Lorre, right at the rim, even now bringing up his crossbow to sight it on the ruins. Trace looked across the gap, saw an opening or window in the lower wall, and a man where he sat working at a table, facing away from Trace and the man with the crossbow. And it was this unsuspecting man's back, clad in a shirt of faded yellow towelling, which was the American's target!

'No!' Trace howled at the top of his voice. *'No!'*

He hurled himself along the ledge between the tower of rock and the chasm, threw himself at the marksman where he kneeled. Mr Lorre glanced in Trace's direction, his thin face white with tension and murderous intent – and then Trace was on him. The crossbow went off even as Trace sent it flying from the other's hands. Its bolt sped across the chasm, clanged harmlessly against the ruin's wall. The two men clawed at each other for a moment, but the American was off balance. He drew back a fist to throw at Trace – and his eyes went wide, wider, bulged as he tilted over backwards.

Trace reached for him – too late. He caught a sleeve of the man's bright shirt – was left with it torn and dangling from his clenched, trembling fist. Trace looked over the rim. Mr Lorre was spinning like an autumn leaf. He made no protest, uttered no sound, simply flew, out of control, to where he struck a projecting rock before plunging out of sight two hundred or more feet below. And at last there came a splash, at once swallowed up in the lapping, grunting sounds of the ocean from some deep, unseen grotto.

And: 'God – oh, Jesus *Christ!*' gasped Trace out loud, horrified. 'I didn't mean to – I didn't *mean* to!' And in the back of his mind a small sarcastic voice cried: *and that's another fine mess you've gotten me into!*

211

'Ho!' came a voice from behind. Trace turned on all fours. It was the Greek youth, built like a bull, his fist a great threatening knot.

'I didn't mean that to happen!' Trace cried, his mouth agape and twisted. The Greek struck him once, right between the eyes, and Trace went out like . . .

Chapter Four

. . . A light!

But brighter than any light had any right to be.

Trace shuttered his eyes, turned them away from it, tried to sit up. He felt nauseous. Where the hell . . . ? *What* the hell . . . ? And then he remembered.

'Christ!' he struggled against a weight on his chest, realized he was stretched flat on his back, turned his face away from what could only be the sun. And now he could open his eyes.

The weight on his chest was the great paw of the Greek who'd hit him, who now sat staring at him with huge, soft brown eyes. Trace was lying on a stone table and the sun streamed in on to him from a large aperture he now recognized: the window in the ruin, into which the American had aimed his crossbow.

'Shit! I *killed* him!' Trace mumbled, his tongue thick and dry as an eraser. Again he tried to rise and this time the Greek let him sit up. Warm in the sunlight but not yet hot, Trace guessed he'd been out no more than a minute or two. His head ached abominably and the flesh of his forehead felt corrugated above his eyes, impressed with a crest of knuckles. He glared at the Greek, who in turn grinned back, then looked about the room.

A second young Greek, who could be the twin brother of the first, stood guarding a door of rough planking, his arms folded across his massive chest. He, too, was grinning. Trace looked at both of them again, carefully climbed down off the table using a stone bench as a step. The youth who was seated there steadied him until he was standing on the solid stone floor. Again Trace blinked, tried to get his eyes in tune with the cool gloom of the room now that he was out of the direct sunlight. And finally he saw the third occupant of this pile. The most important one.

It was the man in faded yellow towelling, which now Trace saw to be a knee-length robe, standing with his back to the room, his hands pensively behind him, staring out of a second window's deep embrasure across the Aegean's serene blue horizon. The man who had been Mr Lorre's target.

Mr Lorre, poor bastard . . .

'I . . . I killed him,' Trace mumbled again, uselessly. 'But I swear I didn't mean to.'

'Of course you didn't,' said the man at the window, turning to stare at him. 'I saw it all. You cried out to warn me, went to deflect his aim. He tried to strike you, overbalanced . . . if he were still alive, then in all likelihood I should now be dead.'

Trace looked across the room at him through the shaft of sunlight, through swirling dust-motes turned to gold in that magic beam of Mediterranean sun. His head was haloed in a softer light from the window. He looked like a saint standing there. So this was the one: the young/old man who lived in the monastery – *him and the thing he watches over* . . .

Trace moved round the table, approached him, closed with him more rapidly and grasped the front of his robe in both hands. The Greek youths were beside him in a moment, effortlessly unclenching his fingers from the robe, pinning his arms to his sides. They looked like, were strong as, idiots. Trace glanced from one to the other and back again. Their eyes were soft and their grins vacuous.

'They *are* idiots,' said the man in faded yellow, as if

214

reading Trace's mind. 'But idiots who love me. Idiots who obey my slightest whim, whose lives are mine, who would kill for me and never count the cost. If I wished it they would cheerfully toss you from this window. Right now – if I wished it.'

'Who are you?' Trace asked.

'More to the point,' said the other, 'Who are you?'

There was only one way Trace would ever get to the bottom of this. 'My name is Charles Trace,' he said. 'Dimitrios Kastrouni sent me.'

'*Dimitrios!*' The other's mouth gaped. He signalled to his men who immediately released Trace and stepped back. 'Dimitrios Kastrouni,' the man in faded yellow said again, nodding. He took hold of Trace's arm and drew him away from the window. And now for the first time Trace could look at him and see him clearly without straining his eyes.

He wasn't old, this man, despite his locks of flowing hair which almost exactly matched his robe, the wrinkles like gouges in his brown, leathery skin. No, for his eyes were young. They were grey-green and young and strange, and paradoxically there was that in them which was ancient. *Like a saint,* Trace thought again. They might have looked into heaven, those eyes, or into hell. And:

'Dimitrios Kastrouni,' he said again, a faint smile tugging the corners of his mouth. 'Oh, yes, he's a hard nut, that one. Too hard for Khumeni's rotten teeth, I think. How is he, Kastrouni?'

Trace looked away, gingerly fingered his forehead. 'You mean, how was he,' he said. And: 'I don't know about Khumeni's teeth, I only saw his hammer!'

Seemingly gnarled fingers gripped Trace's arm tighter, almost in a spasm, actually bruised him. 'Kastrouni?' Trace's host said in a disbelieving whisper. 'Dead?'

Abruptly he released Trace, swayed, staggered to the table and collapsed onto the stone bench. 'Not Dimitrios,' he moaned, shaking his head. 'Lord, let it be a lie!'

'I'm not lying,' Trace followed him. 'I saw it.'

The man in faded yellow looked up at him. 'How . . . ? I mean, what . . . ?'

'Lightning,' said Trace, watching the other's eyes. They flinched; the man's strong yellow teeth showed in a clenched double line as his lips drew back in a snarl of pain, horror; and he squeezed his eyes tightly shut.

'Lightning!' he repeated Trace, coughing the word out like bile. 'Hell-bolt! Demogorgon!'

'That's why I'm here,' Trace sat down beside him. 'Kastrouni told me a story. I didn't believe him. But some of the things he told me, however crazy, rang true. Then things started to happen. I saw Kastrouni killed. And I know now that it wasn't an accident. Lightning killed him, yes, but deliberately! How can that be? I have to know. But before that . . . I didn't give him a chance to tell me all he might have told me. Now I want to know – have to know. He mentioned you and this place, also a wine store in Pighadia. I came to Karpathos and spoke with a man in the town: a fat, jolly man who sold wine. Now he's dead, too. They slit his throat. The police have the wrong man for it. I know who did it: either the thin man who went over the cliff, or another still in Pighadia.' He paused for breath, finally continued:

'That's it, roughly. If you want further proof of what I've said just ask me details and I'll tell you all I know. And then you have to tell me things.'

The man in yellow unscrewed his eyes, looked up through a thin film of tears, seemed to see Trace for the first time. Then . . . it was as if he looked directly into Trace's soul, the way those eyes probed his. And Trace couldn't be at all sure that he approved of what he saw. But:

'Tell me everything,' the man commanded. 'Leave nothing out.' He turned to one of his men, said something in Greek. The youth nodded, went out of the room.

'Before I start,' said Trace, 'I asked you who you were . . .'

'My name is Saul Gokowski,' said the other. 'I don't suppose it will mean much to you. Nor should it. Now, if you don't mind . . . ?'

As Trace organized his thoughts the Greek returned with a huge plate of salad, a loaf of bread and a pitcher of thin wine. 'We can eat as we talk,' said Gokowski, breaking off some bread for himself.

Trace was grateful, the chase had taken a lot out of him. He washed dust from his throat, dipped a chunk of bread in the juices of tomatoes and cucumbers. And then he told Gokowski everything. He told it quickly, breathlessly, tried to omit nothing. He even told him that he, Trace, was a thief; told him about his mother and where she was now; told him about his twin, a freakish thing who was born dead. The one thing he failed to mention was his affaire with Amira Halbstein, for of course she wasn't part of the story.

It took maybe three-quarters of an hour, and then he was finished.

'This twin of yours,' said Gokowski after a moment's thought. 'What was he like?'

'My mother only saw him once, I think, before they took his body away. She said he looked awful. If she said anything else about him, then I've forgotten. Anyway, he was dead . . .'

'Who else knew about him?'

'The doctor who delivered us,' Trace shrugged. 'A nurse or two – how do I know? My mother went into confinement to have a child; when she left the hospital she had me. Why should anyone want to know more than that?'

'Did Kastrouni know?' the other pressed.

'No, he only wanted to know about – ' and Trace realized that he'd left something out of his story after all.

'About you?' said Gokowski urgently. 'Did he ask about marks, stigmata?'

Trace stared at the other, saw the way Gokowski was staring at *him*. 'I am not the son of the antichrist,' he blurted, shaking his head. 'I'm not!'

'But you do have a mark, right?'

Trace started to deny it, saw the other staring at him.

'Right?' said Gokowski again.

'It depends what you call a mark,' he said. And slowly, reluctantly he bared his left foot, showed it to the monastery's master.

Gokowski looked, gazed intently, finally drew air in a great gulp. Trace guessed from his expression that the reality was not so bad as the expectation. He, too, took a deep breath, said:

'Well?'

'That is a club foot,' said Gokowski. 'Not the usual deformity, no, but it is hardly rare in any shape or form. And in this case not even a real deformity. It is not disgusting; at least, it does not seem to trouble you too much.'

'No,' Trace lied, 'it doesn't.'

'Your mother was raped by a beast,' said Gokowski. 'By a monster, something that never should be but is! As God lives, so does the devil, and the hybrid horror which is his bastard on earth impregnated your mother. In this at least Kastrouni was correct. But he did not know about your twin, and for that matter we may assume that Khumeni is also ignorant of that fact. As for your foot:

218

the pregnancy was abnormal, your mother carried a Thing in her womb as well as a child. You are probably lucky it is not worse.'

'So what you're saying is . . . you don't think I'm Khumeni's son?' Trace saw that he was right; relief flooded over him, left him almost light-headed.

'No,' Gokowski shook his head. 'I do not think you are. If you were your evil would show. You say you are a professional thief – but the world is full of thieves! You, Khumeni's son? And would you seek me out and save my life if you were? Would you be interested in saving anyone's life?' Again he shook his head. 'I doubt it.' And at last he smiled. 'No, you are not the son of the antichrist, Charles Trace.'

'And yet my twin was? Is that possible?'

'He was not your twin, not genetically. It's not a frequent occurrence, but women have given simultaneous birth to disparate offspring, yes – and by "disparate" I mean the children of different fathers. You have said you always believed that your father was this Lt Solomon. And I think you are right.'

Trace sighed long and loud, leaned back where he sat and let his head loll backwards. Gazing up at the ancient, high-arching ceiling of stone, he said: 'Well thank goodness for that. And for God's sake, Saul, call me Charlie!'

Eventually Gokowski told his part of it. 'As to what I am – you'll know soon enough. But what I was: I *was* an archaeologist. So was my father before me. In the 30s we excavated at Berbati, Tell Agrab, Megiddo. I say "we", but in fact I was just a boy then. No, not even a boy, a child. Before you ask it, Charlie, I'm fifty-three years old. I look seventy, I know, but that's the way of it . . .

'Anyway, that was my young life, digging in deserts. I developed a love of it. But as the years went by . . . we were Polish Jews and my father smelled a European war brewing. My mother had left us not long after I was born and so we had no commitments that way; Israel was a concept, lacking cohesion, even though the British had been bruiting the idea about ever since World War One; we somehow managed to settle and stay in Palestine right through the war and all the other difficulties. Actually, it wasn't all that hard: Jews had been flooding in for years. From Russia, and now from Uncle Adolf.

'In '52 my father died. I wasn't yet twenty-two years old but I took over his work. He'd been doing a lot of research and translation work for several American institutions, for the French, even for the British Museum. He was an expert, you see? And where Middle-Eastern antiquities were concerned he was local. Ancient inscriptions, hieroglyphs, archaic Arabic, and anything Hebraic since time immemorial. Myself, I'd say he was a genius, who but for the problems of his time and his own personal aggressive attitude – he was both bull-necked and hard-headed – must certainly have gained recognition. Well, that wasn't to be.

'But the point I am making is this: he passed a lot of it on to me. Not only his love of ancient languages and civilizations but his understanding of them. He was a modern linguist, too, and I also got a smattering of that. I was raised a Jew, speaking the old language, but here I am speaking to you in English – do you see? And if you were a Pole or a Frenchman it would make little difference. This is not a matter of any great pride with me, it is merely a talent. However . . .

'In the year before he died, my father, Joseph Gokowski, was visited at his home in Zippori, a town west of Galilee and close to Nazareth, by a white-haired man who gave his name as Jonathan Ben Meiris, a Jew living somewhere in the Greek islands. Let me cut the story

220

short: Meiris was in fact Dimitrios Kastrouni: He brought to my father certain of the contents of Khumeni's saddle-bags, from his donkey, which animal Kastrouni had taken in error in Chorazin some thirteen years earlier.'

'You mean Guigos,' said Trace.

Gokowski smiled grimly at him across the table. 'So,' he said. 'While there are some things you are willing to believe, others defy your acceptance. That is perhaps understandable. Except you must remember, we are dealing with the darkest powers of evil here, with the supernatural, with the antichrist himself. As you point out, I *do* mean Guigos, yes. Also Khumeni, Ab, Goor the Hun, Tirox of Haleb, which is now Aleppi in Syria – and others. As for those "others", we can make educated guesses; those I have named are definite.'

'You're saying that he is in fact a phoenix, just as Kastrouni supposed?' said Trace.

'That is to be poetic. Kastrouni was Greek and of course had poetry in him. Khumeni may well be the *source* of certain phoenix legends, but he is not, in fact, "a phoenix". I repeat: he is the antichrist. But let me get on:

'I was busy with a colleague on some ruins on the western shore of Galilee when Kastrouni stayed with my father in Zippori. I only used to see the stranger at night, when I'd come in off the desert in my American jeep. He was intense but courteous, and he always avoided talking about his business with "Old Joe" – by which my father was fondly known to me. Anyway, he stayed a fortnight, left certain items behind, finally went back I supposed to his Greek islands. I never saw the things he left – not then, anyway – but my father had mentioned that there were books, certain shards, and a smattering of conjectural writings ancient and modern . . .

'But the upshot of his visit was this:

221

'Prior to my father's illness – a heart condition, gradually worsening – he, too, had been working various ruins on the shores of Galilee. We had sometimes worked together during the day; at night he would return to his studies and translations. Now, however, when by rights he should be resting, he took up again his wandering and excavating in the desert with renewed vigour – but on his own, utterly alone. I warned him that he would make himself ill; it made no jot of difference; he was grown as intense, even more so, than his recent visitor.

'Our work being what it was, we had friends in all the lands around. Even in the worst political and international storms – short of actual war, you understand – we could normally gain access to archaeological sites of interest across the local borders. And now, I noticed, my father had renewed certain Jordanian and Syrian contacts. You will appreciate that at that time these were delicate dealings indeed: there had been a war, and others were brewing; Syrian boundaries came right down to the western shore of Galilee; the Jordanian boundary was of course the Jordan south of the lake. Do you see what my father was thinking of, what he was preparing for?'

Trace nodded. 'He wanted to go and have a look at Chorazin, right?'

'Of course! And finally, with the cooperation of our military, that is exactly what he did. I will explain in a moment . . .

'As for myself:

'I was young, fit, my work was hardly important in the grand warlike scheme of things – I was "drafted" into the Army. And when I could arrange it, I was part of the "special operations and scouting parties" which gave escort to my father on his trips across or around Galilee to the northern shores. But would he ever let me go into Chorazin with him? Would he actually let me enter that

222

damned, doomed city of ruins? Never! No, the military must ring the town about, so that he could go and dig and do whatever he did there entirely alone.

'And in a year his work killed him. It happened like this:

'I was serving with a Defence Engineer unit down in Sederot east of the Gaza Strip. We were looking after the Beersheba – Qiryat Gat railway. Then I got news that my father was taken ill at home. I went to him and found him very sick indeed. He told me he was ready to die, that perhaps he was afraid of living! And over and over again before he died, as he rambled weakly about this and that, he would say to me: "He was right, Jonathan Ben – he was right!" And he would say: "Are you strong, son, are you strong?" I would answer, "Yes, I am very strong – what is it that I must do?" Then he would say: "Ah! If only *I* were young and strong again. Then I would do it – or try to do it, or assist in its doing – myself. But I'm old."'

Gokowski leaned forward and bowed his head over the table at this point, and Trace waited a moment before gently probing: 'Yes? What else?'

Gokowski looked up. 'Forgive me,' he said. 'I loved him very much.' He took a deep breath, continued:

'In my father's last moments he called me to him and whispered, "I've been down there, in the secret vault beneath Chorazin. Saul, the proof of it is there. The place *is* evil. Jesus knew it, perhaps He sensed it coming. And just as He was here, so now *he* is here! The antichrist walks amongst men. He has done so since the very hour when Jesus died in Golgotha!" And then he, too, died . . .'

Again Gokowski paused, and after a moment's silence:

'I served a second year and was then released to carry on my father's work. It was the end of 1953 before I could complete his outstanding backlog of translations, which I considered a debt of honour since he'd been paid in advance. After that – then I was a free man, free to do whatever I wanted to do.

'Meanwhile "Jonathan Ben Meiris", Dimitrios Kastrouni, had written to me from Athens commiserating and saying he would try to come and see me soon. But his letter also carried a warning: if I was carrying on my father's work, I would do well to leave alone any explorations or excavations in Chorazin. He had been mistaken to attempt to enlist my father's aid in a certain venture; he had not realized how unwell was the old man; he feared that he may well have given "Old Joe" bad counsel. He would say no more but simply begged that I trust and be guided by him; finally, he strongly advised that I avoid all manner of contact with anyone calling himself George Guigos.

'And within a six-month, what should happen but that a representative of that very creature came to see me! Except that I was not to know it, not then, for this hireling of his called him "Khumeni", a rich Armenian who dealt in purloined and smuggled archaeological antiquities. As openly as that? Not quite. No, he did not simply approach me and say: "My master, George Khumeni, wishes you to dig for him in a certain place and send a certain article you will find there to a certain address, payment for which work will be very generous", but in the space of less than one hour's conversation, that was indeed the gist of his message.

'And where was I to dig? Chorazin! And what was this thing I would find? It was one of two stone tablets graven with letters in a tongue defunct for thousands of years, the most ancient of all Hebraic languages.'

'I know of them!' said Trace, whose mind had been working overtime. 'I read about them in one of the books

224

Kastrouni gave to me. The book was Morgan Selby's *Journey's & Discoveries in the Holy Land*. Ab's witch fostermother inscribed them, one to concentrate the forces of evil and the other to exorcise them.'

Gokowski leaned over the table and gripped his arm. 'Do you still have this book?'

Trace looked glum. 'In England,' he said. For a moment Gokowski looked disappointed. Then:

'It makes no difference. I know of Selby's work – and of his blasphemies – and doubt if there's much that I don't already know. Anyway, you are correct. Now then, this Khumeni wished me to remove one of the Chorazin Tablets and dispatch it somewhere, then close up the place as before and never return there. Which tablet was he interested in, do you suppose?'

Trace thought about it for a second or so, said, 'The text under the ascending node – so that he could summon Satan's power, through Demogorgon, wherever he had the tablet!'

Gokowski shook his head. 'I can follow your reasoning but you are not in possession of all the facts. Ab was born – spawned, littered – in Galilee. 347 years later his first rebirth took place there, and likewise each successive rebirth or renewal ever since. He is *imbued* with the powers of Satan and Demogorgon and can call upon them anywhere, at any time – as you have surely witnessed! But the tablet with the ascending node is all-powerful, all-evil, and as such it is the very instrument of his resurrection!'

'He renews himself through the tablet,' said Trace, 'and the tablet must stay in Chorazin.'

'Indeed! Now think: why has Chorazin never been excavated or more than cursorily explored? If we could check backwards through two thousands of years, I believe we would find that Khumeni – let us continue to call him that – has kept close watch on the place,

225

obstructing all and any such exploration. Now especially, with modern war raging, and the threat of tanks in those high places over Galilee, and perhaps *crashing through* to certain caverns . . . it must have been a worrying time for Khumeni. Still, the tablet under the ascending node must stay there – but what of the other?'

'The tablet of exorcism?' Trace scratched his nose, shrugged. 'What of it?'

'Why, surely, if that should fall into the "wrong" hands what then? Could Khumeni really afford the chance exhumation of that sole, solitary means of his own defeat and destruction? Of course not. The vault had harboured it long enough. It must be taken out of there.'

Trace was puzzled. 'So why didn't he just go back there and get it?'

'Because he may not touch it! It is abhorrent to him! Anathema! Some other must bring it up and deal with it. Someone with access to the place. Very well, you might reason, then why did he not simply supervise the work? Why let some outsider in on the vault's secret? Oh? And how long do you think he intended I should survive *after* I had carried out his wishes?'

'But what would he have done with the tablet anyway?' Trace asked.

'Destroyed it, of course. Crushed it, removed it – and its threat – forever.'

'And you did,' said Trace, nodding. 'Not destroy it, no, but you did bring it up out of there. By which time you were studying the bits and pieces Kastrouni had left with your father, and beginning to piece it all together for yourself. You brought it up and you brought it here. You've appointed yourself its keeper; it is "the thing" you "watch over!"'

'Yes and no,' said Gokowski. 'You go too fast and assume too much. First of all, I was not like you a thief. I

226

was not a looter of tombs. No, I turned Khumeni's offer down. And after that, as you have said, gradually I began to understand something of what Kastrouni had passed on to my father. But as the next four years went by, so too my fortunes changed – drastically!

'First I took to drinking. I must have been, or certainly came close to being, an alcoholic. A woman of Jenin, a high-class whore, seemed to go out of her way to seduce me and keep me seduced. She literally robbed me, both of my senses and of my worldly goods. I was almost bereft by drink, besotted with this woman – bedevilled! Before, I had been a man of means; but by mid-1958 . . . it was as if a curse had descended on me. A black cloud of locusts of the spirit had settled on me, were devouring me. But then –

' – Again word from Kastrouni. A large, rambling letter of many thousands of words, in fact. And this time he told me everything. What's more, he'd been back to Cyprus by then and had met up with Guigos/Khumeni for the second time; and I, too, was told of what he believed he saw that night in the villa north of Larnaca! And what did he want me to do? Go down under Chorazin, set charges, blow the place back to hell!

'Since those events in Cyprus he'd been busy. Khumeni might be stalking him, but so too was he stalking Khumeni. Certainly he had it in for him! He was determined, one way or the other, that the creature must be destroyed. Ah! But just like you, at first I thought Kastrouni must be raving. And anyway, what did I care for him and his crazy fancies? I was still under this cloud; my money was all used up; I was sinking fast. At which time – back came Khumeni's man, and this time his offer was even better than before. My remuneration would be great; all my lost wealth would be restored; I could start life afresh.

'Now then, before I say more, perhaps you are still

wondering why Khumeni did not do his own spadework, as it were? I think I can explain:

'On his last trip to Chorazin as Guigos in 1936, Khumeni had had big problems. Kastrouni was the cause of most of them, first of all when he failed to make himself – available? – and again when he got back to Haifa and worked once more, for a little while, for the then British administration. For then he had actually reported Guigos, had made a statement that he had seen Guigos kill two men – Khumnas and Mhireni – "somewhere" in the desert. He didn't mention Chorazin because that was a place he'd already promised himself he *never* would go back to! But with the accusation of a double murder hanging over him, Guigos – or Khumeni, as he was to become – was now obliged to smuggle himself out of Palestine! When the administration was taken over by the new State of Israel under David Ben Gurion in 1948, so were all the records. And now ten years later they were still extant. Guigos/Khumeni was still wanted for questioning.

'Anyway, for whatever reason, he would not go back himself, not then. But don't believe for a moment that he didn't try other alternatives besides me. There were raiding parties galore sneaking in over the Golan Heights in those days – and who to say that they were all terrorists, eh?

'But once again, let me cut it short for you. As I've explained, I was desperate. I accepted Khumeni's money in advance, used what little authority I had left to go to Chorazin, eventually found that terrible subterranean place and removed the tablet with the descending node. None of this was easy, but somehow I did it. I sealed the place up again, took the tablet home with me overnight in my jeep, did everything as I had been instructed. Yes, and in the morning I would take the stone to a certain house in Haifa, and that would be the end of that. Except –

' – I had read what was written on the stone. And indeed it *was* an exorcism. In the most terrible words you can imagine, in a tongue so ancient that even I had difficulty with the translation, the pronunciation, that stone was the world's ultimate solution to every evil thing! And not only that, it was the catalyst which finally purged me . . .

'Charlie, I do not know if you are a believer. I cannot say if *I* was a believer – until that night. Anyway, I dreamed. And I was . . . visited! I saw . . . something! It was beautiful and it was awesome. It was gentle and it was powerful. It asked me if I had no fear for my soul, and I said I had. It asked me if I desired to be damned above all other men, that my name should rank only with that of Judas. And I said that I did not so desire it. And then it said to me, "When this man's servant returns to you and asks why you have not done his bidding, ask him what is his master's secret name. And when he asks of what you speak, *tell* him his master's secret name. And tell him also that his master's name is Legion!'

Trace nodded. 'I see. So in the morning you didn't go to Haifa with the stone after all.'

Gokowski looked surprised. 'You believe me? About my dream?'

Trace held up his arms helplessly. 'I just can't see you lying, that's all! What difference does it make? You *didn't* do as you were instructed to do, and that's what matters. So what came next?'

'Four days went by,' Gokowski continued, 'and then Khumeni's man returned, demanding the tablet. I asked him about Khumeni, asked him to tell me his master's real name. He looked angry, even frightened, said he didn't know what I was talking about. I told him his master was once called Guigos and he went pale. Then I said: "He's had many names – indeed they are legion." At which I thought he would faint.

'He left at once and without the tablet; I waited for a little while and then I, too, left. I had already made arrangements for the sale of my house, settled my affairs, contacted friends in the USA. All of which I'd accomplished in the four days since my dream. That is the extent to which it had impressed me! And so I went to America to start life afresh. Alas –

' – America wasn't safe. Khumeni was well established there and had both political and Mafia links – which in America are not always especially disparate! I discovered this very quickly, literally had to leave almost everything and get out fast. But where to?

'Well, my father and I had earlier done some work for the Rhodian Antiquarian Research Society whose headquarters is in Rhodes, and a number of the Greek friends I had made then were now in positions of some power – that is to say, politically well-placed – in the Dodecanese group. By routes deliberately mazy and tortuous, finally I came to Karpathos. The monastery required a great deal of work to raise it even to these spartan standards; but it did have the benefit of being remote and, as you have discovered for yourself, very nearly inaccessible. I bought it for a song, hired a man – the father of these backward boys of mine, now dead, God bless him – and now . . . now I believe we're up to date. I have been here for twenty-two years, but it is only in the last ten that Khumeni has discovered my whereabouts.'

Trace considered all he had heard, finally said, 'I'm sorry if this sounds a bit blunt, but frankly it surprises me that you're still alive! He almost got to you in America, you say – and today you again came within an ace – and so . . . ? I mean, how *are* you still alive? If we really are talking about the antichrist, where's all this monstrous power of his?'

'When first he traced me here,' Gokowski answered, 'he did indeed send an assassin. Then, too, I was lucky. My man found him first. Whoever he was, he left this world via the same route as the thin American. I feel no remorse: anyone in league with Khumeni dices with death, and worse, as a natural consequence. Anyway, an attempt had been made on my life; I knew now for a certainty that Khumeni had neither forgotten nor forgiven me; it was time to put into effect an early-conceived plan of mine.

'Khumeni's aim, of course, remained the same: to destroy the tablet of dissolution. I wrote to him, and – ' He paused as Trace gave a snort.

'You did what?'

Gokowski raised his yellow eyebrows. 'Why not? I was in regular contact now with Kastrouni; both of us were aware of Khumeni's American businesses, his various addresses; our intelligence in regards his doings had greatly increased over the years. So, as I say, I wrote to him. I pointed out that it would avail him not at all to kill me, indeed that it would cost him dearly. He, like yourself, mistakenly believed that I had the tablet here with me. I told him he erred, that in fact the stone was buried deep in a secret place, and that my executors – several of them, in various parts of the world – were fully instructed as to their reaction in the event of my death accidental or otherwise. Letters would at once be dispatched to all the world's religious leaders, detailing the nature and the whereabouts of the stone, and more specifically Khumeni's interest in it. Similarly, the location of the Chorazin vault would be declared; the area would soon be aswarm with all manner of men and digs; access to the place, for any projected use of it by Khumeni, would be quite impossible.'

'Stalemate!' said Trace.

'Exactly. He used that very word in his next and last communication. But he also warned that in the event of any pre-emptive action on my part in this respect, then that my death would follow close at heel, when of course he would have nothing to lose by it.'

And now Gokowski leaned back in his seat. 'There you have it. Doubtless you'll have some questions. Ask away . . .'

Trace was looking worried now. He sighed, shook his head as if to clear it, said: 'A moment ago it was all beginning to ring true. Now? Suddenly nothing rings true. I don't know enough, can't put what I do know together. Things seem about to crystallize, then go back to being fuzzy. I think I've tried to take in too much too fast.'

Gokowski shrugged. 'That is why I suggest you ask what questions you will, see if I can throw a little light on the shadowy areas.'

Trace nodded, sat up straighter. 'Very well, First off, what did Khumeni want?'

'Ultimately? The utter destruction of mankind. He wishes to reduce civilization to ashes, then for us to start again in ignorance and bestiality, in the worship of his father, Satan.'

'But he's only one person, one creature!'

'So is President Reagan. So is the leader of the USSR. So is Mrs Thatcher, Colonel Gadafi, the Pope, the Ayatollah. So was Jesus.'

'How will he set about it?'

'He *has* set about it! Wars rage world-wide. They have waged throughout. It is easy to forget in the civilized or peaceful half of this world what is constantly happening in the other half. But it is true, Charlie: half of this world of ours is constantly at war! And this is an atomic age. Did you know that in America Khumeni controls certain nuclear interests? Well, *now* you know! He is "big" in many countries. Not here in the Greek islands. Not so much in England, where money still cannot buy everything, though that day, too, is coming. Not in Australia, which remains largely innocent. But elsewhere he *is* big. He is not heard of in Russia, but there they brew their own poisons, which keeps him content. He is in Japan, in Germany, in South Africa and Spain. He is enormous in France . . .'

Trace was beginning to feel very small. 'Who works against him?'

'I do. Kastrouni – did. You do, I hope. I have "a friend" still in Israel, who keeps a low profile, watches and waits. And there are others. Not many. We have tried to recruit, but – ' He shrugged.

'But?'

'Well try it for yourself! Go back to London, rush out on the streets and yell: "The antichrist is here! You are all doomed, *doomed* unless you listen to me!" And what do you suppose would happen?'

'Nothing,' Trace nodded. 'I've seen them in Speaker's Corner. The old "End is Nigh" gang. No one listens.'

'That is correct,' Gokowski agreed. 'It is not so much that people are without faith – rather that they no longer fear. The supernatural isn't real, Charlie. And what is not real cannot hurt. Ask anyone . . .'

Trace was silent, thoughtful for a long moment. Then:

'This friend of yours in Israel. Would that be the same colleague who was working with you on the west shore of Galilee when Kastrouni came to see your father in Zippori?'

'Why, yes. Why do you ask?'

'Just something that's on my mind. Can you tell me his name?'

'Would that be wise? And is it important?'

'Then let me tell you his name,' said Trace. 'It's Halbstein, isn't it?' He saw from the other's face that he was correct.

'How do you know this?' Gokowski wanted to know.

Trace shrugged, lied: 'Oh, I think Kastrouni must have mentioned it, that's all. It's not really important.'

Then he, too, sat back. He felt like someone had just buried an axe in his chest – possibly in Gokowski's chest, too – but he tried not to show it . . .

Part IV

Chapter One

Perhaps Gokowski suspected something, perhaps not. But from that moment forward as they talked it seemed to Trace that Gokowski's attitude was that much more down to earth, as if suddenly it had dawned on him that his visitor was not quite so naïve or ignorant as he had thought. In any case, when later Trace had left the monastery, his parting words to its sear, yellow-robed master were these:

'Saul, don't put too much faith in England being a country free of Khumeni's taint. There's plenty of the devil in England, believe me. And for that matter even Israel may not be entirely secure. In a war such as the one you are waging, the very closest of friends could be suspect – '

That had been in the late afternoon, when the shadows had been growing toward evening. Then, wanting to get his machine back down to the foot of the cliffs before darkness set in, Trace had taken Gokowski's men with him to manhandle the small motor-cycle between them. At the bottom he'd thanked them both and they had gone back up the path for the second machine. What they intended to do with that Trace couldn't say. He supposed that eventually it would be returned to the workshop in Pighadia.

And as he sped back toward the island's principal town in the fast-falling twilight – and back toward the girl he had almost fallen in love with, whom now he must consider an enemy – he mentally reviewed all that had passed between himself and Gokowski during the second half of their conversation. It had been mainly questions and answers, with Trace asking the questions:

'Where did you bury the tablet? Somewhere in Israel?'

'Oh, yes – but nowhere that Khumeni is ever likely to find it! Indeed, it's best that only I know where – for now. But I will tell you this much: my house in Zippori was purchased by a "business consortium" in Haifa – since when it has undergone extensive rebuilding. Also, I am informed that its gardens were completely excavated before landscaping . . .'

And: 'But how can the tablet do anyone any good buried?'

'The actual *stone* is buried. Only the stone. And don't think for a moment that it's power stops there. No, for of course I copied its legend. Come with me and I'll show you.'

Trace had been guided through the shell of the old building – through rooms which had no ceilings or roofs, and others which had been completely rebuilt – and finally down into cellars whose foundations were the solid rock itself. There, where the windows were cut from a cliff face and looked out over the Mediterranean, at last he was shown the room which served Gokowski as workroom, study and library. And it was at once apparent that his work for the last twenty years had been identical to that of Dimitrios Kastrouni.

For here were theological works from every religion on earth, back to back with pamphlets, books and treatises on every aspect of demonology and devil-worship. Here was Christ, Son of God, His life and works and very *meaning* delineated on paper and parchment, both in cyphers known to Trace and in others utterly beyond his ken; and here Satan similarly encapsulated, encoded. On the one hand day, and on the other night. Light side by side with darkness.

Gokowski had explained.

'To understand one, you must know the other. God is the cleverer of the two, but His adversary is the wilier. Did you think the Orientals were clever at copying, Charlie? Then who can say – perhaps they are closer to Satan than we suspect? For certainly he is a master not only of duplicity but also of duplication. Let me explain:

'God gave the world Jesus. Satan gave us Ab. The Lord gave us His ten commandments, and the devil gave us the first Chorazin tablet. Ah! – but when Ab's witch-mother inscribed the first stone, some external or higher power – the power of God, of His will? – guided her also to inscribe the second. God gave His son supernatural skill, to call upon angels for their strength and counsel. And the devil gave Ab power to call up demons, chiefly Satan's seedbearer, Demogorgon. Moses used plagues to blight Egypt and escape from the wiles of Pharaoh, and Ab and all the others since Ab have used those same plagues in the propitiation or spell-casting of their reincarnations.'

As he had said all of this, Gokowski's tone had gradually grown more doleful and his eyes had settled on Trace almost speculatively. Trace had felt his skin prickling, had sensed a hidden meaning. 'What are you trying to tell me?'

Gokowski had looked away for a moment, saying: 'There is a question you haven't asked me. Oh, there are several I might have expected, but one in particular which you hold back. Possibly because you are afraid of the answer.'

'My part in all this? Is that what you mean? You're right, I do fear the answer – but that's not why I haven't asked it. The reason for that is simple: namely that I don't intend to *have* a part in all this! I know Khumeni

239

doesn't want me dead, because I'm still alive. Therefore I'll simply stay alive and continue to defy him.'

At that Gokowski's eyes had hooded over but he had remained silent, waiting. Trace had felt himself being squeezed into a corner, had felt his anger rising. By saying nothing at all Gokowski had told him that it wasn't that easy, that like it or not he did have a part to play. Which meant of course that he had to know what it was – now more than ever.

'Go on, then,' he had finally grated, 'tell me. What does all of this have to do with me? What part can I possibly play in the devil's plan for the destruction of mankind?'

'Maybe a bigger part than you think, Charlie.' Gokowski had gone to stand beside an ancient bureau of blackened wood, unlocking one of its drawers. He had taken out a single sheet of paper covered with lines of glyphic characters. Then he'd passed it to his guest, studying Trace's face as he glanced at it then peered more closely. The paper was only paper, but it felt slimy, unpleasant to Trace's fingers. He had let it fall to the bureau's top, saying:

'Is that it? That's your transcription from the second tablet? I can't even read it, let alone understand it!' He curled his lip – in distaste? – and continued: 'Anyway, it hardly explains my alleged part in all this.'

But by then Gokowski had also taken out an ugly, squat-bodied machine-pistol from the bureau, which he had cocked in a sharp action before pointing it directly at Trace's chest. 'Pick it up,' he'd quietly ordered then. 'The paper – *pick it up!*'

'What the hell – ?'

'Yes, what the hell,' Gokowski had nodded as Trace once more took up the sheet of paper with the glyphs. But this time he had been more concerned with Gokowski's weapon than the queasy feel of the paper. 'Look at it,' said Gokowski, 'and listen – '

Then he had commenced speaking in a harsh and guttural Arabic tongue, whose sounds were so alien that it seemed hardly likely a man's throat could form them. That on the one hand, and yet on the other Trace felt each foreign word of it sear itself on the surface of his mind. It wasn't painful, rather the deceptive tickle of the dentist's pliers drawing a tooth from a thoroughly deadened jaw.

And moments after Gokowski had finished, still the two men had stood there, sweat rivering their faces. And finally: 'It's hot in here,' Trace had said, wiping his brow. And again, carefully, he had put the sheet of paper down on the bureau.

Gokowski had seemed puzzled, but the gun did not waver in his hands. He narrowed his eyes. 'Perhaps I should ensure here and now,' he'd whispered then, 'that you cannot play your part. For after all, there's a slim chance even now that you are . . .

'. . . But you are not, no.' And to Trace's great relief Gokowski had made his weapon safe, returned it to the bureau.

'Man, you're crazy!' Trace had mumbled then, trembling like a jelly where he had backed up against the stone wall. 'If your hand had slipped on that trigger . . .'

'If I had killed you,' Gokowski had answered, himself trembling, 'it would have been no slip, Charlie Trace. But no, we are agreed, you are innocent. Or let us say that you are not tainted. And so, since I must let you live – because I cannot in all conscience kill you – I'll try to answer your question and tell you where you stand in all of this.

'You have seen how Satan imitates Good to initiate Evil. Very well, then tell me this: how well do you know your Bible?' He waved Trace to a bench where it looked out of the window across the sea far below, sat down close to him.

'As well as most, I suppose,' Trace had answered..'Oh, I can't quote it chapter and verse, but I know the stories.'

'And do you know the one about Abraham and Isaac in Genesis 22?'

'The sacrifice? When Abraham would have given up his son as a burnt offering, in place of a lamb? I know it, yes. At the last moment God stepped in and stopped it. What has that to do with me?'

'Nothing, except perhaps that there would seem to be certain parallels.'

'I don't understand.'

'Each time Ab – or let us say Satan's son, the antichrist – regenerates, three men are "sacrificed", absorbed into him, to fuel him through the years until his next loathsome rebirth. There should have been three in 1936, but Kastrouni escaped it and Guigos took a donkey instead. Unlike Abraham, however, Guigos's · hand was not stayed. It never has been. The evil alternative leaves no room for mercy. The devil enjoys death. So does his emissary, Demogorgon. And so, of course, does the antichrist. That is to say, Khumeni, as he is now. In short, there's to be a "sacrifice", Charlie. Khumeni has three illegitimate sons. At his next and last re-incarnation in this cycle, he intends to absorb all three – just as Kastrouni saw Yakob Mhireni absorbed in 1936!'

At that Trace's mouth had fallen open. 'And he thinks I'm one of them?'

'I would say he's sure of it. And if *I* were that sure – that is to say, if I didn't have evidence to the contrary – you *would* be dead, Charlie. And better dead, believe me! But you have convinced me that he is not your

242

father, and so I see you as an ally. Just how you can be used is difficult to see at this stage, but – '

'Used?' Trace had broken in. 'I don't intend to be used. I'll go after Khumeni in my own way, not in any way you might dream up. Antichrist or not, I now believe that he's the reason my mother is a madwoman. Also, I know he's murdered two men, and that one of them literally gave up his life in order to bring me a warning. What's more, I believe that he's corrupted someone I . . . someone I liked a great deal. So just like you and Kastrouni before me, now I too want him dead.'

'And just how do you propose to kill him?'

'I don't know. I suppose I'd first have to find him, or let him find me. In fact I'm pretty sure he's already found me.'

Gokowski had nodded. 'A reasonable assumption.'

'Yes, but listen to me anyway. You see, Saul, I'm my own man. I'm not yours, and I'm certainly not his. I thank you for your hospitality and for all you've told me, but from now on I'm on my own. That's the way I like it. It's how I work best. Questions? Oh, I've got a lot more questions. But I think I'll ask them of someone else.'

At that Gokowski had stood up, shrugged, reached out to take and shake Trace's hand unstintingly. 'You're a brave young man, Charlie. You've saved my life, and for that you have my thanks. As for the rest, I can only wish you luck.'

Trace might have left it at that but one last thing continued to bother him. 'You said that Khumeni's next reincarnation would be the last of the cycle. What did you mean? It's the only question I have left, for you anyway, and I think it's important.'

'You may believe me that it is,' Gokowski had told him, leading the way back up through the cellars to the upper levels. 'You mentioned a list of dates in Kastrouni's notebook,' he continued, negotiating the ancient passage-ways with an old familiarity. 'They started with "347 A.D. less 20," ended with the date 1936. Is that right?'

Trace clearly remembered the list. He pictured it in his mind's eye:

347 A.D.	– less	20
327	– ..	25
302	– ..	30
272	– ..	35
237	– ..	40
197	– ..	45
152	– ..	50
102	– ..	55

1936

'That's right,' he said. 'What of it?'

'You didn't understand it?'

'Frankly, no.'

'Ab lived for 347 years, but in his second life he was given *twenty years less!* That is to say, he lived 327 years. In his third life –

But at last Trace had seen it. ' – In his third life he lived only 302 years! He was losing five more years each time!'

'Correct. As he ate up the centuries, so they also consumed him, and so his regenerations had to come faster and faster on a steadily accelerating scale. He came again in 1248 as Bodang the Mongol, and this time he lasted only 237 years.'

'So that by the time he reached his eighth rebirth he had only 102 years to come – which took him to 1936!' Trace had got the idea.

'Right again,' Gokowski had nodded. And how long, then, his current span?'

'Less fifty-five,' Trace had whispered then. 'Only forty-seven years. Which means that – '

'It means that this is the year of his next regeneration. 1983, Charlie. When exactly we can't say. Only Khumeni himself knows that. But this is certainly the year. And this will end the cycle. This time he absorbs *flesh of his own flesh!* – which is to say, he sacrifices his own sons – to the will of Satan for his own continuation. And so it starts again. Another Ab, another antichrist, another 347 years of terror. Except . . .'

'Yes?'

'Except it will not last that long. Not this time. An atomic age, Charlie. And Satan the great mimic, eh?'

And as Trace had left the monastery and crossed the bridge with Gokowski's men behind him, so the master of that crumbling pile had commenced to quote a passage he knew intimately – a passage from the Holy Bible. Even skirting the massive rock pinnacle, where soon the monastery itself was lost from view, still Trace had been able to hear Gokowski's voice rising on the still air:

'The heavens shall pass away with a great noise, and *the elements shall melt* with fervent heat, *the earth also* and the works that are therein shall be burned up!'

After which there had been only an echo, quickly dying . . .

'Charlie!'

Amira's husky-honeyed voice was full of concern, astonishment – outrage? It contained, at any rate, a bag of mixed emotions. She was dressed casually in a frilly green blouse which allowed her elastic breasts freedom and a natural buoyancy, and in bottle-green slacks which fitted snugly and emphasized the slenderness of her waist, the sleek lines of her behind. Her feet were bare, agitated on the black and white cobbles of the Villa Ulysses's courtyard.

She stood at the door, having opened it a few inches in answer to his hammering, her almond eyes wide and unblinking.

'Aren't you going to invite me in?' Trace said, his own voice rough-edged. He gave the door a none too gentle shove and brushed past her, pausing just inside. The courtyard's subdued lights were on; Trace found the switch and turned them up full; shadows drew back as he glanced all about the place before striding toward the open door to Amira's rooms. She was after him in a flash, her feet pattering on the cobbles as she hurried to draw level. And now her voice really was outraged:

'Charlie, what the hell do you mean by this? How *dare* you! You . . . you go off for a few hours in the morning to collect your things, come back at night after I've spent most of the day worrying about you, rush in without so much as a – '

'Worrying about me?' Trace snarled over his shoulder. 'Save all that shit for your next victim!' He went inside, checked quickly through the rooms, started toward the wooden, open-plan stairs, and:

'Charlie!' this time she spoke in a furious hiss; she laid a hand taut as a claw on his arm where he stood with one foot on the bottom tread, his hand on the stair rail; he froze still as a statue, glared for a moment at her hand on his arm. Then he turned, his face a mask of fury, white with rage. He went to strike her, checked himself at the last moment, gave her a shove.

Her anger turning to shock, Amira reeled off-balance across the room, came up against the recessed platform with its piled cushions, fell backwards into them with Trace stalking after her. He stood over her where she sprawled, reached down, bunched up the front of her

246

blouse in his fist and tore it free of her body. The blouse came away like, felt substantial as, so much tissue paper in his hand. He tossed it down, stared at her, deliberately studied her breasts where her vulnerability exposed them to their best.

Then he stepped back a pace and quickly stripped.

She saw what he intended and the shock already written on her face turned to incredulity. She started to sit up but he pinned her head against a cushion, his hand rough on her throat. Then he tugged at her green slacks. 'Get them off,' he grunted, and for all his anger, still his voice had thickened with lust. 'Now – or they go the same way as the blouse.'

Struggling to obey him, lifting her buttocks to work the material of her slacks down her thighs, she tried to laugh and almost made it. 'Is this a game?' she panted directly into his face. 'Is this the way you really like to do it, Charlie? You get your jollies pretending you're right? And by dreaming up crazy fantasies about blood and murder and satanists? Is that it? You like to think you have the devil in you? It makes you feel big and brutally strong, and – '

'Your skinny American chum is dead!' Trace cut her off, yanked her slacks the last six inches and off her feet. Her hands were free but she made no attempt to cover herself. Instead a hand flew to her mouth, but she stopped the movement before its conclusion. She wasn't as quick with her expression, though. Her half-sneer disappeared into the great O of her gasp. And still Trace stared at her, at all of her now.

In the soft light of the room and the blue light of stars falling through a high window, her skin gave the illusion of being silvery pale; and now her face grew paler still, grew into a white mask. 'What did you say?' she whispered.

Trace tried to analyze her expression and failed. Surprise? Relief? Gladness? All of these things one on top of the other? It didn't make sense, wasn't what he'd expected. But what had he expected? Maybe the message hadn't sunk in yet.

'He's dead,' he repeated. 'Right off a cliff at the monastery – splash, *squish!* I pushed him.'

She licked her lips and her eyes were wild now, darting all about the room. 'My American chum? I don't know any Americans, Charlie. I – '

'Liar!' he growled. He climbed up on to the pillows between her legs, made as if to enter her. 'You and Laurel and Hardy, you all came out here together. And you were the sweet bait for the big fish – me!'

Her face was all terror now; terror stared out of her eyes at him. Trace had to admire her acting. 'You . . . you really are crazy, aren't you?' she whispered. 'Last night you made love to me, and now you want to rape me!'

'Rape? Well, why not? He raped my mother, didn't he? Your boss? Khumeni? That's why he thinks I'm his son, right? Because he didn't know about my beast brother, who *was* his son! Rape? You object to that? Or maybe it's just that you'd like it better his way? The way of the beast? Is that how he gives it to you? OK, so let's try it – and afterwards you can tell me which of us you prefer, me or the fucking donkey you work for!'

He grabbed her hair, tried to turn her face down. But suddenly she came back to life. The back of her slim hand was hard as a whip as it cut across his face and knocked him flying. It wasn't the weight of the blow, rather its bite, its sheer unexpectedness; and also the fact that Trace was badly positioned, kneeling on the edge of the platform. In any case he flew backwards, arms flailing, went sprawling on his back on the floor.

248

For a second he lay there, fingering his face, his muscles and nerves jumping. Then he sucked at the air, sighed, lay his head back on the boards of the floor. He rolled his eyes down until they stared at her, and:

'You,' he said, his voice dripping poison. 'You and your father: traitors, both of you. And him out there right now, in Israel, digging for Khumeni, looking for the second tablet while you . . . while you use your beautiful whore's body to trap me. And then there's that poor bastard Saul Gokowski, who thinks your father is his "friend"!'

Amira sat up, reached out her arms toward him. And again he couldn't understand the look on her face. 'Oh, Charlie – Charlie, you're so – ' Her eyes widened, lifted from him, looked beyond him. The wooden stairs creaked. 'You're so – *right!*' she finished it.

A tiny foot came down on Trace's lank hair, pinning his head to the floor. Small, that foot, yes – but it weighed a ton. Trace grabbed the ankle, started to swing his legs up and over to kick at the . . . but brought them to a halt in mid-air and let them fall back, unresisting. Mr Hardy was more agile than he looked. He had kneeled, grasped Trace's left ear in pudgy fingers, now held something shiny and cold to his taut throat.

'*Bastard!*' Trace whispered.

'Oh, yes, I really am,' the fat man wheezed. 'But you've seen what I can do, so please don't force me to demonstrate.'

Trace might have shook his head but didn't dare. 'Your freaky boss wouldn't like it if I got hurt,' he said, merely breathing the words, exhaling them.

'Only if it wasn't necessary,' said the fat man, his upside-down face smiling. 'Amira?'

She came off the platform and struggled into her clothes, then stepped out of view. A moment later she was back – with a hypodermic syringe! She tested it and a spray of pearly droplets few from its needle. Then she kneeled beside him and said: 'Hold very, very still, Charlie.'

He didn't have much choice, hardly dared grunt as the needle slid into his arm. He felt it, though – felt its sting, and the cold, cold waves of numbness spreading outward from its point of entry. But after that – after that he didn't feel anything at all . . .

. . . Trace was sitting up.

He sat upright in a high-backed chair staring out of a small window into the Villa Ulysses's courtyard. It was a cane chair and he could feel the lattice of its woven seat against his backside, the ribs of its uprights against his back. He leaned fractionally backward, or was propped in that position, with his head tilted slightly forward and his arms hanging loosely down outside the chair's arms. He wore a dressing-gown that smelled of stale urine.

Trace's eyes were open but he couldn't remember when he'd opened them. Apart from the needle – the hypodermic needle in Amira's treacherous hands, which had put him to sleep – he remembered very little. His 'sleep' or period of unconsciousness had been deep and dreamless, and probably of some duration: his face felt itchy, an old symptom of two or more days' growth of stubble. He *could* feel, hear, smell and probably taste. As for touch: hardly that, for he couldn't move, but he could feel things touching him.

Oh, his perceptions were there, all right, but they certainly weren't working overtime; in fact they felt mysteriously slowed down, dulled, weird and wasted. Only his sight seemed to be anything like normal. He wondered if that were possible: four of his five senses, atrophied. No, of course not, it was only the effect of the drug. But even his thoughts seemed to come slowly.

A fly, landing on his nose, caused him to blink. But the fly's touchdown came moments *before* Trace felt it, and the blink – a very slow thing – came long moments after. In any case, the blink sufficed to scare the fly off: obviously Greek flies didn't have the tenacity of their British cousins . . .

Since Trace wasn't sure what day it was, he gave his attention to the time of day. That wasn't hard: the shadows fell almost vertically out in the courtyard, which meant it must be just about midday. If his captors had put him out there in the sun, under those almost tangibly 'heavy' rays, they would have burned right through to his brain by now. 'Fell asleep in the sun and died.' Easy.

Except they didn't want him dead. Khumeni didn't want him dead. He wanted him . . . absorbed?

Trace's every instinct yelled, 'Get up, run, fly – *fight*, you idle bastard!' But his flesh gave only a slow twitch; several nerves jerked sluggishly in his legs, his arms; and the lattice of the chair's weave continued to impress his backside as before. So: 'Forget it,' he told himself. 'You're not going anywhere, Charlie.'

The courtyard door opened and Amira came through it. 'Bitch!' thought Trace. 'Lorelei . . . lamia . . . Mata Hari . . . Circe . . . no, *Gorgon!* Gorgon, yes – you've turned me to stone!'

She was alone, came hurrying across the courtyard under the vines, looked nervous, frustrated, shiny with sweat. She was a woman in a hurry, with no time to spare. And half-way across the courtyard her eyes focused upon his own, saw that they were open, awake. At that she broke into a run, literally flew the rest of the way to the door to her apartment. Then she was beside him, kneeling in front of him, her almond eyes wide where they gazed into his.

Her concern was 'obvious', 'real', – as real as the concern she'd shown when she stuck the needle in him and did this to him. But wasn't this carrying her acting a bit far?

Bitch! Trace said with his eyes. He tried to say it with his tongue, too, but what little movement he achieved only served to release into his mouth a previously trapped pocket of some vile goo that tasted like bile. She read his mind anyway, whispered:

'Charlie, you're so wrong! Oh, I'm supposed to work for Khumeni, yes, but in fact I'm working against him. My father, too. We know what he *is*, Charlie, so how could we work for him? If you don't believe me – well, that's your business. At this stage of the game it doesn't really matter what you believe. Except to me. But at least you'll hear me out . . .' She paused and bit her lip.

'Except . . . I'm not sure how much of this is getting through to you? And I don't know how much time we have.' She turned her head, cast anxious eyes across the distance to the door at the bottom of the courtyard. 'Decker will be back soon. He's the fat one. He's arranging the details of our flight out of here.' *That'll be a neat trick,* Trace thought. *And how do I go? In a trunk in the cargo hold?*

As if reading his mind a second time, she said: 'You're going as Klein, the man who died at the monastery. Actually, you're not all that dissimilar. His clothes should just about fit you, and we have his passport. And of course, Decker and Klein already had their visas for Israel. For me it's no problem – naturally I've retained my nationality. As for your condition, the story will be this:

'You take these fits, go into a sort of semi-catatonic

252

state. There's a clinic which treats just such ailments in Galilee, and you're already booked in there. But this current attack is six months premature and caught you out on holiday. Anyway, it's made you a wheelchair case. That's no problem: Decker has a very capable, calculating mind. He had a chair flown out from Rhodes yesterday.'

Trace managed a slow blink – but deliberately slow. He kept his left eye closed for long moments before slowly opening it. It conveyed nothing except that maybe he had something to convey. Amira caught on fast. She took his hand, said:

'Can you squeeze?'

Trace slowly, with great effort, squeezed. 'I felt that!' Amira was excited. 'That's good. One squeeze for yes, two for no, OK?'

Trace squeezed.

'Do you believe I'm innocent?'

He squeezed once – then twice more. 'Yes' – and 'no.' He was still uncertain.

'Well, it can't be helped. But surely you must have seen how I was on the point of telling you all of this when Decker came on the scene? If he'd left his entry a second longer he'd have heard everything – and then I would have had to try to kill him! Anyway, you'll believe me soon enough. But before anything else happens – before you make a mistake – there are things you have to know. And they're important, Charlie, because as this thing proceeds they could well make the difference between life and death for you! And where your life is concerned . . . suddenly I care a great deal. I didn't much care before I met you, and I only cared a little having met you, but since then . . .'

Trace squeezed. 'Yes,' he knew what she meant.

She leaned forward, gave him a kiss he could just feel but couldn't respond to in the least, sat back again. 'And you know,' she continued, 'right from the start I couldn't believe you were what you were supposed to be. You were just too naïve – to be the son of *that* thing, I mean! But anyway, now you have to listen, Charlie, and try to understand. You really are going to have to play this thing dumb. No, dumber than that, stupid! I'll explain:

'You have to pretend Kastrouni told you nothing, gave you nothing. Or maybe he mentioned a friend of his who had a wine-shop in Pighadia – just a mention – and when you came here on holiday, naturally you looked him up. As for your trip to the monastery: you were sightseeing, that's all. Maybe Klein picked a fight with you or something, you don't know why, and in the scuffle he fell. Am I getting through to you? Do you understand that these are the things you must say if anyone asks you these questions?'

Trace squeezed. 'Yes,' he understood perfectly. They knew he wouldn't go as a lamb to the slaughter anyway. But if he also knew who was in charge of the slaughter house – and what kind of 'humane killer' was waiting for him there . . . No, he could clearly see how it would be far too dangerous to know too much.

'Good! – that's important. If they think you're mostly ignorant of this thing, then they might not watch you too closely. And that way maybe we'll get the chance to work something out. But if they should ever suspect just how much you really know – which I have a feeling is a deal more than you've said . . .'

Curtains! thought Trace. *Definitely* . . . And perhaps something of the helplessness he felt got through to her.

On her knees, she put her arms round him, hugged him for a moment before drawing back. Again she stared at him, her gaze intense. 'Charlie, you accused me of some things. I want you to know that I've never known Khumeni . . . that way. When you see him you'll know couldn't. I would die first, I swear it! Anyway, he doesn't care for women. Decker says he . . . says he takes animals. What he did that time in Cyprus was out of necessity, to get himself some offspring. Oh, yes, I know about that; Kastrouni has been a friend for some years; we've pooled our information, our resources.'

Then her eyes widened more yet. 'But what you said two nights ago, about not being his son – about having a beast-brother who *was* his son – was that true?'

Trace squeezed.

'And did Saul Gokowski know that?'

He squeezed twice: 'No,' and once more: 'Yes, *now* he knows.'

She thought about it, licked her lips, muttered to herself: 'Kastrouni didn't know, and so – neither does Khumeni!' And to Trace: 'Where is this brother?'

He could only give two squeezes.

'He's dead?'

Another squeeze.

'At birth!'

Telepathy, Trace thought – and again he had doubts about her. But no doubt about the fact that she was one switched-on woman. 'Yes,' he squeezed.

'Thank God!' she let out a great sigh. 'It was my part to seduce you, but when I found myself enjoying it – *before* I knew this – I was beginning to think I really was perverse!'

As her strained face gave way to a faint smile, so quiet footsteps sounded on the concrete path beyond the courtyard's wall. She quickly stood up, put a finger up to her lips (a gesture which, if the situation wasn't so desperate, Trace might have found comical, but which he nevertheless understood perfectly) and turned away from him. And moments later Decker came through the door, wheezed his way across the courtyard and into the apartment.

He stared at Trace with unsmiling, piggy eyes, turned to Amira. 'Is he OK?'

'I think so,' she coldly answered.

'Can he hear and does he understand what's said to him?'

'Yes. Take his hand. One squeeze for yes, two for no.'

Decker took Trace's hand in his fat, sweaty paw. 'Anybody in there?' he said.

Trace squeezed once – wished he could squeeze harder – would have enjoyed squeezing the slimy bastard's windpipe.

'OK, so listen,' Decker wheezed. 'In a couple hours, as the drug wears off, you'll be able to move a bit more. Enough to swallow food at least. That's when you get a little chow – slop, anyway. Soup, you know? And you better eat up, Charlie boy, 'cos that's the last for a couple of days. You follow?'

Trace squeezed.

'After that, this evening, you'll just about be able to stand. That's when we go poo-poos. And that's nice 'cos then you won't have to keep pissing yourself! But just so's you don't get too mobile, then you take a couple of little white pills, to top up on that shit we shot you. You follow?'

Again Trace squeezed.

Decker straightened up, grinned down at his helpless captive, gave his face three deceptively gentle slaps with the flat of his open hand. Trace barely felt them, but they somehow managed to sting him.

'My day's coming, you fat slug!' he silently promised. 'But by God *you'll* feel it – you'll feel all of it – just as soon as I'm able . . .'

256

Chapter Two

But for now Trace was not able, not even if he'd been offered his own weight in gold; and the rest of the day and evening went exactly as Decker had forecast.

Before 'poo-poos', however (for some obscure reason the one event Trace had really dreaded, despite the fact that the none-too-distant future promised to hold terrors beyond imagining, let alone the toilet door), Amira had managed to sneak back to him and take his hand again. This had been while the fat man was in the other half of the villa, but there was no guarantee that he would stay there. Upstairs in the sleeping area there was a small, curtained connecting door between the two apartments. When Trace and Amira had spent the night together, he'd tried the door but it had been locked. Since when he'd forgotten it. A serious omission. That was where Decker had come from to take him by surprise. It was where he could come from again, at any moment. And so:

Very quickly, in a breathless whisper, Amira had said: 'Charlie, however unpleasant things get, just bide your time and don't give up hope. There's more going on than I can tell you. Just believe me, things aren't as desperate as they seem. Not yet, anyway. Do you believe me?'

His squeeze had been a lot stronger by then, and he'd felt that if he tried he might actually manage a nod. Yes, he believed her. He had to believe her. She was all he had.

But then she'd left him and Decker had returned, and an hour after that it had been poo-poos – not quite as dreadful as Trace had thought it would be, and at least as bad for Decker – following which Trace had been almost glad to swallow the 'little white pills'. And then, once again, nothing . . .

After that time became meaningless. For Trace it consisted solely of the often brief moments when he was 'awake' – or more properly when he was conscious. And even then everything was so strange that he could never be sure he wasn't simply dreaming. The first time this happened to him was aboard the Skyvan, which told him that he was somewhere between Karpathos and Rhodes, heading for Rhodes.

He'd forced eyelids that felt weighted down with lead to open, had seen the single narrow aisle of the airplane stretching out before him, weirdly distorted, almost as if to infinity. The passengers had been mainly local island Greeks, but there was also a middle-aged couple immediately in front of Trace and to his right, who were obviously well-to-do English tourists. He had thought at first that they had speech impediments, for as they loudly chatted their deep, horsey voices seemed slowed down to only half the speed of normal conversation, like the dull booming of a gramophone record played one speed too slow. And then, of course, he'd realized that this was simply the effect of the drug again, working in him as before.

With the very greatest of effort he had managed to turn his head a little to the left, at the same time squeezing the hand he barely felt holding his own. And there had been Amira sitting beside him, but on a level an inch or two below his – at which Trace had guessed that he was seated in a high wheelchair, which would also explain his position in the centre of the aisle.

Then the English couple had looked back toward him

258

(had he inarticulately mouthed something or other?), noticed he had his eyes open, nodded to him and to themselves in slow motion, and boomed away at Amira; in answer to which she'd smiled nervously, put a languid finger to her lips, told them:

'S-h-h-h! N-o-o-o e-x-c-i-t-e-m-e-n-t-t-t!'

And Trace had noted, half a mile away in the front of the tiny plane, the broad red neck of Decker falling in a fold over his shirt collar, where he sat sweating right behind the slightly elevated pilot. The fat man had been otherwise engaged, however, and had noticed nothing; he'd seemed intent on peering ahead, out of the forward windows, probably studying the outline of Rhodes as it expanded into view.

Then Amira had leaned toward Trace (frighteningly, for the weird alteration in his vision seemed to make her face suddenly swell up inordinately large, like an approaching airship, as it closed with his) to whisper: 'Ch-ar-lie! Y-o-u m-u-s-t h-a-v-e a h-i-g-h r-e-s-i-s-t-a-n-c-e. A-n e-x-c-e-p-t-i-o-n-a-l t-o-l-e-r-a-n-c-e. T-h-a-t-'s g-o-o-d! A-r-e y-o-u O-K?'

He'd squeezed a 'yes,' – immediately followed by a 'no.' It was all like a very bad LSD trip. He felt terrible, sick to his guts. He could feel bile inching its way up his throat, made infinitely worse through his slowed-down perceptions.

Amira must have seen his Adam's apple bobbing, recognized the sudden parchment colouring of his skin, the beads of cold sweat fast gathering on his brow; anyway, she'd quickly produced a brown paper bag lined with film from somewhere or other. And then Trace had gone through the sheer nightmare of low-metabolism retching and vomiting.

When it was finally over he'd closed his eyes and let his head fall back; and then, light as thistledown, he'd felt

Amira tidying up his mouth, dabbing away the tears which ran in slow motion down his barely cognisant cheeks. Natural tears produced by his stomach's *un*natural violence, the yawning gape of his jaws. But Amira had not known that they were more than that. Only Trace himself had known that.

For they had also been tears of frustration, and of a rapidly mushrooming hatred and loathing. Afterwards, too weak to resist, Trace had once more fallen asleep –

– But this time, as he let the darkness close in on him, he was desperately trying to remember that sequence of alien words he had heard in the old Greek monastery – those words read out aloud by Saul Gokowski – the exorcism from the second Chorazin tablet.

Whatever else happened, and whether or not Amira had been right when she'd said that things weren't as desperate as they seemed, Trace had determined that from now on he'd be ready for any eventuality. And he wasn't going to go out without a fight . . .

Then there was Rhodes: the evening when Trace woke up (how long after the episode on the Skyvan? The same day, maybe – or a week later?) in a garden under a grapevine looking out over a sea of gold as the sun went down and the stars came out. And then for an hour, apparently on his own, he'd fought his paralysis and tried to move his arms, his legs – only to succeed in the end when he accidentally kicked his wheelchair's brake loose. Facing slightly downhill, he'd begun to roll forward, unable to cry out but merely issue a series of high-pitched gurgles or croaks, until his left-hand wheels hit a curb and he was tilted head-first into a patch of lush mint under a lemon tree.

He landed soft but the wheelchair clattered on to its side and skidded squealingly on the inevitable cobbles and a moment later lights went on in a white-walled bungalow at the top end of the garden. Then Amira had come running, crying out to him, and Trace might have sobbed his relief if he'd been able. As it was he could only let her check him over for injury, then breathlessly lever and angle him up again into his chair, finally wheel him to the house and round to its front. And:

'Rhodes,' she'd told him then, where they gazed down on the city's million lights. 'The last time we were here I thought you were . . . someone else. I knew you were going to die and I didn't care much. And now I can't let you die no matter what. Do you think we have a chance, Charlie?'

He'd squeezed once, 'Yes,' *God, I hope so!*

'I was sitting here watching the lights come on and must have fallen asleep,' she continued. 'Then I heard your chair go over and I suppose that woke me up. Thank God you're all right! But what a *crazy* thing to do!' She was angry. 'Was that an accident, Charlie? You better tell me it was an accident. You could so easily have hurt yourself.'

'Yes,' he squeezed once, an accident.

'Well, never mind that now,' she'd told him, not really believing him. And more eagerly: 'In fact I'm glad you're awake. There are things I have to tell you – if for no other reason than that they might give you a little peace of mind, a little hope. Because I know how you must be feeling.'

Do you? Trace thought at her. *Jesus, Amira, but you don't. I feel rough, hungry, ill, unwashed, itchy – and until you've suffered a slow itch that you can't scratch, you can't possibly know how I feel!* And: 'U-urch-ch!' he'd managed, which should have come out as, 'Oh, Christ!'

'What?' She was astonished. 'Charlie, you shouldn't be able to move a fraction, shouldn't even be able to think

261

straight. And here you are upsetting your wheelchair, even trying to speak! Do you know how many doses of those tablets he's given you? Three. The last lot, just a few hours ago, should have kept you under till morning. You're developing an amazing tolerance! But let me tell you about tomorrow:

'At noon you eat again, just enough to keep you ticking over. But if you like, tonight when the place is quiet, I can bring you a little meat? Or soup, maybe? I can do you some soup now, if you think you'd get it down? No? Anyway, after that we're booked on the 2:00 P.M. flight for Israel, getting into Tel-Aviv a little after 3:30. Tomorrow night at this time we'll be in Jenin, half-way between Tel-Aviv and Galilee, and then for the first time you'll meet Khumeni – also the two men he thinks are your brothers, by different women.' She had paused, asked:

'Are you taking this in?'

He had given her a squeeze, said: 'Urk.'

'God, you're a trier, Charlie Trace!' she'd given him a spontaneous hug. 'But let me get on. Tonight I convinced Decker he should relax, go into town and have a drink. The fact is I can't stand him around me. Well, that's OK but he's unpredictable. I don't know when he'll be back, or what mood he'll be in by then . . .'

Trace had continued to listen, had known Amira was going full-steam; but doped to the gills as he was, her words had been hitting him like so much treacle. He could easily get bogged down in them. So far he was taking it in, but it was hard work. And there were so many of his own questions that he wanted answered, if only he had the power to ask them. Chiefly he would like to know what she'd meant back in the Villa Ulysses when she'd told him things weren't desperate. How desperate could things get? What *exactly* was going on? And apart from the more immediate relevance of these questions,

262

certain others seemed to have surfaced or solidified during Trace's unconscious periods. For instance:

If Khumeni and Saul Gokowski had stalemated each other, how come Khumeni had suddenly tried to have the other killed back there on Karpathos? Didn't it worry him any longer that Gokowski had his measure and could alert people in high places in respect of Khumeni's purpose and intentions? Or was it simply that the 'next regeneration' was so close now that Khumeni could afford to take chances; because by the time anyone moved against him – if anyone was sufficiently impressed to move against him it would all be over and he would be someone else? Or rather, three other someone elses would be him . . .

But Amira was off again and Trace had been left behind. And so he'd abandoned his inwardly directed questions for the moment and returned his attention to what she was saying, trying to pick up the thread:

'. . . one of Khumeni's men for a long time,' she'd been saying. 'Well, you've met him. He's fat and ugly and despicable. And he's a dupe, too: he has no idea what Khumeni really is and I haven't tried to enlighten him. He doesn't care, just so long as Khumeni pays him good money. And Khumeni pays *all* his people good money! Decker is also his English connection on the drugs front. He divides his time between England, Amsterdam and the USA, and I suspect Khumeni pulled him in for this job purely as a matter of availability: Decker just happened to be in England at the right time. Not that Decker's incapable or anything: he's very capable! I've only known him this last week, since a few days before we left England – but I know he's hateful. Murder and drugs are only two of the things he does. I believe he's big in prostitution in London, too! And of course Khumeni – well, he's into *all* vice – or as much as he can handle, world-wide . . .'

Amira paused for a moment, looked toward dark alleys where they descended steeply into Rhodes town, listened intently. She heard only cicadas and the throb of the city's heart, began to breathe again. And finally she continued:

'The man you . . . the one who died at the monastery, Phillip Klein, he was on hire to Khumeni from the Mafia. He uses a lot of their people, hires them like we'd hire interior decorators!'

But Trace was growing weary now. And there was something Amira still hadn't told him, which he'd hoped desperately to hear. Namely, if she really was on his side, if she wasn't just a clever whore using her wiles and her body in the interests of the beast Khumeni – then why the hell didn't she just up and push him in his wheelchair out of here right now? She could take him to the local law, couldn't she? Tell them her story – or at least enough of it that they would want to check it out.

She had been looking straight into his eyes as he thought these things, and perhaps she'd seen something of the doubts written there. And again Trace had thought, *telepathy*, as she half-turned her face away, lowered her eyes and bit her lip. But he'd willed her to look at him, and at last she had, saying:

'I know what you're thinking, Charlie, but I can't. *We* can't walk away from it. In order to get my father on his hook, Khumeni threatened him with my life; and to get *me* he threatened my father's life. That's how he works. But it isn't only my father's life that would be in jeopardy if I fouled this up, it's . . . well, a lot more than that. You see, Charlie, Khumeni wants to bring his three sons together in Galilee. Why? Well, you'd know more about that than I do. But the way I understand it, it's the only

264

thing that will get Khumeni *himself* into Galilee. Which is where we want him. So, since he believes you are one of his sons – '

It had all made sense, but the effort of listening had finally taxed Trace beyond his endurance. So he was the lure, was he? The bait in the trap. Part of it, anyway. And what next, after they'd got Khumeni back into Israel? Did they really know and understand what they were dealing with here? Kastrouni had known, probably better than any man, and where was Kastrouni now?

And again Trace had drifted into sleep with Saul Gokowski's rite of exorcism burning in his mind. And whether it was the drug, his fatigue, a combination of both or something else entirely, he couldn't say – but it seemed to him that those alien words were far more familiar to him now, as if repetition was sharpening their definition.

His last memory, however, as the darkness closed in, had been of Amira's voice superimposed over his own imagined chanting, asking: "Charlie? Are you OK? Are you going to sleep again, Charlie?' Then she'd hugged him again, maybe a little desperately, and he'd heard something that could have been a sob; and finally, as from a long, long way away, 'Forgive me, Charlie. Please forgive me . . .'

That night (Trace had reckoned it could only be the same night, for it was the same bungalow, on a hill in Rhodes) when the city slept and the stars were diamond bright in an unbelievably clear sky, she had crept to him and woke him up. He had come awake uneasily to find his chair tilted back at forty-five degrees, panicking just a little as memories flooded in to remind him who he was, and where, and what was happening to him. Then he'd recognized her perfume and felt her kiss on his brow, and he had known it was Amira.

She had lighted a tiny oil lamp, wound his chair upright beside an open window that let in the warm night air. And: 'Soup,' she'd told him in a whisper, producing a bowl of thick, tender meaty chunks in a rich gravy. 'The idea is that you be kept weak, but I'm going to see that you're strong. And if you can somehow manage it, try to avoid taking all of the pills he'll want to give you tomorrow. You can always pretend you're still asleep or dopy or something, and put the pills to the side of your mouth to get rid of later. But whatever you do and however well you may feel, don't try to tackle him! You must promise me that, Charlie.'

'Yes,' he'd squeezed, gulping soup as she fed him with a spoon. Oh, yes, he promised he wouldn't tackle Decker. Actually, that was a laugh. Right now he wouldn't be able to tackle a new-born runt puppy! But for all that, still things weren't as bad as they'd been. Not by a long shot. Still slow, still vague and fudgy, but his five senses were at least fighting the drug now, and fighting with a will.

'What about some exercise? Do you think you could talk?'

Two squeezes. She must be joking! But on the other hand . . . another squeeze, 'Maybe'. Exercise wasn't a bad idea.

She'd helped him up, carefully looping his left arm round her neck and taking his weight. Not too bad, not bad at all! And then they'd stumbled to and fro, weaving their way across the rug-covered floor of the room, to and fro, until the blood got going and he was taken with pins and needles. Then he'd signalled: 'No, enough!' and she'd sat him down again.

'Decker's asleep,' she'd whispered then. 'Out like a

266

light and snoring like a pig. He *is* a pig! He . . . he came back drunk and it looked nasty for a minute or two, but finally he got the message.'

Trace slowly turned his head to look at her. The oil lamp didn't give much light but . . . was that a bruise on her face, under her eye? She'd quickly turned away; and in the next moment she'd reached over, shielded the rim of the lamp's flue, blown the room back into darkness.

'Better sleep now, Charlie, if you can. And remember what I said about not giving yourself away by tackling Decker or doing anything stupid. He's a bad lot and would take great pleasure in hurting you.' Then her kiss again on his forehead, and his chair slowly tilting backward, and her perfume fading as she moved away.

And Trace had reclined there in silence and the light of the stars through the window for a long time before he'd finally slept again . . .

And then it was morning.

'How's Sleeping Beauty this morning?' The fat man's wheezy, imitation-American twang; his footsteps, shuffling close. 'You awake, Charlie boy?'

Trace had kept his eyes shut, his head lolling, but in fact he'd been awake for some little time. He'd just been sitting here, listening to them start to stir, getting up, moving about. Then:

Slap! slap! slap! – Decker's pudgy fingers on his face, and Trace had jerked his head back, his eyes snapping open. Decker had stepped back at once, his own eyes widening and showing how bloodshot they were. He'd had a good drink last night, for sure. And how Trace had cursed himself then. How much had he given away? All of it? Maybe not. Slowly, he let his head loll again, his eyes slowly close.

'For a minute then – ' Decker had wheezed, suspicion

267

in his voice. He'd come closer, Taken Trace's chin and given his head a shake, until Trace half-opened a bleary eye. And: 'Naw!' Decker had grinned at him then. 'Just reaction, that's all. I woke you up nasty, eh, Charlie boy?'

Then Decker had wound him upright and Trace had allowed himself to 'come properly awake.' And:

'Poo-poos,' growled the fat man, grimacing. But Trace had to admit to himself that it sounded like a good idea to him. 'Then shavey-poos, 'cos you're hairy as a badger's arse, and finally bathy-poos to get rid of the stink. Who's a lucky boy, eh?'

You are! Trace had thought. *Lucky I haven't got that cut-throat razor of yours in my hand right now!*

But Decker had been looking at him suspiciously again. 'You know, boy, you look just a mite too damn good. Today I think we up the dosage. Yep, I reckon it's three little white pills for Charlie boy today. Just to be on the safe side, eh?'

Trace's hands were on the arms of his chair. He'd gripped with them and felt his fingers dig in a little. The fat man's words had all been received sharp and clear. Trace could smell the scent of flowers drifting in from the garden, and coffee smells from the kitchen. His vision was almost normal, too, and Decker's slaps had carried more of that sting he remembered from before. They were a taunt and a torment, those slaps . . .

Then Amira had walked in with a tray and steaming mugs of coffee – and Trace had seen at once that she wore dark glasses. They couldn't hide the bruise, though, where it bloomed under her right eye.

'*Bastard!*' Trace had hissed out loud, the word totally involuntary where it slipped off his tongue in an unguarded moment.

Decker's mouth had fallen open at once. 'What?' he

glanced from Trace to Amira, back to Trace. 'You fucking . . . !' And to Amira: 'You hear that? The little shit called me a – ' He loomed over Trace, raising his open palm.

Amira somehow contrived to get between Decker and his target without dropping her tray. 'It's your own fault!' she snapped at Decker. 'He cared for me, remember? That was my job, to get him to care for me. Even now he cares, and he's seen my eye. If Khumeni finds out you hit me, believe me you'll pay for it. But not nearly as much as you would if he thought you'd hit Trace . . .'

Slowly Decker had straightened up, turned to face her where she backed away. 'Little lady, you watch your mouth. You'll tell Khumeni nothing, you hear?' He took a waddling pace toward her – reached out and lifted a mug of coffee from her tray. 'Anyway, you went to bed with this dildo, didn't you? So what's wrong with me, eh?'

'I was *paid* to seduce Trace!' she'd spat at him then.

'Yeah?' Decker's face had puddled into a fat, ugly smile. 'Well, why didn't you say so? I can pay.'

'Oh no you couldn't,' she'd scowled, turning away. 'Not even if you had the keys to Fort Knox!'

Following which it had been time for Trace's ablutions. Decker wasn't too gentle with him, and Trace was sure that when the fat man shaved him he deliberately knicked his chin. Worse, in the bath he'd thought Decker was intent on drowning him. But at last it was over.

Then there had been a little food, and later the pills. Three of them. One went down, washed into his stomach with lemonade while the fat man massaged his throat. But the other two –

Trace had managed to trap them under his tongue. Later he'd spat them into a vase of flowering cactus. The

269

one he'd swallowed had been sufficient, however, to put him out yet again . . .

. . . Later, Trace would remember coming to on the plane, but only very briefly.

. . . And at Tel-Aviv, being wheeled across the airport's tarmac; many soldiers standing around in grey and green uniforms and caps with flat, jutting peaks, and each and every man of them carrying an automatic weapon; the sun burning his hands and wrists where they lay limp on the arms of his wheelchair. And Saul Gokowski's chant echoing in the vaults of his brain.

. . . In a taxi, with his head in Amira's lap; Decker in the front passenger seat wheezing instructions to the driver.

. . . In an ambulance, flat on his back on a stretcher, with Amira sitting beside him, holding his hand. But this time he stayed awake. And he examined himself.

He felt stiff as a board but his senses seemed more or less in order; weak as a kitten, yet eager for action. He couldn't say exactly *how* he felt, but he knew he'd been inactive long enough. Could he talk? There was a sure way to find out.

Amira's head was down, her eyes closed; she leaned half against the wall of the ambulance, half against Trace's stretcher. Her face was drawn, drained. She had been through a lot.

Trace managed without too much difficulty to lift his head an inch or two, looked around the interior of the ambulance. It was a large vehicle but there were just the two of them here in the back, Trace and the girl. Beyond a reinforced, tinted glass panel which separated them from the cab, Decker was driving, his fat red neck unmistakable. A telephone was fixed in a bracket on the

270

wall, for speaking to the driver. Its switch was in the 'off' position.

'Amira!' Trace croaked. 'Hey – *urch-ch* – Amira!'

She started and her eyes shot open. 'Charlie!' She cast a darting glance through the tinted glass partition, then back at Trace. She tried to smile at him. 'How do you feel?'

Trace tried to say 'miserable' but his tongue felt like a furry rubber wedge. He settled for 'Shitty.'

'Me too,' she told him.

He shifted his position, a manoeuvre that required a lot of effort, a deal of concentration, and asked: 'Where . . . ?'

'Where are we? On our way to Jenin. Khumeni will be there, and your "brothers". Others of Khumeni's people will have brought them here – kidnapped, just like you.'

'How do you – *uh!* – know these things?' The inside of Trace's mouth tasted pretty much like he'd expect a toilet to taste. But his words were coming easier now, his mind and body beginning to function better together than at any time since that injection she'd given him.

'George Khumeni never tells anyone everything,' she answered. 'So it's a matter of intelligence. My instructions were to seduce you in London while Khumeni arranged to put some sort of pressure on you. Desiring to get out of London for a spell, you'd come with me to Israel and, eventually, Jenin. You helped matters along a little by booking a holiday in Karpathos; but at the same time that complicated things, because now I would have less time for your seduction. I had to try, then, to get you to change your holiday plans and come with me to Israel. That day you went off into the hills, to Gokowski's monastery, I was going to receive "a message" from my father saying he was ill and could I come home at once. I would be distraught and turn to you for help, and you would bring me home – to Jenin, of course. Decker was in case I failed. He had instructions that if you weren't suited with me, then that he was to help me get you to Israel any way we could. And he, too, had been told your destination: Jenin.

'When Khumeni contacted me in London and gave me my orders, I at once got in touch with my father who told me that the beast had already instructed him to make ready a house in Jenin – a place big enough to accommodate twelve people at least. That is to say, Khumeni himself, Decker and Klein, my father and I, and seven others. My father also told me that Kastrouni had been in touch to say that the "Greek Connection" had already been kidnapped.'

'The Greek connection?' Trace's mind was fully active now, if not his body. 'Khumeni's Greek son?'

'That's right. Kastrouni had had him under observation for a long time, and when he suddenly disappeared – '

'That was a signal to your little group that it was all starting to happen, eh?'

'Yes. The other seven people at Jenin would obviously be yourself, your "brothers", and their minders or kidnappers – two to each of them.'

Trace added it all up. 'That means there'll be Khumeni and five thugs against three captive zombies, a girl and an old man! What good is that?'

'No good at all. It puts the beast ahead – or so it would appear. And that's what we want. He'll think he's in the clear.'

'But he *will* be in the clear!'

'Not by a mile,' she answered, shaking her head. 'I don't know everything, Charlie, but I do know this much: it can only be finished in Chorazin, and so until then we play it exactly the way Khumeni wants it.'

Trace shook his head, however weakly. 'There are still

things I don't see,' he said. 'A lot of them. If Kastrouni was one of your group, why was he working against you? He came to London and gave his life warning me *off* Israel!'

'Psychology!' she smiled tiredly, then shrugged. 'He probably thought you'd want to come and find out for yourself. Anyway, Dimitrios was always the wild one, the driving force. I can't really say why he came to London. Maybe he wanted to bring you out here himself. Remember we're only loosely connected; our communications aren't as good as we'd like them to be. Kastrouni wasn't wasting any time, that's all.'

'And Gokowski – he threatened me, tested me, said if he could prove I *was* Khumeni's son that he'd kill me there and then.'

'Bluff!' again her wan smile. 'Saul wanted to impress you with something of the moment of what was happening. You'd seen two murders, and however inadvertently you'd actually been involved in a third death. His threat was meant to be the last straw on the camel's back – to break any last thread of resistance and make you believe. But he wouldn't have killed you, Charlie, not for anything. He, too, knew you had to come here, meet Khumeni, go with him and the others to Chorazin. It's the only way the beast can be destroyed.'

Trace lay back his head, shook it slowly left and right, tried to get his whirling thoughts in order. '"The beast", you call him. And do you believe, *really* believe, that this man is the antichrist? I mean, I know he's evil – you can't all be wrong – and I know he has . . . powers, for I saw Kastrouni die. But . . .'

'He *is* the antichrist,' she nodded. 'Oh, yes. You'll know it's true the moment he chooses to let you see it's true. Oh, if he wants to charm you he will, and then you could never believe! But if he *wants* you to believe – you will.'

'All of you believe,' said Trace, almost to himself. 'Every one of you that I've met so far, believes completely. The antichrist himself. And you think you have his measure!' He was angry now, tried to struggle upright; Amira put a hand on his chest, held him there easily.

'At least we think we know what we're doing, Charlie.'

'But you're up against the power of Satan! What can you do, any of you? *And what happens to me if you fail?*'

A red light beside the telephone came on. Crackling with static, Decker's voice wheezed electrically: 'Jenin coming up – a few more minutes.' The fat man hadn't looked back.

Trace closed his eyes, flopped back lifelessly, played dead. Amira flipped the 'on' switch, took up the telephone. 'OK,' she answered. 'All's well back here.'

'And how's our boy?'

'He's going to be just fine.'

'Yeah? But for how long!' ·A pause, then: 'Hey, Amira?'

'What is it?'

'Now I know how those old cowboy bounty hunters used to feel.'

'Oh? How was that?'

'Satisfied!' Decker wheezed, and began to laugh.

You bastard, thought Trace. And once more he promised himself: *but if I've got it coming to me, you'd better believe it's coming for you, too, fat man – in spades!*

Chapter Three

Approaching Jenin, Decker took out a sheet of instructions from his pocket and glanced at it, then looked for landmarks. On the eastern extreme of the town, where typically Middle-Eastern dwellings were just beginning to cluster in small knots and the surface of the hitherto dirt road suddenly became metalled, he turned right down an avenue of palms and giant cacti or succulents toward an impressive private building in its own grounds behind high, parapet walls. Tall, wide wooden gates were closed to his vehicle, but as he applied his brakes and the ambulance began to slow down, so the gates swung open easily and a robed figure whose face was hidden by a cowl waved him through and flagged him to a halt.

The gates were then closed and locked and their guardian, a man in a brown, full-length, loose-fitting robe approached Decker's cab. Decker took in the figure's strange lope and his face lost something of its colour. He got down from the ambulance as Khumeni threw back his hood. And looking at that face from close quarters, Decker was glad evening was settling and that the shadows of the carob and almond trees in the garden were long, dusty and heavy.

'Ah, Mr Decker!' said Khumeni, his voice soft and husky and almost pleasant, forming a complete contrast to his awful aspect. 'Punctual as ever. And has all gone well?'

Decker pulled himself together, threw off the morbid cloud that always seemed to settle whenever he was near this man, faced up to him. 'For me, yes,' he wheezed, 'but for Klein, no. He's dead, killed by Trace.'

Khumeni at once reached out a hand like a claw and grasped Decker's shoulder where it joined his neck. 'But you do have Charles Trace?'

Decker jerked back against the ambulance, shook himself free of the other's grip. 'Inside, yes,' he wheezed, suddenly panting. 'The Halbstein girl is with him.'

Khumeni took a deep breath. 'Tell me about Klein later,' he snapped. 'For now drive up to the house. I want to have a look at your passenger.' Without another word he turned and loped toward the house along a gravel drive, and Decker was left to climb back into his cab and follow on behind.

Inside the body of the ambulance, Trace and Amira had heard all of this. Also the girl had been looking through the tinted partition and so out of the cab's windows. As Decker started up the motor again, she said: 'I know this place, Charlie. It belongs to rich friends of my father. It's an arrangement that he can have the run of the place whenever they're away.' She quickly went on to describe the house and grounds, being at pains to explain how difficult it would be to sneak away from here.

Picturing the place as she described it, Trace didn't think so. If he was fit he'd be out of here in a flash – or into it, if he so desired. If he were fit . . .

But then, as the ambulance came to a halt for the second time, he put all such thoughts out of his mind. He heard Decker get out of his cab and go to the rear of the vehicle, heard him cranking down the reinforced central section of the rear panel to form a ramp, then his wheezing as he clambered in and assisted Amira with Trace's trolley.

Then, peering through lids three-quarters shuttered,

276

Trace felt himself wheeled down the ramp on to grating gravel chips, steered up on to solid stone flags, finally guided through doors into a cool, shadowy corridor and so into a room whose louvre-shuttered windows made it gloomy as a cupboard. There Amira lifted his dangling hands up on to the trolley (and doing so gave one of them a covert squeeze) and someone, probably the girl again, threw a blanket over his trunk and lower limbs against the room's cooler temperature. Then:

'So this is our Mr Trace, is it?' Khumeni's voice, faintly accented, quiet in the room's confined space and yet having a husky depth and gritty strength. Trace sensed him moving closer, heard the rustle of his robe and saw him like a dark shadow looming. He steeled himself . . . and sure enough a moment later felt a hand fall upon his brow. 'He seems hot,' said Khumeni, 'feverish almost. Not like the others at all.' There was a hint of suspicion in his voice.

'It was like an oven in the back of that ambulance,' Amira lied. 'And he's not only hot – he also smells and needs a wash. I'll bring a bowl in here and take care of it, if you wish.'

There was a moment's silence and then, through eyes open by the merest crack, Trace saw Khumeni's slow nod. 'Very well. It seems you've formed something of an attachment, Miss Halbstein.'

'I was supposed to, wasn't I?' she was quick to return.

'*Huh!*' came Decker's snort of derision, and then his whispered, 'Whore!'

Khumeni snatched his hand from Trace's brow, turned on the fat man at once. 'From you, Decker? Dealer in drugs, murderer, pimp? You surprise me! Also, you forget yourself. People are not generally outspoken in my presence. Rarely twice, and *never* three times. You would do well to remember that . . .'

All three then left the room, and as they went Khumeni said to Amira: 'Yes, wash him. I need him fit and well, and clean certainly. For now . . . And there's something else you can do for all three of them. I want you to – ' but here the conversation was lost to Trace as the door closed behind them.

Out in the corridor Khumeni finished telling Amira what he wanted done, then turned to Decker who was lingering in the background. 'Was there something, Mr Decker?'

'Er, I was wondering about . . . about the others! I mean, where is everyone? Or is that none of my business, since I won't be staying?'

'That was not what you were wondering at all,' Khumeni brushed him aside, 'and so I will ignore your question.' He turned his back on the fat man, spoke to Amira: 'As for you, Miss Halbstein, I suppose you are wondering about your father. He is not here. He is at the nunnery and clinic in Galilee, once Chinnereth. He prepares the way for me.'

She knew the place he meant: it was run by Italian nuns and stood in the hills, close to Bethsaida's ruins – also close to Chorazin. Her father had told her once that Khumeni had been making donations to the monastery for years, all to this one end. Travel in Israel, especially close to the borders, was restricted. But because Khumeni was one of the nunnery's major patrons, his visa had been stamped to give him access. He was using the nuns to his own ends: irony of ironies, their nunnery was his route into Chorazin! As for the three kidnapped men: ostensibly they were 'potential candidates' for the clinic, which in fact offered no treatment but was simply a refuge for hopeless catatonics. The beast Khumeni's plans were well laid.

'Then my part in all of this is over,' Amira spoke up. 'So . . . am I free to go?'

'No,' Khumeni shook his head, 'for I don't trust you – not while I am here in your country. You have too many friends here, and your father is not without influence. Therefore the two of you are to be my guests until . . . until tomorrow night.'

Decker's wheeze was nervous now: 'But that doesn't include me, eh, Mr Khumeni? As you have stated, I have many other interests, all of which await my urgent attention. This is what I had intended to point out but a moment ago. So, if you'll just pay me what's owed, I'll – '

'Mr Decker, I do not like you,' Khumeni cut him off. 'I have never liked you. I comment upon this strong dislike of mine to impress upon you that each moment spent in your company distresses me just as mine doubt-less distresses you. But at the same time I do admit that you perform your duties efficiently and have never failed me. My present plans involved not only yourself but also Mr Klein, who I note is no longer available. You may tell me about that in a moment. But since I am already short-handed, obviously I cannot afford to lose you, too. And so until tomorrow, in a place other than this and when all is completed, I'm afraid final payment must be delayed.'

'But I – '

'You may of course leave now, at once, but if you do then naturally the second half of your payment is forfeit.'

'What? But – '

' – But if you stay on, for just one more day, then not only will you have your money but also transport out of Israel wherever you wish to go. At my expense.'

Decker thought about it for a moment, said: 'Well, obviously I'll stay.'

'Good! Now then, you'll find four other, er, gentlemen, in the lounge at the rear of the house. One of them will show you your rooms. Sunset is in an hour or so, and the view from the lounge's windows, across a pool with a fountain in the garden, is quite spectacular, I'm told, as the sun goes down. I've arranged a meal for you all for just after sunset, following which I shall join you and detail tomorrow's schedule. One small thing, however: do not attempt to leave this place tonight. The four gentlemen in the lounge are of Mr Klein's, er, organization? Indeed, you might even say they're members of the same "family". They have arranged a shift system of patrolling the grounds; their orders in respect of anyone attempting to leave after sunset are quite specific and leave no room for misunderstanding or error. Now you must excuse me: I wish to take a longer look at my . . . acquisitions?'

'I was going to wash Trace,' said Amira.

'Yes, in a few moments. Five minutes at most. You are most assiduous in your duties – your self-imposed duties – Miss Halbstein. That is very good, or so I most sincerely hope. For your sake . . .' He smiled hideously in the corridor's faint light, turned and went back into the shuttered room.

Trace had been about to get up off his trolley and go to the door. He'd hoped to catch something of the muted conversation from the corridor. Also, there were two other surgical tables in the room and he wanted to have a look at what was lying on them: his 'brothers', he supposed. But as Khumeni came in and closed the door behind him, so Trace was caught red-handed, seated upright on his trolley with one hand to his head, swaying to and fro. For a moment the robed figure stood there uncertainly in the gloom, his hand on the doorknob. Then he strode to Trace's side and gripped his shoulder, gazed into his eyes.

Trace could only act it out, pretend that he had just

280

this moment regained consciousness. But the way he felt, that should not prove too difficult. 'What . . .?' he mumbled. 'Who . . .?'

'Most remarkable!' Khumeni whispered gruffly. 'Remarkable indeed! Now, lie down again, my son, and don't weary yourself. All is well and you are cared for, believe me.' His voice was almost hypnotic. The thin, hard hands on Trace's shoulders forced him unresistingly back; he gazed into Khumeni's sulphurous eyes as his own slowly grew accustomed to the room's gloom. And at last Trace knew what Kastrouni, Gokowski and Amira had meant. Knew, too, that they had been correct.

'So you are the third one, are you?' Khumeni continued, more to himself than to Trace. 'But you are strong, clever, lusty – and a thief. And you are not unhandsome. Perhaps, then, you are not the third but . . . the first?'

His voice *was* hypnotic, Trace knew it. But had to listen to it, could not draw his eyes from Khumeni's eyes or extricate his mind from the sucking aura of this man . . . this Thing? He panicked inside. He *mustn't* listen to his voice! He must find a distraction, another point on which to focus.

Trace drove out the voice from his ears, forced his eyes to unfreeze in their orbits, studied Khumeni's face instead. And yes, now that he could see it properly, that face was as Kastrouni had described it; but not *exactly* as he'd described it. No, for Khumeni was older now by almost thirty years, and they had been years of black, seething evil! Simple flesh, even the stolen, mutated flesh of others, could never stand up to the uses to which this monstrous creature had put it.

Teeth which had been strong and gleaming white – Ihya Khumnas's teeth – were white no longer but yellow as old ivory and jagged as broken fangs. And Khumeni's

281

hooked nose was fallen in a little – though not so badly as George Guigos's before him – and eaten away at the rim of the left nostril. The white blaze of Yakob Mhireni's scar was like a strap of pale leather now against ancient hide, and all hair had receded into coarse white tufts at the rear of an elongated, wolfish skull. The creature wore some cloying scent; but even so a bad-lobster smell, Khumeni's *real* smell, came through it.

Worst of all were his eyes: those volcanic blowholes that smouldered with a rotten phosphorescence, those windows on the sheer hell of the thoughts inside! And again those terrible eyes held Trace captive, and again Khumeni's voice seeped like old oil into his head, his reeling brain:

'But you must tell me all about yourself, Charles Trace, for I perceive that you are not like these other sons of mine. I had thought I knew all there was to know, but now I'm no longer sure. Indeed, I would now say that you were more changeling than even I suspected.' Trace felt the blanket drawn from him, heard Khumeni's treacly voice oozing on:

'For see, although you bear the true mark, you are not crippled. Oh, your brothers have marks, too, but not like this. This was Ab's birthright, his great misfortune – and I know for Ab abides in me even to this day. Aye, and *this* mark has spanned all the centuries between then and now; and now you have it. But what can it mean, Charles Trace? What can it mean?'

Trace could neither close his eyes nor avert them. He was Khumeni's now, the beast's to command. 'Now answer me this,' said Khumeni. 'Am I as wise as I am evil, or am I in fact a great fool? Are you really my son Charles Trace? Are you, or are you perhaps – '

There came a quiet knock at the door, distracting Khumeni and simultaneously setting Trace free of hi spell. Before the beast could deny entry, the door opened and Amira came in. She carried a bowl of steaming water, a towel, soap. Seeing Khumeni standing there beside Trace, she said, 'Oh!'

'Five minutes!' he snapped. 'I said five minutes, Miss Halbstein!'

She looked taken aback. 'But it's been more than that. And until I'm done with these three I can't put my room in order.'

'What?' Khumeni took two loping strides towards her. 'You're to be here for only one night and yet you desire to "put your room in order"? And you can't bear the thought of this one lying here, stinking through the night? Who seduced who, Miss Halbstein? It strikes me you've led far too soft a life! But very well, see to it. I merely indulged an odd fancy, that's all, or would have if you hadn't returned so quickly.' He glanced toward Trace. 'A fancy, yes; but one way or the other, it can make little difference now.' He moved past her, swirled out of the room, let the door slam behind him.

Trace and Amira looked at each other. 'Saved by the belle!' he finally punned. But sweat, miraculously held back until now, suddenly flooded from his pores like water from an overloaded sponge. He felt weak from the narrowness of his escape. For if Amira hadn't come in, surely he would have been obliged to answer the beast's questions. Now he could at least breathe deeply again, lie back, try to compose himself.

Amira started to wash him. 'What did he want?' she asked.

'He asked me if I really was his son,' Trace answered – and heard her gasp.

'Charlie, he *what*? But that means . . . Do you think he's guessed that – '

'No,' he cut her off. 'He seems pretty damn sure this

283

foot of mine is his doing. And as you just heard him say, it would make little difference now anyway. He needs three and I'm to be one of them, son or not. But I reckon he'll try to question me again. He knows there's something fishy about me; he's suspicious, anyway.'

'So you've decided to join us?' she said.

He frowned, looked at her quizzically. 'What?'

'This was your chance,' she shrugged. 'You could have told him about your brother, told him his real son was dead. It's obvious why he's curious about you: he knows Dimitrios Kastrouni came to see you, and if he doesn't know already about your seeing Saul Gokowski, he soon will – when Decker tells him how Klein died. So . . . you *could* have tried to get out of this. I don't think it would have worked, for it's surely too late for him to change his arrangements now, but at least you could have tried. You didn't, so . . .'

'I've joined no one!' Trace's voice was harsh. 'I want this bastard dead just as much as you do – but for purely personal reasons. Mainly, for my mother. Maybe for Kastrouni, too. And at the moment I have the advantage of being not quite so helpless as he thinks. So you see, even if your lot doesn't get him, I shall certainly try. The main worry – something I have no answer for – is that he . . .' he paused and shuddered. 'I don't know; it's like he's hypnotic.'

'He is,' said Amira. 'Not especially so with me, for I'm a poor subject, but he is a powerful hypnotist, yes. You're worried that he'll read your mind, see through you?'

'Something like that.'

'Well, not tonight he won't.' She finished washing him, produced a hypodermic.

'Oh no you don't!' said Trace at once. He made to sit up. 'I know what that stuff will do to me!'

She shook her head. 'Not this time, Charlie. This is a

284

simple sleeping-draught – to put you down for the night. A drug, of course, but nothing like that first jab I gave you in Pighadia. The others get it, too, but in the morning they'll still be feeling pretty rough for they've had the full treatment. You'll be weak – that's only natural – but you'll also be pretty much in control of yourself. It will let you keep the edge you've got.'

Trace warded her off. 'You're not sticking that – '

'Charlie, trust me.'

'Do you know what you're asking?' he grated. 'That I allow myself to be knocked out, put to sleep, in *this* place?'

'This place is safe,' she said. 'And this way we know Khumeni won't be able to get to you. It's Chorazin we have to worry about. Look, Charlie, I know what I'm talking about. At least, God help me, I hope and pray I do! Now give me your arm.'

He knew she was right, gritted his teeth, sat still and turned his face away. 'OK,' he said at last. 'Get it done.'

Feeling the needle go in and deliver its load, he gazed across the gloomy room toward the other trolleys where his 'brothers' lay. For all he knew they might well be equally blameless; he didn't even know what they looked like yet. Then the room began to grow darker, and Trace knew it wasn't just the setting of the sun.

Feeling her hands guiding and lowering his trunk to the trolley's padding, he heard her say: 'I love you, Charlie Trace, and I'll kill myself if anything happens to harm you. But I love the world, too; and though it's an old, old cliche it really is bigger than both of us. If Khumeni were to win, the whole world would be the loser, Charlie . . .

The last thing he felt was her mouth on his as it turned numb and lost all feeling, along with the rest of his body . . .

* * *

Morning came with sounds of movement in the large house. Trace came awake, lay still, listened. People were up and about. On a nearby trolley, one of his 'brothers' groaned. *I know how you feel*, Trace thought, checking out his faculties. Everything seemed to be working. That stuff Amira had put into him had in fact been a sleeping-draught, a sedative, and nothing more.

But stiff! – he felt as if his back and limbs were bolted in position; he could almost hear himself creaking as he slowly, painfully sat up on his trolley. And he was hungry, starving – and thirsty. Especially thirsty! His mouth felt full of decaying fish or something similarly rotten, but he was still very weak. That was all bad enough, but at least he no longer felt sick.

Footsteps outside the door sounded just as he was levering his legs down to the floor. He saw no point in pretending, and in any case had no time to lie down again. He simply froze as the door opened and a stranger came in. The man was short, stockily built, pale-faced. He wore dark spectacles supported on a nose badly broken at some time or other, had 'heavy' written all over him. 'Hey!' he said. 'A live one!'

Decker followed him into the room. 'Oh, he's a live one, all right,' the fat man wheezed. 'Isn't that so, Charlie boy? A right little shagger! But at least he can walk – apparently. Take him to the toilet, Lou, while I start getting these two ready.'

The heavy took Trace's arm in a stubby, hard hand, guided him to the door, half-supported him along the corridor to a toilet and shower. Inside the small room, he said: 'Can you make it on your own? Clean-up, shower?'

Trace nodded.

'OK. I'll be outside. Don't take all day.' His accent was American; New York, Trace guessed. At least it wasn't a Texas drawl or a New England twang, but certainly it was hard-edged.

Trace tossed his dressing-gown in a corner, relieved himself, showered. As he was drying himself broken-nose came in, helped him into a full-length robe of white towelling. 'You need a shave,' the stubby man grunted. And: 'Here,' he stuck a cigarette in Trace's mouth, lighted it. Trace had washed out his mouth in the shower; the cigarette tasted like something exotic, heaven-sent. 'Good, yeah?' said the stubby man. 'So enjoy it.'

Then Trace was led through the house to a cool room with large square windows looking out on a spacious garden with a pool. Beyond the pool a high stone wall was decked with ivy, cacti, flowering plants. Beyond that the tops of tall palms made motionless, dark green umbrellas. Trace collapsed into an easy chair, was handed an electric razor. The man called Lou plugged it in for him, said, 'Shave.'

Trace shaved, taking his time and acting more dopey than he felt, and while he was shaving he checked out the room and the people in it. There was Lou – a Mafia hireling, he'd already decided, – and another heavy with his feet up on an occasional table, panama hat pulled down over his eyes, and a big-nosed Palestinian type fetching and carrying and readying a large table for breakfast. That was it so far. No sign of Amira or Khumeni.

Trace guessed the time would be a little before 10:00 A.M.; half a day left to zero hour. He finished shaving, sat back in his chair. The effort of showering and all had drained him. Which didn't say a lot for the shape his 'brothers' must be in. And despite everything he began to drowse, started up briefly as one of the other zombies was brought in and dumped in a chair, finally fell into a sleep which might have been pleasant – but for Saul

Gokowski's rite of exorcism repeating over and over in his subconscious mind . . .

. . . He came sharply awake.

'Breakfast, Charlie boy,' Decker wheezed, shaking his shoulder. Then Khumeni's unmistakable rustle of a voice:

'You seem to be doing a little better than the others, Charles. And so you may go to the table and feed yourself.' Trace slowly looked up and saw the beast standing just inside the door. Khumeni had on his hooded robe, with the hood up. His eyes were small fires in a shadowy face.

The room had filled up; there was an air of nervous anticipation, expectancy, imminent action. Trace struggled upright unaided, might have fallen (or at least made out that he might), found Amira beside him, holding him up. He said, 'That's, *uh!* OK,' and shrugged himself free. Three swaying paces took him to the table. He sat heavily, slowly turned his head to scan the others already seated. Two of them were in wheelchairs, seemed only half-conscious. No need to ask who they were, but Trace checked them out anyway.

One would be Greek and the other Turkish, he knew that much, but it didn't help him decide which was which. Dressed in robes the same as his own, they even seemed of a similar design to Trace, though much darker, of course. And he felt a certain grim satisfaction: the same man, Khumeni, might well indeed be father to all three. But he wasn't. Amira sat beside one of them, spoon-feeding him and ignoring her own food; the man called Lou looked after the other one. Then there was Decker, seated at the far end of the table.

The thug with the panama sat on Trace's left; his hat lay in his lap now while he slurpingly cleaned up a bowl of soup. Two other men cut of much the same cloth sat to the right of Trace, completing the scene. Khumeni didn't join them but went to stand beside the window while they ate, his back to the room; the house-boy ran to and fro bringing food and drink.

Trace deliberately continued to act half-crippled throughout the meal and wasn't required to speak to anyone; but in any case, there wasn't a deal of conversation. He noticed Amira's eyes on him from time to time – frowning? Perhaps his act was fooling her, too. But while it must have appeared that he ate slowly and with difficulty, in fact he was packing as much food inside him as he could comfortably hold. Something told him he was going to need all the strength he could muster.

Finally Khumeni adjusted shades until the light was dim, turned from his window, began to speak:

'You are all my guests in this venture,' he husked without preamble. 'Until tonight, anyway. For tonight – ' he shrugged, ' – I have a little business in the desert – following which all of you will be paid according to previous arrangements. Gentlemen – ' he paused briefly to nod in Amira's direction. 'Excuse me, and Madame, of course – we are going on a "dig"! I know the spot intimately, also that great wealth lies below. Something of that, too, shall be yours for your troubles, if it is all I expect it to be.'

Liar! thought Trace. *That's the same patter you dished out in 1936!* And it had more or less the same effect: there was a sudden hush, an intense silence, only broken when the man with the panama tossed his spoon down clatteringly upon the table. 'Buried treasure?' he said, his voice harsh with greed. And the way he had said it, it had not been a question but a statement of fact.

Khumeni's eyes blazed on him. 'That which I seek is my business. No more interruptions, if you please . . . When we are finished here – that is, when I have done with talking to you – you will all prepare to leave. Be sure to take everything you brought into this house out with you, leave nothing behind. We travel thus: myself in the ambulance, with Mr Decker driving. Miss Halbstein will attend to her three charges in the body of the vehicle. Mr Lou Gabella and friends will bring up the rear in the ex-Army landrovers standing at the side of the house. They are not in bad order, these vehicles, and carry spares. The way is not long, but the country is rough and I want no breakdowns or emergencies; therefore we travel slowly, at between twenty-five and thirty miles per hour. There may well be military check-points along our route, so have your papers ready. However, I expect no trouble and will not invite any; if you have weapons, please rid yourselves of them as soon as we are in the desert. Only Mr Vittori will retain his weapon, a machine-gun which we have already hidden away in one of the landrovers.' He paused, looked pointedly at the sour-faced man with the panama. This must be Vittori; he wiped his mouth with the back of his hand, nodded his acknowledgement.

'When we get to the nunnery,' Khumeni continued after a moment, 'we shall lock its sweet sisters of mercy away in one of their own dormitories, make ourselves comfortable and complete certain precautionary measures. Then we wait for the fall of night before moving on to . . . the secret place. Then, too, we shall have the additional pleasure of the company of Professor Halbstein, who has been of great assistance to me. He too shall be specially rewarded. However, two of you will be required to stay behind at the nunnery until we return. Someone must guard the Mother Superior and her brood.

'Not me!' said Decker and Gabella almost simultaneously. They had already been seduced by the thought of treasure. Vittori was hot on their heels: 'I'm coming too,' he growled.

Watching Khumeni's face, Trace thought he saw his eyes light up in a smile, as if someone had thrown a log on a low-burning fire. 'Very well,' he slowly nodded, 'then it's decided: Mr Rosco and Mr Lancing will remain at the nunnery.'

The two men on Trace's right remained silent, staring back at Khumeni where he gazed at them quizzically. 'You are satisfied to remain behind?' he finally queried.

'No comment,' one of them shrugged at last. 'We're pros, been in this game a long time. We been paid already, good money. You rip people off – or try to, or even get the urge to – and sooner or later *you* gets ripped off. Honour among thieves, you know? We do what you say.'

Khumeni nodded. 'Very well. And of course there shall be something for you from the spoils. Now, are there any questions?'

Only two or three hundred! thought Trace.

'No? Good! Well then, let's be at it. I want to be out of here within the hour, and at the nunnery near Bethsaida by two-thirty.' He turned away, loped quickly across the room and out of a door, was gone . . .

At 2:25 P.M. exactly, the gates to the house with the high-walled gardens were opened and the ambulance, followed by a pair of drab, grey-green landrovers, exited in clouds of dust. The sun, glancing off the vehicles' mirrors, windows and one or two polished surfaces, glinted blindingly in the eyes of an observer where he watched from the parapet of a minaret in Jenin three-quarters of a mile away.

Dressed in combat clothing and wearing the insignia of a Colonel in the Israeli Army, he lowered his binoculars, rubbed at his eyes for a moment and turned to a Captain who stood beside him. 'That's them. Get on the radio and pull out any check-point personnel or border-patrols on their route. Pull 'em back, out of the way. I don't want any interfering with them. Then radio the nunnery and let them know what's happening. They'll know what to do . . .'

'Yes, sir!' The Captain saluted, ducked through an arched doorway into a small circular room, spoke urgently to the signalman seated there at a table bearing his radio.

The Colonel stayed on the parapet, again trained his binoculars on the tiny convoy, listened to his orders going out in the clipped jargon of radio-procedure. He frowned and pursed his lips. Three vehicles like a trio of dusty beetles, one big one and two little ones, crawling in the blazing sun. Three very important beetles, with a very important cargo. But what was it? The Colonel sucked his teeth, held the binoculars with one hand, patted his right-hand breast pocket, just to be sure his orders were still in there and he wasn't dreaming all of this. Talk about weird tasks!

His orders had come direct from the C-in-C himself, but he was only obeying a joint-instruction, co-ordinating and answering a joint plea. And the counter-signatories to that were – simply unbelievable! It was only a scrap of paper, of course, and the Colonel's copy only a photocopy at that – but he would dearly love to keep it, if only for posterity. He couldn't keep it: the papers were Top Secret and when the job was finished they must be destroyed. But . . . oh, those signatures!

Among them had been those of the Israeli premier himself, the Archbishop of Canterbury, His All-Highness the Dalai Lama, Masaki Shan, the One Priest of Ko-su Ku on Hokkaido, even the Pope! Strange indeed, devilish strange. But the Colonel would have to let it go at that – without ever knowing just how close he'd been . . .

For Trace the first half of the trip went well enough, but the rest of it was a nightmare. He had wondered why he and his 'brothers' were made to lie on mattresses on the floor of the ambulance, but he wasn't kept wondering for long. Somewhere along the way, shortly after Nazareth, which the little convoy skirted, decent road turned first to dirt track then to boulder-strewn scrub and desert as they toiled up into foothills and headed for the heights north of Galilee. Trace was fairly well able to look after himself and hang on to the various fixtures, but Amira was kept more than busy attending to her two.

There was little or no opportunity for talking, not with the vehicle rattling and bouncing about like this, and certainly not with Khumeni sitting up front. Where the way was especially difficult he would look back, scowling through the tinted partition, but other than that he stared straight ahead and studied the terrain. And so, finally, they came to the lonely nunnery where it looked down across the Sea of Galilee, only a mile or so from those ancient ruins which were once Bethsaida.

Bethsaida. Yes, and the Lord had cursed that place, too: Chorazin, Bethsaida, and Capernaum. A trinity of doom. And now Trace wryly wondered: for what they had harboured in His life, or for what He had known they would harbour in some distant future – *this* present time – when His life if not His work in the world was finished? For now Ab, Guigos, Khumeni was come here again; them and all the others he had been and was, returned to the holy land once more and for the last time to renew himself.

By the time the ambulance trundled to a halt, its inside was unbearably hot. Then, when Decker came and let down the ramp at the rear, Amira was glad to be able to climb out into sweet fresh air rising from the lake. Finally the four Mafia types came and carried out Trace and the other two into bright but pleasingly cool daylight; wheel-chairs were unfolded and all three 'invalids' seated in them; now Trace could look about and get some sort of idea where he was and what the country looked like.

In fact the view was wonderful, quite awesome, and Trace was actually sorry he wasn't better able to enjoy it. Rising from the valley of the lake below, a cliff of raw yellow rock extended in a slow curve for miles east and west, gradually bending into the walls of a basin about the lake's contours. Weathered at its rim, the cliff had been rounded into massive domes of rock, between two of which the nunnery seemed suspended over a scree and pebble-strewn slope that gradually grew steeper until, far below, the cliffs went sheer to the lake.

Monks and nuns, thought Trace, *of whatever denomi-nation; all of them seem to have this predilection for high, near-inaccessible places* . . .

The convoy had fetched its halt on a sort of levelled plateau, slightly higher and set back from the dizzy front. Rough, low walls of uncemented stone protected unwary wanderers against approaching its rim too closely. From the plateau down to the nunnery's single arched entrance in an olive-shaded enclosure where a spring welled up from the rock, wide shallow steps had been hewn from the dome itself. And standing at the head of those steps, her forearms crossed in front of her waist and disappearing into the wide sleeves of her habit, the Mother Superior smiled on all and waited as the beast at last stepped forward to introduce himself.

'Khumeni,' he said, extending a hand from the sleeve of his brown robe. 'George Khumeni.'

'Our benefactor,' said the Mother Superior, still smiling – but she made no attempt to take Khumeni's hand. And then Trace noted that her smile seemed frozen on her face, as if painted there. Khumeni noted it, too.

294

He quickly turned from her, cast anxious eyes at the rocky slopes and ridges all about, peered closely at the dust and grit of the levelled area where the vehicles were parked. In the shadow of his cowl, his eyebrows came together in a frown over his ravaged nose. He turned back to her, questions growing on his lips –

– Which she at once cut off with: 'You are all welcome here. I am Anna Chinnova, the Mother Superior, and the sisters are all waiting to meet you below.' But still she made no attempt to offer her hand.

Khumeni was nervous, alert, on guard. He lifted his head and sniffed the air sharply, loped this way and that, several paces in each direction, for a few seconds. And then again he turned to her and asked: 'Are there others here? Have others *been* here – recently?'

'Others?' she raised her eyebrows. 'Your friend Professor Halbstein is here, but – '

Khumeni ignored her, turned to his men. 'There's something here I don't like. A feeling. Something has been wrong ever since we left Jenin. No barriers on the roads, no patrols. Too easy altogether! Vittori, get down there and find Halbstein. And you – ' he grabbed Anna Chinnova's arms, shook her, ' – what outside communications do you have? A radio? A telephone?'

'How *dare* you!' she gasped, struggling free of his grip. Brown eyes in her cream face grew cloudy with anger. 'Are you mad?'

'Telephone!' Khumeni snapped again, his voice changing, becoming clotted and guttural. 'Where is it? Take me to it at once!' He turned to his party. 'The rest of you, get these three below – and see no harm comes to them.' Again he grabbed the Mother Superior's arm. 'Lead on!' he commanded, half-pushing, half-dragging her down the steps.

Vittori had gone ahead with his short-barrelled

machine-gun, unfolding its skeletal metal butt as he raced down the steps. At the bottom he'd rounded up a dozen indignant nuns under the olive trees, then left them crowded there to run into the nunnery. As Khumeni and the Mother Superior reached the bottom, Vittori reappeared with a bearded, slender white-haired man of about fifty-five years of age. Amira's father.

Khumeni nodded a curt, sour greeting, said to Vittori: 'Now search for a telephone or radio – and if you find one or both destroy them!' He rounded on the muttering Italian nuns. 'You lot – a dozen of you, I see, like brain-washed disciples – *be quiet!*' And to his men: 'Get them inside, lock them up.' He pushed Anna Chinnova after them. 'This old cow, too!'

He shouted more instructions, and leaving the three men in their wheelchairs under the olive trees, his hired thugs hurried to obey. Only then did the beast turn his attention to Amira and her father where they hugged and patted each other. Trace was seated close enough to hear what he said:

'These men of mine are paid for, bought,' Khumeni gurgled, quietly threatening, 'and so they will do exactly as I say. I fear no treachery from them. But you two, father and daughter both, were coerced. I know you fear and hate me, and I know why – because you *know* me! Well, know this, too:

'If you have done anything to interfere with my plans I shall see to it that you die slowly and in ways you cannot possibly imagine! Is that perfectly clear? Is it understood? Good! Then help me get my sons inside.'

Inside the nunnery Trace and his 'brothers' were wheeled down stone corridors and through stone rooms to the front, and out on to a balcony that looked out over the Sea of Galilee. As soon as they had been left alone and the door was closed on them, Trace got up, limped to the balcony's ornate stone wall and looked over it – and immediately wished he hadn't. The view was vertiginous. There was nothing below but thin air, and far, far down, rocks and water. Trace could climb like a monkey but he wasn't a fly! Even if he had thought to make an escape, this wouldn't be the place to try it.

Then he tried the stout wooden door and found it locked, finally turned his attention to the other two where they sat in their wheelchairs. They were awake now but still looking very rough. They didn't look much – considering they were sons of the antichrist! He spoke to one of them, who looked at him blankly, sickly, opened his mouth and tried to speak, gave several croaks and finally coughed something out in Turkish. Trace stared at him a moment longer, saw that his eyes weren't quite focusing, shrugged frustratedly and turned to the other. Greek, this one, but he did understand a few words of English. If Trace had had a smattering of Greek they might have got somewhere, but his knowledge of the language was zero. In the end he gave it up.

An hour went by, then two, by which time Trace's patience was short as the fuse on a 5th of November firework. But at least he had been able to exercise some of the stiffness out of his joints, until he now felt about half-way back to normal. His flesh was still weak, yes, but all of his will was back. And some anger. And a lot of fear. For as the sun dipped toward the horizon and the shadows began to lengthen, so an atmosphere was building, and it was one fraught with an unknown weirdness that Trace felt walking on his skin like poisonous spiders.

He went to the door again, went in anger with his fist raised – and the door opened in his face before he could strike it. Khumeni stood there. He looked at Trace's raised, clenched fist and smiled. Under his cowl his face twisted and his eyes burned like coals, and that was his smile. And away in the west clouds passed over the face of the sun and threw the high balcony into shadow . . .

Standing face to face with the beast, Trace felt a sudden compelling urge to strike him. But that would be like spitting at the sun to put it out, or trying to carve a diamond with an eraser. He knew it, but still he wanted to drive his fist into Khumeni's face, ruin his rotting nose beyond repair. He *wanted* to – but the burning eyes under that cowl held him transfixed, immovable.

Then Khumeni reached out, took Trace's fist in long, bony fingers, drew it down to hang naturally at Trace's side and left it there. And Trace sensed the terrible strength in those fingers, sensed what they could command, and knew that indeed Khumeni could tear him limb from limb – or have him torn.

Khumeni advanced a single pace on to the spacious balcony, and Trace backed off a step before him. The beast turned his back and closed the door, and almost in contempt paused before turning back again. 'You continue to surprise me,' he rasped. 'Your anger, so great. But why?'

'Because of my mother!' Trace blurted, the words coming out before he could check them for content, like iron filings drawn from his tongue by a magnet. Khumeni's hypnotic eyes, of course. Trace forced himself to look away.

'You do well not to look at me,' said Khumeni. 'I might take it as a challenge and climb through your eyes into your brain, and read all the thoughts hidden there. Yes, and they might be such as to make me angry; in my anger I might blind you or turn you into a puling idiot, for my amusement. You see? And so you do well to avoid these eyes of mine. They have learned a lot in two thousand years.'

Trace said nothing, and eventually Khumeni continued:

'Now, you say you hate me because of your mother – but I paid her great tribute when I filled her with my seed. Satan's vast beauty and potency earned him his expulsion, so wondrous were they! You should feel honoured to own me for your father, and yet you answer with anger and hatred.'

Trace wanted to deny him, wanted to shout out that he was not Khumeni's son – but that would be to ruin everything. It must be done at Chorazin, could *only* be done at Chorazin. And Trace wanted to be part of it there. He wanted to do it himself if he could, but at the very least be part of it. Still he could not resist a sneer. He glanced at Khumeni and looked away again, but at the same time he sneered. 'Honoured? If you are what they think you are, who could feel honoured to have you for a father?'

'They?' Khumeni gave the word a razor's edge.

Trace thought quickly. 'Kastrouni said you were only half human, a beast.'

'Kastrouni?' the word came like a cough, fired explosively. Khumeni took Trace's shoulders in his hands and forcibly turned him face-on. 'He did speak to you at length, then. And what did he tell you, the Greek?'

'He came – ' Trace avoided looking directly into the other's eyes, ' – to kill me,' he lied. 'But then he weakened. He saw that I was only a man, not the monster he expected, and he couldn't do it. Instead of killing me, he warned me. He said you were my father, and you were evil, and that he would destroy you if he could.'

Khumeni nodded. 'He weakened, yes. *You* weakened him for me. He was so eager to convert you that when I found him his guard was down. And so, finally, I was able to kill him. I have you to thank for that.'

'I saw you kill him,' said Trace. 'But it was a clean

death. It won't be like that for these men, will it? And it won't be like that for me.'

Khumeni looked at the others, stared at them where they lolled, and Trace was glad of the respite from those burning eyes. 'These two,' said the beast, 'they – are little more than fodder. Fuel for my next span of years. But you . . . who can say what lies ahead? And you are thinking: "Ah! But something also lies ahead for you, too", eh? And do you suppose I don't know they have schemed against me? I *do* know! But these others, these "friends" of your – Gokowski and the Halbsteins and the rest – can you really believe they know what they are dealing with? They only *think* they know. I scorn them, and *my* father will not forgive them, even though they know not what they do!'

'Your father is the devil!' Trace blurted. 'Those words on your lips are a blasphemy. And now I understand the meaning of that word. I was never a true believer, but now I am. You might have duped me before, but now that I'm a believer you've lost me.'

Khumeni laughed, like ice on sensitive teeth. 'What? Lost you? Fool! How could you ever really believe in *my* father without first believing in Him? No, I've not lost you, Charles, I've found you!'

Chapter four

Confused, Trace opened his mouth but nothing came out. 'I . . .' he said. 'I . . .'

'Nothing is what it seems, my son,' Khumeni laughed again. 'You talk of winning and losing; but when Satan spins the wheel, *all* the numbers are zeros! Just remember, nothing is what it seems. To win is to gain everything you detest, and to lose is to be bereft of all you hold most dear. And so, how may you win? A riddle for you to play with, perhaps? But before you attempt to fathom it, consider first my power!'

He threw off his robe, stood naked . . . And if there was any single shred of doubt left in Trace, now it was snuffed out like a candle, extinguished at once. A satyr stood there for a moment, Pan chuckled and smiled slyly – then reached out and caught Trace and drew him close. 'So Kastrouni said that I was only half-human, eh?' his voice bubbled like pitch. 'But he was wrong. *Nothing* of me is human, Charles! Can't you understand that the shape you wear is abhorrent to me and mine? For you are made in the image of the Ultimate Enemy. It is ugly! But this . . . *this* is the real beauty. Look at it. Can't you feel it burning? What, revulsion? I felt that, too, at first – but now I feel only power!'

Trace fought with himself, struggled furiously, won. He turned away. Apparently astonished, Khumeni simply released his shoulders.

'What?' he said. 'You defy me? You dare put me behind you? But I will not *be* defied.' On his grotesque beast's legs he loped to the others where they sat, tore open their robes. 'See here, their marks!' The Greek's right leg was covered in coarse black hair from thigh to ankle; in the Turk's left armpit, a full-sized woman's breast, complete with huge nipple, depended like the udder of a witch.

Trace drew back, shuddering, but Khumeni only brayed with laughter. 'Marks, yes,' he nodded his scabrous head, 'devil's signs – but *you* have the true mark, Charles!'

Sudden pain shot through Trace's left leg from his foot. He cried out, staggered, put a hand on the wall of the balcony to steady himself. And he knew that the pain had been sent, that Khumeni had taken control of him just when he thought he was the winner.

'See my power!' the beast was gleeful. 'And you think I might be defeated? But let me show you more. Get up, my son – up on to the wall.'

Trace shook his head, felt sweat break out on him in a moment as he commanded his body to stay still – and it refused! He fought it every inch of the way – uselessly. He got up on to the wall, kneeled there on that narrow stone parapet, slowly stood up. His right leg was straight and strong, despite recent deprivations, but his left trembled violently. Only inches from eternity, he staggered.

'Lean outwards,' said the beast, 'and look down!'

Trace tried to shake his head in denial, but Khumeni's control was now complete. Inwardly screaming *no, no*, still his body leaned outwards. Far below the Lake of Galilee glittered in the rays of a sun three-quarters down the sky; to the north the world's rim was curved; Gravity, invisible, grew angry at Trace's impertinent posturing.

'More yet!' Khumeni rasped.

Trace leaned out on thin air – and felt himself start to slip through it! Khumeni caught his left hand, leaned backward and swung him like a pendulum, turned him inwards even as he toppled. Jelly, he crashed down from the wall on to the balcony's stone floor and lay there crying and wetting himself.

Khumeni put on his robe, turned the cowl up over his head, moved to the door. Before going through it he paused and pointed at Trace, commanding: 'Now resist me no longer but lie there in your piss and sleep. And tonight we shall see what we shall see.'

And once more Trace could only obey him . . .

Consciousness came with cool updraughts from the lake, with a sky turning indigo, in which the ghosts of stars showed as flickering white fireflies, and with the sound of hurried footsteps on stone and a slamming of doors. The nunnery came awake and Khumeni's entourage was on the move again.

Last to leave and climb the steps to the plateau where the vehicles stood under the first stars was Khumeni himself, behind the trio of staggering zombies he called his sons. For under the awesome power of the beast the three were walking now, though Trace knew that only one – namely Trace himself – should be able to walk at all. But though they reeled like drunkards, still his 'brothers' climbed the shallow steps to the plateau and were helped into the back of a landrover, and Trace with them. Amira got in too, keeping as close to Trace as she could get. Decker was the driver and Khumeni sat beside him, leading the way. For no one knew the way better than Khumeni. In the second landrover, Professor Halbstein drove with Gabella and Vittori as his passengers. The ambulance was left behind.

Down below in the small oasis of greenery guarding the nunnery's entrance, Rosco and Lancing watched the dipped headlights of the two vehicles out of sight, then went back inside. For them it was over, simply a matter of waiting now. So they thought.

But in the prison dormitory Anna Chinnova had sensed Khumeni's departure, and already a stone flag in the floor had been prised loose to allow a pair of armed, uniformed figures to clamber stiffly into view. Israeli soldiers, combat-hardened veterans of many campaigns, they silently worked the stiffness out of cramped joints, quietly readied their automatic weapons and moved to the locked door.

Out in the corridor, Rosco and Lancing had resumed their game of poker at a small wooden table. Then there came the banging from within the dormitory, and the Mother Superior's strident voice demanding that they open the door. 'There are no . . . *facilities* in here!' she protested. 'We have our needs, you know.'

Rosco grimaced and stood up, picked up the weapon Vittori had left behind for them, went to the door. 'Is that all they fucking do?' he inquired of Lancing as he turned the key. 'Pester and pray and pee?'

The door burst open on him to reveal the two Israeli crouched there, guns at the ready. Rosco's eyes stood out in his pale face. 'Shit!' he said, swinging up his weapon – but not quite finding the time to pull the trigger. Both Israelis opened up, the yammering stream of concussion deafening as Rosco was picked up by the sleeting lead and hurled away like a rag doll. Lancing, too, was in the line of fire. Half-way out of his chair the withering blast caught him, laced him up and down and sideways, tossed his crimson corpse loose as an empty suit across the corridor.

With blue smoke and the smell of cordite still heavy in the air, and their ears still ringing, the soldiers went about their business. The senior man extended the antenna of his walkie-talkie, coldly and efficiently made his report.

And up on the heights over Chorazin cigarettes were extinguished and silent observers moved back into the shadows of rocks and ruins, and camouflage netting was checked where it broke down the shapes of vehicles and swivel-mounted general-purpose machine-guns, and a half-platoon of Special Forces grew vigilant as night deepened and the first clouds began to gather in ominous thunderheads out of the east . . .

In the lee of a domed hill to the north-east of Chorazin, Khumeni's landrovers sat in silence and shadows until an hour before midnight. Then, at his signal, the engines coughed into life and dipped headlights came on, and the last half-mile of the journey was completed over bumpy ground and through the crumbling ruins of ages. And at last they came to the secret place.

Trace looked out from the back of the landrover at a scene he knew at once: a scene painted on his mind's eye by Dimitrios Kastrouni and still fresh there, accurate in every detail.

Obviously the place had been, long, long ago, a large village or town. The foundations of many houses were still apparent, and in places, low, ruined walls still stood up from the stony ground. Here was the crumbling rim of the dried-out well Kastrouni had mentioned, in a now ghostly plaza under the stars, and here the almost fossilized trunk of a great olive tree, slowly turning to stone in a languid metamorphosis which had already taken more than six hundred years. And in the near-distance, where the cliffs had been split and weathered into an opening by some ancient watercourse, down there in the 'V' of the cleft, Galilee lay silver in moon and starlight. The place had magic, and mystery, and yet it was morbid. The last because Trace knew where he was.

Khumeni and his three thugs, and Amira and her

305

father, gathered in a group beside the vehicle containing Trace and his 'brothers'. And it was then, as the beast began to issue his last instructions, that Trace – probably the others, too – first noticed his rapidly accelerating *deterioration,* the physical and possibly mental decay bloating in him like a monstrous dry-rot mutation.

Words bubbled out of his now shrunken form like pockets of foul gas bursting over a swamp: 'First we open the place up. Decker, I may need your great bulk, the weight of your gross body, and so you shall come below with me and my three. Vittori: you, too, accompany us. Gabella: you stay up here and keep watch. Especially these two, the girl and her father. Watch them well. You see, they have arranged a little trap for us – a puny threat which I shall deal with shortly!'

'A trap?' Decker nervously gazed all about in the dark. 'I see no trap. And what do you mean, "below"? Where below?'

'A dig, I said,' Khumeni chortled evilly. 'And how may one get below without digging, eh? But bring me the length of chain from the back of that vehicle there and I shall show you.'

While Decker got the chain, Khumeni limped to a level area within a square formed by four large boulders. 'Gabella, Vittori!' he called. 'Quickly, bring shovels, dig here.'

The two did as they were told but Gabella grumbled: 'I don't remember being paid to do any digging.'

Khumeni definitely seemed smaller now; his robe trailed a little on the ground under his feet, and the cowl seemed overlarge for his head. He was crumbling into himself as the transformation took hold and his years caught up with him – that rapid decline which forewarned that his time of renewal drew ever closer – but there was still power in his voice and great cunning in his black

306

heart as he answered: 'Payment? I may tell you, Mr Gabella, that you really won't *believe* your rewards for this night's work!'

He stooped, picked up an old bent stick, slowly straightened and leaned on the stick like a crutch while the two Mafia thugs began to dig. Under his cowl the beast's eyes were alive: glittering red points that eagerly watched as every spadeful of dirt was thrown aside. And the night grew darker yet as the thunderheads crept out of the east and began to shut out the stars. An unseasonal chill settled and a breeze blew up that moaned in the old ruins and over the stony hills.

'There!' said Khumeni after a little while, his clotted voice awful in its eagerness. 'There!' And the grunting, grumbling pair of thugs threw down their shovels and stepped aside.

A dozen inches down the outlines of a slab had come into view, with a huge, rust-red iron ring set in one end. 'Take the chain,' the beast instructed. 'Loop it through the ring and secure it to that landrover there. Vittori, get into the vehicle and prepare to haul up the slab.'

In another moment the slab had been hoisted upright and a black hole gaped below. Khumeni hobbled on his stick to the rear of the second vehicle. He glared into the canvas-roofed interior, where Trace kept his eyes averted. 'Out, you three,' the beast husked, his eyes and voice hypnotic in their combined intensity. 'Out into the night, with me, and down to your destinies.'

But things had now proceeded as far as Trace dared let them. He did not know what awaited down there in that black hole, and he didn't intend to find out. Kastrouni had not been down there, and Trace wasn't going either, not if he had anything to say about it. Whatever plan the Halbsteins had worked out between them – whatever 'trap' they had set for Khumeni and his hirelings – now was surely the time to spring it, before the horror started. If not . . . then Trace would have to set things in motion himself.

Since leaving the nunnery he had not sat still for a moment. He had exercised his arms and legs – particularly his left leg – and his entire body as best he might. But perhaps more importantly, he had also exercised his mind. Physically . . . one good punch would probably knock him down. But mentally he was one hundred per cent alert, switched on. And necessarily so, for it was here – right here and now – that the course of Charles Trace's life, or the end of it, would be determined.

He got down with the others from the landrover, imitated their stumbling, jerky walk where they followed Khumeni toward the hole under the raised slab. There the beast paused and turned to face the rest. And while Trace frantically tried to decide what to do next, Khumeni addressed them:

'All of you,' he croaked, 'listen carefully. It is half an hour before midnight. I shall be gone down into this hole for at least that long and perhaps a little longer, and then I shall return. Then, too, the rewards of this night's work shall be seen. Mr Gabella, you will wait and watch as instructed, for these two are devious. I take it you are able to protect yourself if they should think to attack you?'

Gabella shrugged. 'What, an old guy and a broad? No sweat. But just in case they do try it on – ' There came a sharp *click* and Gabella produced a spring-loaded knife with a blade all of six inches long. The ugly weapon had seemed to grow right out of his hand; obviously he would be proficient in its use.

'Good!' Khumeni nodded his approval. But then he glared at Amira and her father and took a hobbling step toward them. He pointed a long forefinger accusingly from the loose sleeve of his robe. 'And you two, father and daughter alike – did you think to fool me? Or more foolish far – did you think to deter me? And as for your "trap": that is the utmost folly!'

'I . . . that is, we, don't know what you're – ' Amira began, her voice shrill with fear.

'But you do!' the beast turned on her, suddenly livid with fury. '*You do!*' Amira fell into her father's arms, apparently driven back by the power of Khumeni's words alone. And now Khumeni snorted like the beast he was, and he directed his next statement at everyone present:

'I *will* be obeyed – now, tonight, and for always – my father's will be done. Whatever is seen or heard or sensed in the next half-hour, it will have been my doing. Gabella, you may well see things up here to frighten you – yes, even you. But you will stay and watch and wait.' He turned his burning gaze on the dark hills nearby. 'Unfortunately there are those who would interfere, coming down on you like jackals in the night when I have gone below and can no longer help you. But I have seen them, and so has my father's familiar on this earth – Demogorgon!'

Demogorgon . . . The word was like an electric shock in Trace's mind. It confirmed everything, brought it all together. It was all going to happen – starting now!

Lightning flickered in an ominous white tracery along the underside of the clouds where they boiled directly overhead. Lightning which crackled audibly but as yet produced no thunder. Khumeni looked up and his cowl fell back. His jaws opened like a hound's and he laughed; and as his ravaged face was lit by the flickering fires above, so he seemed to draw strength from them and his voice became a monstrous bass croaking:

'*Father, I sense your presence in the heavens where you belong. And I know you gaze down on me through the*

309

*eyes of Demogorgon! So be it! The time has come again
when I must descend into the earth, and rise up again to
do your bidding, renewed and replenished. So be it! Except
we are not alone. There are those who would harm me,
and through me, you! As I have kept faith for two thousand
years, so now keep faith with me. Unleash the fires of hell,
let Demogorgon breathe upon mine enemies!'*

'No!' Professor Halbstein shouted. He produced a
pencil-slim torch from somewhere, fell to one knee and
flashed the torch's beam in a desperate code up toward
the hills. A code, a signal, prearranged.

'Father!' Amira shrieked, falling beside him. 'Father –
we're in the line of fire!' But she, too, knew that it had to
be done.

Vittori was closest to the old man and quickest to
react. He stepped forward, rabbit-chopped him – but
Halbstein's message had been passed. Tracers arced
through the sky beneath the boiling clouds, their light
coming split seconds ahead of the chattering explosions
which spawned them. Hot steel raked the ruins a little
beyond Khumeni's party, crept closer as the gunners
corrected their range.

Trace threw himself flat; Decker, Gabella and Vittori,
too. The zombies Khumeni called his sons staggered to
and fro, helpless spastics; but Khumeni himself held up
his spindle arms to the sky and brayed with laughter as
the night was lit with flares which arced ever closer. And
high overhead the lightning in the clouds grew more
intense, formed a web of white light, converged in a
central area – and lanced down!

Trace had seen something like this before, knew what
was coming. One . . . two . . . three. . . four . . . five
blinding lances of lightning smashed down from Demogorgon's living maelstrom; and in those moments when
the sky blazed bright as day, it seemed to Trace that a

310

great horned head and face were outlined in the roiling clouds, whose eyes were seething, sentient pools of energy. And at once the machine-gun fire from the hills was cut off, the tracers stuttered, stopped, and exploding steel grew silent. Then five bomb-bursts of light – five deafening concussions – five mushrooms of fire and smoke gouting up in the shattered darkness of the high hills. For a moment on those near-distant slopes, a handful of antlike figures danced and capered, human torches screaming their agony; secondary explosions sent tremors through the air and rock; the sky grew red from the funeral pyres of half a platoon of Israel's finest.

After that . . . the flickering electrical energies in the clouds slowly grew quiescent once more. But they remained alert. Then:

'Time is wasting,' said Khumeni, his voice a low growl, the satisfied rumble of a sated animal. 'Decker, take that old fool's torch and lead the way.'

But Decker was no longer eager. All of this was beyond him. He understood the unnatural well enough, but the supernatural . . .? He stood up, tried to brush himself down with hands that fluttered like rags, said: 'Me? Down there? Maybe Lou would like to – '

'Decker,' Khumeni's purr cut him off. 'Shall I talk to the sky again? And should I mention your name to the lightnings I command?'

'No, no!' Decker quickly held up his hands. He moved stumblingly to where Amira tended her father, stooped and took up the torch, tested its beam. 'OK,' he said then, trying to control his quavering voice. 'OK, let's go.'

As Decker began to descend the steps under the slab, so Khumeni turned to his charges. He merely beckoned, and Trace's 'brothers' followed the fat man without protest, wooden in their movements and completely under Khumeni's spell. Vittori went among them, and then it was Trace's turn. He made as if to follow – but at the last possible moment grabbed Khumeni's skinny arm and swung him off balance toward the open vault.

The beast staggered, flailed his arms for a moment, fell into the hole. Falling, he threw his arms wide like a cross so that they slammed down on the rim of the opening to support him, kicked with his feet until they found purchase on unseen steps below. His arms might reasonably have broken, but they didn't. And secure there, waist deep in the opening, finally he glared at Trace and pointed a madly trembling hand at him. 'You –' he hissed, unable to find words to express his anger. '*You . . . !*'

From behind Trace there sounded a distinctive *click* – Lou Gabella's knife!

Then . . . several things, all coming simultaneously:

Trace turned; Gabella was almost on him, the blade of his weapon glittering in the light of the distant fires; and: '*No!*' Khumeni's voice was shrilly fearful. 'Do not harm him! I want him alive!' And as Gabella still closed in, threatening, two shadows growing out of Chorazin's ruins and taking on the shape of men. Impossibly familiar men.

'Enemies!' Khumeni rasped.

From below came muffled, quavering queries: Decker and Vittori, panicking. 'Be quiet!' Khumeni snarled. 'Get below and wait!'

Gabella had turned away from Trace to face the newcomers. Dressed in black clothing and with scarves across their faces, they paused – but only for a moment. Then one of them came on, tossed aside his scarf, revealed his face. Khumeni had grabbed up a torch from a ledge under the raised slab; sparks flew from a cigarette lighter in his trembling, knobby fist; ancient, desiccated rags coated in brittle tar burst into life and threw the shadows back. Khumeni held up the torch, took one good look at

312

the face of the man who now closed with Gabella – and his sulphurous eyes seemed to stand out in his face.

'Kastrouni!' he croaked.

Gabella lunged, the glitter of his knife making an arc of light. But Kastrouni was no novice where knives were concerned. And now two sharp blades glittered in the light from Khumeni's torch.

The Greek blocked Gabella's thrust, drew him closer, drove his own knife in and up. It sliced into Gabella's heart, and Kastrouni twisted it there just to be sure, then snatched it back. As Gabella sank to his knees and flopped down on to his face, so his life went out of him in a long '*Ahhhh!*'

Khumeni once more drew strength from the flickering lightnings in the clouds. He held up his arms to the sky, cried: 'Father, I stand in peril. I am surrounded by mine enemies! Now let Demogorgon – '

Kastrouni drew back his arm, let fly his blade. The knife leaped across the space between, thudded keep into the beast's right shoulder just below the collar-bone. Khumeni wore an old wound there, a scar he remembered well, and he knew Kastrouni's aim had been quite deliberate. He reeled, cried out gurglingly, grabbed the knife in his shoulder and drew it out. But Kastrouni wasn't finished. A second knife appeared in his hand, was drawn back, then hurled forward with all the strength he could muster. And this one was intended for the beast's heart.

Khumeni covered his breast with both hands and tried to cower back in that position. The knife pinned his hands together but merely punctured the skin of his chest through his robe. Shrieking hoarsely, he jerked his hands apart and sent the knife clattering on the stony ground. Then, blood spattering darkly as he stepped falteringly down and backwards, and taking up the torch again from where he had let it fall, he controlled his agony and once more turned his mummied face up to the tortured sky.

'Demogorgon,' he gasped, 'guard them well. Keep them here to wait on my return.' And as his voice gathered awful strength and he disappeared into darkness: *'For they have earned themselves ecstasies of agony beyond compare!'*

Trace glanced at the sky, saw the webs of electrical energy forming as before. He found his voice, said: 'Let's get after him – while we can!'

'No!' a familiar voice denied. The second newcomer had removed his scarf: Saul Gokowski. 'No, Charlie,' he repeated, stepping forward, 'let him go. He won't be coming back up out of there, be sure. We've had this moment planned for quite some – ' But that was as far as he got.

Unnatural energies were building. The hair on the heads of men and girl stood up erect and crackling, full of static. The sky was patterned with veins of blue light, pulsating there; and falling now like a curtain on all sides, a fine veil of coruscating strands of living energy descended, caging Trace and the others within its sputtering circumference. They were surrounded in a moment by a wall of shimmering blue fire.

Then the net began to tighten, the curtain closing; and as the circle narrowed down to less than a hundred feet in diameter, so lightning ran in crackling rivulets about its rim, warning of the death lurking there should anyone try to cross.

Amira's father had regained consciousness. He quickly took in what was happening. 'Saul!' he cried. 'The second tablet. If this thing comes any closer, we won't be able to reach it!'

Gokowski drew a deep breath, said, 'Join me, then. You, too, Dimitrios.' And he commenced to chant those unearthly words from the second Chorazin tablet, that rite of exorcism Trace had heard once before in the monastery on Karpathos. Halbstein and Kastrouni at once took up the chant, and as their voices joined so the circle of electrical energy pulsated and throbbed, while ripples of furious red ran through its curtain of hellish fire. The sputtering and crackling grew more intense and the light pulsed brighter yet; evil fed upon itself, drew energy from the boiling clouds, redoubled its strength to defy the puny creatures in the circle. And with only the very briefest pause, again the ring began to close.

'We're losing!' Gokowski's voice was hoarse. He ran to a place where a low, crumbling wall threw black shadows as Demogorgon's mesh closed in. The curtains of energy encroached on the wall, breaching it even as Gokowski got there. Then –

Gokowski had thrown up an arm, as if to shield himself from the curtain of living energy. His hand made contact and he was at once picked up, effortlessly tossed sprawling in the dust.

But at the same time the energies of the curtain had commenced a wild fluctuation, and its ever-shifting webs were laced with gold now and not the red of anger. Golden waves of light washed outwards, curving round the rippling wall away from the spot where Kastrouni had stood – the place where he had buried the second Chorazin tablet!

And then, weakened, Demogorgon's mesh drew reluctantly back, wavered, finally kept an even distance while the ripples of yellow diminished and finally disappeared. The curtain threatened as before – an unearthly aurora, localized into this cage of energy – but the buried tablet's power held it at bay, unable to advance any closer.

Dimitrios Kastrouni ran to Gokowski, went to his knees beside him. Gokowski sat up, his face twisted with pain as he nursed his arm and shoulder. 'It's here,' he pointed at a mound of dust and rubble at the foot of the crumbling wall. 'I buried it here. Now help me get it up. That monster down there thinks he's got us trapped, but in fact we've got him!'

Professor Halbstein joined them as they dug with their hands, but Amira went to Trace. For at the height of the chanting, suddenly overcome by everything he'd been through, Trace had fainted and crumpled on the earth not far from the entrance to the vault. Now she dragged him away from there, gently slapped his face until he came to. He at once tried to stand.

'Better stay still, Charlie,' she told him. 'At least for a moment or two. Nothing more will happen just now – not until midnight.'

Trace looked across to where the other three men cleared rubble at the base of the wall. 'I have to help them,' he mumbled. Despite her protests he got to his feet, limped to them and gave a hand. And in a very short while the second Chorazin tablet came into view, unseen since the day Saul Gokowski had buried it.

The men clawed away more dirt, revealed a stone oblong some five inches thick, almost three feet long by eighteen inches wide. And it was deeply carved with strange glyphs: the exorcism inscribed by Ab's witch-mother-mistress, the runes of righteousness.

Trace's fingers touched the tablet and tingled; he felt its power, felt dizzy as an astronaut pin-wheeling against the stars in nil-gravity, felt small in the presence of previously unbelievable supernatural forces and concepts – in which he now believed, for his life.

'Are you all right?' Saul Gokowski was looking at him curiously.

'No,' Trace answered, 'I'm sick as a dog! What do you expect? I'm sick from lack of regular meals, from the

316

after-effects of drugs and inactivity, from this bloody electrical *thing* that's watching us. And I'm sick with fear!'

'This "bloody electrical thing" is a demon,' Kastrouni joined in, getting to his feet. 'I know because I've met him before – three times. It's Demogorgon, summoned by Khumeni, the antichrist. It is his father's familiar here on earth. Satan's watchdog. And it bites! If we destroy Khumeni, it will go back where it came from. That's what we're trying to do now: trap him down there, using the tablet, and then destroy him. We have to get the tablet over to the vault.'

'The landrover,' Halbstein nodded. 'The vehicle and its tow-chain. Khumeni had the right idea: it's how I got the stone out of that place. I lowered tackle over the cliff, dragged it into the caves through a sort of natural window there, hauled the tablet up the face of the cliff using a landrover.'

'I'll get the vehicle,' Trace said.

He limped to the landrover (his bloody leg again, only worse than ever), started it up with difficulty, drove it jerkily back to where the others waited. Demogorgon's mesh was interfering with the firing of the plugs, causing partial engine-failure. Then he turned the vehicle in a tight, bumpy circle and revved the motor while the others fitted the chain around the tablet. Finally Kastrouni jumped into the passenger's seat, said:

'OK, Charlie, let's go. We've got twenty minutes to midnight. But things are due to start happening any time now!'

Trace drove back to the vault and beyond it, a distance of maybe twenty yards. Not a great distance by any means, but it would have seemed a mile to men carrying the massive granite tablet. Braking to a halt, Trace said:

'Things will start happening? Isn't enough happening right now?'

'You remember what I told you about the flies, the locusts?' Kastrouni shouted over a renewed burst of crackling and hissing from the mesh. 'Well, apparently there's more. It seems I missed the worst of it that night. There'll be frogs, too, and lice. So Saul thinks.'

'What? And we'll see these things?'

'Oh, yes! You remember Khumeni warned that thug he'd see things to frighten him? I heard the conversation from the shadows; anyway, that's what he was talking about. Well, whoever that killer was, he won't be seeing anything now – but we will!'

Kastrouni joined Professor Halbstein and Saul Gokowski where they wrestled with the tablet, laying it lengthwise across the twenty-four-inch width of the vault's entrance. It left gaps at both ends, but that couldn't be helped. Finally they stood back. And:

'That should do it,' said Gokowski, satisfied. 'He won't be able to come up through that. Its weight would never stop him, but its power should.'

It was quarter to midnight. The flickering, hissing, crackling mesh formed its unbroken curtain all around; the sky was still convulsed with writhing clouds; partly obscured by the mesh of demonic energy, the Israeli corpses and weaponry still burned on the dark hillside. And Trace's flesh crept with a monstrous expectancy.

The others felt it, too.

'It's coming,' said Gokowski, his voice a croak.

Trace tugged at the sleeve of Kastrouni's night-suit. 'One thing I have to know before "it" comes: I saw you die.'

'No,' Kastrouni's face was a sheen of blue light reflecting from cold sweat as he shook his head, 'you saw a

318

London taxi struck by lightning – destroyed by Demogorgon. But I wasn't in it. I saw that thing stalking me down the road. When the taxi cornered I went out of the door, rolled, hit the grass verge just as the taxi exploded. The blast did the rest. I was thrown into bushes, knocked unconscious. Demogorgon couldn't smell my fear, thought I was dead. You, too, apparently. Ambulance sirens woke me up and I crept away from there. As for the poor taxi-driver and his other passenger – ' he shrugged. 'What can I say? Their deaths were my fault.'

'Or mine,' said Trace. 'You came to warn me, remember?' And then: 'What other passenger?'

'Someone who flagged us down on our way to your place,' Kastrouni answered. 'I never knew him and I'm glad for that, at least. Anyway, I laid low for a day or so, then went to Karpathos. Saul had had you watched. I got in just after you left with Amira and the fat man. Saul was ready and we followed on immediately. Since then we've been busy.'

'Twelve minutes,' Professor Halbstein came to them. 'I think we should get back from the vault a little way now.' Even as he spoke, small shapes began to squirm up from the gaps at the sides of the tablet where it lay across the hole. All five fearful people got back, huddled behind the landrover, watched.

'Frogs?' Trace gasped. Kastrouni had warned him, but still it was hard to accept. 'But where do they come from? What the hell . . .? *Thousands* of them!'

'A twisted version of the plagues called down by Moses on Egypt,' Professor Halbstein explained. 'Because of the plagues, the Children of Israel were enabled to flee Pharaoh's bondage. This is Khumeni fleeing the bondage of his crumbling flesh – taking on new flesh, just as the Children of Israel took on a new lease of life. It is a blasphemous distortion of a biblical theme.'

Kastrouni was shuddering. Trace could feel it where he crouched beside him. 'You know what this means, Charlie?' the Greek's voice was heavy with dread. 'It means he'll be melting them, absorbing them, *becoming* them! You, too, if you'd gone down there with them. I'm glad you didn't.'

'But you'd have let me, eh?' Trace grunted.

'If you hadn't tried to fight him, that would have been as good as saying he was right,' Kastrouni answered, 'that you were in fact his son. We had to be sure.'

The tide of frogs had washed past the landrover, passing in widening ripples of squamous, squirming life, apparently unafraid, through Demogorgon's curtain of energy. Then came the lice.

Trace had thought he knew what lice were, but he didn't. For one thing, he hadn't known you could see them; or rather, he hadn't guessed they could be so obvious to the eye, so many and so loathsome.

Lice! – millions of lice! – they burst from the vault in leaping, hopping, milling clouds. Jumping this way and that, whole armies of them dashed themselves together in mindless mid-air collisions as they spewed aimlessly outward from the vault's entrance; and then they flowed over the earth, over the landrover, *on to* the five where they shuddered in a huddle behind it.

Amira screamed her disgust, leaped in horror, again and again, slapping at herself like a madwoman. The others, too, all dancing as if on hot coals, trying to dislodge that miniature vampire horde. And not a single bite, not a drop of blood shed or sucked. For the pit-lice, fat and bloated as ticks, had already sated themselves – below.

'Those poor devils down there,' Amira sobbed in Trace's arms when the lice had passed on. 'And you

320

might have been one of them. Oh, Charlie, Charlie! I would have killed myself if – '

'Six minutes,' her father cut her off.

Gokowski took out something that looked like a black plastic transistor radio from his night-suit. 'We'll give him four more minutes,' he said. 'By then the change should be complete. He'll have taken those damned, doomed sons of his by then, and possibly Decker or that other thug, too. The odd man out will most likely be dead. Then he'll start on his way out, and that's when we'll hit him!' He extended an antenna from the device in his hand, turned a small knob until it made a click. A tiny red light began flashing on and off, illuminating a red button.

'You've mined the place!' Trace made a guess.

Professor Halbstein nodded. 'I did, yes. Enough PE to turn the whole damned hell-hole into an inferno. There are pounds of the stuff down there, as much as I dared to use. Any more and he was sure to find it. That firing device of Saul's will set it off.'

'*Shh!*' Amira cautioned. 'What's that?'

Over and above the threatening, crackling electric voice of Demogorgon, there now sounded – screams? Screams, yes, coming up from the caves beneath the earth – but such screams as never were heard before. Or perhaps once before. 'Oh, God!' said Kastrouni, trying to control the tremor in his voice. 'That I should have lived to experience *this* again!'

But then the agonized shrieking was blanketed by a new sound: a mad massed buzzing as of insects in flight.

'Blowflies!' Trace gasped, and knew he was right. 'Your bloody blowflies, Dimitrios. I remember what you told me: "carrion flies – born in rotting meat", born out of Khumeni!' Kastrouni could only nod.

And up they came from the vault in their buzzing

myriads, circling the area within the living curtain like a solid, shining wall of metallic blue chitin, then breaking up and heading outwards, heedless of Demogorgon's hell-spawning energies. And at last the nightmare approached its climax.

'I can't take much more of this,' the words burst from Professor Halbstein's trembling lips. 'At first sight of the locusts, Saul, you press that damned button. For if that monster should somehow manage to break out of there . . .' He left his fears unspoken.

And now, as if summoned by the waxing terror of the five, up came the locusts in an endless stream of whirring ravenous horror – which was all the signal Saul Gokowski needed. Cowering down and warning the others to do likewise, he pressed the red button. The tiny red light winked out and stayed out. Then –

– *Crump! Crump! Crump!* From deep underground three explosions came as muffled rumbles, and a triple shock was transmitted from the earth and through the soles of their feet where the five crouched.

Professor Halbstein's mouth fell open and he clenched his fists. His face took on an expression filled with frustration. 'But there should have been six detonations!' he gasped. 'Three of them have failed . . . or else he found them.'

Saul Gokowski jabbed again and again at the button on his detonator, but uselessly. He uttered a low curse, tossed the dead device aside – at which the ground underfoot gave a shudder, a sudden convulsion. 'It's caving in!' Gokowski cried.

'And he's hurt!' Kastrouni almost danced in his excitement. 'Look! Look at this curtain of hellish fire!' But they were already looking.

Demogorgon's mesh was damaged. It pulsated errati-cally . . . was torn and at once mended itself, only to tear again . . . and now in several places. The curtain of energy billowed and fluttered as if great winds blew upon it; its ever-shifting filaments of fire sputtering and crackling less ferociously; and as the massed, whirring clouds of locusts passed through it and fled, so the mesh's blue light commenced a spastic dimming and flaring, until finally its harsh electrical 'voice' hissed into a stricken silence. Controlled by Khumeni – by an injured Khumeni, whose concern now was concentrated solely on personal survival and nothing else – Satan's storm-born familiar drew back his webs of energy into the writhing sky.

'We . . . we might have won!' Halbstein's breathless voice sounded dinningly loud in the sudden hush.

'And we might not,' Kastrouni growled. He ran into the shadows, in the direction from which he and Gokowski had originally appeared. But in the moment before he ran Trace had seen something in his face: a strange eagerness, or maybe a look of grim, sardonic anticipation.

'Where's he going?' he asked Gokowski.

'We brought something with us,' the other answered. 'Dimitrios's idea. A last wild throw if everything else failed.'

'Midnight,' Halbstein whispered now. 'We'll soon know whether or not we've failed.'

The ground shuddered again; uneven patches of earth around the entrance to the vault began to sink, throwing up clouds of dust; several ancient walls toppled into rubble, and the landrover leaned over a little. From below came the sounds of a thunderous collapse, and puffs of dust and smoke issued from the gaps where the second Chorazin tablet lay partially covering the entrance.

Then – dread sound that set all who heard it gritting their teeth – there came more muted screaming, which this time issued unmistakably from Decker. Decker lived, and he had been driven mad with torture and terror!

With an abrupt and shocking suddenness, the fat man came up from below, toppling the tablet aside as if it weighed nothing at all. Strong as ten men in his madness, he squeezed up from the vault laughing, crying, gibbering – utterly bereft of mind. For a moment he glared all about; then, laughing again in a high-pitched, almost feminine voice, he turned and staggered through the ruins toward the cliffs where they overlooked the Sea of Galilee. How he stayed on his feet at all was a miracle, for he was streaked with blood and dirt, badly burned down one still smouldering side, and his right arm hung dislocated and useless.

For a moment the four who crouched behind the landrover were awed by the madman's sudden appearance and shambling departure, but then Gokowski sprang up. 'Charlie! Professor!' he shouted. 'We have to put the tablet back!'

They ran to the vault's entrance, struggled with the stone, at last got it positioned again. But even as the tablet was replaced, so there came more movement from the darkness below, where stone steps descended into smoke and gloom. The men drew back, cast frightened glances at each other. And in the next moment:

Foul, stinking black pseudopods of tarry, throbbing matter pushed up from the gaps at the sides of the tablet. One of them, a tapering tentacle of oily, glutinous loathsomeness, touched the tablet in its groping – and all members were at once snatched back. From the reeking blackness beneath the slab, hell's own eyes burned red as coals; and then there came a nightmare voice, crying:

'F-F-FATHER, HELP ME! THY WILL BE DONE, MY TIME IS COME, BUT I AM HURT AND WEAKENED. AND STILL I MUST TAKE A THIRD. LET DEMOGORGON AID ME. THOUGH IT DRIVE HIM BACK WHENCE HE CAME, LET HIM NOW

DESTROY THIS HURTFUL STONE FOREVER. I WOULD BE FREE TO RAVAGE AMONGST MINE ENEMIES. FATHER, I PRAY THEE – *LET ME OUT!*'

Overhead the sky was a black disc of whirling cloud, a dizzily revolving turntable of pent power. And as Khumeni begged for help, so the demon hidden in those clouds answered one last time. A single bolt of lightning lashed down from the centre of the churning disc, struck unerringly with a lance of white fire that shattered the second Chorazin tablet to flaming fragments and hurled them in all directions. Tiny shards of rock and chunks big as fists rained down on the men and the girl where they cowered, and when they dared to look up all that remained of the vault's entrance was a smoking crater – in which all the evil of elder earth bubbled and bloated!

What rose up then into view was hardly George Khumeni, and yet it was him. Him and more than him. It was the seed of Satan. It was Ab and it was Gidor the Gadarene, it was Bodang the Mongol Mage and it was Guigos the beast; it was all of these and others unnamed, unguessed. It was a man – or at least composed of men – and it was a monster. It was *the* monster, caught in its own metamorphosis; but there remained one last element – the catalyst – without which his renewal was as yet incomplete.

The antichrist stood upright in the crater. A thing of black slime with a monstrous laughing face; a gigantic thing with a hairy left leg, with a huge slack breast in its armpit, with cloven hooves and a gape-jawed caricature of a head! It stood there and smoked and smouldered, blackened and blistered, a thing which should have been dead for two thousand years. But instead of death, its single thought was of life eternal!

'A THIRD,' the bass croaking burst again from its blackened lips. 'THE THIRD – *YOU!*'

Its steaming, dripping arms *elongated* toward Trace, great fingers hooked to snatch him up. And as those inhuman hands went to close on him, so the beast threw back its shuddering head and bayed its victory to the night through teeth like crooked bone daggers.

Trace stood paralysed, frozen with horror, rigid as a rock – until something hit him from the side and sent him staggering. Kastrouni, with a sack over his shoulder – which without pause he slit open. Inside, a live animal. The creature squealed its terror as Kastrouni whirled it in a circle, released his hold on its hind legs and sent it flying – directly into the bulk of the horror in the crater. And:

'There, you great black bastard!' the Greek laughed like a man deranged. 'There, take your third. Last time it was a poor blameless donkey, but this time I've found you something more fitting. A pig, George Khumeni, or whatever you are – *swine-flesh for a swine!*'

The thing in the crater offered up a gigantic croaking cry of rage and disbelief, then collapsed in upon itself, pig and all.

'Back,' Kastrouni addressed the others then. 'Quick, get back – and try not to watch. You really don't want to see this.' He shepherded the four stumblingly away. But Trace had to know.

'I'm going with you,' he said, as Kastrouni headed back toward the seething crater.

The Greek looked at him hollow-eyed, shrugged tiredly. 'It's your right, I suppose.'

'FATHER!' the shuddering, frothing mass in the crater continued to croak. 'FATHER!' But Satan no longer listened. Exhausted, Demogorgon's clouds dispersed in a sky where stars came out again to pour on the land their clean white light. And:

'There,' said Kastrouni at last. 'Look, it's finished . . .'

Hybrid horror ran squealing from the smoking crater. Its hideous body was huge and grotesque as before, but firmed-out now and without its previous tarriness; and upon its shoulders it wore the head of a great tusked pig! Away toward the cliffs the monstrous thing scrambled, grunting and squealing and going on all fours. Away into the shadows and the ruins of doomed, damned Chorazin, where even now the crazed figure of Decker staggered in starlight and cried like a baby.

Following, Trace and Kastrouni saw the two come together, heard Decker's howl as the beast-thing tore at him. For a moment they were silhouetted as one where they fought on the very rim of the cliff, and then they were gone into the abyss.

And thus it was that the last Gadarene swine was choked in the Sea of Galilee . . .

Epilogue

Trace and Amira spent a little time with her father, but five days after the horror at Chorazin they were back in London. At the moment their plans were very loose: they had decided to stay together for now and see how things worked out, but they did not yet know where they would live. The summer would last for months yet, and autumn to follow, and there was always Greece and/or its magical islands. Also, Professor Halbstein was going to rest for a while, then start a dig up in Chorazin. He intended to unearth the first tablet and destroy it forever, reduce it to powder. That way the invocation under the ascending node could never be used again. Trace had intimated he might like to be there to see that happen – but not just now.

In Richmond, Amira put her flat (her father's flat) up for sale; and then, because it was a beautiful day, they ate in a garden restaurant not one hundred yards from the bridge. After that it was a spin in Amira's little Japanese job to Trace's place, where he had one or two things that required winding up. As she drove, Amira tackled him about something:

'Charlie, there are two things we should get straight right now.'

'Oh?'

'One: I don't think I'd much care to live with a thief. You're clever enough to do anything you want without that. So I'm asking you to give it up.'

He smiled at her, however wrily. 'Clever enough, am I? Well, I don't know about that – but I've certainly go enough money. I can promise to stay out of trouble for a couple of years, anyway. What's the other thing?'

She glanced at him for a moment, a very serious glance, before turning her eyes back to the road. 'Ever since I first met you, you've had trouble with that foot of yours. And I've watched you. You try to hide it, but I can see it gives you trouble. And it isn't getting any better. I think that before we leave London you should have it looked at. By experts, I mean.'

'You're a straight-up kid,' he told her, nodding. 'Too right, you are! Anyway, put your mind at rest. I had already made that decision. You think I like being a cripple? Well, I don't, and I don't intend to be.'

He had phoned ahead to let Betty Kettler know they were coming. She met them at the door, dressed in her habitual housecoat with her habitual cigarette dangling from her lips, all smiles and wrinkles and unspoken innuendo. But she did have her uses.

'Er, Charlie,' she caught at his sleeve as he ushered Amira upstairs. 'Something came for you.' She gave him a letter. 'I can tell you about it, if you like – and about some callers you had . . .' And she passed him a certain look.

He gave Amira the key to the flat and said: 'Go on up. I'll be right there. Put the kettle on.' Then, as she disappeared up the stairs, he turned to Betty. 'What's up?'

'You put your phone on party line,' she told him.

'That's right – so you could handle it if anything important came up. I was waiting for a call from a hospital in Portsmouth. And then there were one or two other things.'

She nodded. 'Well, there's that letter – from St Mary's, Portsmouth. I pretended I was your mum and the postie let me sign for it. It's special delivery, see? And then there was this bloke on the phone – *very* common! What a mouth on him! A Mr Pelham?'

Trace's heart picked up a little, began to beat faster. 'Joe Pelham?'

'That's him,' she nodded. 'Real annoyed about something, he was! Also, he sounded like he was talking round a mouthful of broken teeth – so maybe that's what was annoying him, eh? Anyway, he says you're not to bother to take him any more business – only he didn't quite say it as nice as that . . .'

Trace liked none of this. 'Anything else?'

'Just one thing: during the last couple of days you've had some rather hard looking callers, Charlie. I just thought it might be worth mentioning, that's all.'

'Thanks,' he nodded. 'You're a straight-up lady, Betty.'

She dug into the pocket of her housecoat, gave him a scrap of paper with a number. 'These hard men said you might like to give them a ring,' she told him.

'Thanks,' he said again, and slipped her a fiver.

On his way up the stairs he tore open the envelope, and on the landing he paused to read the contents. Then he shook his head, snapped on the light and read it again. It was very brief, very official, very cold and clinical. And it had been written and signed by the obstetrician who had delivered Trace into this world – delivered him, *and* his brother.

Trace's frown deepened as he read over the letter yet again, before crumpling it up and thrusting it deep into his pocket. Down's Syndrome? Mongolism? Was that all? Then what the hell – ? And:

What the hell? a chuckling, throaty voice repeated his question in the back of his mind. Suddenly cold as ice, he felt dizzy, staggered a little as he entered the flat. Pain shot up his left leg from his gammy foot.

Amira came out of the kitchen, saw his drawn face, the

way he leaned against the wall. 'Charlie? Is something wrong?'

He shook his head, gruffly answered: 'No. I mean, I don't know. Make some coffee, eh?'

She stared hard at him, opened her mouth and closed it again, went back into the kitchen. Trace switched his telephone to personal, dialled the number given him by Betty Kettler.

It was Cat Carter's crowd, as he'd suspected. What he hadn't suspected was that they would have their hands on Jilly. But it was what they said they'd do to her if he didn't show up that clinched it . . .

Trace wasn't a coward, but he didn't exactly feel brave right now, either. When he'd explained to Amira and she said she wanted to come with him, he hadn't argued too much against it. Finally she won, and down inside he was glad. Then he worked out what he was going to say – how he'd bought the locket off some geezer in a pub, and all that crap: his 'alibi' – assuming, that was, they'd give him the chance to say anything at all.

Eight hours later at 11:00 P.M. on a deserted wharf just outside Henley, he found out that they wouldn't. 'See,' the beefy, expensively dressed, extremely cold and emotionless Cat told him, 'with me it's easy. I mean, I can tell just lookin' at you that you're goin' to lie to me. And frankly, I ain't got the time for all that shit. So no matter what you say this time, my boys here are goin' to hurt you. They'll hurt you a fair old bit. And in a couple of weeks they'll do it again. And they'll keep doin' it until you put things straight, right? And listen: it don't matter where you go, son, or where you try to hide, 'cos sooner or later I'll find you and it'll all start again. So you think about it, right – while you're recovering . . .'

And that was that.

It had turned into one of those windy, freaky, stormy summer nights and people were indoors; anyway, even if Trace had had wind to yell, no one would have heard him. So all he could do was take it. What hurt most wasn't the beating: it was Jilly sitting there in the back of Carter's big Mercedes, contentedly necking with one of his hooray sons as they watched it all through the window. That and the sight of Mr 'ex-Guards officer' Willis, once Khumeni's man, who also had a ringside view from his low-slung, sleek black foreign job.

But it wasn't much of a contest: three of them against Trace, and them built like WWII pill-boxes and about as sensitive. The only good thing about it was that they didn't hurt Amira.

But Jilly – the rotten little bitch! Had Trace been *that* hard on her? Hell hath no fury . . .

Oh, but it has, Charlie, it has!

The last boot went in between his legs as they kicked him down a rotting wooden jetty and left him lying there half-in, half-out of the water. And then there was only the pain and Amira's sobbing, and clouds scudding across the face of the moon as she gingerly flopped him over on to his back.

His right ear felt soft as putty and his left eye was a crimson slit in a bruised tomato. She couldn't bear to touch him for fear of hurting him more. Amira, so gentle and good and caring.

But what about the Greek wise woman – i kali gynaikes – or was it simply that she'd seen something of Amira's future? Her future with Trace . . .

'Charlie – oh, Charlie!' Amira's tears washed his face. He tried to lift his head. His ribs were on fire and his balls felt flat as pancakes.

'Oh, God!' he groaned.

Sorry, wrong number! said the sniggering voice in his head. *Try six-six-six.*

'Wrong number,' Trace croaked as thunder rumbled distantly. 'Wrong bloody number!'

'What?' Amira squeezed water from a handkerchief on to his burning brow.

All the numbers are zeros when Satan spins the wheel. So how can you win, Charles?

'Easy – you bet on the bloody zeros!' he grated through broken teeth.

'What?' Amira asked again, believing he was delirious.

Car doors began to slam shut as Trace sat up; coarse, brutal laughter drifted down to him on the wind. Up on the wharf, headlights blinked on, engines roared into savage mechanical life.

Amira looked at Trace in disbelief. He was a bad hospital case, she knew it – but he held out an arm and made her help him to his feet. He staggered there on the rocking, half-submerged jetty, held his broken ribs, turned his torn face up to the night sky. And suddenly the clouds were boiling – and Trace's eyes were sulphur yellow!

Amira's hand flew to her mouth. She stumbled back from him, almost fell into the water, climbed up on to the wharf. And:

'OK,' Trace spoke to the madly milling clouds. 'OK, you win. I want revenge!'

Only ask it, grandson.

'I do ask it. No, I demand it!'

So be it.

Webs of strange lightning gathered on high where Demogorgon wakened in the night. And along the wharf two speeding cars drove straight into the teeth of hell . . . !